TALES
E. T. A. Hoffmann

TALES OF
E. T. A. Hoffmann

EDITED AND TRANSLATED BY

Leonard J. Kent and Elizabeth C. Knight

Illustrated by Jacob Landau

The University of Chicago Press

CHICAGO AND LONDON

TO THE MEMORY OF

Fanny Kent

Tales of E. T. A. Hoffmann was originally published
as volume 1 *(The Tales)* of the two-volume
Selected Writings of E. T. A. Hoffmann
(University of Chicago Press, 1969)

The University of Chicago Press, Chicago 60637
The University of Chicago Press, Ltd., London

International Standard Book Number: 0–226–34789–3
Library of Congress Catalog Card Number: 73–88790

Contents

Illustrations

Introduction

THE CONTEXT

The term "romanticism" not only has various literary meanings, but its usefulness is directly dependent upon its flexibility. It is a comprehensive and imprecise term representing various tendencies for change in such areas as subject matter, attitude, and form. On the one hand, it may be a basically optimistic expression of belief in the natural goodness of man; on the other, it may view man through much darker lenses, see him as a victim of demonic, hostile, and unpredictable forces. In either case, emotions are elevated above reason, the ideal above the actual, and so on. But regardless of the angle of viewing and of the particular tone and mode of expression of romanticism during the later eighteenth and earlier nineteenth centuries, imagination may well be one of the keys to the concept. Coleridge's words supply helpful information:

> The incidents and agents were to be, in part at least, supernatural; and the excellence aimed at was to consist in the interesting of the affections in the dramatic truth of such emotions, as would naturally accompany such situations, supposing them real. And real in this sense they have been to every human being who, from whatever source of delusion, has at any time believed himself under supernatural agency.[1]

The German romantic in general, and Hoffmann in particular, was essentially concerned with the artistic depiction of a world in which the ordinary and the prosaic were imbued with the extraordinary

1. "Occasion of the 'Lyrical Ballads,'" *Biographia Literaria* (1817), chap. 14.

and incomprehensible, where the "supernatural agency" was given full sway.

The deliberate rejection of the prosaic, everyday world led the romantic writer at first to the idyllic past. In Germany this past was synonymous with the medieval world (which surely never existed as the Germans wished to see it), and it led to the world of the fairy tale and the dream, not as these were viewed through the roseate lenses of the English, who had been greatly influenced by Rousseau, but often, most especially in Hoffmann and his contemporaries, through a much darker and more ominous lense.

Unlike the experience in other countries, in Germany romanticism encompassed all fields—art, music, religion, philosophy, history, political science, natural science—and these were no less affected than literature itself.[2] It was the hope of the poets that a large cultural synthesis could be achieved to erase the artificial boundaries separating these intellectual areas so that such polar concepts as intellect and feeling, art and life, reality and illusion, would be fused. This is what the German writer Novalis (Friedrich von Hardenberg) meant when he announced that "The world must be romanticized."

German romanticism was not only a continuation of the German *Sturm und Drang* ("Storm and Stress") literary movement of the 1770s—a violent protest against the precepts of the Enlightenment—but it was, in great measure, a strong reaction against German classicism (despite the fact that the two terms are often united under the name German idealism).[3] Goethe and Schiller had gone beyond the *Sturm und Drang* movement; they reemphasized classical restraint and, by so doing, had more or less isolated themselves.

2. In England, for example, music "had ceased to be a creative art." The English romantic poets seem to have known nothing of Mozart, Beethoven, or Handel. To appreciate how very different the situation was in Germany, one need only look at Hoffmann's wonderful character in *Kater Murr*, Kapellmeister Kreisler, who is a musician *precisely* because Hoffmann and the German romantics saw music as "the highest art, the art which leads us into the dark abysses of our soul and the mystery of the world." (See René Wellek, "German and English Romanticism," *Confrontations* [Princeton, 1965], pp. 3–33, from which the preceding quotations are taken.)

3. The entire matter is far too complex for adequate discussion here, but it may be of interest to observe that the classical and the romantic coincided in Germany, and it is not surprising, therefore, that the first movement to actually call itself romantic, in 1798, focused primarily on criticism and philosophy rather than on highly imaginative and inventive art.

By 1805 great waves of irrationalism dominated Germany: the imaginative, the fantastic, the colorful, the emotional, the ecstatic, the moody, the hyperbolic, and the patriotic were in vogue. A yearning for freedom was reflected not only in lives, but in works. The harmoniously balanced creations in the classical vein now made way for a cascade of moods and inspirations, an extreme variety of works, a formlessness which had as a common denominator the strong desire for something different and better.

The philosophical groundwork for German romanticism was prepared by many—and one always narrows possible sources of indebtedness somewhat arbitrarily—most prominently, by Immanuel Kant, Johann Fichte, and Friedrich Wilhelm Schelling.

Kant had helped to undermine rationalism with his assertion that knowledge is limited.[4] Fichte, his disciple, not only accepted the limitation of the power of human reason, but developed a concept of the limitless potential of the imagination. When he asserted that ego is the only being, he helped prepare the way for a solipsistic world in which one of Ludwig Tieck's characters can proclaim: "Die Wesen sind, weil wir sie dachten" (Beings exist because we thought of them). Fichte did something to shake the fundamental premise that there was both a subjective *and* an objective world. In may ways, objectivity ceased to exist as a separate entity and became a subjective creation.[5] From Schelling the poets adopted the idea of the existence of a harmonious partnership between man and nature —a most appealing pantheistic relationship. If the world is indeed what the poet sees it to be, psychotic states would inevitably be mirrored in the world of nature. Even when the hostile forces in nature conspire to doom man, these forces seem to be projections of a diseased mind. When Hoffmann's eccentric Kapellmeister Kreisler looks into the lake, what he sees is not his own reflection but the face of the insane artist Leonardo.

The German romantic writers turned to the Middle Ages for their subject matter, especially because they saw it as an era in which

4. Another of his arguments, that there are necessary rules and limitations in life, literature, and morals, went unheard, or at least unheeded.

5. It is true that when Fichte wrote about imagination he conceived it primarily as a metaphysical faculty, but it is hardly surprising to discover that the German romantic writer interpreted it to mean something deeply personal and special—the poet's fantasy. They believed the world to be what the poet sees it to be.

society had been unified and made strong by the Catholic Church.
They saw modern Germany as politically bankrupt and Napoleon as
an inexorable threat to their country; and their vision sought an
earlier world of splendor. (Indeed, so attractive was this medieval
world to a number of poets that they became converts to Catholi-
cism.) Hoffmann, who at first considered himself essentially a musician, composed music for the Church. The Grimm brothers collected fairy tales and laid the foundation of philological studies with
their investigation of early Germanic languages. Clemens Brentano
and his brother-in-law Achim von Arnim collected and published
folksongs which were hailed as the "true" expression of man un-
spoiled by society.[6]

The dark side of German romanticism stemmed in part from
the fact that the German *Kunstmärchen* (the art fairy tale) is, perhaps especially clearly in Hoffmann, different from alleged folklore
—for one thing, often taking place in contemporary cafés or in the
busy streets of Dresden, Berlin, Frankfurt, or Paris. The uncanny,
the mysterious, the horrible, the grotesque, and the prosaic merge
and juxtapose with startling and deceptively simple ease. It is this
merging and juxtaposition which account for much of the horror
beneath the surface, because it shocks the reader into the recognition
that the world of the fantastic and the supernatural is *not* comfortably removed from everyday existence. The novella, which flourished in the Germany of the time, also exploited the uncanny and
the mysterious.[7]

It was Novalis who, in one of his novels, verbalized the tenor
of much German literature of the time: "Die Welt wird Traum,
der Traum wird Welt" (The world becomes the dream, and the
dream becomes the world).[8] It was he who celebrated night and

6. This strong concern with the German past was perhaps also responsible for awakening a love for the fatherland, for a growing national consciousness; paradoxically, what had begun as a determined flight from contemporary
reality ultimately led the Germans back to the present, to a clamorous pa-
triotism directed against the French.

7. It is perhaps revealing to note that neither the *Märchen* nor the
novella, two genres which were especially fostered in Germany, seem to have
been generally known or written at that time outside of Germany.

8. At the end of *Der blonde Eckbert* (*Blond Eckbert*), Tieck concludes
the story with the following: "He [Eckbert] could not now solve the riddle,
whether he was now dreaming or whether he had dreamed before of a wife
called Bertha. The marvelous fused with the ordinary, the world around him
was enchanted and he was not capable of thought or memory."

death and expressed ineffable yearning for the "eternal bridal night." For him light represented the finite world, night the infinite world. Death, not life, seemed more desirable, because death, having been conquered by Christ, was no longer to be feared, but rather to be desired.

German romanticism also drew heavily from Anton Mesmer and "scientific" and occultist doctrines. In considerable measure, the development of the double, for example, seems to have stemmed not only from earlier depiction of twin-doubles (in Shakespeare and Molière, among very many others) , but from studies in psychology and from Mesmer's theory of the magnetic union of souls. The German romantics were eager to exploit imagination, and in the whole question of "doubleness" and duality they found material consistent with their mood and taste and eminently susceptible to imaginative treatment.

Closely related to the yearning for night and death was the German romantic's interest in dreams, in part stimulated by the writings of Gotthilf Heinrich von Schubert, who wrote two very influential books—one on the night side of science and one on the symbolism of dreams. He called the language of dreams a "hieroglyphic language," a language which man need not learn because it is innate and understood and spoken by the soul when the soul is released from its imprisonment in the body. In *The Symbolism of the Dream*, Schubert wrote:

> The series of events in our lives seem to be joined approximately according to a similar association of ideas of fate, as the pictures in the dream; in other words, the series of events that have occurred and are occurring inside and outside of us, the inner theoretical principle of which we remain unaware, speaks the same language as our soul in a dream. Therefore, as soon as our mind speaks in dream language, it is able to make combinations that would not occur to us when awake; it cleverly combines the today with the yesterday, the fate of distant years in the future with the past; and when the future occurs we see that it was frequently accurately predicted. Dreams are a way of reckoning and combining that you and I do not understand; a higher kind of algebra, briefer and easier than ours, which only the hidden poet knows how to manipulate in his mind.

The romantic writers knew well how to use this hieroglyphic language to reveal the dark forces within man. They focused on areas not accessible to reason, on the subconscious and all its manifestations.[9] To depict these dark forces artistically, various techniques were employed; but generally the fairy tale, the myth, and the dream were the three elements that fused in the *Märchen*, as in Hoffmann's "The Golden Pot," where the student Anselmus, ostensibly an ordinary, clumsy boy, is inwardly torn apart. He lives in two worlds, that of the everyday, where nothing goes well, and a fantastic and allegorical dream world, where everything succeeds. The struggle for his soul, or his mind, is carried on by fantastic characters on a supernatural field of battle.

The number of dreams in earlier literature is enormous, but before the German romantics brilliantly exploited the substrata of consciousness (of which the dream is a striking manifestation), the dream most often served literature as an effective and highly stylized device of another kind—actually of several other kinds.[10] Perhaps no one prior to the German romantics understood or consistently and fully explored the dream device and its implications as an organic and inseparable part of a literary work; and in Hoffmann the symbolic dream seems to have fulfilled its potential.

The sentimental novel and the Gothic novel, both very popular in eighteenth-century England and France, contributed to German romanticism as well, the first because it may well have redefined the hero image by removing social position and knowledgeability per se as requisites, thus making possible the pathetic and introspective hero of nineteenth-century literature; and the latter because it more or less stumbled on the whole realm of the unconscious and converted reality into nightmare, even as it stimulated the individual imagination.

But possible sources aside, German literature of the period was filtered through a particularly German vision, and it is different from almost all of that produced elsewhere at the time. For example, the castles and moats and twilight so much a staple of the traditional Gothic novel were irrelevant or incidental to the designs of the

9. See L. J. Kent, "Towards the Literary 'Discovery' of the Subconscious," *The Subconscious In Gogol' and Dostoevskij, and Its Antecedents* (The Hague: Mouton, 1969), pp. 15–52.

10. For example, an introductory, "launching" device; an escape-from-reality technique; one admirably suited for allegory, for love and dream visions; a prefiguring (suspense-creating) device.

German authors. The overtly frenetic tone of the English Gothic novel would be relaxed because the Germans knew that a single scream shatters an everyday world as many screams can never affect a world of shrieks. The "Italian" villains of "Monk" Lewis and Ann Radcliffe would reappear in some of Hawthorne and Poe, but it is precisely to the point that the Germans found evil beneath the mask of normality. Their attitude, and the quality of their horror at the realization that "the power of blackness" lurks everywhere, pervade their works.

Given the German romantic's predilection for the uncanny, his essential anti-Rousseauism,[11] his sense of the grotesque, his detachment, his concern for what is now called "alienated man," his loathing for Philistinism and burghers, he could not join Melville's Bartleby ("I prefer not [to become involved]") in his self-imposed asceticism. The American romantics were, after all, believers. The Germans had no need to pay for their share of Original Sin. The world, as they often saw it, was not an evil place because God willed it to be, but simply because it was.

Aside from Novalis, the list of authors leading towards Hoffmann is considerable. Lawrence Sterne, among the English, exerted a very strong influence, and it is hardly accidental that Hoffmann's long title for *Kater Murr* is itself a parody of Sterne's *The Life and Opinions of Tristram Shandy, Gentlemen*.[12] Goethe, to be sure, left a profound and indelible mark on all who followed him. Among the other Germans, Brentano, Arnim, Kleist, Fouqué,

11. Hoffmann's own attitude toward Rousseau seems to have been ambivalent. Kapellmeister Kreisler, a strongly autobiographical character in *Kater Murr*, tells us that he was only twelve when he began reading Rousseau, and in Hoffmann's diary, 13 February 1804, Hoffmann confesses that he was reading the *Confessions* "perhaps for the thirtieth time," etc.; but, if the thrust of Hoffmann's fiction is to be believed, what he loved in Rousseau had much less to do with his pervasive optimism than with Hoffmann's feeling of kinship to his confusion, his love of and ability in music, his strong attachment to nature, his autobiographical bent, and so on.

12. Hoffmann admired Sterne's apparently haphazard technique of narration and saw this purposeful breaking of illusion and "detachment" (romantic irony) as a refined and subtle technique which found a parallel in the willful caprice of many of the German novels of the time, especially Jean Paul's. *Sentimental Journey* was one of Hoffmann's very favorite books because, among other things, Hoffmann admired Sterne's humor and felt that he had developed the storyteller's art to a high degree of perfection. (Hoffmann and his close friend Hippel often called one another Yorick and Eugenius, two characters in Sterne's book.)

Chamisso, Eichendorff, and Kerner also had some influence on Hoffmann, the first two especially in the area of the grotesque; but Jean Paul (Friedrich Richter) and Ludwig Tieck, other contemporaries, seem to have exterted very considerable and direct influence.

Jean Paul's forte is the fantastic, the grostesque, lacerating humor—realism turned inside out—inverisimilitude. It was he who invented the term and exploited the concept of the doppelgänger ("So heissen Leute, die sich selber sehen" [This is what people are called who see themselves]) . His are "little" heroes who utilize lush imaginations to remove themselves to the world of fantasy. In his work there is an intrinsic duality in which an "I" participates in life while another "I" merely observes, both in a state of perpetual coexistence. His depiction of the world as appearance and reality, as wakefulness and dream, as rational and absurd, as disjointed and whole, as lyric and grotesque, appealed greatly to Hoffmann.

In Tieck the fictional world is often kaleidoscopic, bewildering, unfathomable; here, too, as already noted, the worlds of dream and reality change places. Unlike Jean Paul, there is little compassion, little that can be characterized as gentle. Tieck's world is terror-filled and bizarre, one in which peculiarities of personality become manifest simply because characters are forced to react to the unintelligible forces which engulf them. The *Märchen* describe an escapist world, but only ironically, for it is a world of irrational foreboding and of the swift and merciless execution of an inexorable fate.[13] It seems clear that Hoffmann also owed to Tieck something of his fascination for the puppet-man controlled by a capricious or spiteful fate.

In Brentano and Arnim, Hoffmann found, as a direction towards which their tales pointed, the grotesque vision of the world and the artist's concern with its effect on man.

The term "grotesque" has been so injudiciously and widely used that it is often confused with the horrible or the bizarre. Originally used to designate a certain kind of late Roman ornamental painting, later associated with the decorative work of the painter

13. It has been pointed out that Tieck's "success with the *Märchen* genre depends on the more or less successful translation of the dream into literary form, without any necessary reference to real life. . . . This is the reverse conception to Hoffmann's, according to which the dream revealed a higher reality— reality as we know it, but projected in in wondrous dimensions and colouring, so as to transcend present reality, but not to negate it." (Ralph Tymms, *German Romantic Literature* [London, 1955], p. 76).

Raphael (who abolished all rules of reality and deliberately distorted objects), it is the effect of this art on man rather than the pictorial image itself which leads to an understanding of the true nature of the grotesque. In the eighteenth century it was this effect of the work of art on the recipient that became a major point of interest. Whether a work was objectively grotesque was not very important; what was important was that the reader, or the viewer, experience the grotesque in a highly personal way.

The essence of the grotesque is that it erases the boundary separating the human and animal realm[14] and, by so doing, frequently reduces man to an impotent puppet who sinks in the fateful determinism of hostile forces. Through personification, the grotesque extends its range to encompass the mechanical, which develops a threatening life of its own (as in the case of Olympia in Hoffmann's "The Sandman"). Also, most decidedly in Hoffmann, the grotesque is assigned a reality which contradicts reality as we know it, while at the same time being seen as a true reality, a higher reality, even perhaps *the* reality. It is when the unreality described becomes real and the grotesque ceases to become a game that fears become intense and an abyss yawns before us, because we are invaded by the feeling of the true absurdity of the world. We are led to a vision of the world which is topsy-turvy, one in which madness is the only sanity, because the world is itself a lunatic asylum.

In the introduction to his collection *Fantasy Pieces in the Style of Callot,* Hoffmann says of Jaques Callot, a French engraver and etcher of the seventeenth century:

> The irony which mocks man's miserable actions by placing man and beast in opposition to each other only dwells in a deep spirit, and thus Callot's grotesque figures, which are created from man and beast, reveal to the penetrating observer all the secret implications that lie hidden under the veil of the comical.

Shakespeare's plays, beautifully translated by A. W. Schlegel, were a revelation to the Germans—who lacked the advantage of a Shakespeare tradition—not least of all because they felt a strong affinity to his use of supernatural elements and to his view of man

14. See especially Wolfgang Kayser, *The Grotesque in Art and Literature,* tr. Ulrich Weisstein (New York, 1963).

as an actor. Hoffmann, perhaps at least as much as any of his contemporaries, admired Shakespeare. He was extremely sympathetic to the view expressed by the melancholy Jacques in *As You Like It:* "All the world's a stage and all the men and woman merely players."

THE LIFE

E. T. W. Hoffmann
BORN KÖNIGSBERG IN PRUSSIA
ON 24 JANUARY 1776
DIED BERLIN, ON 25 JUNE 1822
LEGAL COURT ADVISOR
EXCELLENT
IN HIS OFFICIAL POSITION
AS WRITER
AS COMPOSER
AS ARTIST
DEDICATED BY HIS FRIENDS

What is interesting about the inscription on Hoffmann's tombstone is not that it supplies some biographical information, which is, of course, readily available elsewhere, but that by listing his official position and avocations in a certain order it establishes priorities which tell us something of what his friends thought of the whole man. Further, the inscription strongly suggests that Hoffmann was very conscientious, versatile, and gifted, a judgment which has been amply and consistently confirmed by his biographers.

Hoffmann's parents were members of the upper bourgeoisie who had been connected with the law and respectability for generations; but theirs was a preposterously ill-fated marriage, and what Hoffmann called "a comedy of domestic dissension" ended in divorce before he was three. The father was a man of charm and professional ability (he had risen to become councillor of the High Court of Justice), and he was a talented musician as well; but he was less than stable emotionally. He married a cousin, a highly nervous and hysterical woman whose rigidity and coldness and addiction to her peculiar family doomed the marriage. Following the divorce, Ernst Theodor Wilhelm, the younger of two surviving sons, remained in Königsberg with his mother; some three years later his father disappeared totally and forever from his life, except as a very occasional memory.

To say that the situation in which the young Hoffmann found himself was something less than conducive to sound mental health is to understate the case. The household in which he lived was, almost without exception, barren, senile, and sickly: the grandmother, "a woman of Amazonian proportions who had spawned a race of pygmies," ventured from her room only rarely, and then primarily to talk with God and get ready for the final journey; his mother seems from all accounts to have specialized in staring vacantly into space; his uncle had once taken a law degree, but after mangling his first and only case, he had withdrawn from the world to engage in compulsive rituals hardly befitting a man who saw himself as a disciple of the great Kant; and there was a maiden aunt, by far the most sympathetic adult member of the bedlam, who was extremely overindulgent and seems not quite ever to have reached emotional maturity.

Despite all this, or perhaps, at least in part, because of it, before Hoffmann was twelve he could play the harpsichord and the violin beautifully, write musical compositions, and draw devastating caricatures. His uncle, who was entrusted with his early education, instructed him in music and developed in him a sense of discipline, regularity, and hard work which was never to leave him.

Hoffmann, most fortunately, met Theodor Hippel, a boy who would soon attend a Lutheran school with him and would become a life-long friend who more than once would rush to help Hoffmann. Probably viewed by the family as a much-needed sobering influence on the irrepressible Hoffmann—what absolute joy Hoffmann got from decorating his grandmother's well-fingered Bible with marvelous pictures of satyrs and hell drawn in its margin!—Hippel was made welcome, and he shared growing up with Hoffmann. The friends continued together the practice of reading which each had years before initiated on his own: Goethe's *Werther* moved them to ecstasy; and there were the wondrous tales of Jean Paul, Sterne's delicious *Sentimental Journey*, the dazzling Shakespeare, the irreverent Smollet, the brilliant and truculent Swift, and, above all, Rousseau's *Confessions* (in a German translation they would pilfer from Uncle's bookshelves and then devour as they spread it open and laid it on the assigned Latin and Greek texts).

Hoffmann was sixteen when he became a law student at the

University of Königsberg. There is ample evidence that he already saw himself primarily as a composer but was willing to pursue law because of the family tradition and the hope that law would ultimately make him independent enough to devote himself wholly to art. There is nothing especially noteworthy about his studies at Königsberg, where Kant was the most illustrious faculty member, and about whom he must have learned something, despite the fact that he avoided formal work with Kant, possibly to spite his uncle. Much of his time was spent reading occult literature, painting romantic landscapes in the style of Salvador Rosa, and giving music and art lessons.

He was nineteen and had passed the preliminary law examination when he fell outrageously in love with one of his piano students, a bored and sentimental married woman who must have found the frantic, temperamental, provocative, and outspoken artist very attractive, notwithstanding his diminutive stature, his shock of curly black hair, the large nose set in a huge head, the tiny hands and feet, and a nervous and mobile face. After all, the eighteenth-century novel of sentiment was still current, and much of the world seemed *souffrant de l'amour*. For his part, Hoffmann worshiped her as "Cora" (the virgin heroine in a contemporary second-rate play who commits the ultimate sacrifice for love); but, having reached heaven, there was nowhere else to go. The relationship was finally and fortunately terminated. Hoffmann, in a frenzy of compensating creativity, finished a novel, *Cornaro*, which was never published, and then another, *Der Geheimnisvolle* [The Mysterious Man], of which only a fragment remains.

After his mother's death and his tragic affair with "Cora," Hoffmann, then twenty-one, left Königsberg for the Silesian town of Glogau, where he was intent upon preparing for the law examinations required by the Prussian civil service. Here he lived with another uncle, became engaged to his cousin (the engagement was to last for four dutiful years, but was never to terminate in marriage), completed an opera, and joined in a local dramatic society. Two years after his arrival in Glogau, the family moved to Berlin; and there Hoffmann passed his final examination with honors. Instead of the desired post in Berlin, however, he was required to begin a probationary period in Posen, an administrative center in Prussian Poland.

Away from his family for the first time and justifiably bitter at a harsh fate and an unreceptive world, Hoffmann engaged in what was once called "dissolute pleasures"—he drank and wenched himself into exhaustion. Further, in an atmosphere where the civil and military officials seemed to be forever engaged in those ugly little quarrels, he did less than endear himself to the various "bigwigs" by drawing savage caricatures of them, which his friends so diligently distributed that they fell into the hands of the governor himself. These capers were expensive: they cost Hoffmann his assignment in Posen. Instead, in 1802 he was sent to Plock, a town of almost Gogolian dreariness. Here, at least partly in desperation, he married a Polish woman who, aside from perseverance and faithfulness—no mean feats—seems to have had as her major talent the ability to speak Polish.

The Hoffmanns were to remain in Plock for two years, during which time Hoffmann saw his first work published, an essay on the use of the classical chorus in drama. He also wrote a comedy, *Der Preis* [The Prize], several operetta texts, a mass for one of the local convents, and a sonata. Hoffmann had therefore managed to begin living two lives, that of the official and that of the artist; but he apparently accomplished this at major cost to his health, for he began to drink more heavily than before and, as he recorded in his diary, began to suffer from anxieties about doubles and from fears and premonitions of death.[15]

At this critical time, Hippel came to the rescue and managed to have Hoffmann transferred to Warsaw, a bustling and vivacious city in which theater and opera and all the arts flourished. Here Hoffmann at last found the peace and the friendship necessary to devote himself seriously to art. The friends were Eduard Hitzig and Zacharias Werner. Hitzig, only recently transferred from Berlin, had studied under A. W. Schlegel and knew a good deal about the new romantic movement. Crucially, it was he who introduced Hoffmann to Brentano, Tieck, and Novalis. Werner, poet, dramatist, mystic, who had as a boy been Hoffmann's neighbor in Königsberg, further encouraged and stimulated Hoffmann's creative impulses. Hoffmann thrived. His official duties were hardly onerous,

---

15. The concept of doubles apparently haunted Hoffmann long before he used it in fiction. While in Plock he wrote an entry in his diary describing his awareness of a "divided self"; and in 1809 he wrote in his diary that "I imagine that I see myself through a multiplying glass—all the forms which move around me are myselfs [ichs]. . . ."

and he was appointed musical director of a newly formed orchestra sponsored by the Warsaw Academy of Music. Not only did he supervise the reconstruction of the ancient building used by the academy, following his own architectural plans, but Hoffmann painted a series of murals for the building as well. Indeed, the enormously energetic Hoffmann seems to have been engaged in a host of only vaguely connected activities. There is no question but that he was successful both as musical director and as legal official, though, to be sure, legal business was often conducted at the academy—sometimes with Hoffmann flat on his back on a scaffold, painting and singing—and the business of the academy was sometimes conducted under strangely official circumstances. Hoffmann had somehow learned to live in his two different worlds. At any rate, more important than the financial success of the academy was Hoffmann's creative activity. At this time he composed what some critics believe to be the first truly romantic music: incidental pieces to Werner's play *Das Kreuz an der Ostsee* [The Cross by the Baltic Sea].

This unwontedly pleasant and rewarding interlude was rudely disrupted in 1806 when Napoleon, having defeated the Prussians, replaced their officials with Frenchmen. Hoffmann tried valiantly to scratch out a living as a professional musician. He wrote his first symphony, several sonatas, and many pieces of chamber music; but it was an impossible situation, and already suffering from poverty and a nervous collapse, he was forced to send his wife and infant daughter to relatives in Posen. Embittered, but never for a moment without principle, Hoffmann refused to take a pledge of allegiance demanded of all Prussian officials by the French, and he departed for Berlin, his wife and daughter remaining behind in Posen.

Hoffmann would literally have died of starvation in Berlin if faithful Hippel had not again intervened, this time supplying the very necessities of life. Hoffmann, as always, was astoundingly industrious, working at musical odd jobs, painting stage sets, nailing props, and so on; but money was almost impossible to come by. When news arrived that his daughter had died of cholera and that his wife was seriously ill, Hoffmann's fate seemed blacker than ever. He was tormented by paranoia and convinced that his ultimate destruction was imminent, but his wife recovered and joined him, and in the spring of 1808 Hoffmann was offered a position as theater-musical director in Bamberg. He gratefully accepted.

Typically, what was begun so enthusiastically was to lead to a string of minor disasters. Bamberg itself proved wonderfully pleasant and colorful, but the orchestra was torn by politics. After two enervating months Hoffmann submitted his resignation as the conductor but agreed to remain behind, at a reduced salary, to compose incidental music and ballets. He supplemented his small income by giving music lessons and doing portraits. He did, however, have the considerable satisfaction of assisting or directing several productions which were notable for their artistic innovation; he also played a major role in staging Shakespeare and Calderón.

Although the theatrical venture faltered in 1809, it was resumed the following year. Hoffmann now became engaged in a variety of capacities and for the first time in his life achieved an income which at least provided a modicum of security. He launched his career as a music critic and wrote what many consider to be impressionistic, perceptive, and surprisingly modern criticism; and he began his literary career in earnest. He also managed to fall in love with a sixteen-year-old piano student. This "heavenly relationship," unlike his affair with "Cora," was decidedly one-sided. Not only was Hoffmann's love not reciprocated, but the girl seems never to have been aware that it even existed.

Hoffmann, now thirty-six and the best drinker in town, had a complexion that already bespoke a decaying liver and a weakening constitution. His one-sided and frustrating love for the young and lovely girl drove him to extravagant fits of self-pity and depression. The spectre of death which had haunted him since his days in Plock returned in earnest to obsess him. In 1812 the theater failed again, and Hoffmann was once more reduced to groveling for his bread. His diary entry of 26 November contains the terse comment that he had "sold [his] coat so that [he] could eat." But in April of the following year, Hoffmann, now supported by a small legacy from his uncle, left Bamberg forever and started out for Dresden, where a job as musical director in the theater awaited him, and where he would also manage to conduct his operatic group.

The strange destiny which always pursued him saw to it, however, that the Napoleonic wars broke out again at this time so that Hoffmann, who so badly needed a stable position, found himself forced to alternate between Dresden and Leipzig for almost two years, his schedule depending primarily on the specific location of troops at any given time. The battles were so much a part of the situation that Hoffmann even managed to be wounded, for frequently he would perversely insist upon observing the fighting from very close range.

Hoffmann's career now focused more and more on criticism and fiction. His most important opera, *Undine,* and his last major piece of music, *Schlachtsymfonie* [Battle Symphony], were recently behind him. It was during this Dresden-Leipzig period, that Hoffmann's first published book appeared, *Fantasiestücke in Callots Manier* [Fantasy Pieces in the Style of Callot], with a preface by Jean Paul. The four volumes contain stories, the first part of a novel, criticism, essays, and reflections. They also contain two of the stories which are in this volume: "Ritter Gluck" (his first published fiction, which had previously appeared in Berlin in 1809) and "Der goldne Topf" ("The Golden Pot").[16]

In the fall of 1814, at the intercession of Hippel, Hoffmann was recalled to Berlin. From this point to the time of his death less than eight years later, Hoffmann continued to produce criticism and fiction with startling efficiency, completing in all twenty-five volumes.

Of the other works appearing in this edition of Hoffmann, "Der Sandmann" ("The Sandman") appeared in part 1 of *Nachtstücke* [Night Pieces], his second collection of tales (1816); "Rat Krespel" ("Councillor Krespel") and "Die Bergwerke zu Falun" ("The Mines of Falun") in volume 1 of *Die Serapions-Brüder* [The Serapion Brethren], his third collection of tales (1819); "Mademoiselle de Scudéri" in volume 2 of the same collection (1820). *Kater Murr* and "Die Doppeltgänger" ("The Doubles") were published separately, the first in 1819 and 1821, the second in 1822.

As attested to by the famous Jean Paul's having written a preface for his first book, E. T. A. Hoffmann[17] was something of a celebrity at least as early as 1814. By 1820 Hoffmann was lionized. Not only were the literary circles taken with the "weird master," but no less a figure than Beethoven wrote him a rare letter expressing his gratitude for Hoffmann's perceptive criticism of the *Fifth Symphony.* Hoffmann, however, was at once honest and arrogant, and he had too long suffered physical and emotional distress to

---

16. For a full list of all of Hoffmann's literary works see the Chronological List, vol. 2, p. 348.

17. Although his name was never officially changed from Ernst Theodor Wilhelm Hoffmann, in 1813 he substituted Amadeus for Wilhelm, in honor of Mozart.

permit this renown to achieve what gallons of wine could not—intoxicate him. If he was a celebrity, he was, as in all things, an unusual one. Superb at repartee, given to the sarcastic broadside when his wit went unappreciated, he had little patience for the throngs who were now so eager to cater to the whims of this larger-than-life diversified genius. Instead, Hoffmann retreated to Lutter's and Wegener's Café, where he more or less allowed himself to be enthroned and where, surrounded by literati and artists and musicians, he presided, in person or in spirit, until his death.

Hoffmann was again a government official, having received his formal appointment as councillor to the Prussian Supreme Court in 1816; and despite the fact that he alternated his life between the court and the cafe, he seems to have been a very effective and fair administrator and judge whose knowledge of law was considerable. In fact, he was steadily promoted in office.

Hoffmann never learned to become a political creature, possibly because he could not bend his sense of honesty, or because there was something self-destructive about the man; in either case, or both, he was to suffer one more major indignity before death robbed the world of one of its favorite scapegoats.

The Prussian king had asked him to conduct an investigation of "subversive activities," but Hoffmann refused to support this nineteenth century version of a witchhunt. He nevertheless was involved in other proceedings in which his attitude made the king much less than happy, despite the king's public support of Hoffmann's position.[18] Also, contrary and mischievous as ever, Hoffmann could not resist satirizing his arch rival in these proceedings in a book he was completing, *Meister Floh,* which was being published in Frankfurt, then a free city outside the jurisdiction of Prussia. Diplomats traveled from Prussia to Frankfurt and from Frankfurt to Prussia in top-level secrecy, all in an attempt to suppress the book.[19] Even Hoffmann was somewhat taken aback at the size of the paper monster he had created and offered to delete and alter the text, but it was much too late. He was arraigned for trial on the

18. Hoffmann was appointed to a commission to investigate "Father" Jahn, the founder of the Turnverein movement, a "front" for patriotic student radicals. Despite his dislike of Jahn, Hoffmann considered him innocent of the charges and fought for his acquittal.

19. On the other hand, the censors never managed to notice Hoffmann's satirical barbs in *Kater Murr.*

charge of unbecoming behavior, but was once more helped by the ever-available Hippel; and since Hoffmann was already obviously moribund, he was merely reprimanded—a rather academic decision considering that he was soon to die.

By the start of the new year, 1822, Hoffmann was in very bad straits indeed. Hippel and Hitzig joined him in his apartment on 24 January to help celebrate his forty-sixth birthday, but under the circumstances it was a grotesque though well-intentioned evening. There was no way the friends could relieve the pall in the room, Hoffmann, drinking mineral water because wine had been forbidden him as long as two years before, over and over reaffirmed his intense desire to stay alive, despite his agony; and he had his wish for five months, existing only to be slowly destroyed by a creeping paralysis.

Industrious even now, he dictated his final story, "Der Feind" [The Enemy] when he found it impossible to hold a pen. Already in agony, he was treated by a doctor who insisted that the application of red-hot pokers to the base of his spine would bring him some relief. It brought no relief, but it did bring forth final proof that his paralysis never extended above the neck, for when Hitzig came to see him a little later that same day, Hoffmann asked him whether he could smell the aroma of roasted meat.

Hoffmann died on 24 June, after he had asked to be turned to the wall. He had little enough reason to turn his face to the world.

THE TALES

While still in Bamberg, Hoffmann sent the manuscript of "Ritter Gluck"[20] to what was then the most important periodical of the kind in Germany, the *Allgemeine musikalische Zeitung* [Universal Music Journal], and it was published in March of 1809. This was the auspicious beginning of Hoffmann's literary career, for the story was well received.[21]

It has been remarked that "Ritter Gluck" is hardly a story at

20. *Ritter* is a title of nobility, equivalent to "knight." The Gluck in the title and the story is Christoph Willibald Gluck (1714–87), the great German composer.

21. And this favorable reception did much to make it possible for Hoffmann to follow up with numerous articles and musical reviews and the first of the *Kreisleriana,* short pieces of fiction and criticism in which there appeared the embryonic depiction of the marvelous half-mad musician so crucial to his novel *Kater Murr.*

all, but rather a cleverly disguised musical essay "adroitly attached to a narrative in the first person."[22] In fact, despite its brevity, it is one of Hoffmann's very best tales and contains many elements which reappear again and again in his works.

Very clearly, Gluck is the musician-hero whose art has removed him from the vulgar realm of the bourgeois and has raised him to the level where the mystery of the world and of his soul are known to him, as they are not to the narrator—if there really is a narrator separate from the musician. A host of questions arises: Is this "chance" acquaintance really not predetermined? Is the musician merely a madman who sees himself as Gluck? Is the "madman" really Gluck? Is he perhaps a reincarnation of Gluck? Is it possible, after all, that the narrator and Gluck are one and the same and hence exist in two worlds simultaneously, the external world of reality and the inner romantic world of the spirit? But what is this "reality"? We are told in the beginning of the story that what follows took place in 1809; however, we know that the composer Gluck died in 1787. How could Gluck, according to our standards of reality, find himself in Weber's Café, in Berlin, twenty-two years after his death? Perhaps, one could argue, there is no Gluck; it is the narrator who is insanely imagining that he exists. But Hoffmann convinces us that this man is Gluck, for he tells us as much himself, in the very last line of the story, with the italicized "*I am Ritter Gluck.*"

All in all, as in much of Hoffmann, we are left with one satisfactory conclusion: the world itself has more than one reality, and different realities may coexist at exactly the same moment; this being so, the world we thought we knew so well is undermined.

This is a seminal story: the fantastic takes place in an accurate and contemporary setting; the whole question of "doubleness" is raised; through music, the spirit is seen as communicating with the Divine; the attack upon the premise that there is but one reality is made; the imaginative, gaining strength because it overlays the prosaic, is already in full power.[23]

22. Harvey W. Hewett-Thayer, *Hoffmann: Author of the Tales* (Princeton, 1948), p. 172.

23. It has indeed been argued that Hoffmann not only may never have written a better story than this, his first, but that his basic technique advanced little. This, of course, is moot. What seems to be an argument more readily substantiated is that Hoffmann the musician was never truly important because his music never got to the level of Mozart's and Gluck's, the two composers so praised in this story.

This story may also be, as a German critic maintains, the key to an understanding not only Hoffmann but of many of the literary works to follow, because we see in "Ritter Gluck" what he calls "the abandonment of duration," which implies no less the abandonment of place and, making possible any and all combinations, projects an "absurd" and frightening, completely open-ended existence.

"The Golden Pot" is a masterpiece, one which Hoffmann considered his best story. In it, the various ingredients which make up Hoffmann's fictional world are blended with amazing success. It is, at least on one level, the story of an artist who rejects Philistia, not only because fantasy promises escape and greater rewards, but also, concomitantly, because the destitute and overwhelmed student Anselmus hardly belongs to this "comfortable" world at all; he is a pariah who rips his coat on a nail, loses his hat while bowing, is forever late, and is always breaking things because, he tells us, he "walks straight ahead, as if he were a lemming." The simile is well-chosen. Like a lemming, he is headed for total destruction. The world he ultimately flees to is one of green-gold snakes and salamanders, of bronze-gold palm trees, and marvelous tropical birds who make music as they fly—the stunning "wonderland of Atlantis." On this level Anselmus may be seen as strongly autobiographical, for he represents Hoffmann as he wrestled with the problem of the artistic soul meeting the gross realities head on and suggests that the world of Philistia can be conquered by the poet, that the denigration and pressure of Philistia recede and disappear under the marvels conjured up by the poetic imagination, and that the poet reaches salvation.

But there are other interpretations, the most obvious one being much blacker; for if the prosaic world is so enervating and destructive and intolerable to the poet, he *must* retreat to the Atlantis he needs for survival. Having retreated, he has renounced his claim to reality and exists only in Atlantis, which, of course, does not exist at all. Unlike "Ritter Gluck," it may not here be a question of simultaneous realities; rather, it may be one in which the very identity of the poet is threatened with extinction.

Given Anselmus's condition as he barely survives in Dresden, perhaps one can agree that the madness of Hoffmann's artists results primarily from their estrangement from the world and symbolizes the very suffering of the world as it, in turn, torments those most

sensitive to its pain.[24] Or, it has been argued that the story is simply
a metaphoric depiction of the development of the artist in which
some of the characters represent various projections of mind, the
apple-woman being fear, and so on.

Perhaps Anselmus is himself merely a projection of the registrar, a projection which disappears when the registrar marries
Veronica and, therefore, no longer has a need to exist in a world of
fantasy. Or is it that parts of a single character assume individual
identities so that Veronica and Serpentina are one, even as Anselmus and the registrar are one?

The story contains allegorical possibilities and may well have
imbedded in it ironical elements which expose to ridicule some
contemporaneous German philosophy; but these elements are nebu-
lous and arcane. There are mythic elements as well, at least one of
which deserves some mention.

The German romantics, as noted, were concerned with a synthesis, with a conception of man living in perfect harmony and
unity with nature. Atlantis perhaps suggests the Biblical Eden and
Paradise before the fall of man (which resulted because "thought"
overcame spirit and soul). Restoration of harmony and Paradise
may, after all, only be possible through the triumph of faith and,
ultimately, poetry.

This is the only one of Hoffmann's many stories dealing with
artists which has a happy domestic ending. It may even be said that
the bourgeois life depicted in "The Golden Pot" is not without its
rewards, if Veronica is any measure. Yet the ending itself may well
be ironical, for even when many of the almost limitless possible interpretations are considered and the story is read again and again,
the final impression is that this world is simply no place for the
poet:

> Be calm, be calm, my friend. Do not lament so! Were you not
> yourself just now in Atlantis, and do you not at least have there
> a nice little farmstead as a poetic possession of your inner mind?
> Is the bliss of Anselmus anything else but life in poetry, the

24. Dostoevsky's Raskolnikov in *Crime and Punishment* reminds us somewhat of Anselmus, as he barely survives in St. Petersberg. Poverty is only one of
the reasons for Raskolnikov's estrangement, and it is true that Dostoevsky con-
demns his titanism; yet he too is driven to dream of an Atlantis, albeit one in
which love is the primary restorative.

poetry to which the sacred harmony of all things is revealed as the most profound secret of Nature?

However it be interpreted, "The Golden Pot" is a wondrous product of the romantic imagination. The soft and teasing haze drifting over it is fully in keeping with a time and an author dedicated to illusion.

"Der Sandmann" ("The Sandman") is at once one of the more perplexing and successful stories Hoffmann wrote. An interestingly constructed work, it is one of the surprisingly few stories in which evil seems unequivocally to win.

The exchange of letters at the beginning is artistically successful in that the reader gains an "unobstructed" view of Nathanael and Klara—of Nathanael as the archetypal romantic, and of Klara as the embodiment of love and domestic virtue. But as the story progresses, the mental deterioration of Nathanael is only sometimes depicted from his point of view. A narrator supplies additional information, but not always evenly, for the narrator is alternately sensitive and sympathetic, and critical and even sardonic. Here the narrative technique supports the questionmarks imbedded in the fabric of the story because it precludes a clear determination as to how much is happening and how much is imagined.

The story may be seen as the projection of a madman's fantasies. Nathanael's description of his childhood—and there is no reason not to believe him—supplies adequate "evidence" of several experiences which could have, given his temperament, led to psychosis. Thus viewed, the fantastic events described support the contention that here a childhood trauma, which may have been temporarily suppressed in the subconscious, finally asserts itself and results in distortion and death.

Possibly more in keeping with Hoffmann is a reading which sees Coppelius-Coppola—if, indeed, they are one and the same—as a malicious agent of a hostile fate which exists both in Nathanael's mind *and* in external reality. Nathanael is, then, powerless to ward off this evil, this implacable horror which corrupts and destroys. Is it not this evil force which pushes Nathanael into irreversible madness when he discovers that the woman he loves is in fact what he is only metaphorically, an automaton? Created by Coppelius, she is no less fate's evil emissary.

This may be, at least in part, an archetypal revenge story, for Nathanael as a child had looked upon what was forbidden and had seen the secrets of the soul. An eye motif runs through the story: there are eyes during the forbidden experiments; Coppelius threatens to remove Nathanael's eyes; when Olympia is destroyed, her eyes fall out; "coppola" is the Italian word for "eye-socket," and so on.[25] Are the eyes all symbols of Nathanael's punishment for trespassing? Are they rather merely a symbol for the occult, for magic?

It is difficult to determine the degree of Hoffmann's satiric intentions in this story, primarily because the attitude lacks consistency or full development; yet it is unmistakably present. Nathanael, on the one hand a tragic victim of fate, is an absurd romantic as well, not because he would reach for Atlantis, but because his fervent speeches and his soulful poetry are directed at an automaton who can only respond to "How profound is your mind. Only you, only you understand me" with a literally mechanical "Ah."

A critic has written perceptively that

It is possible to give comic expression to the fact that he mistakes a doll for a human being, thinks that she loves him, and confesses his love to her, but Hoffmann's presentation of the matter is so genuinely grotesque that its effect upon us is humorous and horrible at the same time.[26]

Nathanael is no less estranged from reality than Anselmus, and even as in "The Golden Pot," there is some objective basis for understanding what may be viewed as a flight from reality —in Anselmus' case, his marginal existence in Dresden; in Nathanael's, his traumatic experiences as a child. But one should keep in mind that in Hoffmann objectified material serves well because it enriches the range of potential interpretations but does not exhaust them. There is nothing in "The Sandman" which explains, for example, Coppelius' uncanny power over Nathanael; nor should there be.

On any level, Nathanael is in mortal turmoil: he is a poet possessed by a demon, whether it be internal or external, or both. He

25. The use of the spy glass, itself an eye, when Nathanael first sees Olympia enables him to see her with a clarity not before possible, and it is only when looking at her through the spy glass that her eyes are animated. One of the deeply disturbing aspects of the story has to do with the lens which animates the automaton, but which, when focused on Klara, reduces her to a wooden doll. It is this final vision of Klara which leads directly to Nathanael's suicide.

26. Wolfgang Kayser, *The Grotesque in Art and Literature*, p. 75.

is a romantic who carries within himself his own destruction. He must try to reach beyond reality, but having once done so, he may have reached too far ever to be able to return. Besides, Coppelius stands ever ready to block his way.

"Rat Krespel" ("Councillor Krespel") is particularly noteworthy because Krespel is one of Hoffmann's great characters. Humorously and affectionately depicted at first as merely a charming eccentric whose physical appearance is comic rather than sinister, as one "who waltzed a little with the builders' wives and then sat down with the town musicians, took up his fiddle, and conducted the dance music until daybreak," he is yet the artist who invariably finds the ordinary stifling and restrictive. His eccentric, "crazy," behavior is here most effectively depicted as his only way of avoiding madness. In many ways, what so shocks one about Krespel at the conclusion of the story is the realization that he may be the most sane of any of Hoffmann's artists; hence, his estrangement from the everyday world has about it a condemnatory power less obvious and convincing in other depictions of the artist as one who truly seems on the brink of madness. That Hoffmann may see Krespel as sane suggests, quite aside from its other implications, that he viewed him as strongly autobiographical.

It is a dark story from which the supernatural has been excluded but in which the occult functions, especially in the implication of prenatal influence and Antonia's fatal connection and the singular violin.[27] Antonia is destined to die: dedicating herself to art with her lover means death, but abandoning art to remain with her father is also a form of death.

The tragedy, however, is Krespel's, for he, hostile to all interference, still desires to interfere and manipulate, and ultimately he comes to recognize this for the evil it is. He twice accuses himself of having tried to play God, the Father, and once accuses the narrator of considering himself to be God, the Son. Both Krespel and the narrator have interfered in Antonia's life—Krespel by treating his daughter as a mechanical object, another violin, which he can dissect and direct; the narrator by wishing to save Antonia from

27. Antonia's identification with the violin is not merely symbolic. When she hears Krespel playing the violin, she joyfully exclaims, "Why, that is me— I am singing again!"

her father. The evil involved is identical to that of which Kapell-meister Kreisler accuses Meister Abraham in *Kater Murr*.

It is again impossible to determine where Krespel's dream be-gins and how much of what we read is to be taken as having hap-pened; but one of the major themes can here be isolated, and what it tells us is as pessimistic as anything in Hoffmann: art and love cannot coexist.

"Die Bergwerke zu Falun" ("The Mines of Falun") is a marvel of the fantastic and an expression of the German romantic's con-ception of the miner as a man of almost superhuman quality because he has access to secrets hidden from others. The very secrets of crea-tion are his because he works deep within the bowels of earth and is, hence, by virtue of his intimacy, heir to her mysteries and treasures.

The story opens with sunshine and gaiety, but the tone shifts, first when Elis discovers that his mother is dead, then, immediately following, when an old miner excoriates him for despising the mines — "an enchanted garden"—which he has never known. Signifi-cantly, the old miner concludes, "I have uncovered for you, Elis Fröbom, all the glories of a calling Nature did truly intend for you . . . do as your judgment dictates." It is at this point that Elis, enticed by a surpassingly lovely dream, enters a fantastic world which ultimately claims him as a victim.

Like Nathanael in "The Sandman," who "sees" with his spy glass what others cannot, Elis "sees" in the mines metals which are hidden from others. For both Nathanael and Elis the bourgeois world of love and marriage becomes the determining factor that drives them to the world of fantasy and to their doom (in neither story is fantasy equated with the world of art). There is no recon-ciling Atlantis.

Hoffmann is here interested in revealing the agony of the split personality, and he achieves this not only through the description of events, but also through a particularly marvelous dream[28] that foreshadows the action and reveals Elis's inner dissension, the cause of which Hoffmann typically ascribes to an occult power op-

---

28. It also suggests that love may be death itself. There is, too, much in the dream which seems patently erotic and oedipal. When, for example, he looks up at the queen, he hears the voice of his mother. "HE THOUGHT HE SAW HER FIGURE THROUGH THE CLEFT. But it was a charming young woman," etc.

erating outside the individual and controlling him mercilessly. In the end, Elis succumbs, as does Nathanael, imminent marriage precipitating catastrophe.

"Mademoiselle de Scudéri" is one of Hoffmann's greatest stories, not primarily because it is an early example of detective fiction, or because it contains a splendidly exciting plot and is set in a Paris which is described in wonderful and accurate detail,[29] but because, along with the magnificent Madeleine de Scudéri, it also contains René Cardillac, one of Hoffmann's most sinister artists because he unites in his person the artist and the criminal (a motif later to be developed by Thomas Mann).

Cardillac carefully plans and commits numerous murders, each time plunging a dagger into the heart of a victim for whom he has created a masterpiece of the jeweler's art. Why does he commit such crimes? Because art has become a curse and creativity has become the ultimate selfishness. Councillor Krespel destroys his violins and silences his daughter's voice to keep her for himself; Cardillac cannot give up his masterpieces, and when he must, he murders to retrieve them. This is a self-conscious, uncontrollable drive, for he refuses to make jewelry for those whom he admires, and it is this that creates great suspense when Mademoiselle de Scudéri neglects to rid herself of the mysterious jewels that come into her possession.

This is one of Hoffmann's best-constructed stories; it is also one of the few works in which suspense is so intense and into which it is directly and quickly introduced. The opening scenes are masterful and, from the first knock on the door at midnight until the resolution of the crimes, Hoffmann manages to resist the dreamlike atmosphere so typical of him and to proceed with sharp and deft strokes.

Mademoiselle de Scudéri is surely, in several ways, one of the most admirable "detectives" in all fiction, not because of her skill

29. It should not be overlooked that Hoffmann almost invariably endows his stories with a realism born of specificity and minute detail; further, he is known to have done research to assure the accuracy of his depictions. His detailed and accurate presentation of places and, as in this story, characters, adds to their believability and, of course, enhances the fantastic. It is, in part, the very blending of romanticism and what might almost be called "scientific realism" which is Hoffmannesque.

—it is her "bungling" which is so endearing––but because of her humanity and nobility of character. Further, she is an especially effective character because she is Cardillac's foil. Her steps are determined but sometimes wavering, in marked contrast to the fixed and mechanical movements of Cardillac. Hoffmann is able in this story to exploit his strength at characterization as he quickly fills in details that individualize and give life to his cast.

Perhaps because this story is less dreamlike than many of the others, we may find the love affair between Madelon and Olivier less acceptable in its details than we would were it transferred to a fantastic setting. Hoffmann's depiction of love tends to be so highly romantic and stylized that one wonders whether the pearly tears staining a white bosom are intended ironically, as Nathanael's professions of love to the automaton Olympia in "The Sandman" may be. But one rejects that idea in this story and concludes that it was impossible for the romantic Hoffmann to see this aspect of life any more realistically than he could see other aspects.

But the "tear-stained white bosom" aside, this is a splendidly provocative and sympathetic story in which goodness triumphs in a manner as disarming as it is convincing. As with no other story by Hoffmann, one is left with a feeling that madness may not be the only answer to the world, that evil spirits can be exorcised by virtue. "Mademoiselle de Scudéri" suggests that the "power of blackness" may yet be overcome.

"Die Doppeltgänger" ("The Doubles") is one of Hoffmann's final stories and was not published until the year of his death. Here again there are puppets; but, interestingly and crucially, they are not metaphors but exist within the reality of the story. Hoffmann not only conceives of his leading characters as puppets, but sees himself as their master, as perhaps the dark fate to which he so often alludes.

Thus, not only does George Haberland, a puppeteer, inject himself onto the stage, where he appears as a monstrous, grotesque, and disembodied head, but the puppets actually discuss him. Hoffmann, in the person of Haberland, is able to inject himself into the story by making his characters motionless, by freezing them in the scene in the seventh chapter when the doubles confront each other: they "stopped in horror and remained rooted to the floor." Hoff-

mann goes back in time to supply the reader with what he con-
siders necessary information, then suddenly releases his characters
with a powerful "So!" The action then continues.

Nowhere else in Hoffmann do we so clearly see the arbitrari-
ness of life. On the stage of life, action begins or stops according to
the whim of some irrational power which controls us even as it
mocks and is unresponsive to us. Man is seen as a manipulated
puppet who dances to the pull of strings he neither sees nor can
begin to understand.

This is not a supernatural story. Untypically, no battle rages for
the very soul of man. The outside forces are mute. The doubles, the
two young men who look alike, are not doubles in the sense that
Ritter Gluck and the narrator of his story may be. They look alike
because they were fathered by the same man at the same instant, one
physically, the other spiritually. Further, their resemblance is only
superficial, for they are different in taste and temperament and
perception. One is truly a *Fürst* (prince), a man of affairs, a man of
the world—hardly a desirable calling from Hoffmann's point of
view. The other, more positively portrayed, is a maturing artist. Both
carry in their imaginations the same dream of Natalie, a notion so
horrifying to her that she commands them to renounce her and then
retreats to a nunnery; and neither Schwendy, the true *Fürst*, nor
Haberland, the true artist, finds this difficult to accept. The former
will find happiness in reigning; the latter will find his inspiration in
his art. Woman, Hoffmann seems to be saying, has no place in either
life.

If the supernatural is absent from this story, the occult is not;
for Hoffmann, as suggested by "Rat Krespel" and "Mademoiselle de
Scudéri," believed in prenatal influence, even to the extent that it
would produce a child physically identical to one produced by
means more traditional than spiritual love.

There is much about "The Doubles" which is humorous and
satirical. The innkeepers are marvelously drawn as absurd men
who spend much of their lives arguing and fighting, primarily
because it has become a delightful habit which each finds indispensable. The world they inhabit is no less entertaining and compre-
hensible. They and their world serve as effective relief until the
problem of the doubles is "solved." Typically in Hoffmann, it is
the human quality of these men and their existence which give to

the raven and all it represents a very special veneer of the mysterious and of potential horror.

The question of influence is rarely so clear and direct as it may seem; and one must be cautious, always aware that a host of circumstances and coincidences may conspire to make one author appear to be much indebted to another. Yet, this said, Hoffmann's strong historic importance seems very firmly established.

The artist in conflict with society, alienated man, the detective novel, the theme of split personality, the full exploitation of the subconscious and its striking manifestations, the particular use of the fantastic and the grotesque, the use of automatons and puppets, a peculiar vision of a deterministic world, the detachment of the author—these are only some of the elements that can, at least partially, be traced back to Hoffmann.

Without going into a prolonged and unnecessarily detailed analysis, it should be noted that, outside of Germany, Hoffmann's influence on literature was most strongly felt in the United States, Russia, and France.

Irving, Hawthorne, and Poe were among those in America who were acquainted with his works (Irving had spent some time in Germany and knew the language; Hawthorne and Poe could, if necessary, have read Hoffmann in English, for translations of his stories were serialized in *Blackwoods* magazine as early as 1824). In Irving the influence seems essentially general, though specific legends used by Hoffmann can be identified. Hawthorne's use of the ancestral curse stems from Hoffmann's "Das Majorat" ("The Legacy"). Poe, in whom the Hoffmann influence seems pronounced, wrote a very good story, "William Wilson," which seems singularly indebted to Hoffmann's use of the double.[30]

In Russia, Hoffmann seems to have had an all-pervasive influence and, by 1830, to have been the object of something like a "cult." Pushkin, Turgenev, Gogol, and Dostoevsky were among those who strongly admired him. In Dostoevsky this influence is most consistent and clear, especially in Dostoevsky's use of the subconscious. It is hardly surprising, therefore, that Dostoevsky, in a

30. To illustrate the extent and depth of Hoffmann's influence in America, one should read Longfellow's prose romance *Hyperion,* in which full passages of fantastic description were borrowed from Hoffmann.

letter to a friend, wrote that he and a companion "talked of Homer, Shakespeare, Schiller, and Hoffmann—particularly Hoffmann."[31]

In France, Hoffmann's fame was such that Sainte-Beuve, George Sand, and Baudelaire were among those who either directly or indirectly reflect something of Hoffmann's works or ideas.[32] Interestingly, Hoffmann's influence in France seems to have diminished after 1855, at which time Baudelaire's translation of Poe appeared.

Hoffmann appears to have had less luck across the Channel, where Scott's essay "On the Supernatural in Fictitious Compositions and Particularly on the Works of E. T. A. Hoffmann" may have further poisoned a climate already somewhat hostile by creating the impression that Hoffmann was a superficial teller of gruesome tales; and despite the fact that Carlyle saw fit to translate Hoffmann's "Der goldne Topf," a superb story, his introduction to it is rather condescending and less than enthusiastic. But "Teutonic romanticism" left its mark—on the Brontës, for example, and, in Scotland, on Robert Louis Stevenson, whose *Dr. Jekyll and Mr. Hyde* and *Markheim* are very Hoffmannesque.

In Germany, for many years following Hoffmann's death, the critical estimate of his work was hardly more positive than it was on the other side of the Channel. Goethe, for one, agreed with Scott and wrote that he had been saddened to see "that the morbid works of this sick man for many years had had an influence in Germany and [that] such aberrations have been inoculated upon healthy spirits as highly beneficial innovations." But the advantage of distance allows one to understand this. The pendulum of taste, always in movement, had already swung away from romanticism before Hoffmann's death; and some critics argue that in Germany Hoffmann and romanticism probably died simultaneously. At any rate, many of the literary works that immediately followed in Germany were imbued with a social and political consciousness that can perhaps be appreciated through this comment made in 1853, directed at the German romantics in general and at Hoffmann in particular: "One lived in an artist's world of dreams; one did not even read the newspaper." But this taste or course, would change too.

31. Dostoevsky considered *Kater Murr* Hoffmann's greatest work. He said of Hoffmann that he is "immeasurably greater [than Poe]," that "there is an ideal [in Hoffmann] . . . there is purity, there is a genuine beauty. . . ."

32. There is more than a trace of Hoffmann in Hugo. Also, Dumas adapted one of his tales; then there were the mystical novels and *Contes Philosophiques* of Balzac, and so on.

Ultimately, we think it is not pushing too hard to suggest that, specific influences aside, the whole literary world of psychological fiction owes Hoffmann an inestimable debt. Hoffmann shifted the scene of man's incessant conflict from the external world to the mind, where the struggle for identity and survival takes place on a level and with a consistency and intensity absent from earlier literature, and where its significance is greatly increased. There is no question but that Hoffmann anticipated much of what psychologists were later to uncover. Hoffmann seems to have been aware of organic and functional psychoses long before modern science defined them and twentieth-century literature exploited them; but, of course, his interest was primarily esthetic and not scientific.

Hoffmann had a divided allegiance. On the one hand, his pursuit of the irrational and the mysterious, his preference for the enigma rather than the solution, suggests that he was a true romantic; but there is more than a hint that he was not unaffected by the Enlightenment, for the seemingly miraculous is sometimes explained—on one occasion, much to the chagrin of Kapellmeister Kreisler in *Kater Murr*, who is peeved at Abraham for a rational explanation of what he preferred to think of as supernatural. The occult attracted the romantic Hoffmann because it satisfied him emotionally and because it enabled him to exercise his imagination to the limits of its potential, thus exorcising the detestable world of the philistine. For Hoffmann, the occult and the fantastic seem to have meant nothing less than the ultimate emancipation from mediocrity, from what he called "too much reality."

Hoffmann's fictional world is incredibly rich; it is one in which anything can happen, where dream and reality, the conscious and the unconscious, the prosaic and the fantastic may occur simultaneously and reflect each other. It is a world where the virtuous and the criminal, the mediocre and the brilliant, the charlatan and the scientist, the merchant and the artisan, the philistine and the artist all live, sometimes in a single body. It may be a sinister and terrorizing world, but it is often one that is animated by brilliant humor and satire too.

Above all, Hoffmann's fictional world is worth knowing because in it is to be found his complex vision of humanity, of man engaged in an archetypal struggle to establish identity in a hostile, absurd, and remarkably modern world.

TALES OF
E. T. A. Hoffmann

Ritter Gluck

A Recollection from the Year 1809

Usually there are still several lovely days in the late fall in Berlin.
The cheerful sun breaks out of the clouds, and the moisture in the
soft breezes that drift through the streets quickly evaporates. A
gaudy stream of people wanders along the Lindenstrasse to the Zoological Gardens—dandies, solid citizens with their wives and adored
children, all dressed in their Sunday best, clergymen, Jewesses,
junior barristers, prostitutes, professors, milliners, dancers, officers,
etc. Soon all the tables at Klaus's and at Weber's[1] are occupied; the
coffee steams, the dandies light their thin cigars; everyone chats,
quarrels about war and peace, about Mademoiselle Bethmann's[2]
shoes, whether they were recently gray or green, about the closed
commercial state and the bad pennies,[3] etc., until everything dis-
solves into an aria from *Fanchon*,[4] in which a harp that is out of
tune, a couple of untuned violins, a consumptive flute, and a spas-
tic bassoon torment themselves and the people nearby. Close to
the railing that separates the crowd at Weber's from the Heerstrasse
are several small round tables and garden chairs. One can breathe
fresh air here, observe those coming and going; one is remote from
the cacaphonic racket of that execrable orchestra. That is where I

1. Two well-known cafés in Berlin.
2. Friederike Auguste Caroline Bethmann (1760–1815), a famous actress.
3. A reference to a writing of Fichte's ("Der geschlossene Handelsstaat"
[The closed commercial state], 1800) which was a general topic of conversation
at the time. Added by Hoffmann's editor, Friedrich Rochlitz, who was obviously not indifferent about increasing the young Hoffmann's "topicality."
4. A popular light opera by Friedrich Heinrich Himmel (1765–1814).

3

sit, abandoning myself to playful reveries in which sympathetic figures appear with whom I chat about learning, art, everything that is supposedly dearest to man. The crowd of strollers weaves past me more and more gayly, but nothing disturbs me, nothing can scatter my imaginary companions. Only the damned trio from an extremely vile waltz drags me from my dream world. I hear only the screeching upper register of the violins and flute and the snoring bass of the bassoon; the sounds rise and fall, keeping firmly to octaves that lacerate the ear, and I cry out involuntarily like a person seized by a burning pain, "What insane music! What abominable octaves!" Someone murmurs next to me, "Accursed fate! Another octave-chaser!"

I looked up and only then became aware that a man had sat down at the same table, his eyes riveted on me; I could not take my eyes off him.

I had never seen a face, a figure, which had made such an impression on me so quickly. A gently curved nose was attached to a wide, open forehead, which had noticeable swellings above the bushy, partly gray eyebrows, beneath which eyes blazed forth with an almost youthful fire (the man was probably over fifty). The delicately formed chin was a strange contrast to the closed mouth, and a ludicrous smile produced by the curious play of muscles in his sunken cheeks seemed to rebel against the deep, melancholy seriousness which rested on his forehead. There were only a few gray locks of hair behind his large ears which stuck straight out from his head. A very wide, modern frock coat enveloped his large gaunt frame. Just as my glance met his, he cast down his eyes and continued the occupation that my exclamation had evidently interrupted. With evident satisfaction, he was shaking out some tobacco from various little paper bags into a large tin can that was in front of him and was dampening it with red wine from a quarter liter bottle. The music had stopped; I felt compelled to address him.

"It is a relief that the music has stopped," I said. "It was unendurable."

The old man cast a fleeting glance at me and shook out the last paper bag.

"It would be better not to play at all," I continued. "Isn't that your opinion?"

"I don't have an opinion," he said. "You are a musician and connoisseur by profession—"

"You are mistaken. I am neither. I once learned how to play the piano and the thorough bass, as one must as part of a good education; and at that time I was told, among other things, that nothing produced a more unpleasant effect than having the bass pace the soprano in octave intervals. I accepted that at that time as authoritative and I have since found it always verified."

"Really?" he interrupted me, as he stood up and strode slowly and thoughtfully towards the musicians while frequently striking his forehead with the flat of his hand, his face upturned, like someone trying to awaken a recollection. I saw him speaking to the musicians whom he treated with lordly dignity. He returned and had scarcely sat down when they began to play the overture to *Iphigenia in Aulis*.

With half-closed eyes, his folded arms resting on the table, he listened to the *andante*. Tapping his left foot gently, he signaled the entrance of the voices; then he raised his head—quickly casting a glance around—he rested his left hand with fingers spread apart on the table as if he were playing a chord on a piano, and he raised his right hand up high. He was the Kapellmeister signalling the orchestra the start of a new tempo—his right hand dropped and the *allegro* began! A burning glow flushed his pale cheeks; his eyebrows met on his wrinkled forehead; an inner storm inflamed his wild expression with a fire that increasingly consumed the smile that still hovered around his half-opened mouth. Then he leaned back and raised his eyebrows; the play of muscles around his mouth began again; his eyes shone; a deep inner pain was released in a voluptuous pleasure that convulsively shook his inner being. He drew a breath from deep within his lungs; drops formed on his forehead; he signalled for the entrance of the *tutti* and other major places; his right hand kept the beat, and with his left he pulled out a handkerchief and wiped his face. Thus he clothed with flesh and color the skeleton of the overture played by the pair of violins. I heard the soft, melting elegy which the flute utters when the storm of the violins and the bass viols has exhausted itself and the thunder of the drums is silent; I heard the softly played tones of the cello and the bassoon which filled the heart with ineffable sadness; the *tutti* returned, the *unisono* strode on like a sublime and lofty giant, the somber lament died away under his crushing tread.

The overture was over; he let his arms fall, and he sat there with his eyes closed like a person exhausted by excessive exertion.

His bottle was empty; I filled his glass with Burgundy, which I had meanwhile ordered. He sighed deeply and seemed to be awaking from a dream. I urged him to drink, which he did without ceremony, and while he dashed off the glass in one swallow, he cried, "I am satisfied with the performance! The orchestra performed very nicely!"

"And yet," I interrupted, "and yet, only the pale outline of a masterpiece that has been composed with vivid colors was presented."

"Do I judge rightly? You are not a Berliner!"

"Quite right. I only stay here from time to time."

"The Burgundy is good. But it is getting cold here."

"Let's go inside and finish the bottle."

"A good suggestion. I don't know you; but on the other hand, you don't know me either. We will not ask each other's name; names are sometimes a nuisance. I will drink the Burgundy; it costs me nothing and we are comfortable together and that is enough."

He said all this with a good-natured cordiality. We had entered the room. When he sat down, he opened his frock coat and I noticed with surprise that he was wearing under it an embroidered waistcoat, long coattails, black velvet britches, and a quite small dagger. He buttoned the coat again carefully.

"Why did you ask me if I was a Berliner?" I began.

"Because in that case I would have been obliged to leave you."

"That sounds mysterious."

"Not in the least, as soon as I tell you that I—well, that I am a composer."

"I still can't guess what you mean."

"Then forgive my remark, for I see you do not understand anything about Berlin and Berliners."

He rose and paced violently up and down a few times; then he stepped to the window and scarcely audibly sang the chorus of the priestesses from *Iphigenia in Tauris,* while tapping on the window pane from time to time at the entrance of the *tutti* passage. With astonishment I noticed that he gave certain different directions to the melody that were striking in their power and novelty. I let him go on. He finished and returned to his seat. Quite taken by the man's strange behavior and the extraordinary signs of a rare musical talent, I remained silent. After a while he began.

"Have you never composed?"

"Yes. I have tried my skill; only I found that everything which

I had written in moments of inspiration afterwards seemed to be flat and boring. So I gave it up."

"You acted wrongly. The very fact that you rejected your own attempts is no bad sign of your talent. One learns music as a boy because father and mother wish it. So one fiddles and bangs away; but without noticing it, one's senses become more receptive to melody. Perhaps it was the half-forgotten theme of a little song which one now sang differently, the first thought of one's own; and this embryo, laboriously nourished by strange powers, grew to be a giant which consumed everything around and was transformed into your blood and marrow. Ah—how to suggest the thousand ways by which one can come to composing! It is a wide highway: everyone romps around on it and exults and shouts, 'We are the sacred people! We have attained the goal!' One enters the kingdom of dreams through the ivory gate: only a few even see the gate, even fewer pass through! It looks strange here. Absurd figures hover here and there, but they have character—one more than the other. They cannot be seen on the highway; they can only be found behind the ivory gate. It is difficult to get out of this kingdom; monsters block the way as they do in front of Alzinen's castle[5]—everything spins, turns—many dream away the dream in the kingdom of dreams—they dissolve in dreams—they do not cast a shadow any longer, for otherwise, by the shadow, they would know about the ray of light that passes through this kingdom; but only a few, awakened from the dream, arise and stride through the kingdom of dreams—they attain the truth—the highest moment is there: contact with the eternal, the ineffable! Look at the sun; it is the triad from which the chords, like stars, shoot out and entwine you with threads of fire. You lie as in a cocoon of fire until the soul swings up to the sun."

He jumped up at the last words, cast his eyes upward and raised his hand. Then he sat down again and quickly emptied his refilled glass. A silence arose which I did not want to break for fear of getting the extraordinary man off the track. Finally he continued more calmly.

"When I was in the kingdom of dreams, a thousand aches and worries tortured me. It was night and I was terrified by the grinning larvae of the monsters who dashed out at me and sometimes dragged me into the ocean's abyss, sometimes carried me high into

5. See Ludovico Ariosto, *Orlando Furioso* (1532), canto 6, 11, 61–67.

the sky. Rays of light shot through the night and these rays of light were tones which encircled me with delightful clarity. I awoke from my pains and saw a large, bright eye that was looking into an organ; and as it looked, tones sounded forth and shimmered and entwined themselves in marvelous chords that had never before been conceived. Melodies streamed back and forth, and I swam in this stream and was about to drown. Then the eye looked at me and sustained me above the roaring waves. It became night again; two colossi in gleaming armor strode towards me: the Tonic and the Dominant. They snatched me up, but the eye said smiling, 'I know what fills your heart with yearning. The gentle, soft youth Tierce will walk among the colossi; you will hear his sweet voice; you will see me again and my melodies will be yours.' "

He stopped.

"And you saw the eye again?"

"Yes, I saw it again. For many years I sighed in the kingdom of dreams—there—indeed, there—I sat in a marvelous valley and listened to the flowers singing together. Only a sunflower was silent and sadly bowed her closed calyx to the ground. Invisible bonds drew me to her—she raised her head—the calyx opened and shone toward me from within the eye. Now tones, like rays of light, flowed from my head to the flowers, which greedily drank them. The leaves of the sunflower grew bigger and bigger—fire streamed from them—encompassed me—the eye had vanished and I was in the calyx."

With the last words he sprang up and hurried out of the room with a quick, youthful stride. I awaited his return in vain; I decided, therefore, to go back to the city.

When I was near the Brandenburg Gate, I saw a lanky figure striding along in the darkness and immediately recognized my odd friend. I spoke to him.

"Why did you leave me so quickly?"

"It got too hot and THE 'EUPHON'[6] began to sound."

"I don't understand you!"

"All the better."

"All the worse, for I would like to understand you completely."

"Don't you hear anything?"

6. Even Hoffmann's major editors disagree as to what this means. H. v. Müller suggests that this is the designation of the imaginary sound Ritter Gluck hears.

"No."

"It is gone! Let us go. Usually I don't like company, but—you do not compose—you are not a Berliner."

"I cannot fathom why you are so prejudiced against Berliners. Here, where art is respected and practiced widely, I would think a man with your artistic soul would feel happy."

"You are mistaken! I am damned to wander here as my torment in barren space, like a departed spirit."

"In barren space, here, in Berlin?"

"Yes, it is barren around me, for no kindred spirit joins me. I am alone."

"But the artists! The composers!"

"Away with them! They carp and niggle—refine everything to the smallest measure; rake through everything just to find one wretched thought. From chattering so much about art and artistic sensitivity and what have you—they never get around to creating, and if they do happen to feel as if they had to bring a few wretched thoughts to light, the fearful coldness reveals their great distance from the sun—it is Laplandish work."

"Your criticism seems much too harsh to me. At least the splendid productions in the theater must satisfy you."

"Once I prevailed upon myself to go to the theater to hear the opera of my young friend—what is it called? Oh, the whole world is in this opera! The spirits of hell stride through the bright crowd of elegant people—everything in it has a voice and an all-powerful sound—the devil, I mean *Don Juan!* But I couldn't last through the overture, which was spewed forth *prestissimo,* without meaning or understanding; and I had prepared myself for it with fasting and prayer because I know that the 'Euphon' is much too moved by these masses and has an impure appeal."

"Even if I have to admit that Mozart's masterpieces are mostly neglected here in a way scarcely explicable, still Gluck's works certainly enjoy a dignified performance."

"You think so? I wanted to hear *Iphigenia in Tauris* once. As I entered the theater, I heard how the overture of *Iphigenia in Tauris* was being played. Hm—I think, a mistake. *This Iphigenia* is being given! I am astonished when the *andante* with which Iphigenia is received in Tauris begins and the storm follows. Twenty years lie in between! The whole effect, the tragedy's whole well-planned exposition is lost. A quiet set—a storm—the Greeks are cast on land, the opera is there! Well, do you think the composer tossed out the overture so that one can blow it how and where one wants to, like a little trumpet piece?"

"I admit the blunder. Still, everything is done to promote Gluck's works."

"Oh, yes indeed!" he said curtly and then smiled bitterly and ever more bitterly. Suddenly he rose, and nothing could stay him. He vanished in a moment, and for several days I sought him in vain in the Zoological Gardens.

Several months had passed. One cold rainy night I had been delayed in a remote section of the city and was hurrying to my home in the Friedrichstrasse.[7] I had to pass the theater. The sound of music, of trumpets and drums, reminded me that Gluck's *Armida* was being performed, and I was on the point of going in when a strange soliloquy by the windows, where almost every tone of the orchestra could be heard, aroused my attention.

"Now the king is coming—they are playing the March—Drum away! Just drum away! That's very gay! Yes, they have to do it eleven times today—otherwise the parade isn't enough of a parade. Ah ha!—*maestoso*—poke along, boys. Look, there's a super with a shoelace dragging. Right, for the twelfth time and always striking the dominant. O ye eternal powers! It is never going to end! Now he is making a bow—Armida very humbly acknowledges the applause—. Once again? Right. Two soldiers are still missing. Now they are banging into the recitative. What evil spirit holds me here in his spell?"

"The spell is dissolved," I cried. "Come along!"

I quickly seized my odd friend from the Zoological Gardens— for the soliloquist was none other—by the arm and dragged him off with me. He seemed surprised and followed me in silence. We had already reached the Friedrichstrasse when he suddenly stopped.

"I know you," said he. "You were in the Zoological Gardens. We did a lot of talking—I drank wine—and became heated—afterwards the 'Euphon' rang for two days. I endured a great deal—it is past!"

7. Hoffman lived in the Friedrichstrasse, number 179, during his second stay in Berlin, 1807–1808.

"I am delighted that chance has led me to you again. Let us become better acquainted with one another. I don't live very far from here. How would it be—"

"I cannot and may not go to another's house."

"No. You won't escape me. I will come to you."

"Then you will still have to walk a few hundred steps with me. But didn't you want to go to the theater?"

"I wanted to hear *Armida*, but now—"

"You shall hear *Armida* right *now!* Come along!"

We walked along the Friedrichstrasse in silence; he suddenly turned into a cross-street, and I was scarcely able to follow him, because he ran down the street so quickly until he finally stopped in front of a modest house. He knocked for rather a long time before the door was finally opened. Feeling our way in the dark, we found the stairs and then a room in the upper floor, the door of which my guide carefully locked behind us. I heard another door being opened. Soon he came back with a light, and the appearance of the strangely furnished room surprised me not a little. Chairs ornamented with an old-fashioned richness, a wall clock with a gilded case, and a broad, cumbersome mirror gave everything the gloomy appearance of a past splendor. In the middle stood a small piano on which were a porcelain inkstand and several sheets of paper lined for music. A closer glance at these materials convinced me, however, that nothing had been written for a long time, for the paper was quite yellowed, and thick spiderwebs covered the inkstand. The man stepped over to a cupboard in the corner of the room which I had not noticed before, and when he pulled aside the curtain, I saw a row of beautifully bound books with golden letters: *Orfeo*, *Armida*, *Alceste*, *Iphigenia*, etc.; in brief, I saw Gluck's masterpieces standing together.

"You have Gluck's complete works?" I cried.

He did not answer; but his mouth twisted in a convulsive smile, and in a flash the play of muscles in his sunken cheeks distorted his face to a fearful mask. His somber glance directed fixedly at me, he seized one of the books—it was *Armida*—and strode solemnly toward the piano. I opened it quickly and set up the music stand. He seemed pleased with that. He opened the book and—who can describe my astonishment—I saw music paper, but without a single note written on it.

He said, "Now I will play the overture. Turn the pages at the right moments!" I promised to do so; then he played marvelously and masterfully, with complete chords, the majestic *tempo di marcia* with which the overture begins, almost completely true to the original. The *allegro*, however, merely had Gluck's main thoughts woven into it. He introduced so many new and inspired twists that my astonishment grew and grew. His modulations were especially striking without becoming harsh, and he knew how to add so many melodic *melismas* that they seemed to be recurring in ever-rejuvenated form. His face glowed; sometimes his eyebrows were drawn together and a long restrained anger seemed about to burst forth; sometimes his eyes swam in tears of deepest melancholy. At times he sang the theme with a pleasant tenor voice while both hands were working at artistic *melismas*. Then, in a quite special way, he knew how to imitate the hollow sound of the drum. I turned the pages industriously by watching his glance. The overture was over and he fell back in his chair exhausted, his eyes closed. But soon he leaned forward again and said in a hollow voice, while hastily turning more empty pages of the book, "I wrote all this, my good sir, when I came from the kingdom of dreams. But I betrayed that which is holy to the unholy and an ice cold hand reached into my glowing heart! It did not break. Then I was damned to wander among the unholy like a departed spirit—formless, so that no one would recognize me until the sunflower should raise me again to the eternal. Ah—now let us sing Armida's scene!"

Then he sang the final scene of *Armida* with an expression that penetrated my soul. Here too he deviated noticeably from the true original; but the transformed music was the Gluck scene in a higher power. He recapitulated powerfully in sound, and in the highest measure, everything that hate, love, despair, madness can express. His voice seemed to be that of a young man, for it swelled up from the deepest groan to a penetrating power. All my fibers trembled—I was beside myself. When he had finished, I hurled myself into his arms and cried in a strained voice, "What is it? Who are you?"

He stood up and measured me with an earnest, penetrating glance; but when I wanted to ask more, he had vanished with the light through the door and left me in the darkness. Almost a quarter of an hour passed; I had despaired of ever seeing him again and was seeking to open the door, oriented by the position of the piano, when he suddenly returned in an embroidered court dress, with a rich waistcoat, his dagger at his side and the light in his hand.

I was paralyzed. Solemnly he strode towards me, seized me gently by the hand, and said, smiling strangely, *"I am Ritter Gluck!"*

The Golden Pot

A Modern Fairy Tale

FIRST VIGIL

The Misfortunes of the Student Anselmus,
Assistant Dean Paulmann's Medicinal Tobacco,
and the Gold-green Snakes.

About three in the afternoon on Ascension Day, a young man in
Dresden came running out through the Black Gate, directly into a
basket of apples and cakes which a hideous old woman was offering
for sale, so that everything fortunate enough to survive the tremendous crush was scattered to the winds, and urchins in the street
joyously divided the booty that was thrown their way by this precipitous gentleman. At the shriek of "Murder!" unleashed by the
hag, her cronies deserted their cake-and-brandy tables, encircled the
young man, and cursed him with such vulgarity that, speechless
from chagrin and shame, he merely offered his small and by-no-
means especially full purse, which the hag clutched greedily and
quickly pocketed. Now the tightly closed circle around him opened,
but as the young man dashed out, the hag shouted after him: "Yes,
run! Run, you spawn of the Devil! Run into the crystal which will
soon be your downfall—run into the crystal!" There was something
frightful about the shrill, creaking voice of the woman that caused

Sections of this rendering clearly and intentionally reflect Thomas
Carlyle's frequently brilliant (and always suitably poetic) 1827 translation of
this stunning story.

14

strollers to freeze in amazement; and the laughter, which had at first been general, suddenly was silenced.

Despite the fact that he did not begin to understand these extraordinary phrases, the student Anselmus—and the young man was none other—nevertheless felt himself gripped by a certain involuntary dread, and he quickened his pace even more in an attempt to escape the curious looks the multitude cast upon him from all sides. As he worked his way through the crowd of well-dressed people, he heard them murmuring on all sides: "The poor young man! Oh, the damned old hag!" Peculiarly enough, the hag's cryptic words had cast over this amusing adventure an aura of the tragic, so that the youth now provoked a certain sympathy, even though he had before remained unnoticed. Because he was a splendid figure of a man and had a face whose handsomeness and expressiveness were enhanced by the anger which glowed within him, the ladies forgave him not only his clumsiness but even the clothing he wore, though it was completely out of fashion. His pike-grey coat was cut as if the tailor had only known of contemporary styles from hearsay, and his worn and shiny black satin trousers gave him a certain schoolmasterish air which was at odds with the gait and bearing of the wearer.

When the student had almost reached the end of the alley which leads out to the Linke Baths,[1] he was almost out of breath and he began to walk instead of run; but he hardly dared to raise his eyes from the ground because he still saw apples and cakes dancing on all sides of him, and every sympathetic look bestowed upon him by this or that pretty girl seemed to be only a reflex reaction to the laughter which had mocked him at the Black Gate. It was in this frame of mind that he ultimately arrived at the entrance to the baths, which were usually thronged by one group of festive visitors after another. The music of a brass band resounded from within, and the din of merrymaking grew increasingly louder. Tears were about to flow from the poor student because he too had expected to take part in the festivities in the Linkean paradise. Ascension Day had invariably been a family celebration for him; indeed, he had even intended to go so far as to indulge in half a pot of coffee laced with rum and to have a bottle of strong beer. To assure proper dissipation, he had even put more money into his

1. The places mentioned in this story are historical. The Linke Baths was a popular dining place outside of Dresden.

purse than was either altogether convenient or advisable. And now, because of his unfortunate step into the apple basket, all that he had carried with him had simply vanished. Of coffee, of beer, of music, of looking at beautifully-dressed girls—in short, of all of his anticipated pleasures—there was nothing more to be thought. He slipped slowly past the baths and finally turned down the road along the Elbe River, which happened to be deserted at the time. Beneath an elder tree that had sprouted through a wall, he found an inviting, grassy resting place. He sat down here and filled his pipe from the canister containing the medicinal tobacco that had recently been given to him by his friend, Dean Paulmann. Immediately before him the golden waves of the beautiful Elbe rolled and tossed; behind this, lordly Dresden rose, boldly and proudly stretching its luminous towers into the fragrant sky, which, in the distance, dipped down toward flowery fields and fresh spring woods, while a range of jagged mountain peaks revealed Bohemia in the dim distance. But the student Anselmus, unmindful of all of this, stared ahead gloomily and puffed smoky clouds into the air until, finally, he articulated his misery, saying, "In truth, I was born unlucky. Even as a schoolboy I could never win a prize; I always guessed wrong at odds and evens; my bread and butter always fell butter side down—I will not say anything about all these miseries. But isn't it a frightening fate that assures that even now when I have become a student in spite of everything, I remain a clumsy fool. Do I ever wear a coat without immediately staining it with tallow or catching it on some poorly fastened nail or other and tearing an accursed hole in it? Do I even greet any councillor or any lady without hurling my hat away, or even slipping on the smooth pavement and stumbling disgracefully? Didn't I, while in Halle, regularly have to pay a total of three or four groschen for broken pottery every shopping day, because the devil instilled in my head the need to walk straight ahead, like a lemming? Have I ever managed to get to class—or to any other place where an appointment had been arranged—on time? What good did it do me to start out a half hour early and stand at the door, for just as I was about to knock—swish! —some devil emptied a washbasin on me—or made me bump against some fellow coming out and got me involved in endless quarrels, and so I was late for everything? Ah! Where have you flown, you blissful dreams of future fortune, when I so proudly thought I might even rise to the height of Privy Secretary! Has not my evil star estranged me from my best patrons? I know that the Councillor to whom I have a letter finds cropped hair intolerable; with enormous effort the barber attaches a small plait to the back of my head, but at the first bow the unhappy knot surrenders and a little pug dog that has been blithely sniffing all around me frolics to the Privy Councillor with the plait in his mouth. Horrified, I dart after it, only to stumble against the table where he has been working while breakfasting, so that cups and plates and inkwell all tumble to the floor with a clatter, even as a flood of chocolate and ink flows over the important public document he has just been writing. 'Sir, has the Devil gotten into you!' the incensed Privy Councillor bellows and shoves me out of the room.

"What good does it do me that Dean Paulmann has made me hopeful about a secretaryship? Will the malicious fate that hounds me everywhere allow it to happen? Just today—think about it! It was my intention to celebrate a happy Ascension Day with appropriate cheer; for once I was prepared to stretch a point and would, like any other guest, have gone into the Linke Baths and proudly have called out, 'Waiter, a bottle of beer, the best in the house please!' I might have sat there till late in the evening, moreover, quite close to this or that splendid group of beautifully-dressed girls. I know it! Courage would have come; I would have been an entirely different man. I would certainly have pulled it off so well that when one or another of the young ladies asked, 'What time is it?' or 'What is it they are playing?' I would have gracefully sprung to my feet—without overturning my glass or stumbling over the bench—and, bowing, moving forward one and a half steps, I would have responded, 'By your leave, Mademoiselle, it is the *Donauweibchen* overture,'[2] or 'It is just about to strike six.' Could anyone in the world have thought badly of me for this? I say, no!— for the girls would have glanced in my direction and smiled that mischievous smile they always show when I muster the courage to let them know that I too am acquainted with the light tone of society and with the manner in which ladies should be amused. But Satan himself directed me right into the damned apple basket, and now I sit here in solitude, with only my tobacco—"

Suddenly the soliloquy of the student was interrupted by a singular rustling and crackling which began near him in the grass,

2. A popular light opera of the time by Ferdinand Kauer (1751–1831).

but which soon glided up into the leaves and branches of the elder tree spreading over his head. First it seemed as if an evening breeze were shaking the leaves, then as if little birds were twittering on the branches, their small wings mischievously fluttering to and fro. Then a whispering and a lisping began, and it seemed as if the sound of little crystal bells was coming from the blossoms. Anselmus listened and listened. Then—he himself knew not how—the whispering and the lisping and the tinkling turned into half-heard words:

"Betwixt, between, betwixt the branches, between the blossoms, shooting, twisting, twirling we come! Sister, sister, swing in the shimmer—quickly, quickly, in and out. Rays of sunset, whispering wind of evening, sounds of dew, singing blossoms—we sing with the branches and the blossoms; stars soon to sparkle—we must descend; betwixt, between, twisting, turning, twirling, sisters we!"

And thus did the confusing, hypnotic sounds continue. Anselmus thought, "It is only the evening wind which tonight whispers distinct words." But at that instant there was a sound over his head—like a triad of pure crystal bells. He glanced up and saw three little snakes, glistening in green and gold, which had twisted around the branches and stretched forth their heads toward the evening sun. Again there came the whispering and the twittering in the same words as before, and the little snakes went sliding and slithering up and down and through the leaves and the branches; and because their movements were so quick, it was as though the elder tree was scattering a thousand sparkling emeralds through the dark leaves.

"It is the rays of the evening sun playing in the elder tree," Anselmus thought; but the bells once more sounded, and Anselmus saw that one snake was stretching its little head out toward him. A shock like electricity raced through his every limb; he quivered all over, stared upwards, saw a pair of marvelous blue eyes looking down at him with unspeakable desire, so that an unknown feeling of both supreme bliss and deepest sorrow seemed to tear his heart apart. And as he continued to stare, imbued with intense longing, into those charming eyes, the crystal bells sounded harmoniously and the playing, sparkling emeralds fell, encircling him in a thousand glittering flames like golden threads. There was movement in the elder tree, and the tree spoke: "You were lying in my shadow;

my perfume surrounded you, but you did not understand me. Fragrance is my speech when it is kindled by love."

The evening wind drifted by, saying, "I played round your temples, but you did not understand me. The breeze is my speech when it is kindled by love."

The sunbeams broke through the clouds, their rays burning with words, as if to say, "I drenched you with glowing gold, but you did not understand me. That glow is my speech when it is kindled by love."

More and more deeply absorbed in gazing into those glorious eyes, his longing grew stronger, his desire more passionate, and everything rose and moved around him as if all were awakening to joyous life. Flowers and blossoms released their odors about him—the fragrance was like the heavenly singing of a thousand flutelike voices; and what they sang was, like an echo, carried on the evening clouds of gold which sailed away with them into remote lands. But as the last ray of sun suddenly sank behind the hills and the twilight's veil covered the scene, a voice which was hoarse and deep seemed to reach Anselmus from a great distance:

"Hey there! What kind of gossiping and whispering is going on up there? Hey there! Who is seeking my ray behind the hills! Sufficiently sunned, sufficiently sung. Hey there! Through bush and grass, through grass and mist. Hey there! Come dow-w-wn, dow-w-wn!"

Thus the voice faded away, as if in the murmur of distant thunder, but the crystal bells shattered in sharp discord. All became mute; and Anselmus saw how the three snakes, shimmering and sparkling, slipped through the grass towards the river. Gliding, sliding, they rushed into the Elbe; and a green flame crackled over the waves where they had vanished, a green flame which, glowing obliquely ahead, vaporized in the direction of the city.

SECOND VIGIL

How the Student Anselmus was Taken for a Drunk and a Madman. The Crossing of the Elbe. Kapellmeister Graun's Bravura. Conradi's Medicinal Cordial, and the Bronze Apple Woman.

"The gentleman is mad!" said a respectable citizen's wife, who had paused as she was returning from a walk with her family, and now, with her arms crossed, was observing the mad antics of Anselmus. He had clasped the trunk of the elder tree and was continuously calling up to the branches and leaves, "Oh, gleam and glow one more time, you dear golden snakes. Let me once more hear your little bell voices! Oh, you lovely blue eyes, look once more upon me, once more or I must die in agony and longing!" And, along with this, the most pitiful sighing and sobbing escaped from the deepest recesses of Anselmus's soul while, eager and impatient, he shook the elder tree back and forth. But the tree, rather than replying, merely rustled its leaves somberly and inscrutably and seemed as if it were mocking Anselmus and his sorrows.

"The gentleman is mad!" the citizen's wife repeated. And Anselmus felt as if he had been shaken from a deep dream, or as if someone had poured icy water on him to rouse him suddenly from sleep. Only then did he clearly perceive where he was, and only then did he remember what a strange apparition had assaulted his senses so that he had been forced to begin talking loudly to himself. He gazed at the woman in amazement. At last, snatching up his hat, which had fallen off him to the ground, he was about to dash off. Meanwhile, the citizen himself had approached; after placing on the grass the child he had been carrying in his arms, he rested on his staff, listening and staring at the student in astonishment. Now he picked up the pipe and the tobacco which Anselmus had dropped, and extending them to the student, he said, "My worthy sir, do not behave so abominably or take to alarming people in the dark when in fact there is really nothing the matter with you except that you have had a drop too much. Go home and sleep it off like a good lad."

Anselmus was deeply ashamed, and only a very pitiful "Ah!" escaped from him.

"There, there," the citizen continued, "don't take it so to heart. Such a thing can happen to the best of us. On good old Ascension Day it is easy for a man to forget himself in his happiness and to guzzle one drink too many. It can happen even to a clergyman. I take it, my worthy sir, that you are a *candidatus*. But, with your permission, sir, I will fill my pipe with your tobacco. I used all of mine a short while ago."

The citizen uttered this last sentence as Anselmus was about to put his pipe and tobacco away; and now the good citizen cleaned his pipe slowly and deliberately, and just as slowly began to fill it. Several girls from the neighborhood had approached, and they were talking confidentially with the citizen's wife and each other, giggling as they glanced at Anselmus. For the student it was like standing on prickly thorns and glowing hot needles. Just as soon as his pipe and tobacco were returned to him, he rushed off as quickly as he could.

All of the incredible things that he had seen were completely wiped from his memory; he could only remember having babbled all kinds of foolishness beneath the elder tree, and this he found especially horrifying because he had long had an aversion to all soliloquists. His Dean had once said that it is the Devil himself who chatters out of these people, and Anselmus had sincerely believed him. But to be regarded as a *candidatus theologiae* and as being drunk on Ascension Day!—the thought was intolerable. He was about to turn into Poplar Lane near Kosel Garden when a voice behind him called out: "Anselmus! Anselmus! In heaven's name, where are you running so quickly?" The student stopped as if rooted to the spot, because he was certain that some new misfortune was now about to descend upon him. The voice was heard again: "Anselmus, come back, we are waiting for you by the water!" And now Anselmus realized that the voice he heard belonged to his friend, Dean Paulmann. He returned to the Elbe and found the Dean and both of his daughters and Registrar Heerbrand about to embark in a boat. Paulmann extended an invitation to Anselmus to join them in crossing the Elbe and to spend the evening at his house in the suburb of Pirna. Anselmus very happily accepted this invitation, thinking that it was a good way to escape from the evil destiny which had all day pursued him.

By chance, a display of fireworks was taking place on the far bank, in Anton Garden, just as they were crossing the river. Sputtering and hissing, the rockets soared on high, scattering blazing stars through the air, a thousand crackling sparks and flashes bursting all about. Anselmus was sitting near the helmsman, lost in thought; but when he saw the reflection of the darting and crackling sparks and flames in the water, it seemed to him as if the little golden snakes were playing in the waves. All of the marvels which he had seen under the elder tree now once more came alive in his heart and his thoughts, and he was again seized by that ineffable desire, that glowing passion which had shaken him before.

"Ah, my little golden snakes, is it you again? Just sing, sing! Let those lovely, dear dark blue eyes once more come to me through your song. Ah, ah! Are you then beneath the waves!"

Thus cried Anselmus, while at the same instant moving violently, as if he were about to plunge into the river from the boat.

"Is the gentleman mad?" the helmsman shouted and grabbed him by his coattails. The girls, who were close to him, screamed in fear and escaped to the other side of the boat. The Registrar said something in Dean Paulmann's ear, to which the latter lengthily responded, but of which Anselmus could only understand the words: "Attacks like this— Haven't you noticed them?" Immediately following this, the Dean rose and then sat down beside Anselmus, with a certain earnestness, seriousness, and official air, taking his hand and saying to him "How are you feeling, Anselmus?" The student was almost fainting because deep within himself there had risen an insane conflict which he desired in vain to reconcile. He clearly saw now that what he had assumed to be the gleam of golden snakes was really nothing more than the reflection of the fireworks being fired in Anton Garden. But a feeling he had never before known, one he could not identify as either rapturous or painful, convulsed his heart; and when the helm sliced through the water so that the waves, curling as if in anger, splattered and foamed, Anselmus heard a soft whispering in their sound: "Anselmus! Anselmus! Do you not see how we glide ahead of you? Little sister is looking at you again. Believe, believe, believe in us!" And he thought that he could see three streaks of glowing green in the reflected light; but when he gazed somberly into the water to see whether the lovely eyes would not once more look up at him, he saw only too well that the gleam was merely a reflection emanating from the windows of neighboring houses. He sat there, silent, engaged in a struggle with himself. And now Dean Paulmann repeated more sharply, "How are you feeling, Anselmus?"

Utterly despondent, the student answered, "Ah, my dear sir, if only you knew what I, while completely awake and with my eyes wide open, have just dreamed under an elder tree close to the garden of Linke Baths, you would not blame me for being a little absent-minded."

"Well, well, now, dear Anselmus!" the Dean interrupted, "I have always believed you to be a steady young man, but to dream— to dream while your eyes are wide open—and then to suddenly want to leap into the water, this, if you will allow me to say so, is only possible for lunatics or fools!"

Anselmus was extremely distressed by his friend's harsh talk; then Veronica, Paulmann's eldest daughter, a truly lovely, blooming girl of sixteen, said, "But my dear father, surely something extraordinary must have happened to Herr Anselmus. Perhaps he only thinks he was awake when, in truth, he may really have been asleep—and therefore all kinds of foolishness entered his head and still remain in his thoughts."

"And, dearest Mademoiselle, worthy Dean!" Registrar Heerbrand added, "is it not possible for one to sink sometimes into a kind of dreamy state even while awake? I have myself had such an experience; for instance, one afternoon while at coffee, in the kind of mood produced by that special time of salutary physical and spiritual digestion, I suddenly remembered—as if by inspiration—where a misplaced manuscript lay—and only last night a magnificent large Latin paper came dancing before my open eyes in the very same way."

"Ah, most revered Registrar," the Dean responded, "you have always been inclined to the *poetica*, and one thus lapses into fantasies and romantic flights." But Anselmus felt better that anyone should side with him in this very perplexing situation while he was in peril of being considered either drunk or crazy. Despite its already being quite dark, for the first time he noticed that Veronica truly had very lovely dark blue eyes—and he noticed this without recalling the marvelous eyes which he had seen in the elder tree. On the whole, the adventure which had taken place under the elder tree had again completely disappeared from his thoughts. He felt at ease and happy; indeed, he became so high spirited that he offered a helping hand to Veronica, his lovely advocate, as she was stepping from the boat, and when she put her arm in his, he readily escorted her home with such skill and good fortune that he only slipped once—this being the only wet spot in the entire road—Veronica's white gown merely being slightly spattered by the accident.

Dean Paulmann observed this happy change in Anselmus. His fondness for him returned immediately, and he begged to be forgiven for the harsh words which had earlier escaped him. "Yes," he admitted, "there are many examples we possess which indicate that certain fantasies may appear to a man and then prey upon and truly plague him. But this is a physical disease, and leeches are beneficial for it—if they are applied to one's bottom, as proved by a certain learned physician who is now deceased."[3]

Anselmus did not know whether he had been drunk or crazy or sick—in any event, the leeches seemed absolutely superfluous because these alleged fantasies had completely disappeared. The more Anselmus found himself successful in bestowing a variety of delicate attentions on the pretty Veronica, the happier he became.

As usual, there was music after the modest meal. Anselmus had to sit at the piano, and Veronica, her voice pure and clear, sang. "Dear Mademoiselle," Registrar Heerbrand said, "you have a voice like a crystal bell!"

"Indeed not!" Anselmus exclaimed, for a reason unknown to himself; and they all looked at him in astonishment and perplexity. "Crystal bells in elder trees make a wondrous sound—wondrous!" Anselmus continued, half murmuring to himself.

Veronica laid her hand on his shoulder and asked, "What is it you are saying now, Anselmus?"

The student immediately became wide awake again and started to play. Dean Paulmann looked at him morosely, but Registrar Heerbrand placed a sheet of music on the stand and enchantingly sang one of the bravura airs by Kapellmeister Graun.[4] Anselmus played the accompaniment, as he did for many other songs that followed; and a fugue duet played by him and Veronica, which had been composed by Dean Paulmann himself, once more restored everyone to very good spirits.

It had grown rather late; Registrar Heerbrand was reaching for his hat and cane when the Dean secretively drew near him and said, "Hm, do you not wish, honored Registrar, to mention to Anselmus himself—hm!—that about which we spoke before?"

"With enormous pleasure," Registrar Heerbrand replied, and after they had sat down in a circle, he began as follows without further ado:

"There is in this locality an old, strange, noteworthy man. They say that he engages in all manner of occult sciences, but since

3. A reference to a treatise by Friedrich Nicolai (d. 1811), the arch rationalist of Germany, in which he described in detail how he cured an attack of seeing things (in which he did not believe) by applying leeches to his bottom. Goethe similarly poked fun at Nicolai in *Faust I*, in the Walpurgis Night scene.

4. Karl Heinrich Graun (1701–59), an orchestra conductor in Berlin and a composer of popular operas.

no such sciences exist, I take him for an antiquarian, and also for an experimental chemist. I mean none other than our Privy Archivist Lindhorst. As you know, he lives alone in his old and remote house, and when he is not engaged in working in his office, he is to be found in his library or his laboratory, which, however, he permits no one to enter. He owns, aside from many rare books, a number of manuscripts which are partly in Arabic or Coptic, and some of them are written in exotic letters which belong to no known language. He desires to have the latter meticulously copied, and he needs a man who can draw with the pen and reproduce these markings on parchment in ink with precision and accuracy. This work is done in a separate room in the house, under his supervision; in addition to a free dinner during working hours, he pays a taler every day and promises a considerable reward when the copying is properly completed. The hours are from twelve to six daily; between three and four there is a rest period, and you have your dinner. Having experimented with one or two young people without success, Herr Archivarius Lindhorst has finally requested that I find him a master at ink drawing; and then I thought of you, Anselmus, because I know that you not only write neatly but that you are very expert at drawing with a pen. If, in these grim times, and until you are able to establish yourself permanently, you wish to earn a mint taler a day and, in addition, the gift promised for the job successfully completed, you may call exactly at noon tomorrow upon Herr Archivarius, with whose house you are no doubt familiar. But be on your guard against any inkblot; if a blot stains your copy, you will have to start again, and if ink falls on the original, Herr Archivarius, who is a hotheaded man, is likely to fling you out of the window."

Registrar Heerbrand's proposition made Anselmus very happy because not only did he write and draw beautifully with the pen but he had a passion for the painstaking calligraphy required of this kind of copying. He therefore expressed his grateful thanks and promised not to miss the noon appointment scheduled for the next day.

That night Anselmus saw nothing but shining taler coins and heard their delightful clink. Who could reproach this unfortunate youth, who had been deprived of so many aspirations by a capricious fate and had been forced to deliberate about the expenditure of every penny and to do without all those pleasures desired by a youthful heart? Early in the morning he had already searched out his pencils, his quills, and his India ink—never could the Archivist invent superior materials, he felt. More important than anything else, he gathered and arranged his drawings and his masterpieces of calligraphy, intending to exhibit them to the Archivist as evidence that he was competent to accomplish the work desired by that demanding gentleman. Everything proceeded well; an extraordinary and felicitous star seemed to be watching over him. His cravat was properly arranged at the first attempt; not a seam burst; not a thread tore in his black silken hose; and his hat did not even fall into the dust after he had brushed it clean. In short, at exactly half past eleven Anselmus was standing in Conradi's shop in Castle Street, dressed in his elegant grey coat and black satin trousers, with a roll of calligraphies and pen drawings in his pocket, drinking one—two—glasses of the very best medicinal cordial, for here, he thought, slapping his still-empty pocket, here there will soon be the clinking of talers.

Despite the distance to the remote street where Archivarius Lindhorst's ancient house was located, Anselmus was at the front door before twelve struck. There he stood, looking at the beautiful large bronze knocker; but then, when he raised his hand to grip the knocker, precisely as the last stroke of the clock in the church steeple boomed loudly through the air, the glowing, blue eyes rolled horrifyingly, and the metal face became contorted into a sneering smile. Oh! It was the apple woman from the Black Gate! The sharp teeth clattered together in the flabby jaws, and in the clattering there was a rasping which seemed to say: "You fool—fool—fool! Wait, wait! Why did you run away? Fool!" Terrorstruck, Anselmus tumbled backwards; he tried to grasp the doorpost, but his hand gripped the bell rope and tugged it, and piercingly discordant, the bell rang out more and more loudly while the entire empty house echoed, as if to mock him, "Soon your downfall into the crystal!"

Horror possessed Anselmus and thrilled through his limbs. The bell rope reached downward and changed into a white diaphanous, enormous serpent which encircled and crushed him, its coils squeezing him more and more tightly until his fragile and paralyzed limbs cracked into pieces and his blood gushed from his veins and into the transparent body of the serpent, dyeing it red. "Kill me! Kill me!" he tried to scream in his terrible agony, but the scream was only a muffled groan. The serpent lifted its head and placed its long, pointed tongue of glistening brass on Anselmus' chest; then a cutting pain pierced the artery of life, and he lost consciousness.

When he regained his senses, he was on his own poor bed, and Dean Paulmann was standing before him, saying: "In heaven's name, what is this madness that possesses you, my dear Anselmus?"

THIRD VIGIL

Accounts concerning Archivarius Lindhorst's Family.
Veronica's Blue Eyes. Registrar Heerbrand.

"The Spirit looked upon the water, and the water moved and churned in frothy waves and, thundering, dashed itself into the abysses, which swallowed it greedily after opening their black throats. Like victorious conquerors, granite rocks lifted their jagged crowns to protect the valley until the sun gathered it to her maternal bosom[5] and cherished and warmed it while embracing it with her rays, as if they were glowing arms. Then a thousand seeds awoke from their profound sleep under the sands of the desert and stretched their leaves of green and their stalks toward the maternal face above; and, like smiling children in cradles of green, the little flowers rested in their buds and blossoms until they were also awakened by the mother, who, in order to please them, tinted the lights with which they bedecked themselves a thousand different hues.

"But there was a black hill in the middle of the valley which rose and fell like the breast of a man inflamed by passion. Vapors billowed up from the abysses and rolled together into stupendous masses in a malevolent effort to hide the face of the mother; but the mother called upon the storm, which, flying to her service, dispersed the vapors. And when the dreary hill was touched again by the rays of the pure light, a superb fire-lily, exulting in its bliss, burst from the hill, its lovely leaves forming like soft lips eager to receive the mother's kiss.

"Now a dazzling light entered the valley; it was the youth Phosphorous. The lily was imbued with warm desire upon seeing him, and besought him: 'Be forever mine, fair youth! I love you and must die if you forsake me!' Phosphorous responded: 'Lovely flower, I will be yours, but then you will, like a naughty child, for-

5. In German, the sun is feminine.

sake your father and mother. No longer will you know your playmates, for you will endeavor to be both greater and stronger than
those who now share your joy. The salutary desire which now en-
gulfs you will be split into hundreds of rays and will torture and
trouble you, for senses will be born of sense, and the ultimate bliss,
which will be kindled by the spark I ignite in you, will be the hopeless agony through which you will be destroyed, only to rise again
in a different shape. This spark is thought!'

" 'Ah,' the lily lamented, 'can I not be yours in this glow, even
as it now flames within me? Can I love you more than now, and if
you destroyed me, could I again look upon you as I do at this moment?' Phosphorous kissed her, and the lily, as if pierced through
with light, went up in flames, out of which an alien being issued,
soaring quickly from the valley and wandering into infinite space,
unmindful of childhood playmates or of the loved youth. And, as
he had loved her too, so he mourned for the loss of his beloved.
Love of the beautiful lily had brought him to the desolate valley.
The rocks of granite lowered their heads as they joined him in
his anguish. But one of the rocks opened itself, and a dragon with
black wings flew from it, saying, 'My brothers, the metals, sleep
within, but I am forever awake and active, and I will help you.'
Winging to and fro, the dragon finally captured the being which
had sprung from the lily, carried it to the hill, and locked it
within his wing—then it was the lily again; but thought, which
had remained, tore at its heart, and the love for Phosphorous was a
cutting pain before which, as if being breathed upon by poisonous
vapors, the little flowers, previously rejoicing in the presence of the
lovely lily, withered and died.

"Phosphorous dressed himself in a resplendent coat of mail
that sported with the light in a thousand hues, and he battled with
the dragon, which beat on the mail with his black wing until it rang.
And the little flowers sprang to life at this loud clang, and like multi-
hued birds, they fluttered about the dragon. His strength ebbed, and
thus vanquished, the dragon hid himself in the bowels of the earth.
The lily was freed. Phosphorous, full of glowing desire and heavenly
love, embraced her. The flowers and the birds—indeed, even the
towering rocks of granite—joined in a jubilant anthem paying hom-
age to her as queen of the valley."

"Forgive me, my worthy Herr Archivarius, but this is Oriental bombast," Registrar Heerbrand said, "and we beg you to offer us, as you frequently have, something about your entirely extraordinary life, something about your adventures while travelling, particularly something true."

"Well, what then?" Lindhorst responded. "What I have been telling you is the truest I can serve up, and, in a certain respect, is part of my life because I come from that valley, and the fire-lily which ultimately reigned there as queen was my great-great-great-great grandmother; thus, I myself am actually a prince." Everyone burst into resounding laughter. "Yes, have a good laugh," Archivarius Lindhorst continued; "what I have told you in a most scanty and abbreviated fashion probably seems to you to be senseless and mad, yet it is nevertheless intended to be anything but incoherent or allegorical; rather, it is literally true. If, however, I had been aware that this beautiful love story, to which I owe my very existence, would have so little pleased you, I would instead have told you something of the news my brother brought me during his visit yesterday."

"What is this? Do you have a brother, Herr Archivarius? Where is he? Where does he live? Is he also in the service of the Crown? Is he perhaps an independent scholar?" they all asked from every side.

"No!" the Archivarius answered, while taking a pinch of snuff very serenely and composedly, "he has joined the bad side and has gone over to the dragons."

"We implore you, dear Herr Archivarius, to tell us what you mean?" Registrar Heerbrand interjected. "Over to the dragons?"

"Over to the dragons?" resounded from all sides, like an echo.

"Yes, over to the dragons," Archivarius Lindhorst continued, "apparently in absolute desperation, I think. Gentlemen, you are aware that my father has only recently died—at the most about three hundred and eight-five years ago; therefore, I am still in mourning. I was his favorite son, and he left me a beautiful onyx which my brother desired with his whole heart. We argued about it over the corpse of my father, in so unbecoming a manner that the deceased, his patience depleted, arose and threw my evil brother down the stairs. This vexed my brother and he joined the dragons immediately. He now lives near Tunis, in a cypress forest. There he must watch a famous mystic carbuncle, which a devilish necromancer who has set up a summer house in Lapland is after, which is why my brother can get away only for about a quarter of an hour at a time— while the necromancer is taking care of the bed of salamanders in his garden. It is during this period of time that my brother rushes to tell me what is new at the sources of the Nile."

For the second time everyone burst into laughter; but the student Anselmus was growing very uneasy, and he could hardly look into Archivarius Lindhorst's fixed and serious eyes without shuddering internally in a way he himself could not comprehend. Also, there was something about the harsh and strangely metallic tone of Archivarius Lindhorst's voice which was mysteriously penetrating. Anselmus's very bones and marrow tingled as the Archivarius spoke.

The specific purpose Registrar Heerbrand had in mind when he took Anselmus to the café now appeared to be unattainable. Anselmus had steadfastly refused to be induced to attempt a second visit subsequent to the incident at Archivarius Lindhorst's door, because he was utterly convinced that nothing but luck had saved him from death, or at least from madness. Dean Paulmann happened to be strolling through the street at exactly the moment when Anselmus was lying at the door, unconscious, and an old woman who had placed her basket of apples and cakes aside was busily attending to him. The Dean had immediately secured a chaise and, in this manner, had managed to have Anselmus carried home. "You may think anything you like of me," Anselmus said, "you may consider me to be a fool or not, as you wish, but I insist that the accursed face of that witch at the Black Gate was grinning at me from the door knocker. I would rather not talk about what followed, but if I had regained consciousness and seen that execrable apple-hag next to me (for the old woman was none other), I would that very instant have suffered a stroke or have gone completely insane." Every effort at persuasion or attempt at rational argument tried by Dean Paulmann and Registrar Heerbrand failed. Not even blue-eyed Veronica herself could extricate him from the profound state of moodiness into which he had sunk. In fact, they considered him mentally ill, and in an attempt to divert his thoughts, Registrar Heerbrand thought nothing could be more effective for him than copying the manuscripts of Archivarius Lindhorst. It was therefore necessary only to introduce Anselmus to Lindhorst, and to this end Registrar Heerbrand, who knew that the Archivarius frequented a specific café

almost every night, invited Anselmus to accompany him nightly to
that very café, there to join him in a glass of beer and a pipe at his
expense until the Archivarius Lindhorst would somehow or other
get to know him and conclude the deal for the copying—an offer
which Anselmus had accepted with great gratitude.

"Worthy Registrar, God will reward you if you bring the young
man to his senses!" Dean Paulmann said. "God will reward you!"
Veronica echoed as she piously lifted her eyes to heaven, busily
thinking that Anselmus was already a most pleasing young man,
even without his senses!

Accordingly, as Archivarius Lindhorst, intending to leave, was
heading for the door with his hat and cane, Registrar Heerbrand
gripped Anselmus by the hand and, obstructing the way, said, "Most
revered Herr Archivarius, here is Anselmus the student who has
unusual calligraphic and drawing talent and will take the assignment of copying your rare manuscripts."

"I am most delighted to hear this,'" Archivarius Lindhorst
answered quickly, throwing his three-cornered hat on his head,
shoving Registrar Heerbrand and Anselmus off to a side, and dashing noisily down the stairs, leaving both the Registrar and the student standing in utter bewilderment, gaping at the door which had
been slammed in their faces so that its hinges rattled.

"That is a remarkably eccentric old man," Registrar Heerbrand said.

"Remarkably eccentric old man," Anselmus stammered, feeling that he was being turned into a statue by an icy stream flowing
through his veins. But the other guests all laughed, saying, "Archivarius was in an exceptionally whimsical state today, tomorrow
he will be as gentle as a lamb, will utter not a word, will watch the
smoke clouds raised by his pipe, or read the newspapers. You must
not pay attention to such things."

"This is true too," Anselmus thought. "Who would pay attention to such a thing? Didn't the Archivarius tell me that he was
especially delighted to hear that I would copy his manuscripts? And
why did Registrar Heerbrand step right in his way when he wanted
to leave for home? No, no, he is basically a good man, this Herr
Archivarius Lindhorst, and surprisingly liberal; somewhat strange
in his phraseology, but how does this harm me? I will go to see him
at the stroke of twelve tomorrow, even if a hundred bronze apple-
women try to stand in my way!"

FOURTH VIGIL

Anselmus's Melancholy. The Emerald Mirror.
How Archivarius Lindhorst Flew off in the
Shape of a Vulture and Anselmus Met Nobody.

Gentle reader, may I ask you a question? Have you not had hours, even days and weeks, during which all your accustomed activities caused you nothing but annoyance and dissatisfaction, when everything you normally held to be of worth and significance seemed valueless and trivial? You did not know, at such times, what to do or where to turn. A vague feeling suffused your mind that you had more lofty desires which must be attained, desires which transcended the immediate pleasures of this world but were yet desires which your spirit, like a strictly brought-up, frightened child, dared not even express. In this desire for an unidentifiable something, which hovered over you regardless of where you were, like a diaphanous dream that vanished whenever you sought to examine it, you lost interest in everything around you here. You moped around with the disturbed look of a hopeless lover, and no matter what you saw being tried or gained in the bustle of varied existence, neither sorrow nor joy could be awakened in you—it was as though you no longer belonged to this world.

Gentle reader, if such a mood has ever possessed you, you know the state into which Anselmus had fallen. With all my heart I wish it were in my power to present Anselmus to you with complete vividness, gentle reader, for in these vigils in which I describe his extraordinary story there remains so much more of the marvelous (which jolted the lives of ordinary people into the unknown) that I am fearful that in the end you will believe neither in Anselmus nor in Archivarius Lindhorst; indeed, you may eventually have some doubt as to Registrar Heerbrand and Dean Paulmann, despite the fact that these two honorable people, at least, are still walking the streets of Dresden. Gentle reader, make an effort while you are in the fairy region full of glorious marvels, where both the highest rapture and deepest horror may be evoked, where the earnest goddess herself lifts her veil so that we think we see her face, but a smile often glimmers beneath her glance, a playful, teasing smile that enchants us just as that of a mother playing with her dearest children. While you are in this region that is revealed to us in dreams at least, try, gentle reader, to recognize the familiar shapes which hover around you in the ordinary world. Then you will discover that this glorious kingdom is much closer to you than you ever imagined. It is this kingdom which I now strive with all my heart to reveal to you through the extraordinary story of Anselmus.

Thus, as stated, Anselmus had, ever since that evening when he met Archivarius Lindhorst, been submerged in dreamy musing which made him insensitive to every external contact with the ordinary world. He felt that an ineffable something was awakening within his inmost soul and provoking that pain of rapture which is the longing that promises man the existence of a more exalted Being. His greatest pleasure came when he would wander in solitude through the meadows and the woods; and as if freed from all which chained him to his everyday impoverished existence, he could, so to speak, once more find himself in the manifold images which arose from his soul.

Once, while returning from a long walk, he happened to pass that notable elder tree under which, as if possessed by magic he had once gazed upon such numerous wonders. He was peculiarly attracted to the familiar green grass, but he had no sooner seated himself upon it than the entire vision which he had once viewed as if in a heavenly trance and which had, as though through some alien influence, been blotted from his mind, once more floated before him in the most vivid colors, as if he were looking upon it for the second time. Indeed, it was clearer to him than before, that the mild blue eyes belonged to the gold-green snake which had slithered its way through the heart of the elder tree and that those marvelous crystal tones which had so filled him with rapture must have emerged from the turnings of its tapering body. Now, as on Ascension Day, he again embraced the elder tree and cried into the branches and leaves, "Oh, once more slide forth and twine and wind yourself amidst the branches so that I may once more see you, you little lovely green snake! Once more cast your gentle eyes upon me! I love you, and if you do not return, I must perish in agony and sorrow!" But everything remained completely mute and still. As before, the branches and the leaves of the elder tree rustled unintelligibly. Anselmus, however, now felt as if he knew what it was that was alive and striving within his heart; he now knew what was lacerating his heart with the agony of infinite desire. "What else can it be," he said, "than that I love you with all my heart and soul, that

I love you to the very death, you glorious golden little snake; indeed, that I cannot survive without you and must die in forlorn misery if I fail to find you again, if I don't possess you as my beloved! But I know that you will be mine and that then everything my glorious dreams have promised me of another and loftier world will be fulfilled."

From then on Anselmus could be found every evening, when the sun scattered its sparkling golden rays over the tops of the trees, under the elder, pitiably calling from deep within his heart to the branches and the leaves for a sight of his little beloved gold-green snake. Once when he was behaving in this way, there suddenly appeared before him a tall, thin man wrapped in a wide, light grey coat who, looking upon him with large flaming eyes, said, "Hey, there! What kind of whining and wailing is going on here? Hey, there! This is Herr Anselmus who is supposed to copy my manuscripts." Anselmus was more than a little frightened upon hearing this powerful voice, because it was the same voice which had on Ascension Day called, "Hey, there! What kind of chattering and gossiping is this," and so on. Anselmus was so terrified and astounded that he could not utter a word. "What is the matter with you, Herr Anselmus?" Archivarius Lindhorst (the stranger in the light grey coat was none other) continued. "What do you want from the elder tree, and why haven't you come to me to begin your work?"

In truth, Anselmus had been unable to persuade himself to go to Archivarius Lindhorst's house for a second time, despite the fact that that very evening he had strongly resolved to do so. But, at this moment when his beautiful dreams were being shattered by the hostile voice which once before had snatched his beloved from him, a kind of despair seized him, and he burst out violently: "You, Herr Archivarius, may consider me insane or not—it makes no difference to me—but here in this very tree, on Ascension Day, I saw the gold-green snake, my soul's beloved, and she spoke to me in heavenly crystal tones; but you, you, Herr Archivarius, shouted and called so frighteningly across the water."

"What's this, my dear fellow?" Archivarius Lindhorst interrupted while taking snuff and smiling very oddly.

Anselmus felt an ease coming to his heart now that he had been successful in starting to tell this strange story, and he felt completely right in placing upon the Archivarius the entire blame, because he felt that it was he and no one else who had so thundered from afar. Pulling himself together, he continued: "Well, I will tell you all about the mysterious events which happened to me on Ascension Evening, and then you may say and do and think anything you like about me." He described the marvelous adventure in its entirety, from his unfortunate stumbling into the apple basket to the moment when the three gold-green snakes fled across the river, and how the people after that considered him to be either drunk or mad. Anselmus ended by saying, "I really saw all of this with my own eyes, and deep within my heart those precious voices I heard still echo. It was not a dream; and if I am not to perish of desire, I must believe in these gold-green snakes, though, Herr Archivarius, your smile tells me that you believe that these snakes really are no more than figments of my feverish and overwrought imagination."

"Not at all," Archivarius Lindhorst responded with great serenity and composure, "the gold-green snakes which you saw in the elder were simply my three daughters; and it is now very clear that you have fallen head over heels in love with the blue eyes of Serpentina, the youngest of these. To be sure, I knew it myself on Ascension Day, and when—at that time I was busily writing at home —I grew annoyed with all the chattering and gossiping going on, I called to the lazy flirts to tell them that it was high time to leave for home because the sun was setting and they had sung enough and had drunk enough of the sunbeams."

Anselmus felt as if he now was hearing articulated something of which he had long dreamed; and although he imagined that the elder and the wall and the grass and everything surrounding him were now beginning to spin slowly around, he pulled himself together and was about to speak again when Archivarius Lindhorst prevented him from doing so by quickly tugging the glove off his left hand and holding before Anselmus's eyes a ring with a stone which glittered with strange sparkles and flames, saying, "Look here, worthy Herr Anselmus, what you can see here may bring you joy."

Anselmus looked in the stone and, wonder of wonders! the stone cast up a cluster of beams as from a burning circle, forming a gleaming crystal mirror in which, now slithering, now fleeing, now twisting together, the three golden snakes were dancing and prancing; and when their tapering shapes, which glittered with a thousand sparkles, touched each other, there came forth from them glorious tones as of crystal bells; and the snake in the middle stretched her little head from the mirror as if possessed by passion and longing, her dark blue eyes saying, "Do you know me? Do you believe in me, Anselmus? Only in belief is there love. Can you indeed love?"

"Oh, Serpentina, Serpentina," Anselmus cried, with insane passion. Archivarius Lindhorst, however, suddenly breathed on the mirror and the rays dissolved with an electric sputter; and on his hand only a little emerald remained, which Archivarius covered by pulling on his glove.

"Did you see the little golden snakes, Herr Anselmus?" asked Archivarius Lindhorst.

"Oh, heavens yes!" the student responded, "and lovely dear Serpentina."

"Quiet!" Archivarius Lindhorst said. "Enough for today. By the way, if you should decide to work for me, you may see my daughters often enough, for I will grant you this true satisfaction if you are well behaved and stick to your task—that is, if you copy every mark with the greatest neatness and accuracy. But, Herr Anselmus, you have not come to me at all despite Registrar Heerbrand assuring me that you would come right away, and I have waited for several days in vain."

As soon as Archivarius Lindhorst mentioned Registrar Heerbrand's name, Anselmus once more felt that he had both feet on the ground, that he really was Anselmus the student, and that the man who stood before him was in fact Archivarius Lindhorst. The stark contrast between the indifference in the tone of Lindhorst's speech and the marvelous visions which the latter had evoked as a true necromancer caused a certain horror in the student which was only heightened by the piercing look of those fiery eyes which glowed from their bony sockets in the drawn and puckered face, as if from a leather case. Once more the student was inexorably gripped by the same unearthly feeling which had possessed him in the café when Archivarius Lindhorst had told such a wild tale. Anselmus retained his composure through a great effort, and when Archivarius Lindhorst once more asked, "So why is it that you did not come?" the student gathered all his courage and told him what had happened at his door.

"My dear Herr Anselmus," Archivarius Lindhorst said when the student was finished, "my dear Herr Anselmus, I know this apple-woman of whom you speak. She is an evil creature who plays all kinds of ugly tricks on me; but that she would change herself into bronze and into the shape of a doorknocker to frighten welcome visitors away is very irritating indeed and not to be tolerated. Worthy Herr Anselmus, if you come at noon tomorrow and again notice anything of this grinning and growling, would you be good enough to put a drop or two of this liquid on her nose. Everything will return to normal immediately. For now, adieu, dear Herr Anselmus. I must hurry, and I cannot, therefore, suggest that you return with me to the city. Adieu, till tomorrow at noon.''

Archivarius Lindhorst had given the student Anselmus a small vial with a yellow-golden liquid in it, and he walked quickly away so that he appeared, in the deepening dusk, to be floating down to the valley rather than to be walking. He was already drawing close to Kosel Garden when the wind entered his wide overcoat and caused the coattails to spread out, so that they fluttered in the air like a pair of huge wings. To Anselmus, who was watching Archivarius Lindhorst with a look of utter amazement, it was as if a large bird were spreading its wings for a fast flight. And now, while the student gazed steadfastly into the oncoming dusk, a white-grey vulture soared high into the air with a creaking cry; Anselmus clearly saw that the white flutter he had thought to be the retreating Archivarius Lindhorst must have been this vulture, although he still could not understand where the Archivarius had vanished so abruptly.

"But he may have flown away in person, this Herr Archivarius Lindhorst," Anselmus said to himself, "because I now clearly see and feel that all these strange shapes which have entered my waking life and are having their games with me come from a distant world of marvels which I never before saw except in particularly remarkable dreams. But be that as it may! You, my beautiful, gentle Serpentina, thrive and glow in my heart. Only you can quiet the endless desire which lacerates my soul. Oh, dear, dear Serpentina, when will I again see your lovely eyes!" Anselmus cried aloud.

"That is a despicable, un-Christian name!" mumbled a bass voice nearby which belonged to a man who was returning from a walk. Anselmus, remembering where he was, rushed off while thinking to himself, "Wouldn't it now be a real misfortune if Dean Paulmann or Registrar Heerbrand were to meet me?" But he met neither of them.

FIFTH VIGIL

Frau Court Councillor Anselmus.[6] *Cicero de Officiis.*
Long-tailed Monkeys and Other Vermin. The Equinox.

"There is nothing in the world that can be done with this Anselmus," Dean Paulmann said. "All my good advice, all my reproofs are fruitless. He does not wish to apply himself to anything, though he has a splendid classical education which is the basis for everything." But Registrar Heerbrand, smiling roguishly and mysteriously, replied, "Dear Dean, do allow Anselmus to take his time. He is a peculiar subject, this Anselmus, but there is a great deal in him; and when I say a great deal, I mean a Privy Secretary or even a Court Councillor."

"Court—" Dean Paulmann began, the words sticking in his throat in his astonishment.

"Quiet, quiet!" Registrar Heerbrand went on. "I know what I know. He has these two days been copying manuscripts at Archivarius Lindhorst's, and only last night, upon meeting me at the café, Archivarius Lindhorst said, 'You have recommended me a sound man, worthy sir, something will come of him!' Now think of the connections of Archivarius Lindhorst— Quiet, Quiet! We'll discuss this a year from now." With these words the Registrar left the room, the same roguish smile on his face, leaving behind the Dean, whose astonishment and curiosity had rendered him speechless, and who, as if under a spell, was transfixed in his chair. But on Veronica this conversation made a very special impression. "Haven't I all along known," she thought, "that Herr Anselmus is a very clever and attractive young man who is destined for something great? If only I could be sure that he really cares for me! Didn't he press my hand twice that night when we crossed the Elbe? And during our duet, didn't he look at me with glances which pierced my heart? Yes, yes, he really likes me and I—" as young girls tend to do, Veronica totally surrendered to the sweet dreams of a joyous future. She was Frau Court Councillor; she lived in a magnificent house on Castle Street, or in New Market, or in Moritz

6. Veronica, who dreams of marrying Anselmus, would thus be addressed as his wife when Anselmus attained the position of Court Councillor (German *Hofrat*). In Germany a woman uses her husband's title, preceded by *Frau* ("Mrs.").

Street. Her stylish little hat and her new Turkish shawl were wonderfully becoming; she was having her breakfast on the balcony, dressed in a smart negligee, giving her cook orders for the day: "And please take care that you do not spoil that dish. It is the Court Councillor's favorite." Young dandies who are passing by glance up, and she clearly hears, "Well, isn't that wife of the Court Councillor a divine creature! How well her little lace cap suits her!" Frau Privy Councillor Ypsilon sends her servant to inquire if it would suit the pleasure of Frau Court Councillor Veronica to drive with her to the Linke Baths today. "Many thanks. I am terribly sorry, but I have a previous engagement for tea with Frau President Tz." Then Court Councillor Anselmus, who has gone out early on business, returns. He is dressed in the height of fashion: "Already ten," he declares, looking at his gold watch and bestowing upon his young wife a kiss. "How are you, my little wife? Can you guess what I have for you?" he says teasingly, taking a pair of lovely earrings designed in the latest style from his vest pocket and substituting them for her old ones. "Oh, what lovely, dainty earrings!" Veronica cries aloud, jumping up from her chair and throwing her embroidery aside in order to look at those lovely earrings in the mirror with her own eyes.

"Well, what's all this about," Dean Paulmann said, deep in his study of *Cicero de Officiis,* and nearly dropping his book. "Are we having fits like Anselmus?" At precisely this moment Anselmus, who, contrary to his habit, had not been seen for several days, entered the room, much to Veronica's amazement and fright because he seemed, in truth, completely changed. Much more precisely than was usual, he spoke of the new possibility life opened to him which had recently become clear to him, and of splendid prospects which were now available to him but which many were quite unable to recognize. Dean Paulmann, remembering the cryptic speech of Registrar Heerbrand, was even more thunderstruck, and barely a syllable could escape his lips before Anselmus had already made his exit, after dropping hints of some important business he had at Archivarius Lindhorst's, and after he had kissed Veronica's hand with foppish facility.

"That was already a Court Councillor," Veronica murmured to herself, "and he kissed my hand without slipping on the floor or stepping on my foot, as he always used to! And he threw me the tenderest look as well. Yes, he truly loves me!"

Once more Veronica surrendered to her reverie, but now it seemed as if a hostile figure was invading these beautiful visions of her future life as Frau Court Councillor, and as if this figure were mocking her, saying to her, "This is all terribly stupid and ordinary business, and false to boot, for Anselmus will never ever be a Court Councillor and your husband. He does not love you even a little, despite your blue eyes and your splendid figure and your lovely hand." An icy stream then froze Veronica's soul, and a profound dismay swept aside the pleasure with which she had imagined herself in her little lace cap and her stylish earrings just a short while before. Tears almost welling in her eyes, she said aloud, "Ah! it is only too true. He does not love me, and I shall never ever be Frau Court Councillor!"

"Romantic rot, romantic rot!" Dean Paulmann cried, and then, snatching up his hat and his cane, he indignantly and hurriedly left the house. "That's the last straw," Veronica sighed; and she was annoyed at her twelve-year-old sister because she sat and kept sewing unconcernedly at her embroidery frame as if nothing had happened.

It was almost three o'clock, time to tidy the room and set the coffee table because the Mademoiselles Oster had sent word that they were coming to call. But from behind every box that Veronica moved, behind the music books that she took from the piano, behind every cup, behind the coffee pot that she brought from the cupboard, peeped that malicious figure, like a little mandrake, laughing mockingly while snapping its tiny spidery tendrils and crying, "He will not be your husband! He will not be your husband!" Finally, when Veronica had fled into the middle of the room, leaving everything, she saw it again with a long nose and colossal bulk behind the stove, and it growled and snarled, "He will not be your husband!"

"Don't you hear or see anything, sister?" Veronica cried, trembling with fright, not daring to touch anything in the room. Fränzchen arose from her embroidering very gravely and quietly, saying, "What troubles you today, sister? You're rattling and banging everything. I see that I must help you."

But at this moment the visitors, gay and laughing briskly, came tripping in; and at the very same instant Veronica saw that she had mistaken the stove top for the figure and the creaking of the poorly-shut stove door for those malicious words. She was, nevertheless, beside herself with terror and could not immediately recover her composure, so that her friends could not help seeing her unusual agitation which her paleness and her expression betrayed. They immediately terminated their cheerful chatter and insisted that she tell them what in heaven's name had happened. She was forced to confess that while she had abandoned herself to quite special thoughts, she had been possessed by an abnormal fear of ghosts, which was quite unlike her. Her description of how a little grey mandrake had peeped out of the corners of the room mocking and torturing her was painted in such vivid colors that the Mademoiselles Oster peered around with timid glances and began to experience all kinds of unearthly feelings. Fränzchen, however, came into the room at this very moment with the steaming coffee pot, and the three, composed again, laughed at their foolishness.

Angelica, the elder of the Osters, was betrothed to an officer. The young man had joined the army, and news of him had so long failed to reach his friends that there was no question but that he was dead, or at the very least critically wounded. This had plunged Angelica into the most profound sorrow; but she was happy today, even exuberant, a condition which so surprised Veronica that she could not help but talk about it quite unreservedly.

"Dear girl," Angelica said, "do you believe that my Victor is out of my heart and out of my thoughts? He is the reason why I am so happy. Oh Lord! So happy, so completely blissful! For my Victor is well and will soon be home, having been promoted to captain, and having been decorated with the honors his heroism earned. He is prevented from writing by a deep but by no means serious wound in his right arm, inflicted upon him by the sword of a French Hussar, and also, the rapid movement of the army—he refuses to leave his regiment—still makes it impossible for him to send me news. But tonight he will be ordered to return home until his wound heals. He will start out for home tomorrow, and at the precise moment when he is stepping into the coach, he will be informed of his promotion."

"But my dear Angelica," Veronica interrupted, "how do you know all this?"

"Do not mock me, my friend," Angelica continued, "and you will certainly not laugh lest you be punished by the little grey mandrake who might peep out at you from behind the mirror there. I cannot relinquish my belief in certain mysterious things, because

I have often enough seen them in life. I do not, for example, consider it so remarkable as many others do that there are people who are gifted with a certain clairvoyance. There is an old woman in the city here who has this talent to a great degree. She uses neither cards nor molten lead nor coffee grounds, as do ordinary fortune tellers, but after taking certain steps in which you yourself participate, she uses a polished metallic mirror, and the weirdest combination of intermingled figures and forms appear in it. These she interprets, and answers your questions. I was with her last night and was told this news of my Victor, which I do not for a moment doubt."

Angelica's story cast a spark into Veronica's soul, which quickly flared to the thought of consulting this same old woman about Anselmus and her aspirations. She discovered that this old woman was called Frau Rauerin and that she lived on a secluded street near Lake Gate—also, that she could only be seen on Tuesdays, Wednesdays, and Fridays, from seven in the evening, but then, to be sure, during the whole night until sunrise. She also preferred her customers to come unaccompanied. It was Wednesday now, and Veronica resolved, under the pretext of taking the Osters home, to visit this old woman, which she actually did. Thus, she had scarcely said goodbye to her friends, who lived in Neustadt, at the Elbe bridge, when she rushed towards Lake Gate and, before long, had come to that remote and narrow street which had been described to her. There, at the very far end of it, she saw the little red house in which Frau Rauerin was supposed to live. As she approached the door, she could not rid herself of a dread, a kind of horror. Finally, in spite of her reluctance, she summoned her courage and pulled the bell. The door opened and she groped her way through the dark passage toward the stair which lead to the second story, as Angelica had told her to do. "Does Frau Rauerin live here?" she called into the deserted hallway when no one appeared. But instead of an answer there was a long and clear "Meow!" and a large black tomcat, its back arched, its tail whisking back and forth in wavy coils, gravely preceded her to the door of the room, which opened at the sound of a second meow.

"Ah, see—daughter, are you here already? Come in, come in," called an approaching figure whose appearance rooted Veronica to the floor. A tall bony woman covered in black rags!—and while she spoke, her pointed, protruding chin wagged this way and that.

Her toothless mouth, overshadowed by a bony hawknose, contorted into a sneering smile, and glowing cat's eyes sparkled behind large eyeglasses; black wiry hair protruded from the motley shawl wrapped around her head; but two large burn scars, which traversed her face from the left cheek across her nose, deformed her face horribly. Veronica's breath stuck in her throat, and the scream which struggled to escape became a profound sigh as the skeletal hand of the witch clutched her and pulled her into the room.

Here everything was awake and astir—there was nothing but noise and tumult and squealing and meowing and croaking and piping, everything at once, and from everywhere. The old witch pounded the table with her fist and screamed, "Peace, you wretches!" And the monkeys whimpered and climbed to the top of the four-poster bed; and the guinea pigs all dashed beneath the stove; and the raven fluttered up to the round mirror; and the black tomcat, as if the rebuke concerned him not at all, sat comfortably on the upholstered chair into which he had jumped immediately after entering the room.

Veronica gained courage as soon as the room grew quiet. She was less frightened now than she had been while in the hall; indeed, the hag herself did not seem so repulsive now, and for the first time Veronica gazed about at the room. All kinds of obnoxious stuffed animals were suspended from the ceiling; weird household implements which she had never seen before were spread in confusion on the floor; there was a meager blue fire burning in the grate which occasionally sputtered and sent forth yellow sparks, and every sputter was accompanied by a rustling noise from above, and monstrous bats with human faces frozen in contorted laughter flew back and forth; and at times the flame leapt up from the grate, onto the sooty wall; and then there arose the sound of piercing, howling tones of anguish which gripped Veronica and shook her with terror. "By your leave, Mam'selle," said the old woman smirking and grabbing a brush with which she sprinkled the grate after having dipped it in a copper skillet. The fire died and the room grew black as pitch, as if filled with thick smoke. The hag, who had gone into a little room, returned with a lighted lamp; and now Veronica saw that there were neither beasts nor household implements around. It was rather a common, coarsely furnished room. The hag approached her and, with a creaking voice, said, "Little daughter, I know what it is that you wish. You would have me tell you whether or not you will be married to Anselmus when he is a Court Councillor."

Veronica froze with astonishment and fear, but the hag continued: "You told me about it all at home, at your father's, when the coffee pot was beside you. I was the coffee pot. Didn't you recognize me? Little daughter, listen to me. Give up this Anselmus, give him up because he is a nasty person. He stepped on my little sons' faces, my dear little sons, and crushed them to pieces—the red-cheeked apples that steal away after people have bought them right out of their pockets and then roll into my basket again. He sides with the old man; only the day before yesterday he poured that damned golden pigment on my face and nearly blinded me with it. You can still see the burn marks. Little daughter, you must give him up, give him up! He does not love you; he loves the gold-green snake; he will never be a Court Councillor because he has gone over to the salamanders and he intends to marry the green snake. Give him up, give him up!"

Veronica, who was possessed of a firm and steadfast spirit, and who could overcome girlish terror, drew back a step and spoke seriously and resolutely: "Old woman, I have heard of your gift for gazing into the future, and I wished—possibly too curiously and too soon—to find out from you whether Anselmus, whom I love and treasure, could ever be mine. If you continue troubling me with your foolish and absurd babble instead of fulfilling my wish, you are doing wrong. For I ask you to do nothing for me which you do not do for others, as I am well aware. Since you are apparently familiar with my deepest thoughts, it should have been a small matter for you to reveal to me much of that which now causes me anguish and troubles my mind, but after your pointless slander of the good Anselmus, I no longer wish to find out more from you. Goodnight!"

Veronica was about to leave quickly, but the crone fell on her knees, crying and lamenting, and holding the girl fast by her dress, and said, "Veronica, Veronica, have you then forgotten old Liese, the nurse who so often carried you in her arms and fondled you?"

Veronica could barely believe her eyes. Then, indeed, she recognized her old nurse who was deformed only by advanced age and the two scars—old Liese who years before had vanished from

Dean Paulmann's house, no one knew where. The crone also looked different now. Instead of the patched motley shawl, she wore a presentable cap; instead of the black rags, she wore a gaily printed garment—she was neatly dressed, as she used to be.

She arose from the floor and, taking Veronica in her arms, said, "What I have told you now may seem utterly insane, but it is too true, unfortunately. Anselmus has caused me much harm, though it is not his own fault. He has fallen into the hands of Archivarius Lindhorst, who intends to have him marry his daughter. Archivarius Lindhorst is my greatest enemy, and I could tell you all sorts of things about him which you would, however, be unable to comprehend, or which would horrify you frightfully. It seems that he is the Wise Man, but I am the Wise Woman—so be it! Now I see that you are in love with Anselmus, and I will help you with all my strength in order that you may find happiness and marry him as you desire."

"But for heaven's sake, Liese, tell me—" Veronica interrupted.

"Hush! Hush, child!" the old woman cried. "I know what you want to say to me. I have become what I am because I had to. I couldn't help it. Well, I know how to cure Anselmus of his foolish love for the green snake and to lead him, the handsomest Court Councillor, directly into your arms, but you must help too."

"Liese, tell me. I love Anselmus with all my heart, and I will do anything and everything!" Veronica whispered, hardly audibly.

"I know you," the crone continued, "to be a courageous child. I could never frighten you to sleep with the bogeyman, for as soon as I tried, you opened your eyes to see the bogeyman. Also, you entered the blackest room without a candle, and many times you terrified the children of the neighbors by wearing your father's dressing gown over your head. So then, if you are serious about using my art to defeat Archivarius Lindhorst and the green snake, if you are serious about calling Anselmus Court Councillor and husband, then at the next equinox, about eleven at night, you are to steal from your father's house and come here. I will accompany you to the crossroads that intersect the field close by. We will do what is necessary, and the marvels you may chance to see will do you no harm at all. And now, little daughter, good night. Papa already waits for you at supper."

Veronica went quickly away. She was firmly determined not to miss the night of the equinox because, she thought, "Old Liese was right. Anselmus has become chained in strange fetters. But I will deliver him from them, and I will call him mine forever. He is mine and he shall be my Court Councillor Anselmus."

SIXTH VIGIL

Archivarius Lindhorst's Garden, including Some Mockingbirds.
The Golden Pot. English Script.
Messy Scratchings. The Prince of the Spirits.

"After all, it may be," Anselmus said to himself, "that the very fine medicinal cordial of which I greedily drank at Monsieur Conradi's might really be the reason behind all these shocking fantasies which so tortured me at the door of Archivarius Lindhorst. I will, therefore, stay quite sober today and defy whatever additional trouble may attack me."

On this occasion, as before, while preparing for his first visit to Archivarius Lindhorst, Anselmus put into his pocket his pen sketches and his masterpieces of calligraphy, his jars of India ink, and his well-sharpened pens of crows' feathers. He was about to depart, when his eye alighted upon the vial of yellow liquid which Archivarius Lindhorst had given him. There suddenly rose up in his mind, in glowing colors, all of his strange adventures, and an ineffable feeling of rapture and pain shot through his heart. With a piteous voice he involuntarily exclaimed, "Isn't it only for the sight of you, dear lovely Serpentina, that I go to Archivarius Lindhorst's?" At that moment he felt that Serpentina's love might be the prize awarded him for a difficult and hazardous task which he had to undertake, and as if the task were nothing other than that of copying Lindhorst's manuscripts. He expected that at the moment he entered the house or, to be more accurate, even before his entrance into it, all kinds of mysterious things would, as before, occur. No more did he think of Conradi's powerful drink, but instead, he quickly put the vial of liquid into his vest pocket so that he could follow Archivarius Lindhorst's directions to the letter should the bronze apple woman again decide to make faces at him.

At the stroke of twelve, as Anselmus raised his hands to the knocker, didn't the hawk-nose twitch, didn't the cat's-eyes actually glower from it? Now, however, without ado, he sprinkled the liquid on the despicable face and it contracted and immediately remolded itself into the gleaming round knocker. The door opened, the bells sounding delightfully throughout the house—"cling-ling—young-ling—in—in—spring—spring—cling-ling." He mounted the beautiful wide steps in good spirits and relished the odor of some exotic incense which wafted through the house. Hesitantly, he stopped in the hall, for he did not know on which of these many fine doors he was supposed to knock. Then Archivarius Lindhorst, dressed in a white damask dressing gown, came out and said, "Well, I am delighted, Herr Anselmus, that you have finally kept your word. Follow me, this way, won't you please. I must take you directly into the laboratory." Saying this, he walked quickly through the hall and opened a small side door which led into a corridor. Anselmus, in good spirits, followed behind Archivarius Lindhorst. From this corridor they entered a hall or, more properly, a majestic greenhouse. All kinds of rare and marvelous flowers grew there on both sides, all the way up to the ceiling; indeed, there were massive trees with exotically shaped blossoms and leaves. A magical dazzling light spread over everything, but it was not possible to determine its source, for there was no visible window. As Anselmus peered through the bushes and flowers, long avenues seemed to open toward remote distances. In the deep shade of thick cyprus groves there glistened marble basins from which there arose fantastic figures, spouting crystal jets which gently splashed into the gleaming lily chalices. Strange voices rustled through the forest of marvelous plants, and lovely odors wafted up, then down.

Archivarius Lindhorst had disappeared, and Anselmus saw nothing but a gigantic bush of gleaming fire-lilies. Anselmus was transfixed to the spot, intoxicated by the sight and the delicious odors pervading this fairyland garden. Suddenly, from all sides a giggling and a laughing began, and delicate little voices teased and mocked him: "Herr Studiosus, Herr Studiosus, how did you get here? Why are you so stylishly dressed, Herr Anselmus? Will you chatter a minute with us and tell us how Grandmother sat down on the egg and the young master spotted his Sunday vest? Are you able now to play the new tune which you learned from Daddy Starling, Herr Anselmus? You look splendid in your glossy wig and thin boots." Thus the little voices chattered and teased from every corner, even immediately next to the student himself. And Anselmus now saw that all varieties of bright-colored birds were fluttering about him and mocking him. At that moment, the fire-lily bush moved toward him, and he saw that it was Archivarius Lindhorst, whose flowered dressing gown, glittering in yellow and red, had deceived him.

"I ask your forgiveness, worthy Herr Anselmus," Archivarius Lindhorst said, "for leaving you alone. I desired, in passing, to take a peep at my beautiful cactus, which is due to blossom tonight —but how do you like my little indoor garden?"

"O Lord! It is unbelievably beautiful," the student said, "but these bright colored birds have been mocking me a little."

"What kind of chattering is this?" the Archivarius cried angrily into the bushes. Then a huge grey parrot fluttered out and perched itself on a bough of myrtle near the Archivarius and, looking at him with unusual seriousness and gravity through glasses which sat on its hooked bill, creaked, "Don't be offended, Herr Archivarius, my high-spirited children have been a little playful, but the Herr Studiosus is himself to blame because—"

"Be quiet, be quiet!" Archivarius Lindhorst interrupted. "I know the culprits, but you really must keep a tighter rein on them, my friend. Now, let us go on, Herr Anselmus."

The Archivarius stepped through many an exotically decorated room so that Anselmus, in following him, could hardly glance at the gleaming marvelous furniture and other things he had never before seen which filled up all the rooms. They finally entered a large room where the Archivarius, after casting a glance upward, stopped; and Anselmus had time to feast upon the heavenly sight which the simple decorations of this hall provided. From the light-blue colored walls there jutted the trunks of stately palm trees with trunks of golden bronze, their colossal leaves, glittering like sparkling emeralds, arching across the ceiling far above them. In the middle of the room, placed on three Egyptian lions cast of dark bronze, there lay a porphyry plate; and on this plate there was a simple golden pot, from which Anselmus could not avert his eyes from the moment he saw it. It seemed as if, in a thousand shimmering reflections, countless shapes were playing on the brilliant polished gold. He often saw his own reflection, arms outstretched in desire—oh! beneath the elder tree—Serpentina darting and winding up and down, looking at him once more with her lovely eyes. Anselmus was beside himself with mad rapture.

"Serpentina!" he cried aloud, and Archivarius Lindhorst suddenly turned around and said, "What is it, worthy Herr Anselmus? I believe you intended to call my daughter, who is at the very opposite side of the house in her room and is having her piano lesson now. Come, let us go on."

Anselmus followed behind, hardly knowing what he was doing. He neither saw nor heard anything more until Archivarius Lindhorst suddenly grasped his hand and said, "Here we are!" Anselmus, awaking as if from a dream, now saw that he was in a high-ceilinged room which was lined on all sides with bookshelves, a room not different from an ordinary library and study. In the middle of the room there was a large writing table, an upholstered armchair in front of it.

"For the present," Archivarius Lindhorst said, "this is to be your workroom. I cannot yet tell you whether you will at some future time work in the blue library where you suddenly called my daughter's name. I would now like to be convinced of your ability to complete this task you are undertaking in the manner which I desire and require."

Anselmus summoned all of his courage and, not without self-satisfaction at his ability to please Archivarius Lindhorst, he took out the drawings and samples of his penmanship from his pocket. But Archivarius Lindhorst had no sooner cast his eye on the first sheet, which contained writing in the finest English style, than he smiled most peculiarly and shook his head. He repeated these actions every time a leaf was presented, and Anselmus could feel the blood rushing to his face until, finally, when the smile had grown utterly sardonic and contemptuous, Anselmus poured out his irritation: "Herr Archivarius does not seem very pleased by my meager talent."

"My dear, Herr Anselmus," Archivarius Lindhorst said, "you do in fact have a considerable talent for the calligraphic art, but it is apparent that, for the meantime, I must depend more upon your industry and good intentions than upon your accomplishments. Perhaps it is the fault of the inferior materials you use."

Anselmus spoke at length of his ability in his art, which had so often been acknowledged. He spoke about his fine India ink and the crow quills which were of the finest quality. Archivarius Lindhorst, however, handed him the sheet containing the English script. "Judge this for yourself!"

When Anselmus saw his handwriting, he felt as if a thunderbolt had struck him. The script was unspeakably wretched. The curves were not rounded, the hairstroke failed to appear where it should have been; capital and small letters could not be distinguished; in truth, the messy scratchings of a schoolboy intruded, frequently ruining the best drawn lines.

"Also," Archivarius Lindhorst continued, "your ink is not permanent." Dipping his finger into a glass of water, he ran his finger over the lines and they disappeared, leaving not a trace behind. Anselmus felt as if some monster were choking him; not a word could escape from his throat. With the wretched sheet in his hand, he stood there, but Archivarius Lindhorst laughed out loud and said, "Don't be upset, Herr Anselmus. What you could not do well before you will probably be able to do better here. You will, at any rate, have the use of better supplies than those to which you are accustomed. Just begin confidently."

Archivarius Lindhorst first drew a black fluid out of a locked trunk, from which a very strange odor escaped; he also drew out well-pointed pens of a peculiar color, and a sheet which was extraordinarily white and smooth. Finally, he brought out an Arabic manuscript. As Anselmus sat down to begin his work, Archivarius Lindhorst left the room. Anselmus had frequently had occasion to copy such Arabic writing before. It did not seem to him, therefore, that the first assignment would be difficult to do. "How those scratches got on my fine English script, the Lord and Archivarius Lindhorst know best," he said, "but I will swear to the death that they were not done by *my* hand!"

Every fresh word which now stood beautifully and perfectly on the parchment increased his courage, and as his courage increased, so did his dexterity. In truth, the pens he was using wrote superbly well, and the mysterious ink flowed smoothly, as black as jet, onto the bright white parchment. In addition, as Anselmus worked along industriously and concentrated upon the work before him, he began to feel increasingly comfortable in the remote room; and he had very much adjusted to his work, which he intended to complete successfully, when at the stroke of three he was called by Archivarius Lindhorst to partake of a delicious dinner. At dinner Archivarius Lindhorst was in an especially good mood. He asked about Anselmus's friends, Dean Paulmann and Registrar Heerbrand, and he told many gay stories about the Registrar. Anselmus found the good old Rhine wine particularly delightful, and he grew more talkative than usual. Exactly at the stroke of four he rose from the table to resume his work, and Archivarius Lindhorst was very pleased by this punctuality.

If Anselmus had been doing well in copying these Arabic symbols before dinner, he now did even better. In truth, he could not understand the speed and the ease with which he was able to transcribe the convoluted strokes of these foreign characters. It was as if, deep within him, he could hear a whispering voice: "Ah, could you really work so well if you were not thinking of her, if you did not believe in her and in her love?" Then, throughout the room, whispers floated, as in low undulating crystal tones: "I am near, near, near! I am helping you. Be brave. Be steadfast, dear Anselmus! I am working with you so that you may be mine!" And as soon as Anselmus heard these sounds with inner rapture, the unfamiliar characters grew ever clearer to him, and he hardly needed to look at the original script at all; in fact, it seemed as if the characters were already outlined on the parchment in pale ink and there was nothing more for him to do but fill them in with black. Thus he worked on, surrounded by those precious inspiring sounds, that soft sweet breath, until, at the stroke of six, Archivarius Lindhorst entered the room.

He approached the table with a peculiar smile. Anselmus silently rose, Archivarius Lindhorst continuing to look at him with a derisive smile. But he had no sooner glanced at the copy than this smile was converted to an expression of deep seriousness. No longer did he seem the same. His eyes, which customarily glowed with sparkling fire, now looked at Anselmus with ineffable gentleness; a soft flush colored the pallid cheeks; and instead of the sarcasm which had previously shaped the mouth, his lips, now gently curved and graceful, seemed to be parted to express sententious and persuasive speech. His body seemed taller and statelier, the wide dressing gown spread over his breast and shoulders like a royal mantle unfurling in broad folds, and a narrow streak of gold wound through the white locks which lay on his high brow.

"Young man," Archivarius Lindhorst began solemnly, "I knew before you dreamed of them all the secret relationships binding you to my dearest and holiest concern! Serpentina loves you. An extraordinary destiny spun by the fateful threads of hostile powers will be fulfilled if she becomes yours and when you receive the golden pot as a necessary dowry which properly belongs to her. But your happiness will only arise from struggle and toil; hostile forces will attack you, and only the inner force within you, accustomed to withstand these conflicting powers, can spare you from disgrace and ruination. By working here, you will surmount your apprenticeship. Belief and complete knowledge will lead you to the goal, but only if you keep to that which you have so well begun. Carry her always and faithfully in your thoughts, she who loves you, and then you will see the marvels of the golden pot, and happiness will be yours forever. Farewell. Archivarius Lindhorst expects you in his room tomorrow at noon. Farewell."

And with these words Archivarius Lindhorst gently pushed Anselmus out of the door, which he then locked; and Anselmus found himself in the room where he had enjoyed dinner. One door of the room led into the hallway.

Absolutely bewildered by these cryptic events, Anselmus lingered at the street door. He heard a window opening above him, and he looked up. It was Archivarius Lindhorst, who was once more a very old man, again dressed in his light grey gown, who now looked as he usually did. The Archivarius called to him: "Well, worthy Herr Anselmus, what are you pondering down there? Ah, the Arabic is still on your mind. Extend my compliments to Dean Paulmann if you see him, and come tomorrow exactly at noon. Your wages for this day will be found in the corner of the right hand pocket of your vest."

Anselmus immediately found the silver taler exactly where he had been told it would be, but he did not derive pleasure from it. "I do not know what will come of all this," he said to himself, "but even if I am in the grasp of some insane delusion and have been seized by a spell, my precious Serpentina will live in my heart even more strongly than before; I will die rather than leave her, for I know that my love and the thought of her are with me forever and that nothing hostile can change that; what else is this thought but Serpentina's love?"

SEVENTH VIGIL

*How Dean Paulmann Knocked the Ashes from His Pipe
and Retired to Bed. Rembrandt and Breughel.
The Magic Mirror and Doctor Eckstein's
Prescription for an Unknown Disease.*

Dean Paulmann finally knocked the ashes out of his pipe and said, "Now it is time to go to bed."

"Absolutely," Veronica replied, frightened by the fact that her father was up so late, the clock long ago having struck ten. Accordingly, no sooner had the Dean withdrawn to his study and bedroom, and Fränzchen's heavy breathing indicated that she was asleep, than Veronica, who, to keep up appearances, had also gone to bed, rose softly, very softly, dressed herself, and throwing a coat about her, slipped out of the door.

Anselmus had been continuously before her eyes from the moment she had left old Liese; it was as if a mysterious voice which she could not recognize kept repeating in her soul that his resistance resulted from an antagonistic force which kept him prisoner, and that he might be freed through some occult, magical art. Every day her confidence in old Liese increased; and even her earliest impressions of unearthliness and terror had by degrees diminished, so that the mystery and the strangeness of her relationship with the old witch now appeared to her only in the light of something extraordinary and fictional and, hence, not completely unattractive. She had, therefore, firmly stuck to her resolve, even at the risk of being missed at home and encountering a thousand inconveniences, to go on with the adventure of the equinox. And now, at last the fateful night on which old Liese had promised to offer comfort and aid had arrived. Veronica, who had long been accustoming herself to the idea of this night adventure, was infused with courage and hope. She flew through the deserted streets, unmindful of the storm which howled through the air and was already dashing thick raindrops in her face.

The church tower clock struck eleven with a stifled, droning clang as Veronica came to old Liese's house, her clothes soaked through with rain. "Well, my dear! Already here! Wait, my love, wait!" a voice cried from above her; and in a moment the old woman, weighed down with a basket and attended by her cat, was standing at the door.

"Now we will go and do what is proper to do and thrives in the night, which is favorable to our work." Thus speaking, the crone seized the shivering Veronica with her cold hand and gave her the heavy basket to carry while she herself took out a little cauldron, a three-legged iron stand, and a spade. By the time they reached the open field, the rain had stopped, but the wind had grown stronger. It howled all about them with a thousand voices. A horrible, heart-piercing wailing seemed to resound from the black clouds which rolled together in their speedy flight and veiled everything in the world in densest darkness.

But the hag quickly stepped forward and in a shrill harsh voice cried, "Light! Light, my boy!" Then blue gleams quivered and sputtered before them like forked lightning, and Veronica saw that the sparks were coming from the cat and were leaping forward to light the way while his doleful and ghastly wails punctuated the momentary pauses of the storm. Veronica's heart almost stopped beating. It was as if icy talons were ripping into her soul; but, with enormous effort, she composed herself and, pressing closer to the old hag, said, "It must all be done, come what may!"

"True, true, little daughter!" the hag responded, "stand firm and I will give you something beautiful, and Anselmus to boot."

At last the old hag stopped walking and said, "This is the place!" Using the spade, she dug a hole in the ground and then shook coals into it, placed the iron stand over them, and the cauldron on top of the stand. She did all this while gesturing weirdly, the cat circling around her. Sparkles continued to sputter from its tail, and these sparkles formed a circle of fire. The coals ignited, and finally blue flames leapt up around the cauldron. Veronica was told to remove her coat and her veil and to crouch down beside the old woman, who, seizing her hands, pressed them hard while glaring at the girl with fiery eyes. Before long the exotic materials —and nobody could have determined whether they were flowers, or metals, or herbs, or animals—which the crone had taken from her basket and flung into the cauldron began to seethe and to bubble. The hag now left Veronica and, gripping an iron ladle, plunged it into the glowing mass which she then began to stir, while Veronica, following orders, continued to stare steadily into the cauldron and to focus her thoughts on Anselmus. Now the witch again added shining metals to the cauldron, a lock of hair which Veronica had cut from her head, and a little ring which she had long worn. Meanwhile she uttered fearful howling noises into the night, and the cat whimpered and whined as it ran around incessantly.

Gentle reader, I sincerely wish that you had been traveling towards Dresden on this twenty-third day of September. The people at the last station had tried futilely to keep you there when night fell, enveloping the earth; the friendly host at the inn had assured you that the storm and the rain were too violent to be dealt with and, further, that for supernatural reasons it was simply not safe to dash away in the dark on the night of the equinox; but you had refused to listen, thinking to yourself, "I will tip the coachman a whole taler and will reach Dresden by one o'clock at the latest;

and there in the *Golden Angel* or the *Helmet* or in the *City of Naumburg*, a delicious supper and a soft bed await me."

Now, as you are heading toward the city through the dark, you suddenly see a strange flickering light far off in the distance. Approaching, you can distinguish a ring of fire and in its center, next to a cauldron out of which a thick vapor pours with quivering red flashes and sparks of light, you also see two contrasting figures sitting. Your road cuts directly through the fire, but the horses snort and stomp and rear; the coachman curses and prays and beats the horses with his whip, but they will not move from the spot. Then, without thinking, you leap from the stagecoach and rush toward the fire. Now you can clearly see the dainty, gentle child who, in her thin white night dress, kneels by the cauldron. Her braids have been untied by the storm, and her long, chestnut brown hair flies freely in the wind. Her angelic face hovers in the dazzling light cast by the flickering flame under the trivet, but in the icy terror which has overcome it, the face is as stiff and white as death; and you realize her fear, her complete horror, from the eyebrows which are drawn up, and from the mouth, vainly opened to emit the shriek of anguish that cannot find its way from a heart oppressed with indescribable torment. She holds her soft, small hands aloft; they are pressed together convulsively as if in prayer to her guardian angel to spare her from the monsters of Hell, which, obedient to this all-powerful spell, are about to appear. She kneels there, as still as a marble statue. Opposite her, cowering on the ground, is a tall, shriveled, copper-colored crone with a peaked hawk-nose and glittering cat-eyes; her bony naked arms stick out from the black cloak which is pulled around her, and she stirs the hellish brew while laughing and shrieking through the roaring, bellowing storm with her croaking voice.

I can imagine, gentle reader, that although you are usually unfamiliar with terror and fear, that your hair might have stood on end at the sight of this picture by Rembrandt or Breughel which was actually taking place in true life. But your eyes could not be averted from the gentle child entangled in these hellish pursuits, and the electric shock quivering through all your nerves and fibers with the speed of lightning would kindle in you the courageous thought of standing up to the mysterious powers possessed by the monstrous circle of fire and your terror would disappear at this thought. You would feel as if you yourself were one of those guardian angels to whom this almost mortally frightened girl was praying, even as if you were forced to draw your revolver and blow out the hag's brains without further ceremony. But while you were so clearly thinking about this, you would probably have cried out "Hello!" or "What's going on here?" or "What are you doing?" Then, at a reverberating blast from the coachman's horn, the witch would have somersaulted into her brew and in a flicker all would have disappeared in thick smoke. I cannot tell you whether you would have found the girl for whom you desperately searched in the darkness, but you certainly would have destroyed the spell of the witch and would have broken the magic circle that Veronica had thoughtlessly entered.

Alas, gentle reader, neither you nor anyone else drove or walked this way on the twenty-third of September during that stormy night so favorable to witches; and Veronica was forced to stay by the cauldron, overcome with terror, until the work neared its completion. She did indeed hear all that howled and raged about her, all kinds of despicable voices which bellowed and bleated and howled and hummed, but she did not open her eyes because she felt that the very sight of the abominations which encircled her might drive her into an incurable, devastating insanity.

The witch had stopped stirring the brew, and the smoke rising from it grew dimmer and dimmer until, finally, nothing but a light spirit-flame burned in the bottom. Then the crone cried, "Veronica, my child, my dearest, look there into the bottom! What is it you see? What do you see?" But Veronica could not answer, and yet it seemed to her that all kinds of intermingled shapes were whirling in the cauldron. Suddenly, with a friendly look and an outstretched hand, Anselmus rose up from the very depths of the cauldron, and Veronica cried, "It is Anselmus! It is Anselmus!"

The old hag immediately turned the petcock attached to the bottom of the cauldron, and molten metal gushed forth, boiling and bubbling into the tiny mold which she had placed beneath it. Now the hag leapt into the air and, darting about wildly and gesturing horribly, shrieked, "It is done, it is done! Thank you, my boy! You kept guard. Hey—hey—he is coming! Bite him to death! Bite him to death!" But now a loud sweeping sound rushed through the air—as if a gigantic eagle were swooping down and beating all around him with his wings. And a stupendous voice boomed, "Hey there, wretches! It is over, it is over! Get home!" The hag, bitterly bewailing her fate, sank down to the earth. Veronica lost all consciousness.

When she regained her senses, it was bright daylight. She was in her bed; Fränzchen, standing before her with a cup of steaming tea in her hands, was saying, "Tell me, sister, what in the world is wrong with you? I have been standing here for an hour, and you have been unconscious, as if in a fever, moaning and whimpering until we were all scared to death. Father missed his class this morning because of your illness. He will very soon be here with the doctor."

Veronica drank her tea silently; even as she drank it, the tormenting images of the night came vividly before her. "So it was all nothing but a wild dream which tormented me? But surely, I did go to that old woman last night. It certainly was the twenty-third day of September. Well, I must have been terribly sick last night and have imagined all of this. It is my constant thinking about Anselmus and the strange old woman who pretended to be Liese but wasn't and made a fool of me, which is responsible for my illness."

Fränzchen, who had left the room, now returned with Veronica's dripping wet coat in her hand. "But look, sister," she said, "look at the condition of your coat! Last night's storm blew open the shutters and knocked over the chair upon which your coat was hanging, and the rain came in and drenched it." These words weighed heavy on Veronica's heart because now she knew that it was not a dream which had tormented her but that she had, in fact, been with the witch. The very thought caused terror and anguish to seize her, and a feverish chill quivered through her body. Shuddering convulsively, she drew the bedclothes tightly around her, but in so doing she felt something hard pressing on her breast, and when she grasped it it seemed to be a medallion, which as soon as Fränzchen left with the wet coat, she pulled out. It was a small round brightly polished metallic mirror. "This is a gift from the old woman!" she cried eagerly. And it was as if flaming rays were darting from the mirror and penetrating into the deepest recesses of her soul with benevolent warmth. The fever chill left, and through her whole being an inexpressible feeling of serenity and contentment streamed. She could not help but remember Anselmus; and as she thought about him more and more intensely—behold!—his friendly face smiled at her out of the mirror, as if she held in her hand a living miniature portrait.

But before long she felt that it was no longer Anselmus's image which she saw, but rather that it was Anselmus himself, alive and in the flesh. He was sitting in a stately room which was peculiarly furnished, and he was industriously writing. Veronica was about to step forward to tap him on the shoulder and to say to him, "Herr Anselmus, turn around; it is me!" but she could not, for it was as though he was surrounded by a circle of fire; yet when she stared more closely, she could see that this circle of fire consisted of nothing but large gilt-edged books. Finally, Veronica managed to catch Anselmus's eye. It seemed as if, while glancing at her, he needed to recall who she was; but at last he smiled at her and said, "Oh, dear Mademoiselle Paulmann, is it you? But why is it that you sometimes desire to appear as a little snake?"

Veronica could not keep from laughing aloud at these peculiar words, and with this she awoke as from a profound dream. She quickly hid the little mirror because the door opened and Dean Paulmann and Doctor Eckstein entered the room. Doctor Eckstein stepped to the side of her bed, felt and long studied her pulse, then said, "Ai! Ai!" and wrote a prescription; once more he felt her pulse, again said "Ai! Ai!" and left his patient. But from this information provided by Doctor Eckstein, Dean Paulmann could not clearly understand what it was that ailed his daughter Veronica.

EIGHTH VIGIL

The Library of Palm Trees. The Fortunes of an Unfortunate Salamander. How a Black Quill Caressed a Beet and Registrar Heerbrand Got Drunk.

Anselmus had now been at work with Archivarius Lindhorst for several days, and these hours were for him the happiest of his life. Still surrounded by lovely sounds, forever encouraged by Serpentina's voice, he was filled to overflowing by a perfect delight that often mounted to the highest rapture. Every problem, every need of his impoverished existence, had disappeared from his mind, and in this new life which now unfolded before him with its sun-filled brilliance, he understood all of the wonders of a loftier world which had before merely filled him with astonishment, even with fear. His copying work proceeded quickly and easily because he felt more and more as if he were copying characters which he had long known and he hardly needed to glance at the manuscript while he perfectly reproduced it.

Archivarius Lindhorst only appeared occasionally, except at dinner time, and his appearance always exactly coincided with the precise moment when Anselmus had completed the final character of some manuscript. At these times Archivarius Lindhorst would hand him another sheet and, without uttering a word, would immediately leave, after having stirred the ink with a little black stick and having replaced the old pen with newly sharpened ones. One day when, at the stroke of twelve, Anselmus had as usual climbed the stairs, he discovered that the door through which he usually entered was locked. Archivarius Lindhorst approached, dressed in his strange, flowered dressing gown, calling aloud, "Today you are to come this way, good Herr Anselmus, because we must go to the room where *Bhagavad-Gita*'s masters await us."

He walked along the corridor, leading Anselmus through the same rooms and halls the student had passed on the occasion of his first visit. Anselmus was once more astounded by the splendid beauty of the garden, but now he realized that many of the exotic flowers which were suspended on the dark bushes were really marvelously colored insects that fluttered up and down on their little wings, as dancing and swirling in groups, they caressed each other with their antennae. Again, on the other hand, the pink and azure-colored birds were now seen to be fragrant flowers, and the perfume they scattered about seemed to rise from their cups in low and lilting sounds which, when mingled with the splashing of fountains in the distance and the sighing of the high groves of trees, merged into mysterious, deep, inexpressible longing. The birds which had unmercifully mocked and jeered him before were again fluttering to and fro over his head and calling incessantly with their sharp little voices, "Herr Studiosus, Herr Studiosus! Don't be in such a hurry! Don't peer into the clouds as you do—you might fall on your nose. Ha, ha, Herr Studiosus! Put on your bath robe. Cousin screech owl will curl your wig for you!" And thus they continued with all kinds of absurd banter until Anselmus left the garden.

At last Archivarius Lindhorst stepped into the azure room. The porphyry with the golden pot was gone and had been replaced in the middle of the room by a table which was covered by violet-colored satin; and upon this cover lay the writing equipment familiar to Anselmus. An armchair upholstered with the same material was beside it.

"Dear Herr Anselmus," Archivarius Lindhorst said, "you have now copied a number of manuscripts for me quickly and accurately, to my great satisfaction. You have gained my confidence, but the hardest is still to be done, and that involves the transcription, or rather, the painting of certain works which are written in strange characters. I keep them in this room, and they can only be copied here. You will, therefore, in the future, work here, but I advise you to pay great heed because if you make a false penstroke or—heaven forbid!—if you should allow a blot to fall on the original, you will be plunged into misfortune."

Anselmus saw that small emerald leaves projected from the golden trunks of the palm trees. Archivarius Lindhorst took hold of one of these leaves, and Anselmus perceived that the leaf was, in fact, a roll of parchment, which the Archivarius unfolded and spread out on the table before the student. Anselmus was more than a little struck by these singular intertwined characters, and as he studied the numerous points, strokes, dashes, and twirls in the manuscript, which sometimes represented plants or mosses or animals, he almost despaired of ever copying them accurately.

"Courage, young man!" Archivarius Lindhorst cried, "If you continue to maintain your belief and your true love, Serpentina will help you."

His voice resounded like ringing metal, and as Anselmus, suddenly terrified, glanced up, he saw the Archivarius standing before him in the same majestic form he had assumed during his first visit to the library.

Anselmus felt as if he must sink to his knees in deep reverence, but the Archivarius climbed up the trunk of a palm tree and vanished high among the emerald leaves. Anselmus realized that the Prince of the Spirits had been speaking with him and had left to return to his own study, perhaps intending, by using the beams which had been sent to him as envoys by some of the planets, to send back word about what the fate of Anselmus and Serpentina was to be.

"It might also be," he thought, "that he is awaiting news from the sources of the Nile, or that a magician from Lapland is visiting

him. In any case, it is in my interest to begin diligently working." Saying this, he began to study the exotic characters contained on the roll of parchment.

He heard strange music coming from the garden, and he was surrounded by sweet and lovely fragrances; and he could hear the birds too, still mocking and twittering, but he could not make out their words, a state of affairs which pleased him immensely. At times it also seemed to him that the emerald leaves of the palm trees were rustling and that the clear crystal tones which Anselmus had heard under the elder tree that eventful Ascension Day were dancing and flitting through the room. Marvelously strengthened by this sparkling and tinkling, Anselmus increasingly and more intensely focused his eyes and his thoughts on the writings on the roll of parchment, and before long, almost as in a vision, he realized that the characters therein could represent nothing other than these words: "About the marriage of the salamander and the green snake." Then the air reverberated with a strong triad of clear crystal bells, and the words "Anselmus, dear Anselmus!" floated down to him from the leaves and—wonder of wonders!—the green snake glided down the palm tree trunk.

"Serpentina, lovely Serpentina!" Anselmus cried in the madness of absolute bliss, because as he gazed more intently, he discovered that he was looking at a lovely and glorious maiden who was coming towards him from the tree, looking at him with ineffable longing with those dark blue eyes which lived in his heart. The leaves appeared to reach down and to expand; thorns sprouted on every side of the trunk, but Serpentina twisted and twirled herself deftly between them and so skillfully drew her fluttering robe, with its ever-changing colors, along with her, that, clinging to her dainty form, it nowhere was caught on the points and prickles of the palm tree. She sat down on the same chair with Anselmus, clasped him in her arms, and pressed him to her so that he could feel the breath coming from her lips and the electric warmth of her body as it touched his.

"Dear Anselmus," Serpentina began, "now you will be completely mine. You will win me for your bride through your belief and your love, and I will bring you the golden pot which shall assure our happiness together forever."

"Oh, dearest, lovely Serpentina!" Anselmus cried. "What

need have I of anything else if I have you! When you are mine, I will happily surrender to all of these inexplicable mysteries which have beset me ever since the moment I first saw you."

"I know," Serpentina continued, "that the strange and mysterious things which my father—often simply to indulge his mood —has caused to happen to you have provoked in you distrust and fear, but now I hope this will be no more, for at this very moment I have come to tell you, dear Anselmus, everything, from the bottom of my heart and soul, down to the smallest detail which you need to know in order to understand my father and so that you may clearly comprehend what our circumstances really are."

Anselmus felt as if he were so completely in the grasp of the gentle and lovely form that he could neither move nor live without her, and as if her beating pulse throbbed within him. He listened to every word she uttered until it resounded in his heart and then, like a burning ray, kindled divine bliss within him. He had put his arms around her very dainty waist, but the strange, ever-changing cloth of her robe was so smooth and slippery that it seemed as though she might writhe out of his arms at any moment and, like a snake, glide away. The thought made him tremble.

"Oh, do not leave me, lovely Serpentina!" he cried involuntarily. "You alone are my life!"

"Not now," said Serpentina, "not until I have told you all that you, because of your love for me, will be able to understand:

"Dearest one, know then that my father is of the marvelous race of salamanders, and that for my existence I am indebted to his love for the green snake. In primeval times, in the fairyland of Atlantis, the powerful Prince of the Spirits, Phosphorous, ruled, whom the other spirits of the elements served. Once upon a time the salamander whom the prince loved more than any of the others (it was my father) happened to be walking in the splendid garden, which had been decorated by Phosphorous's mother in the most marvelous fashion with her finest gifts; and the salamander heard a tall lily softly singing: 'Close your little eyelids until my lover, the morning wind, wakes you.' He approached it, and touched by his glowing breath, the lily spread her leaves, and he saw the lily's daughter, the green snake, lying asleep in the kelch of the flower; then the salamander became enflamed with passionate love for the lovely snake and he took her away from the lily, whose perfumes futilely called for her beloved daughter throughout all of the garden in ineffable anguish. The salamander had carried her off to the palace of Phosphorous and there besought Phosphorous: 'Marry me to my beloved and she shall be mine forever.' 'Madman, what are you asking?' the Prince of the Spirits said. 'Know that the lily was once my mistress and ruled with me, but the spark which I cast into her threatened to destroy the lovely lily, and it was only my victory over the black dragon, whom the spirits of the earth keep chained, which preserves her so that her leaves are able to remain strong enough to enclose this spark and to guard it; but if you clasp the green snake, your fire will consume her body and a new being, rapidly springing from her dust, will soar away and leave you!'

"The salamander did not listen to the warning of the Prince of the Spirits. Filled with passion he enfolded the green snake in his arms, and she crumbled into ashes, and a winged being who was born from her dust soared away through the sky. Then the madness of despair gripped the salamander, and he dashed through the garden spouting fire and flame, in this absolute frenzy destroying this lovely garden until the fairest flowers and blossoms it possessed hung limp, black, and scorched, their wailing filling the air. The angry Prince of the Spirits seized the salamander in his wrath and said to him, 'Your fire has burned out. Your flames are extinguished. Your rays are darkened—sink down to the spirits of the earth; let these jeer at you and mock you and keep you their prisoner until such time as the fire element will again be rekindled and will glow with you, a new being, from the earth.'

"Extinguished, the poor salamander sank down, but now the irritable old Earth Spirit, who was Phosphorous's gardener, approached and said, 'Master, is there anyone who has greater cause to complain about the salamander than I do? Had not all the lovely flowers which he has scorched been decorated with my gayest colors? Had I not carefully tended them and nursed them and expended many a fair color on their leaves? Yet I must take pity upon the poor salamander, for it was nothing but love, in which you, O Master, have often been entangled, which drove him to the despair which resulted in the destruction of the garden. Revoke his punishment; it is too severe!'

" 'For the present,' said the Prince of the Spirits, 'his fire is extinguished, but in a time devoid of happiness, when degenerate man will no longer be able to understand the voice of Nature, when the spirits of the elements, exiled into their own regions, will only speak to him from a great distance, in faint echoes; when banished from the harmonious circle, an infinite desire alone will give him news of the Kingdom of Marvels, which he once inhabited when there was belief and love in his soul—in this hapless time the fire of the salamander will again be ignited. But he will be permitted to rise as a man, and completely entering man's prosaic existence, he will learn how to endure its needs and its oppressions. And not only will he continue to remember his first state, but he will again attain a sacred harmony with all of nature; he will comprehend its wonders, and the power of his fellow spirits will be at his command. He will find the green snake in a lily bush again, and the fruit of his marriage with her will be three daughters which will appear to men in the shape of their mother. In the springtime they will hang in the dark elder tree and will sing with their lovely crystal voices. Then, if during that coarse age, a youth is found who understands their song—yes, if one of the little snakes looks at him with gentle eyes; if this look awakens in him an anticipatory vision of distant wondrous lands to which he can courageously soar when he has cast away the onerous lot of common place life; if, with his love of the snake, there arises in him vividly a belief in the marvels of nature, rather, a belief in his own existence amid these marvels, the snake will be his. But not until three such youths have been found and married to the three daughters may the salamander cast away his oppressive burden and return to his brothers.'

" 'If I may, Master,' the Earth Spirit said, 'I would bestow a gift upon these three daughters which will make their lives with the husbands they will find glorious. Let each of them receive from me a pot of the most beautiful metal which I possess. I will polish each pot with light borrowed from the diamond, and our Kingdom of Marvels will glitter in it as it presently exists in the harmony of universal nature; and on the day of the wedding, from its interior a fire-lily will spring forth which will embrace the worthy youth with its eternal blossoms and sweet wafting perfume. Also, he will soon come to learn the lily's speech and will understand the marvels of our kingdom, and he and his beloved will dwell in Atlantis itself.'

"You understand, dear Anselmus, that the salamander of whom I speak is none other than my father. Despite his lofty nature he has been forced to subject himself to the meanest aspects of everyday existence and, therefore, he is often provoked into that perverse mood which causes troubles to so many. Now and then he has told me that for the temperament which the Prince of the Spirits Phosphorous stipulated as a condition of marriage with me and my sisters men have a name, which, to tell the truth, they often enough misapply. They call it a childlike poetic nature. He says that this character is often to be discovered in youths who, because of the extreme simplicity of their way of life and their complete lack of what this world calls worldliness, are mocked at by the common rabble. Oh, dear Anselmus, you understood my glances and my song beneath the elder tree. You loved the green snake and you believe in me; you will be mine forever. From the golden pot the lovely lily will bloom and we, happy, joined together, truly blessed, will dwell in Atlantis together!

"But I must not keep you from knowing that in its mortal battle with the salamanders and the spirits of the earth, the black dragon burst from their grasp and quickly flew off through the air. It is true that Phosphorous once more holds him in bonds, but hostile spirits arose from the black feathers which rained down upon the ground during the struggle, and these spirits have on all sides aligned themselves against the salamanders and the spirits of the earth. That woman who hates you so intensely, dear Anselmus, and who, as is well known to my father, strives to possess the golden pot; that woman owes her very existence to the love of such a feather (plucked from the dragon's wing during the battle) for a certain beet, beside which it dropped. She is aware of her origin and of her power because the secrets of many a mysterious constellation are revealed to her through the moans and convulsions of the captured dragon. She uses every means and makes every effort to work from the outside to the inside, while my father battles her with the beams which shoot forth from the spirit of the salamander. All the destructive powers which exist in deadly herbs and the venom of poisonous beasts are collected by her, and when she mixes these under favorable astrological conditions, she is able thereby to cast many a wicked spell which overwhelms man's soul with trembling and trepidation and makes him vulnerable to the power of those demons produced by the dragon as it was vanquished in battle. Dear Anselmus, beware of that old woman! She loathes you because your childlike innocence and your reverent character have made many of her evil charms impotent. Stay true! Stay true to me! You will soon reach the goal!"

"Oh, my Serpentina, my own Serpentina!" Anselmus cried, "how could I leave you? How would it be possible for me not to love you forever?" A kiss was burning on his lips. He awoke as if from a deep dream. Serpentina had vanished. The hour of six was striking, and he felt oppressed because he had not copied a single letter.

Deeply troubled, fearful of the reproaches of Archivarius Lindhorst, he looked at the sheet before him—Oh wonder!—the copy of the mysterious manuscript was perfectly completed, and upon examining the letters more closely, that which was written was nothing other than the story Serpentina had told about her father, who was the favorite of Phosphorous, the Prince of the Spirits of Atlantis, the Kingdom of Marvels.

Archivarius Lindhorst entered the room now, wearing his light grey coat and carrying his hat and his cane. He looked at the parchment on which Anselmus had been working, allowed himself a hefty pinch of snuff, and with a smile said, "Exactly as I thought! Well, Herr Anselmus, here is your silver taler. Now if you will only follow me, we will go to the Linke Baths!" Saying this, the Archivarius walked quickly through the garden, which was now so full of the din raised by singing, whistling, and chattering that Anselmus was made completely deaf by the noise and gave thanks when he again found himself on the street.

They had hardly walked twenty paces when they met Registrar Heerbrand, who joined them in a companionable fashion. At the gate they filled their pipes, which they had brought with them, and Registrar Heerbrand complained that he had forgotten his tinderbox and could not strike fire. "A tinderbox!" Archivarius Lindhorst said scornfully. "Here is enough fire, fire to spare!" and he snapped his fingers, from which streams of sparks flew and immediately lit the pipes.

"Do observe the chemical knack of some men!" Registrar Heerbrand said. But, not without inward awe, Anselmus thought of the salamander and his story.

At the Linke Baths Registrar Heerbrand drank so much beer that, despite the fact that he was usually a well-mannered and quiet man, he began singing student songs in a high-pitched tenor voice. Irritably, he asked everyone whether he was his friend or not, and he finally had to be taken home by Anselmus, long after Archivarius Lindhorst had left.

NINTH VIGIL

*How Anselmus Gained Some Sense. The Punch Party.
How Anselmus Mistook Dean Paulmann for a
Screech Owl and the Latter Felt Greatly Hurt
Thereby. The Ink Blot and Its Consequences.*

Anselmus had completely withdrawn from his normal life because of the strange and mysterious events which happened to him daily. No longer did he visit any of his friends, and he waited with impatience every morning for the hour of noon so that he could unlock the gate to his paradise. But despite the fact that his entire being was focused on gentle Serpentina and the marvels of Archivarius Lindhorst's enchanted kingdom, he could not help thinking occasionally about Veronica; indeed, it often seemed as if she appeared before him and blushingly confessed how she loved him with her whole heart and how desperately she wished to rescue him from the phantoms which ridiculed and confused him.

He felt at times as if some external power that suddenly interrupted his thoughts drew him irresistibly toward the forgotten Veronica, and as if he must pursue her wherever she chose to lead him, as though he were tied to her with an unbreakable bond. That very night after Serpentina had appeared before him in the shape of a lovely maiden, after the marvelous secret of the salamander's wedding with the green snake had been revealed, Veronica appeared before him more clearly than ever before. In fact, it was not until he awoke that he was fully aware that he had only been dreaming, because he was convinced that Veronica was truly beside him, complaining very sorrowfully to him, in a way which pierced him to the heart because he was sacrificing her profound and faithful love for fantasies which were born only in his distraught mind and which would, moreover, finally prove to be his ruination. Veronica was more beautiful than he had ever seen her, and he could not drive her from his thoughts. It was in this troubled mood that he rushed from the house, hopeful that a morning walk would help him escape his agony.

An occult magical influence directed him to Pirna Gate, and he was about to turn into a cross-street when Dean Paulmann, coming after him, called out, "Ai! Ai! Dear Herr Anselmus— *Amice! Amice!* In heavens name, where have you buried yourself for so long? We never see you at all. Do you know that Veronica is very anxious to play another duet with you? So, come along now, you are on the street leading to our house anyway."

Anselmus, forced by this friendly aggressiveness, accompanied the Dean. Upon entering the house they were greeted by Veronica, who was dressed so elegantly and with such obvious care that Dean Paulmann, himself amazed, asked, "Why are you so decked out? Were you anticipating visitors? Well then, I bring you Herr Anselmus."

Anselmus, while delicately and elegantly kissing Veronica's hand, felt it exert a gentle pressure which shot through his body like a flash of fire. Veronica was the epitome of gaiety and hospitality, and when Paulmann left them to enter his study, she contrived, using various coquetteries, to encourage Anselmus so that he finally forgot all about his shyness and actually chased the wild girl around the room. But once again his old demon awkwardness possessed him, and he stumbled against the table, Veronica's pretty little sewing box tumbling to the floor. Anselmus picked it up; the lid had fallen open and his attention was attracted by a little round metallic mirror into which he looked now with special pleasure. Veronica, softly walking up to him, placed her hand on his arm and, pressing close to him, looked over his shoulder into the mirror with him. Suddenly, Anselmus felt as if a battle were commencing in his soul. Thoughts and images flashed before his eyes—Archivarius Lindhorst—Serpentina—the green snake. But the tumult finally abated and this chaos was clearly converted into consciousness. Now it seemed obvious to him that he had always thought of no one but Veronica; indeed, that the shape which had appeared before him yesterday in the blue room had been none other than Veronica, and that the wild story of the marriage between the salamander and the green snake had simply been copied by him from the manuscript and was not at all related to what he had heard. He wondered more than a little about all those dreams, and he ultimately attributed them solely to the feverish state of mind into which he had been thrown by Veronica's love, as well as to the work he had done in Archivarius Lindhorst's room where, in addition, there were so many strangely intoxicating odors. He could only laugh heartily at the insane whim which had caused him to fall in love with the little green snake and at mistaking the well-nourished Archivarius Lindhorst for a salamander.

"Yes, yes, it is Veronica!" he cried aloud, and then, upon turning his head, he looked directly into her blue eyes, from which there beamed the warmest love. A soft, "Ah!" escaped from between her lips as they now burningly pressed upon his.

"Oh, how fortunate I am!" the blissful student sighed; "today I have in my possession that which last night was only a dream!"

"But will you really marry me when you are a Court Councillor?" Veronica asked.

"Indeed I will!" Anselmus replied. And at that moment the door creaked open and Dean Paulmann entered. "Now, my dear Anselmus, I will not let you get away today," he said. "You will have dinner with us, and then Veronica will make us delicious coffee, which we will share with Registrar Heerbrand, for he has promised to come here."

"Oh, kind Dean Paulmann," Anselmus answered. "Don't you know that I must go to Archivarius Lindhorst and copy manuscripts?"

"But *amice*, look!" Dean Paulmann said, holding up his watch which pointed to half past twelve.

Anselmus realized that it was now much too late to begin working at the Archivarius's and he eagerly complied with the wishes expressed by the Dean, especially because he could now be hopeful of having an opportunity to look at Veronica all day long and to obtain from her many fleeting and meaningful glances and gentle pressures of the hand—even perhaps to succeed in stealing a kiss. Anselmus's desires had now reached these lofty heights, and he grew more and more contented in his heart the more completely he was able to convince himself that he would soon be rescued from all of the fantastic things he had imagined, those things which he now thought might sooner or later have made him quite insane.

As promised, Registrar Heerbrand came after dinner, and when coffee was over and dusk had fallen, puckering up his face and happily rubbing his hands, he announced that he had something with him, which if properly composed and reduced into form— paginated and entitled by the fair hands of Veronica—might entertain them all on this October evening.

"Come on, then, tell us about this mysterious thing which you have with you, most valued Registrar!" Dean Paulmann cried. Then Registrar Heerbrand shoved his hand into his deep pocket and, after three such trips, brough forth a bottle of arrack, two lemons, and some sugar; and before half an hour had flown, a savory bowl of hot punch was steaming on Dean Paulmann's table. Veronica drank to their health in a sip of the punch, and before long there was much gaiety and good-natured talk among the friends. But Anselmus, the drink getting to his head, once more felt that the images of those marvels which he had experienced these last few weeks were invading his mind. He saw Archivarius Lindhorst in his damask dressing gown, which glowed like phosphorous in the dark; he saw the azure room and the golden palm trees; indeed, now it seemed to him as if he must still believe in Serpentina. A raging ferment of conflict stirred his soul. Veronica handed him a glass of punch, and while taking it from her he gently touched her hand. "Serpentina! Veronica!" he sighed to himself. He surrendered to deep reverie, but Registrar Heerbrand loudly cried, "This Archivarius Lindhorst is a strange old gentleman no one can fathom, and he will always be. Well, long life to him! Your glass, Herr Anselmus!"

It was then that Anselmus awoke from his dreamy state and, as he touched glasses with Registrar Heerbrand, said, "That follows, respected Herr Registrar, from the fact that Archivarius Lindhorst is really a salamander who has in his fury destroyed the garden of Phosphorous, the Prince of the Spirits, because the green snake had fled from him."

"What?" Dean Paulmann asked.

"It is true," Anselmus continued, "and for this reason he is sentenced to be a royal Archivarius and to keep house here in Dresden with his three daughters, who are, after all, nothing more than little gold-green snakes which bask in the elder tree and perfidiously sing and, like so many sirens, seduce very many young people."

"Herr Anselmus! Herr Anselmus!" Dean Paulmann cried. "Are you out of your mind? In heaven's name, what idiocy is this you are babbling?"

"He is right, he is right," Registrar Heerbrand interrupted. "That fellow Archivarius is a damned salamander who strikes fiery flashes from his fingers which burn holes in your coat like red hot tinder. Yes, absolutely, you are right, my little brother Anselmus, and whoever says 'No!' to you is saying 'No!' to me." And with these words, Registrar Heerbrand hit the table so mighty a blow with his fist that the glasses rang out.

"Registrar, are you crazy too?" the indignant Dean cried. "What is this you are all babbling about?"

"As for you," said the student, "you are nothing but a bird. You are a screech owl who curls toupees, Dean Paulmann!"

"What? I'm a bird? A screech owl? A toupee-curler?" the Dean screamed in rage. "Sir, you are insane, absolutely mad!"

"But the old witch will get her hands on him," Registrar Heerbrand said.

"Yes, she is powerful, that old hag," Anselmus interrupted, "even though she is of low birth. Her father was nothing more than a ragged wing feather, and her mother was only a dirty beet; but she owes most of her powers to all kinds of destructive creatures —poisonous vermin which she keeps in her house."

"What horrible slander!" Veronica cried, her eyes blazing with anger. "Old Liese is a wise woman, and the black cat is not a pernicious creature but is rather a sophisticated young aristocrat possessing elegant manners and is her own blood cousin."

"But can he eat salamanders without singeing his beard and dying like a snuffed out candle?" Registrar Heerbrand cried.

"No, no!" Anselmus shouted, "he could never do that, never in the world; and the green snake loves me for I have a childlike nature and I have looked into Serpentina's eyes."

"The cat will scratch them out!" Veronica exclaimed.

"Salamander—Salamander—conquers them all, every one of them," Dean Paulmann roared in the height of fury. "But I must be in a lunatic asylum. Have I gone crazy myself? What kind of gibberish am I uttering? Yes, I am mad! I am also insane!" And saying this, Dean Paulmann jumped up, tore his wig from his head and flung it against the ceiling so that the battered locks flew about and, becoming completely entangled and utterly disordered, rained down their powder all over the room. Then Anselmus and Registrar Heerbrand seized the punch bowl and the goblets and, hallooing and shouting, also threw them up against the ceiling, and the pieces of glass jingled and jangled about their ears.

"*Vivat* the salamander! *Pereat, pereat* the witch! Smash the metal mirror! Dig out the cat's eyes! Birds, little birds in the air— *Eheu—Eheu—Evoe—Evoe*—salamander!" the three men shrieked and screamed and bellowed as if they were totally mad. Fränzchen ran out, loudly crying, but Veronica remained behind and sobbed out her pain and sorrow on the sofa.

At this moment the door opened and everything instantly grew still. A little man in a small grey coat entered. His nose, on which a colossal pair of glasses nestled, seemed to be entirely different from any nose that had ever before been seen. He wore a most singular wig, too—one that looked more like a feather cap than a wig.

"Ai, I bid you good evening!" the comical little man crackled. "Is the student Anselmus among you gentlemen? I extend to you the compliments of Archivarius Lindhorst, who today waited vainly for his calligraphist; but he most respectfully requests that you ask Anselmus not to miss his appointment tomorrow."

At this he left, and they all now clearly realized that the serious little man was in fact a grey parrot. Dean Paulmann and Registrar Heerbrand burst into guffaws which echoed through the rooms, punctuated by the sobs and the moans coming from Veronica. As for Anselmus, the madness of an internal horror was pervading his very soul and, unconscious of what he was doing, he rushed out the door and along the street. Mechanically he reached his house, his garret, and before long Veronica came there to see him, in a peaceful and friendly mood, and she asked him why he had so worried her with his tipsiness. She implored him to be on his guard against fantastic hallucinations while working at Archivarius Lindhorst's.

"Good night, good night, my beloved friend," Veronica whispered so softly that she could hardly be heard, and breathed a kiss on his lips. He stretched out his arms in an attempt to clasp her, but the dream-like shape had disappeared, and Anselmus awoke, cheerful and refreshed.

He could not help but laugh uproariously at the effects of the punch, but when he thought of Veronica, he felt full of a most delicious sense of warm contentment. He said to himself, "To her alone I owe my recovery from mad delusions. In truth, I was little better than the man who believed himself to be made of glass; or the one who would not dare leave his room because he thought he was a barleycorn and was afraid that the hens would eat him! But just as soon as I am a Court Councillor I will marry Mademoiselle Paulmann and be happy; and that will be the end of it!"

And at noon, as he once more walked through the garden of Archivarius Lindhorst, he could not help but wonder at how all of this had once appeared to him to be so exotic and marvelous, because nothing that he now saw seemed at all extraordinary: earthen flower pots, quantities of geraniums, myrtle, and so on. Instead of the gleaming multicolored birds which once teased him, now there were only a few sparrows fluttering about that broke into a twittering at the sight of him which was both unpleasant and unintelligible. The azure room also looked entirely different now, and he could not understand how that garish blue and those artificial golden trunks of the palm trees with their shapeless glistening leaves could ever have thrilled him for a moment. Archivarius Lindhorst looked at him with a very strange and ironical smile, then asked, "Well, how did you enjoy your punch last night, good Anselmus?"

"Oh, you have no doubt heard from the grey parrot how—" Anselmus answered, completely ashamed; but he hesitated when he remembered that the appearance of the parrot was only a part of his intoxication.

"I was there myself," Archivarius Lindhorst said. "Didn't you see me? But you almost crippled me with those mad pranks because I was sitting in the punch bowl at the precise moment when Registrar Heerbrand got his hands on it to fling it against the ceiling, and I had to retreat quickly into the bowl of the Dean's pipe. Now, adieu, Herr Anselmus! If you are diligent, you will also have a silver coin for the day you missed, because your previous work has been so good."

"How is it that Archivarius Lindhorst can babble such drivel?" Anselmus thought to himself while sitting at the table and preparing to copy the manuscripts, which, as usual, had been spread before him by Lindhorst. But he saw so many strange crabbed strokes and twirls all twisted together in inexplicable confusion, perplexing the eye, that it seemed to him to be almost impossible to transcribe this exactly; indeed, in looking it all over you might have thought that the parchment was in fact nothing but a piece of thickly-veined marble, or a stone which had been sprinkled with mosses. He nevertheless resolved to do his very best and boldly dipped his pen in the ink, but regardless of what he tried, the ink would not flow. He impatiently flicked the point of his pen and—O heavens!— a huge blot fell on the outspread original! Hissing and foaming, a blue flash flew up from the blot; crackling and wavering, it shot up through the room to the ceiling; and then a thick vapor rolled from the walls. The leaves began to rustle as if torn by a storm, and glaring basilisks darted down from them in sparkling fire, and these lighted the vapor, the masses of flame then rolling around Anselmus. The golden trunks of the palm trees changed into gigantic snakes which knocked their frightful heads together with a piercing metallic clang and wound their scaly bodies round the distracted student.

"Madman! Now you must suffer the punishment for that

which you have done in your bold irreverence!" cried the terrifying voice of the crowned salamander who, like a glittering beam in the middle of the flame, appeared above the snakes. And now cataracts of fire were poured on Anselmus from the gaping jaws of the snake; but suddenly it seemed as if the cataracts of fire were congealing about his body and turning into a solid icy mass. And while Anselmus's limbs were more and more pressed and contracted together and were hardening into powerlessness, consciousness deserted him. When he came to himself, he could not move a muscle. It seemed to him that he was surrounded by a glistening brilliance which he struck if he so much as tried to lift his hand. Alas! He was sitting in a well-corked crystal bottle on a shelf in the library of Archivarius Lindhorst.

TENTH VIGIL

Sorrows of Anselmus in the Glass Bottle. Happy Life of the Scholars of the Church of the Holy Cross and the Law Clerks. The Battle in the Library of Archivarius Lindhorst. Victory of the Salamander and Deliverance of Anselmus.

Gentle reader, I may rightly doubt whether you ever found yourself sealed up in a glass bottle, unless you have been oppressed in a vivid dream by such magic tricks. If this has been the case, your appreciation of poor Anselmus's woeful situation will be very sharp, but if you have never even dreamed of such things, then for Anselmus's sake and for mine, your imagination may still cooperate enough so that it finds itself enclosed in crystal for a few moments.

You are surrounded by brilliant splendor; everything around you appears illuminated and imbued with the hues of a beaming rainbow; all that you see quivers and shimmers and hums in the magic sheen; you swim, devoid of motion and power in a firmly congealed ether which so presses your limbs together that your mind gives orders in vain to your dead body. The mountainous burden lies upon you with more and more weight, and your every breath consumes more and more of the modicum of air which still drifts in the narrow space around you; your pulse throbs wildly, and cut through with anguish, every nerve tenses and trembles in this mortal agony.

Gentle reader, take pity on Anselmus! This unspeakable torture gripped him in his prison of glass, but he knew only too well that even death could not save him, for did he not recover from the profound unconsciousness into which he had been thrown by excessive pain just as the morning sun brightly shone into the room, and didn't his martyrdom begin again? No limb could he move, but his thoughts bounced against the glass and stunned him with their discordant vibrations. Instead of the words which the spirit once spoke from within him, he now could hear only the muffled din of madness. In his agony he exclaimed, "O Serpentina, Serpentina! Save me from this hellish torture!" And it was as if faint sighs breathed around him, spreading over the glass like the translucent green leaves of the elder; the clanging stopped, the dazzling bewildering glitter disappeared. Anselmus was now able to breathe more freely.

"Am I not myself to blame for my unhappiness? O most kind and beloved Serpentina, haven't I sinned against you? Haven't I given way to gross doubts about you? Haven't I lost my belief and, along with it, everything that was going to make me so blissful? Alas! Now you will never ever be mine. And the golden pot is now lost to me as well, and I will never again behold its marvels. Alas, if I might just see you once more; only once more, my lovely Serpentina, hear your sweet and tender voice!" Thus, lamented Anselmus, pierced through by this profound sorrow; and then he heard a voice close to him, "I don't know what you want, Herr Studiosus. Why are you lamenting so, beyond all measure?" And now for the first time Anselmus noticed that there were five other bottles on the same shelf, and he could see three Scholars of the Church of the Holy Cross and two Law Clerks.

"Ah, gentlemen, my companions in misery!" he cried. "Tell me how it is possible for you to be so calm, even happy, as I see you are by your cheerful look. You are also sitting here corked up in glass bottles, and you can no more move a finger than I can. Like me, you cannot think a reasonable thought but that there arises such a murderous cacaphony of ringing and humming, and such a rumbling and roaring in your head, that it is enough to drive you insane. No doubt you do not believe in the salamander or in the green snake!"

"You are talking drivel, Herr Studiosus," one of the Church scholars replied. "It has never been better for us than it is now, because the silver coins which the insane Archivarius paid us for all kinds of confusing scripts are still in our pockets. Now we no longer have to learn Italian choruses by heart. Each day we go to Joseph's or some other pub where the beer is fine enough, and we can look a pretty girl in the face. So we sing like real students, *Gaudeamus igitur,* and we are absolutely content!"

"That is absolutely correct," a law clerk added. "I am also well provided with coins, as is my dearest colleague beside me. Now we walk about on the Weinberg instead of being occupied by copying nasty briefs within the confines of four walls."

"But my worthiest masters," Anselmus said, "can you not see that all of you are corked up in glass bottles and cannot move, let alone go for walks."

And now the Scholars of the Church of the Holy Cross and the Law Clerks began to guffaw loudly and cry, "The student is out of his mind! He imagines that he is sitting hunched in a glass bottle, and here he is standing on the Elbe bridge, looking right down into the water. Let us leave this madman and continue on our way!"

"Ah," the student sighed, "they have never seen the tender and lovely Serpentina. They do not know what freedom means nor what it is to live with love and belief; therefore, because of their own foolishness and unimaginative natures, they feel no oppression as a result of their imprisonment. But I, miserable I, must perish in want and in woe if she whom I love beyond all words does not save me."

Then, wafting to him in faint tinkles, came Serpentina's voice through the room: "Anselmus! Believe! Love! Hope!" And every sound beamed into Anselmus's prison, and the crystal yielded to his pressure and expanded until the heart of the prisoner once again felt as if it could stir in his breast.

The agony of his situation grew less acute, and he understood now that Serpentina still loved him and that she alone made it possible for him to tolerate his imprisonment. No more did he trouble himself about his foolish companions in misfortune, but instead he concentrated all his thoughts upon gentle Serpentina. Suddenly, however, on the other side of him there arose a muffled, croaking, loathsome murmur, and he could soon observe that it emanated from an old coffee pot, with a lid which was half broken, which stood opposite him on a little shelf. As he looked at it more carefully, the ugly features of a withered old woman were gradually disclosed, and in a few moments the apple woman of Black Gate stood before him. She smirked and laughed at him screeching "Ai! Ai! My handsome boy, must you now suffer? Into the crystal is your downfall. Isn't this what I predicted long ago?"

"Mock and jeer at me, you damned witch!" Anselmus said. "You are responsible for it all, but, the salamander will catch you, you nasty beet."

"Ho ho!" the hag replied, "don't be so proud! You have squashed my little sons; you have scarred my nose—but I still like you, you rascal, for once you were a handsome young fellow; and my little daughter likes you too. You will never escape from the crystal unless I help you, but my friend the rat that lives close behind you will chew the shelf in half. Then you will tumble down, and I will catch you in my apron so that not only will your nose remain unbroken but your splendid face will not be injured in any way; and then I will carry you off to Mam'selle Veronica, to whom you will be married when you become a Court Councillor."

"You offspring of the Devil, get away from me!" Anselmus cried in anger. "It was your hellish tricks that led me to commit the sin for which I now am forced to expiate. But I will patiently bear it all, for I choose to remain here, where gentle Serpentina surrounds me with her love and her consolation. Wretched hag, listen and despair! I defy your power! I love none other than Serpentina; I will not be a Court Councillor; I will not look at Veronica who seduces me to evil through your influence; I will die in sorrow and desire if the green snake cannot be mine. Away with you, you filthy old changeling!"

And the old woman laughed until the room echoed. "Sit and die, then!" she cried, "but now it is time for me to begin my work. I have other business to pursue here." And throwing off her black coat she stood in loathsome nakedness. Then she ran in circles, and large folios tumbled down on her. Out of these she ripped parchment leaves and, quickly piecing them together in an artful combination and attaching them to her body, she was soon dressed in a weird multicolored armor. Out of the inkwell dashed the black cat, fire spitting from its mouth, and it ran meowing towards the hag, who screamed in shrill triumph and disappeared through the door with it. Anselmus saw that she was going towards the azure room, and he immediately heard a hissing and a tumult in the distance. The birds in the garden were crying and the parrot called, "Help! Help! Thieves! Thieves!" At that moment the horrible old woman bounded back into the room carrying the golden pot in her arms and repulsively gesturing all the while. She shrieked fiercely through the air, "Joy! Joy! Little son! Kill the green snake! At her, at her, son!"

Anselmus thought he heard a deep moaning; he thought he heard the voice of Serpentina; then he was seized by despair and, gathering all his strength, he dashed wildly—as if his nerves and arteries were bursting—against the crystal. Suddenly a loud clang resounded through the room, and the Archivarius in his bright damask dressing gown appeared in the door.

"Hey, Hey! Wretches! Mad delusion! Witchcraft! Hey, there! he shouted. Then the hag's black hair stood up like coarse bristles. Her red eyes gleamed with hellish fire; and gnashing the pointed fangs of her hideous jaws together, she sputtered, "Quick, at him! Hiss at him! Hiss!" She laughed and bleated scornfully, pressed the golden pot firmly against her body and from it threw handfuls of sparkling earth on the Archivarius; but as the earth touched his dressing gown, its particles changed into flowers, which rained down on the floor. Then the lilies on the dressing gown flickered and flared, and the Archivarius caught these blazing lilies and flung them on the witch. She howled in agony, but as she leaped into the air and shook her armor of parchment, the lilies' fire was extinguished, and they fell away as ashes.

"Quick, my boy!" the hag screeched again, and the black cat hurtled through the air clear over the Archivarius's head towards the door; but the grey parrot quickly flew out to confront him and, catching him by the nape of the neck with his crooked bill, he tore at him until red fiery blood burst from its neck—and Serpentina's voice cried out, "Saved, saved!"

At this the witch, her mouth foaming with rage and desperation, threw herself at the Archivarius. She threw the golden pot behind her, and baring the long talons of her bony hands, she tried to clutch the Archivarius by the throat. He, however, instantly removed his robe and threw it over her. Then hissing and sputtering, blue flames leapt from the leaves of parchment which were the armor of the hag, and she rolled on the floor in agony trying desperately to secure fresh earth from the pot and fresh leaves of parchment from the books so that she could suffocate the blazing flames. And whenever earth or leaves touched her body the flames were extinguished. But now from inside Archivarius's body there issued forth fiery crackling tongues of flame which lashed out at the hag.

"Hey, hey! Victory to the salamander!" the Archivarius's voice reverberated through the room, and a hundred fiery bolts whirled in burning circles around the shrieking hag. Ripping and spitting, the cat and the parrot again flew at each other, locked in their ferocious combat; but finally the parrot, using his powerful wings, flung the cat to the ground, and transfixing the cat with his claws, he held his enemy—which, in the agony of death, uttered terrifying meows and shrieks—and pecked out the glowing eyes of the cat with his sharp bill, burning froth spouting from the eyes. Then thick vapor steamed up from the spot where the horrible old hag lay hurled to the ground under the enchanted dressing gown. Her howling, her terrible, piercing cries of defeat and woe died away, as in the remote distance. And the smoke which had permeated the room with its stench blew away. The Archivarius lifted his dressing gown; a nasty beet lay beneath it.

"Most honored Archivarius, may I offer you the vanquished enemy?" the parrot said, extending a black hair which he held in his beak to Lindhorst.

"Very good, my dear friend," the Archivarius replied, "and here also lies my vanquished enemy. Be so kind as to take care of that which remains. This very day as a small reward you shall have six coconuts—and a new pair of glasses, because, as I see, the cat has villainously cracked the lenses of your old ones."

"Yours forever, most revered friend and patron," the delighted parrot answered, and then the parrot took the beet in his bill and flew with it out of the window which Lindhorst had opened for him.

And now the Archivarius retrieved the golden pot, and in a powerful voice cried, "Serpentina, Serpentina!" But as Anselmus, rejoicing in the destruction of the loathsome witch who had cast him into misfortune, looked at the Archivarius, he was once more amazed, for here again stood the tall and majestic form of the Prince of the Spirits regarding him with an expression of ineffable grace and dignity.

"Anselmus," the Prince of the Spirits said, "it was not you but a hostile principle which attempted destructively to penetrate your nature and divide you against yourself, and which was to blame for your lack of belief. You have proved your loyalty. You are to be free and happy!"

A brilliant flash quivered through Anselmus's mind; the glorious triad of the crystal bells sounded more powerfully and more loudly than he had ever heard it, and his nerves and his senses quivered. As the melodious tones rang through the room, swelling higher and higher, the glass which enclosed Anselmus shattered, and he dashed into the arms of his dear and gentle Serpentina.

ELEVENTH VIGIL

*Dean Paulmann's Anger at the Madness Which Had
Broken Out in His Family. How Registrar Heerbrand Became
a Court Councillor and Walked About in Shoes and Silk Stockings
in the Sharpest Frost. Veronica's Confessions. Betrothal
over the Steaming Soup Tureen.*

"But tell me, worthy Registrar, how could the damned
punch last night have gone so to our heads and driven us to all
kinds of incredible foolishness!" Dean Paulmann demanded the
next morning as he entered his study, which was still full of broken
glass, while his hapless wig, separated into its original elements,
floated in the punch. After Anselmus had rushed from the house, the
Dean and the Registrar had continued running and hobbling up
and down the room, shouting like lunatics and bashing their heads
together until Fränzchen, with enormous effort, dragged her very
tipsy papa off to bed. Then Registrar Heerbrand, utterly exhausted,
had collapsed upon the sofa which Veronica had deserted in order to
take refuge in her bedroom.

Registrar Heerbrand had tied his blue handkerchief around
his head. He looked terribly pale and sad, and he groaned an answer,
"Oh, worthy Dean, it was not the punch which Mam'selle Veronica
brewed to such perfection. No! It was simply that damned student
who is responsible for all the trouble. Have you not observed that he
has long been *mente captus*? And are you not aware of the infectious
nature of madness? One fool begets twenty—excuse me, that is an
old proverb. Especially when you have had a glass or two to drink,
you fall easily into madness; then you proceed to perform involuntary capers and go through your exercises exactly as the cracked-
brained leader directs. Dean, would you believe that I still get
dizzy when I think about that grey parrot?"

"Nonsense!" the Dean interrupted. "It was really nothing
but Archivarius Lindhorst's little old librarian who had flung a
grey coat over himself and was looking for Anselmus."

"That may be," admitted Registrar Heerbrand, "but I must
admit that I feel very wretched. All night long there was a terrible
booming of organ notes and whistling in my head."

"That was me," the Dean said, "I snore very loudly."

"Well, that may be so," the Registrar admitted again. "But

Dean! Oh Dean! It was not without reason that I tried to convey an atmosphere of good cheer among us last night—and that Anselmus has ruined everything! You don't know—Oh Dean! Oh Dean!" And with this, Registrar Heerbrand sprang up, snatched the blue handkerchief from his head, embraced the Dean warmly, and pressed his hand. Again, in a voice completely heartrending, he cried, "Oh, Dean, Dean!" and quickly taking up his hat and cane, he dashed out of the house.

"This Anselmus will never again cross my threshold!" Dean Paulmann said, "for it is very clear to me that this madness of his robs the best people of their senses. Now the Registrar is stricken with it! Up to now I have escaped, but the devil who knocked so hard last night at the door of our carousal may ultimately get in and play his games with me. So *apage, Satanas!* Away with Anselmus!"

During this conversation Veronica had grown very thoughtful. She spoke not a word, but only smiled occasionally, and then very peculiarly. And as time wore on she persisted in this surprising mood—a gay, gregarious girl who now preferred to be left alone. "She also has Anselmus on her mind!" the Dean said, fuming with indignation. "But it is a good thing that he does not come here. I know that he is afraid of me and that this is why he will not come."

Dean Paulmann had spoken these concluding words aloud, and the tears welled in Veronica's eyes. Sobbing, she said, "Oh, how can Anselmus come here when he has for a long time been corked up in the glass bottle?"

"What's that!" Dean Paulmann cried. "Oh heavens, heavens! She is driveling now just like the Registrar. Soon she will have an attack! Oh, you damned, loathsome, Anselmus!"

He dashed quickly out to find Doctor Eckstein, but the physician only smiled and once more said, "Ai! Ai!"

This time, however, he prescribed nothing at all, but merely added the following words to the little he had said. "An attack of nerves! Takes care of itself. Go outdoors; walks; entertainments; theater—go see *Sonntagskind, Schwestern von Prag.*[7] It will take care of itself."

"I have rarely seen the Doctor so eloquent," Dean Paulmann thought. "He is really talkative, I must admit."

---

7. Operettas by Wenzel Müller (1767–1835).

And now, days and weeks and months passed. Anselmus had disappeared. Registrar Heerbrand also failed to make an appearance. It was not until the fourth of February that the Registrar, dressed in a stylish new coat made of the finest material, wearing handsome, thin shoes and silk stockings, despite the sharp frost and carrying a large bouquet of fresh flowers in his hand, entered the parlor of Dean Paulmann exactly at noon, the Dean being more than a little astounded upon seeing his friend so grandly attired. Registrar Heerbrand walked up to the Dean most solemnly, embraced him with the most earnest courtesy, and said, "Now at last, on the saint's day of your beloved and most honored Mam'selle Veronica, I will straightforwardly tell you what I have long kept locked in my heart. That evening—that unfortunate evening—when I carried the ingredients of our explosive punch in my pocket, it was my intention to tell you a bit of good news and to celebrate the happy day convivially. I had already learned that I was to be appointed a Court Councillor—and for that promotion I now have the papers, *cum nomine et sigillo Principis*, in my pocket."

"Ah, my dear Registrar—Court Councillor, I mean," the Dean stammered.

"But it is you, you alone, most revered Dean, who can complete my joy," the new Court Councillor continued. "I have for a long time been secretly in love with your daughter, Mam'selle Veronica, and I can boast of many a kind look which she has bestowed upon me, obvious proof that she would not reject my attention. In a word, revered Dean, I, Court Councillor Heerbrand, do now entreat you for the hand of your most amiable Mam'selle Veronica, whom I, if you do not oppose it, intend to marry shortly."

Dean Paulmann, immeasurably astounded, clapped his hands together and cried again and again, "Ai! Ai! My good Registrar—Court Councillor I mean. Who would have thought of it! Well, if Veronica really does love you, there are no objections on my part. In truth, it may be that her present moodiness is really nothing but the effect of her secret love for you, Court Councillor! You know what whims can possess girls!"

At this moment, pale and troubled as she now always was, Veronica entered. Court Councillor Heerbrand immediately rose to his feet and went up to her and in a nice little speech said something about her saint's day and gave her the fragrant bouquet, and with it a little package. And when she opened it, a pair of brilliant earrings sparkled up at her. A swiftly fleeting blush colored her cheeks and, her eyes gleaming with happiness, she cried, "Oh, gracious heaven, these are the same earrings I wore several weeks ago, those which pleased me so!"

"But my dearest Mam'selle, how can this be?" the Court Councillor interrupted, rather alarmed and hurt, "when I bought these jewels less than an hour ago for cash in Castle Street?"

But Veronica did not heed his words; she was already before the mirror to look at the trinkets, which she quickly fixed in her lovely little ears. Dean Paulmann, however, grave of countenance and solemn of tone, told her about his friend Heerbrand's promotion and his present proposal, and Veronica turned to the Court Councillor and, with a searching look, said:

"I have known for a long time that you desired to marry me. So be it! I promise you my heart and my hand; but now I must reveal to you—I mean, to both of you, to you, my father, and to you, my promised bridegroom—much of that which is heavy on my heart, and I must tell you now, even if the soup should get cold—which Fränzchen, I see, is now placing on the table."

And without waiting for the Dean or the Court Councillor to reply—although words were clearly forming on the lips of both—Veronica continued:

"Best of fathers, you may believe me. I loved Anselmus from the depths of my heart, and when Registrar Heerbrand, who has himself become a Court Councillor, assured us that Anselmus would very probably reach some such height, I determined that he and none other should be my husband. But then it seemed as if alien, hostile beings were resolved to steal him away from me. At that time I went to old Liese, who had once been my nurse but has since become knowledgeable in necromancy and has become a great enchantress. She promised to help me and to deliver Anselmus completely into my hands. At midnight, on the equinox, we went to the crossroads on the highway. She conjured up hellish spirits, and with the help of the black cat, we produced a little metallic mirror in which I, after focusing my thoughts on Anselmus, had only to look in order to completely dominate his heart and his mind. But now I wholeheartedly repent having done this," Veronica added, "and I now repudiate all satanic arts. The salamander has vanquished old Liese. I heard her shriek, but there was nothing I could do to help her, for as soon as the parrot had eaten the beet, my metallic mirror broke in two."

Veronica took both pieces of the mirror and a lock of hair out of her sewing box and after handing them to Court Councillor Heerbrand, continued:

"Court Councillor, take the fragments of the mirror, and tonight at twelve o'clock throw them into the Elbe from the bridge, at the spot where the cross stands; the stream is not frozen there. Do, however, keep and wear that lock of my hair. I now repudiate all magic," she repeated, "and I wholeheartedly wish Anselmus all joy and good fortune, since he is now married to the green snake who is more beautiful and rich than I am. Dear Court Councillor, I will love you and revere you as befits a true and faithful wife."

"Alas! Alas!" Dean Paulmann cried, full of sorrow. "She is mad, she is mad! She can never be Frau Court Councillor because she is mad!"

"But not in the least," Court Councillor Heerbrand interrupted. "I well know that Mam'selle Veronica has felt some kindness for the bumbling Anselmus; and it may be that she has, during some fit of passion, had recourse to the old witch who, as I realize, can be none other than the cards-and-coffee fortuneteller of Lake Gate—in brief, old Rauerin. Nor can it be denied that there are cryptic arts which exert their all too baleful influence on men. We read of them in the most ancient writings, and no doubt there still are such. As far as what Mam'selle Veronica wishes to say about the victory of the salamander and Anselmus's marriage to the green snake, in truth, I take this to be nothing but a poetic allegory, like a poem in which she celebrates her final complete farewell to the student."

"Take it for what you will, most revered Court Councillor," Veronica said, "perhaps for an extremely stupid dream."

"I will not do that," Court Councillor Heerbrand replied, "for I well know that Anselmus possesses secret powers which torment him and drive him to all the insane capers one can think of."

Dean Paulmann could stand this no longer. He burst out with: "Stop! For the love of heaven, stop! Have we once more imbibed too much of that damned punch, or has Anselmus's lunacy possessed us as well? Court Councillor, what rubbish is this coming from your mouth? I suppose, however, that love haunts your brain. Marriage will soon take care of this. I should otherwise be fearful that you too were plunging into a degree of madness, most revered Court Councillor. What would then become of the future branches of the family, inheriting as they do the *malum* of their parents? But now,

I bestow upon this happy union my paternal blessing and permit each of you as future bride and bridegroom a joyous kiss."

Thus they immediately kissed, and so it was that before the soup had a chance to grow cold, the formal betrothal was completed. In a few weeks, Frau Court Councillor Heerbrand was in fact what she had been in her vision—she was sitting on the balcony of a splendid house in Neumarket and, with a smile, was looking down upon the dandies, who in passing turned their glasses up to her and said, "She is a divine creature, the wife of Court Councillor Heerbrand."

TWELFTH VIGIL

Account of the Estate to Which Anselmus Withdrew as
Son-in-Law of Archivarius Lindhorst, and How He
Lived There with Serpentina. Conclusion.

How deeply I felt within my spirit the blissful happiness of Anselmus, who was now inwardly united with his gentle Serpentina, and who had withdrawn to the mysterious KINGDOM of Marvels which he recognized as the home toward which his heart, filled with strange foreknowledge, had always yearned. In vain I tried, gentle reader, to set before you those glories which surrounded Anselmus, or even to create in the faintest degree an impression of them in words. I was reluctantly obliged to admit to myself the feeble quality of all my attempts at expressing this. The meanness of commonplace life made me feel chained and silent. I grew sick in the torture of my own futility; I wandered about as if in a dream. In brief, I plunged into the identical condition that engulfed Anselmus, and which I tried to describe to you in the Fourth Vigil. When I looked over the eleven vigils, which are now fortunately completed, it grieved me to the heart to think that inserting the Twelfth Vigil, the very keystone of the whole, would never be permitted me, for whenever I tried during the night to complete the work, it was as if mischievous spirits (they might indeed be blood cousins of the slain witch) were holding a polished and gleaming piece of metal before my eyes in which I could behold my own mean self—pale and anxious and melancholy, like Registrar Heerbrand after his bout with the punch. And then, I flung down my pen and got quickly into bed so that I might at least in my dreams once again see happy Anselmus and lovely Serpentina. This had continued for several days and nights when at last, completely unexpectedly, I received the following letter from Archivarius Lindhorst:

Respected Sir: I am familiar with the fact that you have, in eleven vigils, written about the extraordinary fate of my good son-in-law, Anselmus, erstwhile student, now poet, and that you are at present most sorely tormenting yourself so that in the twelfth and final vigil you may write something about his happy life in Atlantis, where he now lives with my daughter on a pleasant estate which I own in that country. Now, notwithstanding my great regret that my own singular nature is hereby revealed to the reading public (seeing that this may expose me to a thousand inconveniences in my office as Privy Archivarius; indeed, it may even, in the Collegium, provoke the question of how far a salamander may justly bind himself through an oath, as a state servant, and how far, generally, he may be entrusted with vital affairs of state since, according to Gabalis[8] and Swedenborg,[9] the Spirits of the elements are not to be trusted at all, and notwithstanding the fact that I realize that my closest friends must now avoid my embrace, fearing that I might in some sudden anger dart out a flash or two and singe their wigs and Sunday coats), notwithstanding all of this, I say, it is my intention to help you complete the work, since much good of me and my dear married daughter (if only the other two were also off my hands!) has been said therein. If you would, therefore, write your Twelfth Vigil, descend your damned five flights of stairs, leave your garret, and come over to me. In the blue palm tree room already known to you, you will find suitable writing materials, and then in a few words you can describe to your readers what you have seen—a better plan for you than any long-winded account of a life about which you know only through hearsay. With esteem,

Your obedient servant,
The Salamander Lindhorst
Pro tempore Royal Privy Archivarius

This somewhat abrupt but, on the whole, friendly note from Archivarius Lindhorst gave me enormous pleasure. In truth, it

8. Seventeenth-century author of a treatise on the spirits of the elements and their relationship to people.
9. A Swedish theosophist (1688–1772).

seemed clear enough that the extraordinary manner in which his son-in-law's good fortune had been revealed to me and which I, sworn to silence, must keep even from you, gentle reader, was well known to this strange old gentleman; yet he did not take it as badly as I might readily have feared. On the contrary, he was here offering me a helping hand to complete my work. And I might, from this, fairly conclude that he was at heart not opposed to having his wondrous existence in the world of spirits revealed through the printed word.

"It may be," I thought, "that through this means he perhaps expects to get his two other daughters married sooner. Who knows but that a spark may fall in the heart of this or that young man and therein kindle a desire for another green snake—whom he will immediately seek out and discover on Ascension Day, under the elder tree? From the woe which was Anselmus's lot when he was held captive in the glass bottle, he will be forewarned to be doubly and trebly on his guard against all doubt and unbelief."

I extinguished the lamp in my study at exactly eleven o'clock and made my way to Archivarius Lindhorst, who was already waiting for me in his hallway.

"Have you arrived, my worthy friend? Well, I am pleased that you have not mistrusted my good intentions. Please follow me."

And saying this he led the way through the garden, which was now filled with lustrous brightness, and into the azure room where I saw the very violet table at which Anselmus had been writing.

Archivarius Lindhorst disappeared, but soon he returned, carrying in his hand a lovely golden goblet out of which there arose a tall, sparkling blue flame. "Here," he said, "I bring you the favorite drink of your friend Kapellmeister Johannes Kreisler. It is burning arrack into which I have thrown a little sugar. Do take a sip or two of it. I will remove my dressing gown, and to amuse myself and enjoy your worthy company while you sit looking and writing, I will just bob up and down a little in the goblet."

"As you wish, honored Herr Archivarius," I answered, "but if I am to keep sipping the liquor, there will be none for you."

"You need have no such fear, my good fellow," Archivarius Lindhorst said. Then, quickly throwing off his robe, to my great amazement he climbed into the goblet and vanished in the flames. I enjoyed the drink without fear, softly blowing back the fire. The drink was truly delicious!

Are not the emerald leaves of the pa!·n trees gently moving, softly sighing and rustling, as though kissed by the breath of the morning wind? Awakened from their sleep, they stir and mysteriously whisper of the wonders which, from the far distance, approach like tones of melodious harps! The azure abandons the walls, but dazzling beams shoot through the fragrance. And whirling and dancing in childish happiness, the vapor rises to measureless heights and weaves back and forth above the palm trees; but ever brighter shoots beam on beam until, in boundless expanse, a grove opens before my eyes, and there I behold Anselmus.

Here glowing hyacinths and tulips and roses raise their heads, and their perfumes are like the loveliest of sounds which call to the joyous youth: "Come, wander, wander among us, beloved, for you understand us! Our perfume is the longing of love. We love you and are forever yours!" And then these golden rays seem to chant in vibrant tones: "We are fire, kindled by love. Perfume is longing, but fire is desire; and do we not dwell in your heart? We are your own!" And the dark bushes and the tall trees rustle and whisper, "Come to us, beloved happy one! Fire is desire, but hope is our cool shadow. Lovingly, we rustle round your head, for you understand us because love dwells in your heart." And the brooks and the fountains murmur and patter: "Beloved, do not walk by so quickly; look into our crystal! Your image lives in us, and we preserve it with love, for you have understood us." In the triumphal choir, bright birds are singing: "Listen, listen! We are joy, we are delight, the rapture of love!" But Anselmus eagerly turns his eyes to the glorious temple which rises behind him in the distance. The stately pillars seem to be trees, and the capitals and friezes seem to be acanthus leaves, which, in wondrous wreaths and figures, form splendid decorations. Anselmus walks to the temple, and with inward delight he views the variegated marble, the steps with their strange veins of moss. "Ah, no!" he cries, as if in the excess of bliss. "She is not far from me now; she is near!"

Then Serpentina advances, in the fullness of beauty and grace, from the temple. She carries the golden pot, from which a bright lily has sprung, and the inexpressible rapture of infinite longing glows in her gentle eyes. She looks at Anselmus and says, "Oh, my beloved, the lily has sent forth her lovely cupped flower; the highest is now fulfilled. Is there a happiness which is the equal of ours?"

Anselmus clasps her with all the tenderness of passionate devotion. The lily glows in flames over his head; and the happy whispering of the trees and the bushes grows louder; clearer and more happy is the rejoicing of the brooks; the birds and the shining insects dance in the waves of perfume; a gay, joyous tumult in the air, in the water, in the earth, is celebrating the festival of love! Now sparkling gleams dance over the bushes; diamonds peer up from the ground, like shining eyes; high fountains sparkle from the brooks; strange fragrances drift on sounding wing; they are the spirits of the elements who pay tribute to the lily and announce the happiness of Anselmus. And now, Anselmus raises his head as if encircled with a glorious halo. Are they glances? Are they words? Are they songs? Do you hear the sound? "Serpentina! Belief in you, love of you, has unfolded to my soul the inmost spirit of nature! You have brought me the lily which sprang from gold, from the primeval force of the world, before Phosphorous had kindled the spark of thought; this lily is knowledge of the sacred harmony of all beings; and I will live in this knowledge with the greatest bliss forevermore. Yes, I, most fortunate of all, have perceived what is highest: I must indeed love you forever, O Serpentina! Never shall the golden blossoms of the lily grow pale; for, like belief and love, this knowledge is eternal!"

For the vision in which I now beheld Anselmus bodily in his freehold of Atlantis I stand indebted to the arts of the salamander; and it was fortunate that when everything had dissolved in air, I found a paper lying on the violet table with the foregoing account written beautifully and distinctly by my own hand. But now I felt myself as if pierced and lacerated by a sharp sorrow.

Ah, happy Anselmus, who has cast away the burden of everyday life! Who in the love of charming Serpentina flies with bold wings and now lives in rapture and joy on his freehold in Atlantis, while I —poor I—must soon, yes, just in a few moments, leave this beautiful hall which is itself far from being a freehold in Atlantis, and again be transplanted to my garret, where enthralled by the paltriness of existence, my heart and my sight are so bedimmed by a thousand mischiefs as by a thick fog, that I will never, never behold the lily.

Then Archivarius Lindhorst patted me gently on the shoulder and said, "Be quiet, be quiet, my revered friend. Do not lament so!

Were you not yourself just now in Atlantis, and do you not at least have there a lovely little farmstead as a poetic possession of your inner mind? Is the bliss of Anselmus anything else but life in poetry, poetry where the sacred harmony of all things is revealed as the most profound secret of Nature?"

End of the Fairy Tale

The Sandman

NATHANAEL TO LOTHAR

You certainly must be disturbed because I have not written for such a long, long time. Mother, I am sure, is angry, and Klara will imagine that I am spending my time in dissipation, having completely forgotten my pretty angel whose image is so deeply imprinted on my heart. But it's not so; I think of you all every day and every hour, and my lovely Klärchen appears to me in my sweet dreams, her bright eyes smiling at me as charmingly as when I was with you. Alas, how could I write to you in the tormented frame of mind which has disrupted all my thoughts! Something horrible has entered my life! Dark forebodings of some impending doom loom over me like black clouds which are impervious to every ray of friendly sunshine. I will now tell you what happened to me. I must tell you, but the mere thought of it makes me laugh like a madman. Oh, my dearest Lothar, how can I begin to make you realize, even vaguely, that what happened a few days ago really could have so fatal and disruptive an effect on my life? If you were here you could see for yourself; but now you will certainly think I am a crazy man who sees ghosts. In brief, this horrible thing I have experienced, the fatal effects of which I am vainly trying to shake off, is simply this: A few days ago, on October 30th, at twelve noon, a barometer dealer came into my room and offered me his wares. I bought nothing and threatened to kick him down the stairs, whereupon he left of his own accord.

You will surmise that only associations of the strangest kind that are profoundly entangled in my life could have made this incident significant, and that the character of this wretched dealer must have had an evil influence on me. In fact, this is the case. I will, with all my strength, pull myself together and calmly and patiently tell you enough about my early youth so that everything will appear clearly and distinctly to your keen mind. But just as I am about to begin, I can hear you laugh, and I can hear Klara say: "This is all childish nonsense!" Laugh! I beg you, have a good laugh! But, my God, my hair is standing on end, and it is in mad despair that I ask you to laugh at me—as Franz Moor asked Daniel.[1] But back to my story.

Except at the noon meal, my brothers and sisters and I saw little of our father during the day. His work must have kept him very busy. After supper, which was served at seven in the old-fashioned way, we all went into father's workroom and sat at a round table. Father smoked and drank a large glass of beer. He often told us marvelous stories, and he would get so carried away that his pipe would keep going out and I would relight it for him with a piece of burning paper, which I thought was great fun. But there were occasions when he'd put picture books in our hands and sit silently in his armchair, blowing out billows of smoke till we all seemed to be swimming in clouds. Mother was very sad on such evenings, and hardly had the clock struck nine when she would say: "Now, children, off to bed with you! The Sandman is coming, I can already hear him." And at these times I always really did hear something clumping up the stairs with a heavy, slow step; it must have been the Sandman. Once, this dull trampling step was especially frightening; and as my mother led us away, I asked her: "Oh, Mama, who is this nasty Sandman who always drives us away from Papa? What does he look like?"

"My dear child, there is no Sandman," my mother answered. "When I tell you that the Sandman is coming, it only means that you are sleepy and can't keep your eyes open any longer, as though someone had sprinkled sand into them."

Mother's answer did not satisfy me, for in my childish mind I was certain that she denied that there was a Sandman only to keep us from being afraid of him—I had surely always heard him coming up the stairs. Full of curiosity to learn more about this Sandman and what his connection was with us children, I finally asked

1. A reference to one of Schiller's popular plays, *Die Räuber,* 1781.

the old woman who took care of my youngest sister what kind of man the Sandman was.

"Oh, dear Thanael," she replied, "don't you know that yet? He is a wicked man who comes to children when they refuse to go to bed and throws handfuls of sand in their eyes till they bleed and pop out of their heads. Then he throws the eyes into a sack and takes them to the half-moon as food for his children, who sit in a nest and have crooked beaks like owls with which they pick up the eyes of human children who have been naughty."

A horrible picture of the cruel Sandman formed in my mind, and in the evenings, when I heard stumbling steps on the stairs, I trembled with fear and dread. My mother could get nothing out of me but the stammered, tearful cry: "The Sandman! The Sandman!" Then I ran into the bedroom and was tortured all night by the horrible apparition of the Sandman. I was old enough to realize that the nurse's tale of the Sandman and his children's nest in the half-moon couldn't be altogether true; nevertheless, the Sandman remained a frightful specter; and I was seized with utmost horror when I heard him not only mount the stairs, but violently tear open the door to my father's room and enter. Frequently, he stayed away for a long time; then he came many times in succession. This continued for years, and I never got used to this terrible phantom. My image of the horrible Sandman grew no paler. His intimacy with my father occupied my imagination more and more. An insurmountable reluctance prevented me from asking my father about him; but if only I—if only I could solve the mystery and get to see this fantastic Sandman with my own eyes—that was the desire which increased in me year by year. The Sandman had directed my thoughts toward marvels and wonders which can so easily take hold of a childish mind. I liked nothing better than to hear or read horrible tales about goblins, witches, dwarfs, and such; but at the head of them all was the Sandman, of whom I was always drawing hideous pictures, in charcoal, in chalk, on tables, cupboards, and walls.

When I was ten my mother moved me from the nursery into a small room which opened off the corridor and was close to my father's room. As always, on the stroke of nine, when the mysterious step could be heard in the house, we had to scurry out. From my room I could hear him enter my father's, and soon thereafter I seemed to detect a thin, strange-smelling vapor spreading through the house. As my curiosity to know the Sandman grew, so did my courage. When my mother had left, I would sneak out of my room into the corridor; but I could never discover anything, because the Sandman had already gone through the door by the time I got to a spot from which he would have been visible. Finally, driven by an uncontrollable impulse, I determined to hide in my father's room itself to await the Sandman.

I could tell one evening from my father's silence and my mother's sadness that the Sandman was coming. I pretended, therefore, to be very tired, left the room before nine o'clock, and hid in a dark corner close to the door. The front door groaned. Slow, heavy, resounding steps crossed the hall to the stairs. My mother hurried past me with the rest of the children. Softly, softly I opened the door of my father's room. He was sitting as usual, silent and rigid, his back to the door; he didn't notice me. I slipped quickly behind the curtain which covered an open cupboard in which my father's clothes were hanging. Closer, ever closer resounded the steps—there was a strange coughing, scraping, and mumbling outside. My heart quaked with fear and expectation. Close, close to the door, there was a sharp step; a powerful blow on the latch and the door sprang open with a bang! Summoning up every drop of my courage, I cautiously peeped out. The Sandman was standing in the middle of my father's room, the bright candlelight full on his face. The Sandman, the horrible Sandman, was the old lawyer Coppelius[2] who frequently had dinner with us!

But the most hideous figure could not have filled me with deeper horror than this very Coppelius. Picture a large, broad-shouldered man with a fat, shapeless, head, an ochre-yellow face, bushy grey eyebrows from beneath which a pair of greenish cat's eyes sparkled piercingly, and with a large nose that curved over the upper lip. The crooked mouth was frequently twisted in a malignant laugh, at which time a pair of dark red spots would appear on his cheeks and a strange hissing sound would escape from between clenched teeth. Coppelius invariably appeared in an old-fashioned coat of ash grey, with trousers and vest to match, but with black stockings and shoes with small agate buckles. His little wig barely extended past the crown of his head, his pomaded curls stood high over his big red ears, and a broad hair bag stood stiffly out from his neck so that the silver clasp which held his folded cravat was visible.

2. *Coppo* is Italian for "eye socket."

His whole appearance was loathsome and repulsive; but we children were most revolted by his huge, gnarled, hairy hands, and we would never eat anything they had touched. He noticed this and took pleasure in touching, under some pretext or other, some piece of cake or delicious fruit which mother had slipped on our plates, so that, tears welling up in our eyes, we were unable to enjoy the tidbit intended for us because of the disgust and abhorrence we felt. He did the same thing on holidays when each of us received a glass of sweet wine from our father. He would pass his hand over it or would even raise the glass to his blue lips and laugh demoniacally, and we could only express our indignation by sobbing softly. He always called us "the little beasts"; and when he was present, we were not to make a sound. How we cursed this horrible man who deliberately and malevolently ruined our slightest pleasure! Mother seemed to loath the repulsive Coppelius as much as we did; the moment he appeared, her gaiety, her lightheartedness, and her natural manner were transformed into dejected brooding. Father behaved toward him as if he were a superior being whose bad manners must be endured and who must be humored at any cost. Coppelius needed only to hint, and his favorite dishes were cooked and rare wines were served.

When I now saw this Coppelius, then, the terrible conviction that he alone was the Sandman possessed me; but the Sandman was no longer the hobgoblin of the nurse's tale, the one who brought the eyes of children for his brood to feed upon in the owl's nest in the half-moon. No! He was a horrible and unearthly monster who wreaked grief, misery, and destruction—temporal and eternal—wherever he appeared.

I was riveted to the spot, spellbound. At the risk of being discovered and, as I could clearly anticipate, severely punished, I remained watching, my head stretched out through the curtain. My father greeted Coppelius ceremoniously. "To work!" Coppelius cried in a hoarse, jarring voice, throwing off his coat. Silently and gloomily my father took off his dressing gown, and both of them dressed in long black smocks. I did not see where these came from. My father opened the folding door of a wall cupboard, but what I had always believed was a cupboard was not. It was rather a black recess which housed a little hearth. Coppelius went to the hearth, and a blue flame crackled up from it. All kinds of strange utensils were about. God! As my old father now bent over the fire, he looked completely different. His mild and honest features seemed to have been distorted into a repulsive and diabolical mask by some horrible convulsive pain. He looked like Coppelius, who was drawing sparkling lumps out of the heavy smoke with the red-hot tongs he wielded and then hammering the coals furiously. It seemed as if I saw human faces on all sides—but eyeless faces, with horrible deep black cavities instead.

"Give me eyes! Give me eyes!" Coppelius ordered in a hollow booming voice. Overcome by the starkest terror, I shrieked and tumbled from my hiding place to the floor. Coppelius seized me. "Little beast! Little beast!" he bleated, baring his teeth. He dragged me to my feet and flung me on the hearth, where the flames began singeing my hair. "Now we have eyes, eyes, a beautiful pair of children's eyes!" he whispered. Pulling glowing grains from the fire with his naked hands, he was about to sprinkle them in my eyes when my father raised his hands entreatingly: "Master! Master!" he cried, "leave my Nathanael his eyes!" "Let the child keep his eyes and do his share of the world's weeping," Coppelius shrieked with a shrill laugh, "but now we must carefully observe the mechanism of the hands and feet." He thereupon seized me so violently that my joints cracked, unscrewed my hands and feet, then put them back, now this way, then another way. "There's something wrong here! It's better the way they were! The Old Man knew his business!" Coppelius hissed and muttered. But everything around me went pitch black; a sudden convulsive pain flashed through my nerves and bones—I felt nothing more.

A gentle, warm breath passed across my face, and I awoke as from the sleep of death, my mother bending over me.

"Is the Sandman still here?" I stammered.

"No, my dearest child, he left long ago and will do you no harm," my mother said, kissing and cuddling her reclaimed darling.

Why should I bore you, my dear Lothar? Why should I go into such copious detail when so much remains to be said? Suffice it to say that I had been caught spying and had been manhandled by Coppelius. My fear and terror had brought on a violent fever, which kept me ill for many weeks. "Is the Sandman still here?" were my first words after regaining consciousness, the first sign of my recovery, my deliverance. I have only to tell you now about the most horrible moment in all the years of my youth; then you will be convinced that it is not because of faulty vision that everything seems devoid of color to me, but that a somber destiny has really hung a murky veil over my life, which I will perhaps tear through only when I die.

Coppelius was not seen again; it was said that he had left the town.

It was about a year later, when we were once more sitting at the round table as was our custom. Father was very cheerful and was telling us entertaining stories about his youthful travels. As the clock struck nine, we suddenly heard the front door groan on its hinges and slow, leaden steps resounded across the hall and up the stairs.

"It's Coppelius," my mother said, growing pale.

"Yes, it is Coppelius," father repeated in a faint, broken voice. Tears welled in mother's eyes.

"But Father, Father!" she cried, "must it be like this?"

"It is the last time!" he answered, "I promise you this is the last time he will come here. Now go, take the children with you. Go, go to bed! Good night!"

I felt as if I had been turned into cold heavy stone—I couldn't catch my breath! But as I stood there, motionless, my mother seized me by the arm. "Come, Nathanael, do come!" I let myself be led to my room. "Calm yourself, calm yourself and go to bed!" my mother cried to me. "Go to bed and go to sleep. Sleep!" But tormented by an indescribable fear, I couldn't close my eyes. The destestable and loathsome Coppelius stood before me with fiery eyes, laughing at me malevolently. I tried in vain to obliterate his image from my mind. It must have been about midnight when there was a terrifying explosion—like the firing of a cannon. The entire house resounded with the detonation; there was a rattling and clattering past my door. The front door slammed shut violently.

"That is Coppelius!" I cried in terror, springing out of bed. Then there was a shriek, a wail of heart-rending grief. I rushed to my father's room. The door was open, and suffocating smoke rolled towards me. The maid shrieked: "Oh, the master! Oh, the master!" My father lay dead in front of the smoking hearth, his face charred black and his features hideously contorted; my brothers and sisters were sobbing and moaning around him—my mother unconscious beside him! "Coppelius, you vile Satan, you've murdered my father!" I cried, and lost consciousness.

When my father was placed in his coffin two days later, his

features were once more serene and gentle, as they had been in life. My soul drew consolation from the thought that his alliance with the satanic Coppelius could not have thrust him into everlasting perdition.

The explosion had awakened the neighbors; the tragedy was talked about and reached the ears of the authorities, who wanted to proceed against Coppelius and hold him accountable. But Coppelius had vanished from town without leaving a trace.

So, my dear friend, when I now tell you that this barometer dealer was the infamous Coppelius himself, you will not blame me for regarding this apparition as foreboding some frightful disaster. He was dressed differently, but Coppelius's figure and face are too deeply etched on my mind for me possibly to make a mistake. In addition, Coppelius has hardly changed his name. I have been told that he claims to be a Piedmontese skilled craftsman, Giuseppe Coppola.

I am determined, regardless of the consequences, to deal with him and to avenge my father's death.

Do not tell my mother anything of this loathsome monster's presence here. Give my love to dear, sweet Klara. I will write to her when I am in a calmer frame of mind. Farewell, etc., etc.

KLARA TO NATHANAEL

Despite it's being true that you have not written for a long time, I believe that I am still in your thoughts. You surely had me most vividly in mind when you intended sending your last letter to Lothar, because you addressed it to me instead. I opened the letter with delight and did not realize my error until I read: "Oh, my dearest Lothar." I should have stopped reading and given the letter to your brother. Even though you have often reproached me, in your innocent, teasing manner, for being so serene and womanly in disposition that if the house were about to collapse I would quickly smooth a misplaced crease out of a curtain—like the woman in the story—before escaping; nevertheless, I can hardly tell you how deeply the beginning of your letter shocked me. I could barely breath; everything swam before my eyes. Oh, my dearest Nathanael, what horrible thing has entered your life? To be parted from you, never again to see you—the thought pierced my breast like a red-hot dagger. I read on and on. Your description of the repulsive Coppelius horrifies me. For the first time I learned about the terrible, violent way your dear old father died. My brother Lothar, to whom I gave this letter, tried with little success to calm me. The horrid barometer dealer Giuseppe Coppola followed my every step, and I am almost ashamed to admit that he even disturbed my normally sound and restful sleep with all kinds of horrible dream images. Soon, however—by the very next day, in fact—I saw everything differently. Do not be angry with me, my dearest one, if Lothar tells you that despite your strange presentiment that Coppelius will harm you, I am still cheerful and calm.

I will frankly confess that in my opinion all the fears and terrors of which you speak took place only in your mind and had very little to do with the true, external world. A loathsome character old Coppelius may have been, but what really lead to the abhorrence you children felt stemmed from his hatred of children.

Naturally, your childish mind associated the dreadful Sandman of the nurse's tale with old Coppelius—who would have been a monster particularly threatening to children even if you had not believed in the Sandman. The sinister business conducted at night with your father was probably nothing other than secret alchemical experiments, which would have displeased your mother because not only was a great deal of money being squandered, but, as is always the case with such experimenters, your father's mind was so imbued with an illusory desire for higher knowledge that he may have become alienated from his family. Your father, no doubt, was responsible for his own death through some carelessness or other, and Coppelius is not guilty of it. Let me tell you that yesterday I asked our neighbor, an experienced chemist, whether experiments of this kind could possibly lead to such a sudden lethal explosion. "Absolutely," he replied, and continued, at length and in detail, to tell me how such an accident could occur, mentioning so many strange-sounding names that I can't recall any of them. Now, you will be annoyed with your Klara and will say: "Such a cold nature is impervious to any ray of the mysterious which often embraces man with invisible arms. Like the simple child who rejoices over some glittering golden fruit which conceals a fatal poison, she sees only the bright surface of the world."

Oh, my dearest Nathanael, do you not believe that even in gay, easygoing, and carefree minds there may exist a presentiment of dark powers within ourselves which are bent upon our own destruction? But forgive me, simple girl that I am, if I presume to tell you what my thoughts really are about such inner conflicts. I will not, to be sure, find the right words; and you will laugh at me—not because what I say is foolish, but because I express my ideas so clumsily.

If there is a dark power which treacherously attaches a thread to our heart to drag us along a perilous and ruinous path that we would not otherwise have trod; if there is such a power, it must form inside us, from part of us, must be identical with ourselves; only in this way can we believe in it and give it the opportunity it needs if it is to accomplish its secret work. If our mind is firm enough and adequately fortified by the joys of life to be able to recognize alien and hostile influences as such, and to proceed tranquilly along the path of our own choosing and propensities, then this mysterious power will perish in its futile attempt to assume a shape that is supposed to be a reflection of ourselves. "It is also a fact," Lothar adds, "that if we have once voluntarily surrendered to this dark physical power, it frequently introduces in us the strange shapes which the external world throws in our way, so that we ourselves engender the spirit which in our strange delusion we believe speaks to us from that shape. It is the phantom of our own ego, whose intimate relationship, combined with its profound effect on our spirits, either flings us into hell or transports us to heaven." You see, dear Nathanael, that my brother Lothar and I have fully discussed the matter of dark powers and forces—a subject which I have outlined for you not without difficulty and which seems very profound to me. I do not completely understand Lothar's last words; I have only an inkling of his meaning, and yet it seems to be very true. I beg you to cast the hateful lawyer Coppelius and the barometer man Giuseppe Coppola from your thoughts. Be convinced that these strange figures are powerless; only your belief in their hostile influence can make them hostile in reality. If profound mental agitation did not speak out from every line in your letter, if your frame of mind did not distress me so deeply, I could joke about Sandman the lawyer and barometer dealer Coppelius. Cheer up, please! I have decided to be your guardian angel, and if ugly Coppola takes it into his head to plague you in your dreams, I will exorcise him with loud laughter. Neither he nor his revolting fists frighten me at all; as a lawyer he is not going to spoil my tidbits, nor, as a Sandman, harm my eyes.

Ever yours, my dearest beloved Nathanael, etc., etc., etc.

NATHANAEL TO LOTHAR

I am very sorry that Klara recently opened and read my letter to you through a mistake occasioned by my distraction. She has written me a very thoughtful and philosophical letter in which she proves, in great detail, that Coppelius and Coppola exist only in my mind and are phantoms of my ego that will vanish in a moment if I accept them as such. As a matter of fact, one would not think that Klara, with her bright, dreamy, child-like eyes, could analyze with such intelligence and pendantry. She refers to your views. The two of you have discussed me. No doubt you are giving her lessons in logic so that she is learning to sift and analyze everything very neatly. Do stop that! By the way, it is probably quite certain that the barometer dealer Giuseppe Coppola cannot possibly be the old lawyer Coppelius. I am attending lectures by the physics professor who just came here recently and who, like the famous naturalist, is called Spalanzani and is of Italian origin. He has known Coppola for many years; besides which, one can tell from his accent that he is really a Piedmontese. Coppelius was a German, but, it seems to me, not an honest one. I am still a little uneasy. You and Klara may still consider me a morbid dreamer; however, I cannot get rid of the impression that Coppelius's damned face makes on me. I am very happy that he has left the city, as Spalanzani told me. This professor is an eccentric fellow. A small, chubby man with big cheekbones, a thin nose, protruding lips, and small piercing eyes. But better than from any description, you can get a picture of him if you look at a picture of Cagliostro as painted by Chodowiecki in any Berlin pocket-almanac.[3] Spalanzani looks just like that.

Recently, when I went up the steps, I noticed that the curtain which usually covers the glass door was not completely drawn across. I do not even know why I was curious enough to peek, but I did. A tall, very slender, beautifully dressed, beautifully proportioned young lady was sitting in the room in front of a small table, on which she had placed her outstretched arms, with hands clasped. She was sitting opposite the door, so I could see her divinely beau-

---

3. There was in fact a picture of Count Alessandro di Cagliostro (1743–95), Italian charlatan, painted by Daniel Nikolaus Chodowiecki (1726–1801), in the Berlin Genealogical Calendar of 1789. Hoffmann, typically, is using accurate material.

tiful face. She did not seem to notice me; indeed, her eyes seemed fixed, I might almost say without vision. It seemed to me as if she were sleeping with her eyes open. I became very uneasy and therefore stole quietly away to the neighboring lecture room. Later, I discovered that the figure which I had seen is Spalanzani's daughter, Olympia, whom he, for some strange reason, always keeps locked up so that no one can come near her. Perhaps, after all, there is something wrong with her; maybe she is an idiot, or something like that. But why do I write you about all this? I can tell you better and in greater detail when I see you. By the way, I am planning to visit you in two weeks. I must see my dear, sweet, lovely Klara again. The irritation which, I must confess, possessed me after the arrival of that disagreeable analytical letter will have vanished by then. For this reason I am not writing to her today. A thousand greetings, etc., etc., etc.

Gentle reader, nothing can be imagined that is stranger and more extraordinary than the fate which befell my poor friend, the young student Nathanael, which I have undertaken to relate to you. Have you, gentle reader, ever experienced anything that totally possessed your heart, your thoughts, and your senses to the exclusion of all else? Everything seethed and roiled within you; heated blood surged through your veins and inflamed your cheeks. Your gaze was peculiar, as if seeking forms in empty space invisible to other eyes, and speech dissolved into gloomy sighs. Then your friends asked you: "What is it, dear friend? What is the matter?" And wishing to describe the picture in your mind with all its vivid colors, the light and the shade, you struggled vainly to find words. But it seemed to you that you had to gather together all that had occurred—the wonderful, the magnificent, the heinous, the joyous, the ghastly—and express it in the very first word so that it would strike like lightning. Yet, every word, everything within the realm of speech, seemed colorless, frigid, dead. You tried, tried again, stuttered and stammered, while the insipid questions asked by friends struck your glowing passion like icy blasts until it was almost extinguished. If, like an audicious painter, you had initially sketched the outline of the picture within you in a few bold strokes, you would have easily been able to make the colors deeper and more intense until the multifarious crowd of living shapes swept your friends away and they saw themselves, as you see yourself, in the midst of the scene that had issued from your soul.

Sympathetic reader, no one, I must confess, asked me about the history of young Nathanael; you are, however, surely aware that I belong to that remarkable species of authors who, when they carry something within themselves as I have just described it, feels as if everyone who approaches—indeed, everyone in the whole world—is asking "What is it? Do tell us, dear sir!"

I was most strongly compelled to tell you about Nathanael's disastrous life. The marvelous and the extraordinary aspects of his life entirely captivated my soul; but precisely for this reason and because, my dear reader, it was essential at the beginning to dispose you favorably towards the fantastic—which is no mean matter—I tormented myself to devise a way to begin Nathanael's story in a manner at once creative and stirring: "Once upon a time," the nicest way to begin a story, seemed too prosaic. "In the small provincial town of S——, there lived"—was somewhat better, at least providing an opportunity for development towards the climax. Or, immediately, *in medias res:* " 'Go to hell!' the student Nathanael cried, his eyes wild with rage and terror, when the barometer dealer Giuseppe Coppola—" In fact, that is what I had written when I thought I noticed something humorous in Nathanael's wild look—but the story is not at all comic. There were no words I could find which were appropriate to describe, even in the most feeble way, the brilliant colors of my inner vision. I resolved not to begin at all. So, gentle reader, do accept the three letters, which my friend Lothar has been kind enough to communicate, as the outline of the picture to which I will endeavor to add ever more color as I continue with the story. As a good portrait painter, I may possibly succeed in making Nathanael recognizable even if the original is unknown to you; and you may feel as if you had seen him with your own eyes on very many occasions. Possibly, also, you will come to believe that real life is more singular and more fantastic than anything else and that all a writer can really do is present it as "in a glass, darkly."

To supply information necessary for the beginning, these letters must be supplemented by noting that soon after the death of Nathanael's father, Klara and Lothar, children of a distant relative who had likewise died and left them orphans, were taken in by Nathanael's mother. Klara and Nathanael soon grew strongly attached to each other, to which no one in the world could object; hence, when Nathanael left home to continue his studies at G———, they were engaged. His last letter is written from G———, where he is attending the lectures of the famous professor of physics Spalanzini.

I could now confidently continue with my story, but even at this moment Klara's face is so vividly before me that I cannot avert my eyes, just as I never could when she gazed at me with one of her lovely smiles. Klara could not be considered beautiful; all who profess to be judges of beauty agreed on that. Nevertheless, architects praised the perfect proportions of her figure, and painters considered her neck, shoulders, breasts almost too chastely formed. Yet on the other hand, they adored her glorious hair and raved about her coloring, which reminded them of Battoni's Magdalen.[4] One of them, a veritable romantic, elaborated an old comparison between her eyes and a lake by Ruïsdael,[5] in which the pure azure of a cloudless sky, the woodlands and flower-bedecked fields, and the whole bright and varied life of a lush landscape are reflected. Poets and musicians went even further and said: "That is nonsense about a lake and a mirror! Can we look at the girl without sensing heavenly music which flows into us from her glance and penetrates to the very soul until everything within us stirs awake and pulsates with emotion? And if we cannot then sing splendid tunes, we are not worth much; the smile flitting about her lips will tell us this clearly enough when we have the courage to squeak out in her presence something which we profess to be a song when, in fact, it is only a disconnected jumble of notes strung together."

And this really was the case. Klara had the spirited imagination of a gay, innocent, unaffected child, the deep sympathetic feelings of a woman, and an understanding which was clear and discriminating. Dreamers and visionaries had bad luck with her; for despite the fact that she said little—she was not disposed to be talkative—her clear glance and her rare ironical smile asked: "Dear friends, how can you suppose that I will accept these fleeting and shadowy images for true shapes which are alive and breathe?" For this reason, many chided Klara for being cold, without feeling, and unimaginative; but others, those whose conception of life was clearer and deeper,

4. The reference is to "The Repentent Magdalen," a painting by Pompeo Battoni (1708–87) which Hoffmann frequently saw in Dresden.

5. Jacob van Ruïsdael (1628–82), one of the greatest landscape painters of the Dutch school.

were singularly enamored of this tenderhearted, intelligent, and child-like girl, though no one cared for her so much as Nathanael, who had a strong proclivity for learning and art. Klara clung to her lover with all of her soul, and when he parted from her, the first clouds passed over her life. With what delight she flew into his arms when he returned to his native town (as he had promised he would in his last letter to Lothar) and entered his mother's room. It turned out as Nathanael had believed it would: the instant he saw Klara again thoughts about the lawyer Coppelius or Klara's pedantic letter —all his depression vanished.

Nevertheless, Nathanael was right when he wrote to his friend Lothar that the abhorrent barometer dealer Coppola had exercised a disastrous influence on his life. This was evident to everyone for even in the first few days of his visit Nathanael seemed completely changed; he surrendered to gloomy brooding and behaved in a manner more strange than they had known before. All of life, everything, had become only a dream and a presentiment; he was always saying that any man, although imagining himself to be free, was in fact only the horrible plaything of dark powers, which it was vain to resist. Man must humbly submit to whatever fate has in store for him. He went so far as to insist that it was foolish to believe that man's creative achievements in art or science resulted from the expression of free will; rather, he claimed that the inspiration requisite for creation comes not from within us but results from the influence of a higher external principle.

To the clear-thinking Klara all this mystical nonsense was repugnant in the extreme, but it seemed pointless to attempt any refutation. It was only when Nathanael argued that Coppelius was the evil principle that had entered him and possessed him at the moment he was listening behind the curtain, and that this loathsome demon would in some terrible way destroy their happiness, that Klara grew very serious and said, "Yes, Nathanael, you are right; Coppelius is an evil and malignant principle. His effect can be no less diabolical than the very powers of hell if they assume living form, but only if you fail to banish him from your mind and thoughts. He will exist and work on you only so long as you believe in him; it is only your belief which gives him power."

Nathanael was greatly angered because Klara said that the demon existed only in his own mind, and he wanted to begin a disquisition on the whole mystic doctrine of devils and sinister powers, but Klara terminated the conversation abruptly by making a trivial remark, much to Nathanael's great annoyance. He thought that profound secrets were inaccessible to those with cold, unreceptive hearts, without being clearly aware that he included Klara among these inferior natures; and therefore he did not cease trying to initiate her into these secrets. Early in the morning, when Klara was helping to prepare breakfast, he would stand beside her and read to her from various occult books until she begged: "But my dear Nathanael, what if I have to accuse you of being the evil principle which is fatally influencing my coffee? For if I please you and drop everything to look into your eyes as you read, my coffee will boil over and no one will have breakfast." Nathanael slammed his book shut and rushed to his room indignantly.

Nathanael had formerly possessed a notable talent for writing delightful and amusing stories, to which Klara would listen with enormous pleasure; now, however, his tales were gloomy, unintelligible, and shapeless so that although Klara spared his feelings and did not say so, he probably felt how little they interested her. Above all, Klara disliked the tedious; and her uncontrollable drowsiness of spirit was betrayed by her glance and by her word. In truth, Nathanael's stories were really very boring. His resentment of Klara's cold, prosaic disposition increased; she could not conquer her dislike of his dark, gloomy, and dreary occultism; and so they drifted farther and farther apart without being conscious of it. Nathanael was forced to confess to himself that the ugly image of Coppelius had faded in his imagination, and it often cost him great effort to present Coppelius in adequate vividness in his writing where he played the part of the sinister bogeyman. Finally it occurred to him to make his gloomy presentiment that Coppelius would destroy his happiness the subject of a poem. He portrayed himself and Klara as united in true love but plagued by some dark hand which occasionally intruded into their lives, snatching away incipient joy. Finally, as they stood at the altar, the sinister Coppelius appeared and touched Klara's lovely eyes, which sprang into Nathanael's own breast, burning and scorching like bleeding sparks. Then Coppelius grabbed him and flung him into a blazing circle of fire which spun round with the speed of a whirlwind and, with a rush, carried him away. The awesome noise was like a hurricane furiously whipping up the waves so that they rose up like white-headed black giants in a raging inferno. But through this savage tumult he could hear

Klara's voice: "Can't you see me, dear one? Coppelius has deceived you. That which burned in your breast was not my eyes. Those were fiery drops of the blood from your own heart. Look at me. I have still got my own eyes." Nathanael thought: "It is Klara: I am hers forever." Then it was as though this thought had grasped the fiery circle and forced it to stop turning, while the raging noise died away in the black abyss. Nathanael looked into Klara's eyes; but it was death that, with Klara's eyes, looked upon him kindly. While Nathanael was composing his poem he was very calm and serene; he reworked and polished every line, and since he fettered himself with meter, he did not pause until everything in the poem was perfect and euphonious. But when it was finally completed and he read the poem aloud to himself, he was stricken with fear and a wild horror and he cried out: "Whose horrible voice is that?" Soon, however, he once more came to understand that it was really nothing more than a very successful poem, and he felt certain that it would arouse Klara's cold nature, although he did not clearly understand why Klara should be aroused by it or what would be accomplished by frightening her with these hideous visions which augured a terrible fate and the destruction of their love.

They were sitting in his mother's little garden. Klara was extremely cheerful because Nathanael had not plagued her with his dreams and foreboding for the three days he had devoted to writing the poem. Nathanael also chatted gaily about things which amused her, as he had in the past, so that Klara remarked: "Now I really do have you back again. Do you see how we have driven out the hateful Coppelius?"

Nathanael suddenly remembered that the poem which he had intended to read to Klara was in his pocket. He took the sheets from his pocket and started reading while Klara, anticipating something boring as usual and resigning herself to the situation, calmly began knitting. But as the dark cloud of the poem grew ever blacker, the knitting in her hand sank and she stared fixedly into Nathanael's eyes. But Nathanael was carried inexorably away by his poem; passion flushed his cheeks a fiery red, and tears flowed from his eyes. When he finally finished, he uttered a groan of absolute exhaustion; he grasped Klara's hand and sighed, as though dissolving in inconsolable grief: "Alas! Klara, Klara!"

Klara pressed him tenderly to her bosom and said in a voice at once soft but very slow and somber: "Nathanael, my darling Na-

thanael, throw that mad, insane, stupid tale into the fire." Nathanael
then sprang indignantly to his feet, thrust Klara away, and cried,
"You damned, lifeless automaton;" and ran off. Klara, deeply hurt,
wept bitter tears, sobbing, "He has never loved me because he does
not understand me."

Lothar came into the arbor; Klara had to tell him everything
that had happened. He loved his sister with all his soul, and every
word of her complaint fell like a fiery spark upon his heart so that
the indignation which he had long felt toward the visionary Nathanael flared into furious rage. He ran to find Nathanael and in
harsh words reproached him for his insane behavior towards his
beloved sister. Nathanael, incensed, answered in kind, "Crazy, con-
ceited fool," and was answered by "Miserable commonplace idiot."
A duel was inevitable, and they agreed to meet on the following
morning behind the garden and to fight, in accordance with the local
student custom, with sharpened foils. They stalked about in silence
and gloom. Klara, who had overheard and seen the violent argument, and who had seen the fencing masters bring the foils at dusk,
suspected what was to happen. They both reached the dueling
ground and cast off their coats in foreboding silence, and with their
eyes aglow with the lust of combat, they were about to attack when
Klara burst through the garden door. Through her sobs she cried:
"You ferocious, cruel beasts! Strike me down before you attack each
other. How am I to live when my lover has slain my brother, or my
brother has slain my lover?"

Lothar lowered his weapon and gazed in silence at the ground,
but in Nathanael's heart the affection he had once felt for lovely
Klara in the happiest days of youth reawoke with a lacerating sorrow.
The murderous weapon fell from his hand, and he threw himself at
Klara's feet: "Can you ever forgive me, my one and only, beloved
Klara? Can you ever forgive me, my dear brother Lothar?" Lothar
was touched by his friend's profound grief, and all three embraced
in reconciliation, with countless tears, vowing eternal love and
fidelity.

Nathanael felt as if a heavy burden which had weighed him
to the ground had been lifted, as if by resisting the dark powers that
had gripped him he had saved his whole being from the threat of
utter ruin. He spent three blissful days with his dear friends and
then returned to G——, where he intended to remain for another
year before returning to his native town forever.

Everything that referred to Coppelius was kept from Nathanael's mother, for they knew that it was impossible for her to think of
him without horror, since like Nathanael, she believed him to be
guilty of her husband's death.

Upon returning to his lodgings, Nathanael was completely
astonished to find that the whole house had been burned down;
nothing remained amid the ruins but the bare outer walls. Although
the fire had started in the laboratory of the chemist living on the
ground floor and had then spread upwards, some of Nathanael's
courageous and energetic friends had managed, by breaking into
his room on the upper floor, to save his books and manuscripts and
instruments. They had carried them undamaged to another house
and had rented a room there, into which Nathanael immediately
moved. It did not strike him as singular that he now lived opposite
Professor Spalanzini, nor did it seem particularly strange to him
when he discovered that by looking out of his window he could see
where Olympia often sat alone, so that he could clearly recognize
her figure, although her features were blurred and indistinct. It did
finally occur to him that Olympia often sat for hours at a small table
in the same position in which he had seen her when he had first
discovered her through the glass door, doing nothing and incessantly gazing across in his direction. He was forced to confess to
himself that he had never seen a lovelier figure, although, with
Klara in his heart, he remained perfectly indifferent to the stiff and
rigid Olympia; only occasionally did he glance up from his book
at the beautiful statue—that was all.

He was writing to Klara when there was a soft tap at the door.
At his call, the door opened and Coppola's repulsive face peered in.
Nathanael was shaken to the roots. Remembering, however, what
Spalanzini had said to him about his compatriot Coppola and what
he had solemnly promised his sweetheart regarding the Sandman
Coppelius, he felt ashamed of his childish fear of ghosts and force-
ably pulled himself together and said as calmly as possible, "I don't
want a barometer, my good friend, do go away."

Coppola, however, came right into the room and said in a
hoarse voice, his mouth twisted in a hideous laugh, his little eyes
flashing piercingly from beneath his long, grey eyelashes, "Oh, no
barometer? No barometer! I gotta da eyes too. I gotta da nice eyes!"
Horrified, Nathanael cried, "Madman, how can you have eyes?

Eyes?" But Coppola instantly put away his barometers and, thrusting his hands in his wide coat pockets, pulled out lorgnettes and eyeglasses and put them on the table. "So, glasses—put on nose, see! These are my eyes, nice-a eyes!" Saying this, he brought forth more and more eyeglasses from his pockets until the whole table began to gleam and sparkle. Myriad eyes peered and blinked and stared up at Nathanael, who could not look away from the table, while Coppola continued putting down more and more eyeglasses; and flaming glances crisscrossed each other ever more wildly and shot their blood-red rays into Nathanael's breast.

Overcome by an insane horror, Nathanael cried, "Stop, stop, you fiend!" He seized Coppola by the arm even as Coppola was once more searching in his pocket for more eyeglasses, although the table was already covered with them. Coppola gently shook him off with a hoarse revolting laugh and with the words "Oh! None for you? But here are nice spyglasses." He swept the eyeglasses together and returned them to the pocket from which they had come and then produced from a side pocket a number of telescopes of all sizes. As soon as the eyeglasses were gone Nathanael grew calm again, and focusing his thoughts on Klara, he clearly saw that this gruesome illusion had been solely the product of his own mind and that Coppola was an honest optician and maker of instruments and far removed from being the ghostly double and revenant of the accursed Coppelius. Besides, there was nothing at all remarkable about the spyglasses that Coppola was placing on the table now, or at least nothing so weird about them as about the eyeglasses. To make amends for his behavior, Nathanael decided actually to buy something, picked up a small, very beautifully finished pocket spyglass, and in order to test it, looked through the window. Never in his life had he come across a glass which brought objects before his eyes with such clarity and distinctness. He involuntarily looked into Spalanzini's room. Olympia, as usual, sat before the little table, her arms upon it, her hands folded. For the first time now he saw her exquisitely formed face. Only her eyes seemed peculiarly fixed and lifeless. But as he continued to look more and more intently through the glass, it seemed as though moist moonbeams were beginning to shine in Olympia's eyes. It seemed as if the power of vision were only now starting to be kindled; her glances were inflamed with ever-increasing life.

Nathanael leaned on the window as if enchanted, staring stead-

ily upon Olympia's divine beauty. The sound of a throat being
cleared and a shuffling of feet awakened him from his enchantment.
Coppola was standing behind him. "*Tre zechini*—three ducats,"
Coppola said. Nathanael had completely forgotten the optician. He
quickly paid the sum requested. "Nice-a glass, no? Nice-a glass?"
Coppola asked in his hoarse and revolting voice, smiling maliciously. "Yes, yes, yes," Nathanael answered irritably. "Goodbye,
my friend." But only after casting many peculiar sidelong glances at
Nathanael did Coppola leave the room. Nathanael heard him laughing loudly on the stairs. "Ah," thought Nathanael, "he's laughing
at me because I overpaid him for this little spyglass." But as he
quietly voiced these words he seemed to hear a deep sigh, like a
dying man's, echoing through the room. Terror stopped his breath.
To be sure, it was he who had deeply sighed; that was obvious.
"Klara is absolutely right," he said to himself, "in calling me an
absurd visionary, yet it is ridiculous—more than ridiculous—that
I am so strangely distressed by the thought of having overpaid Coppola for the spyglass. I see no reason for it." Then Nathanael sat
down to finish his letter to Klara, but a glance through the window
showed him that Olympia still sat as before, and as though impelled
by an irresistible power, he jumped up, seized Coppola's spyglass,
and could not tear himself away from the alluring vision of Olympia
until his friend Siegmond called for him to go to Professor Spalanzini's lecture. The curtain was tightly drawn across the fateful door
so that he could not see Olympia; nor could he see her for the next
two days from his own room, despite the fact that he scarcely ever
left his window and, almost without interruption, gazed into her
room through Coppola's glass. Moreover, on the third day curtains
were drawn across the window, and Nathanael, in despair, driven
by longing and ardent passion, rushed out beyond the city gates.
Olympia's image hovered before him in the air, emerged from the
bushes, and peered up at him with great and lustrous eyes from
the shining brook. Klara's image had completely faded from his
soul. He thought of nothing but Olympia, and he lamented aloud,
in a tearful voice, "Oh! My loftly and lovely star of love, have you
arisen only to disappear again and leave me in the gloomy night of
dark despair?"

As he was about to return home, he became aware of great
noise and activity in Spalanzini's house. The doors were open and
various kinds of gear were being carried in. The first floor windows

had been removed from their hinges, maids with large dust mops were busily rushing about, sweeping and dusting, while inside the house carpenters and upholsterers were banging and hammering. Nathanael stood absolutely still in the street, struck with amazement. Siegmund then joined him and asked with a laugh: "Well what do you think of our old Spalanzini now?" Nathanael assured him that he could say nothing, since he knew absolutely nothing about the professor, but that, much to his astonishment, he had noticed the feverish activity which was taking place in the silent and gloomy house. Siegmund told him that Spalanzini was going to give a great party, a concert and a ball, the next day and that half the university had been invited. Rumor had it that Spalanzini was going to present his daughter Olympia to the public for the first time, after so long having carefully guarded her from every human eye.

Nathanael received an invitation, and at the appointed hour, when carriages were driving up and lights gleamed in the decorated rooms, he went to the professor's house with palpitating heart. The gathering was large and dazzling. Olympia appeared, elegantly and tastefully dressed. No one could help but admire her beautifully shaped face and her figure. On the other hand, there was something peculiarly curved about her back, and the wasplike thinness of her waist also appeared to result from excessively tight lacing. There was, further, something stiff and measured about her walk and bearing which struck many unfavorably, but it was attributed to the constraint she felt in society. The concert began. Olympia played the piano with great talent and also skillfully sang a *bravura* aria in a voice that was high pitched, bell-like, almost shrill. Nathanael was completely enchanted; he was standing in the back row and could not precisely distinguish Olympia's features in the dazzling candlelight. Surreptitiously, he took Coppola's glass from his pocket and looked at her. Oh! Then he perceived the yearning glance with which she looked at him, and he saw how every note achieved absolute purity in the loving glance that scorched him to his very soul. Her skillful roulades appeared to him to be the heavenly exaltations of a soul transfigured by love; and, finally, when the cadenza was concluded, the long trill echoed shrilly through the hall and he felt as if he were suddenly embraced by burning arms. No longer able to contain himself, rapture and pain mingling within him, he cried: "Olympia!" Everyone looked at him; many laughed. The cathedral organist pulled a gloomier face than before and simply said, "Now, now!"

The concert was over. The ball began. Oh, to dance with her! That was his one desire. But how could he summon up the courage to ask her, the queen of the ball, to dance with him? And yet, without really knowing how it happened, just as the dance began he found himself standing close to her and she had not yet been asked to dance. Barely able to stammer a few words, he grasped her hand. It was cold as ice. A deathly chill passed through him. Gazing into Olympia's eyes he saw that they shone at him with love and longing; and at that moment the pulse seemed to beat again in her cold hand, and warm life-blood to surge through her veins. In Nathanael's heart, too, passion burned with greater intensity. He threw his arms around the lovely Olympia and whirled her through the dance. He had thought that he usually followed the beat of the music well, but from the peculiar rhythmical evenness with which she danced and which often confused him, he was aware of how faulty his own sense of time really was. Yet he would dance with no other partner, and he felt that he would murder anyone else who approached Olympia to ask her to dance. But this occurred only twice; to his amazement Olympia remained seated on each occasion until the next dance, when he did not fail to lead her out to the dance floor. If Nathanael had had eyes for anything but the lovely Olympia, there would inevitably have been a number of disagreeable quarrels; for it was obvious that the carefully smothered laughter which broke out among the young people in this corner and that, was directed towards the lovely Olympia, whom they were watching curiously for an unknown reason. Heated by the quantity of wine he had drunk and by the dancing, Nathanael had cast off his characteristic shyness. He sat beside Olympia, her hand in his, and with fervor and passion he spoke of his love in words that no one could understand, neither he nor Olympia. But perhaps she did, for she sat with her eyes fixed upon his, sighing again and again, "Ah, ah, ah!" Whereupon Nathanael answered: "Oh, you magnificent and heavenly woman! You ray shining from the promised land of love! You deep soul, in which my whole being is reflected," and more of the same. But Olympia did nothing but continue to sigh, "Ah, ah!"

Professor Spalanzini passed the happy couple several times and smiled at them with a look of strange satisfaction. It seemed to

Nathanael, although he was in a very different, higher world, that
it was suddenly getting noticeably darker down here at Professor
Spalanzini's. When he looked around him, it was with great con-
sternation that he saw that only two lights were burning in the
empty room and that they were about to go out. The music and the
dancing had ceased long ago. "We must part, we must part!" he
cried in wild despair, then kissed Olympia's hand. He bent down to
her mouth; icy lips met his burning ones. Just as when, touching her
cold hand, he had felt a shudder seize him, the legend of the dead
bride flashed suddenly through his mind.[6] But Olympia drew him
close to her, and the kiss seemed to warm her lips into life. Professor
Spalanzini walked slowly through the empty room, his steps echoing
hollowly, and in the flickering light cast by the candles, his figure
assumed a sinister and ghostly appearance.

"Do you love me? Do you love me, Olympia? Just one word!
Do you love me?" Nathanael whispered.

But as she rose, Olympia only sighed, "Ah, ah!"

"Yes, you, my lovely, wonderful evening star," said Nathanael,
"you have risen for me and will illuminate and transfigure my soul
forever."

"Ah, ah!" Olympia replied as she walked away. Nathanael followed her; they stood before the professor.

"You had a most lively conversation with my daughter," the
professor said with a smile. "If you enjoy talking with this silly
girl you are welcome to come and do so."

Nathanael left, his heart ablaze with all of heaven.

Spalanzini's ball was the talk of the town for the next few days.
Despite the fact that the professor had done everything to put on a
splendid show, the wags found plenty of fantastic and peculiar
things to talk about. Their favorite target was the rigid and silent
Olympia, who, her beautiful appearance notwithstanding, was
assumed to be hopelessly stupid, which was thought to be the reason
Spalanzini had so long kept her concealed. Nathanael heard all this,
not without inner fury, but he said nothing. "What would be the
use," he thought, "of proving to these fellows that it was their own
stupidity which precluded them from appreciating Olympia's profound and beautiful mind."

6. A reference to Goethe's ballad, "Braut von Korinth" ("Bride of Cor-
inth"), in which the hero unwittingly makes love to a revenant and must die.
Nathanael's subconscious may be warning him.

"Do me a favor, brother," Siegmund said to him one day, "and tell me how it is possible for an intelligent fellow like you to have fallen for that wax-faced, wooden puppet across the way?"

Nathanael was about to lose his temper, but he quickly gained control of himself and replied: "Tell me Siegmund, how do you account for the fact that a man who is able so readily to discern beauty has not seen the heavenly charms of Olympia? Yet, thank heaven you are not my rival, for if you were a rival, the blood of one of us would be spilled."

Siegmund, seeing how things were with his friend, adroitly switched tactics, and after commenting that there was no point in arguing about the object of a person's love, he added: "It's very strange, however, that many of us have come to the same conclusion about Olympia. She seems to us—don't take this badly, my brother —strangely stiff and soulless. Her figure is symmetrical, so is her face, that's true enough, and if her eyes were not so completely devoid of life—the power of vision, I mean—she might be considered beautiful. Her step is peculiarly measured; all of her movements seem to stem from some kind of clockwork. Her playing and her singing are unpleasantly perfect, being as lifeless as a music box; it is the same with her dancing. We found Olympia to be rather weird, and we wanted to have nothing to do with her. She seems to us to be playing the part of a human being, and it's as if there really were something hidden behind all of this."

Nathanael did not surrender to the bitterness aroused in him by Siegmund's words; rather, mastering his resentment, he merely said, very gravely: "Olympia may indeed appear weird to you cold and unimaginative mortals. The poetical soul is accessible only to the poetical nature. Her adoring glances fell only upon *me* and irradiated my feelings and thoughts. I discover myself again only in Olympia's love. That she does not indulge in jabbering banalities like other shallow people may not seem right to you. It's true that she says little; but the few words she does utter are in a sacred language which expresses an inner world imbued with love, with the higher, spiritual knowledge gathered from a vision of the world beyond. But you have no feeling for these things; I am wasting my breath."

"God protect you, brother," said Siegmund very gently, almost sadly. "It does seem to me that you are moving in an evil direction. You may depend upon me if—no, I'll say nothing more." It suddenly dawned upon Nathanael that his cold, unimaginative friend Siegmund sincerely wished him very well, and so he warmly shook his outstretched hand.

Nathanael had completely forgotten that there was in the world a Klara whom he had once loved; his mother, Lothar—all had disappeared from his mind. He lived only for Olympia, beside whom he sat every day, hour after hour, carrying on about his love, about mutual sympathy kindled into life, and about their psychic affinity —and Olympia listened to all of this with great reverence. From deep within his desk, Nathanael dug up everything he had ever written—poems, fantasies, visions, romances, tales—and the number was increased daily by a plethora of hyperbolic sonnets, verses, and canzonets; and all of this he read to Olympia tirelessly for hours at a time. Never before had he had such a splendid listener. She neither embroidered nor knitted; she did not look out of the window nor feed a bird nor play with a lapdog or kitten; she did not twist slips of paper or anything else around her fingers; she had no need to disguise a yawn by forcing a cough. In brief, she sat for hours on end without moving, staring directly into his eyes, and her gaze grew ever more ardent and animated. Only when Nathanael at last stood up and kissed her hand and then her lips did she say, "Ah, ah!" and then add, "Goodnight, my dearest."

When Nathanael returned to his own room, he cried, "How beautiful, how profound is her mind! Only you, only you truly understand me." He trembled with rapture when he thought of the marvelous harmony which daily grew between him and Olympia; it seemed to him as if she expressed thoughts about his work and about all of his poetic gifts from the very depth of his own soul, as though she spoke from within him. This must, to be sure, have been the case, for Olympia never spoke any word other than those already recorded. But even in clear and sober moments, those, for example, which followed his awaking in the morning, when Nathanael was conscious of Olympia's utter passivity and taciturnity, he merely said: "What are words? Mere words! The glance of her heavenly eyes expresses more than any commonplace speech. Besides, how is it possible for a child of heaven to confine herself to the narrow circle demanded by wretched, mundane life?"

Professor Spalanzini appeared to be most pleased by the intimacy which had developed between his daughter and Nathanael, and he gave Nathanael many unmistakable signs of his delight.

When, at great length, Nathanael ventured to hint delicately at a possible marriage with Olympia, the professor's face broke into a smile and he said that he would allow his daughter to make a perfectly free choice. Emboldened by these words, and with passion inflaming his heart, Nathanael determined to implore Olympia the very next day to put into plain words what her sweet and loving glances had long told him—that she would be his forever. He searched for the ring his mother had given him when he had left. He intended to present it to Olympia as a symbol of his devotion and the joyous life with her that had flowered. While looking for the ring he came upon his letters from Klara and Lothar; he cast them aside indifferently, found the ring, put it in his pocket, and hurried with it across to Olympia.

While still on the stairs, he heard a singular hubub that seemed to come from Spalanzini's study. There was a stamping, a rattling, pushing, a banging against the door, and, intermingled, curses and oaths: "Let go! Let go! Monster! Villain! Risking body and soul for it? Ha! Ha! Ha! Ha! That wasn't our arrangement! I, I made the eyes! I made the clockwork! Damned idiot, you and your damned clockwork! Dog of a clockmaker! Out! Let me go!" The voices causing this uproar belonged to Spalanzini and the abominable Coppelius. Nathanael rushed in, seized by a nameless dread. The professor was grasping a female figure by the shoulders, the Italian Coppola had her by the feet, and they were twisting and tugging her this way and that, contending furiously for possession of her. Nathanael recoiled in horror upon recognizing the figure as Olympia's. Flaring up in a wild rage, he was about to tear his beloved from the grasp of these madmen when Coppola, wrenching the figure from the professor's hand with the strength of a giant, struck the professor such a fearful blow with it that he toppled backwards over the table on which vials, retorts, flasks, and glass test tubes were standing—everything shattered into a thousand fragments. Then Coppola threw the figure over his shoulder and with a horrible, shrill laugh, ran quickly down the stairs, the figure's grotesquely dangling feet bumping and rattling woodenly on every step. Nathanael stood transfixed; he had only too clearly seen that in the deathly pale waxen face of Olympia there were no eyes, but merely black holes. She was a lifeless doll. Spalanzini was writhing on the floor; his head and chest and arm had been cut by the glass fragments and blood gushed from him as if from a fountain. But he summoned up all his strength: "After him, after him! What are you waiting for! Coppelius—Coppelius has stolen my best automaton. Worked at it for twenty years—put everything I had into it—mechanism—speech—movement—all mine. The eyes—the eyes stolen from you! Damn him! Curse him! After him! Get me Olympia! Bring back Olympia! There are the eyes!"

And now Nathanael saw something like a pair of bloody eyes staring up at him from the floor. Spalanzini seized them with his uninjured hand and flung them at Nathanael so that they hit his breast. Then madness racked Nathanael with scorching claws, ripping to shreds his mind and senses.

"Whirl, whirl, whirl! Circle of fire! Circle of fire! Whirl round, circle of fire! Merrily, merrily! Aha, lovely wooden doll, whirl round!"

With these words Nathanael hurled himself upon the professor and clutched at his throat. He would have strangled him if several people who had been attracted by the noise had not rushed in and torn the raging Nathanael away, thus saving the professor, whose wounds were then bandaged. As strong as he was, Siegmund was unable to subdue the madman, who continued to scream in a horrible voice, "Wooden doll, whirl round!" and to flail about with clenched fists. Finally, several men combined their strength and flung Nathanael to the ground and tied him up. Nathanael's words turned into a heinous bellow, and in a raging frenzy, he was taken away to the madhouse.

Before continuing my narration, gentle reader, of what further happened to the unhappy Nathanael, I can assure you, in case you are interested in Spalanzini, that skillful craftsman and maker of automatons, that his recovery from his wounds was complete. He was, however, forced to leave the university because Nathanael's story had caused a considerable scandal and because opinion generally held that it was an inexcusable deceit to have smuggled a wooden doll into proper tea circles, where Olympia had been such a success, and to have palmed it off as a human. In fact, lawyers held that it was a subtle imposture and considered it felonious because it had been so craftily devised and was directed against the public so that, except for some astute students, it had gone undetected, notwithstanding the fact that everyone now claimed wisdom and pointed to various details which they said had struck them as suspicious. They did not, however, bring any clues to light. Why, for

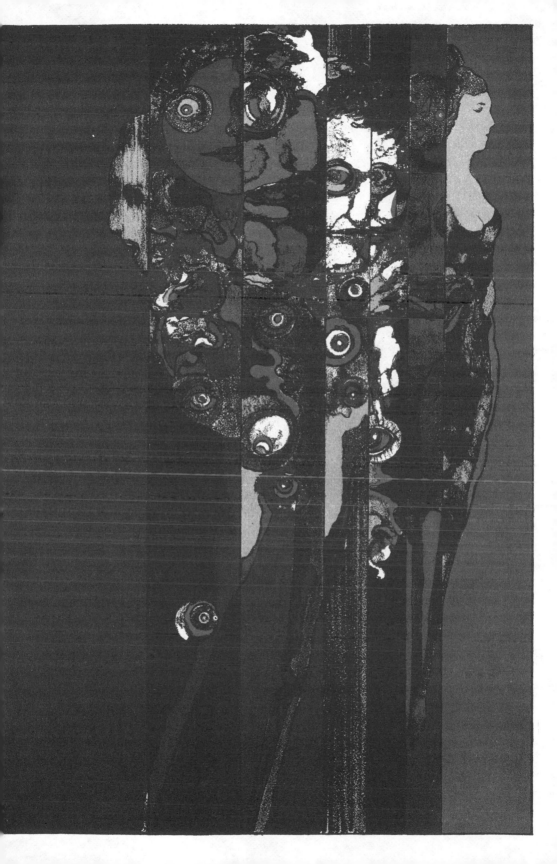

example, would anyone have had his suspicions aroused by the fact that Olympia, according to an elegant tea party-goer, had sneezed more often than she had yawned? This elegant gentleman was of the opinion that the sneezing had really been the sound of the concealed clockwork winding itself up—concomitantly, there had always been an audible creaking—and so on. The professor of poetry and rhetoric took a pinch of snuff, snapped the lid shut, cleared his throat, and solemnly declared: "Most honorable ladies and gentlemen, do you not see the point of it all? It is all an allegory, an extended metaphor. Do you understand? *Sapienti sat.*"

But many honorable gentlemen were not reassured by this. The story of the automaton had very deeply impressed them, and a horrible distrust of human figures in general arose. Indeed, many lovers insisted that their mistresses sing and dance unrythmically and embroider, knit, or play with a lapdog or something while being read to, so that they could assure themselves that they were not in love with a wooden doll; above all else, they required the mistresses not only to listen, but to speak frequently in such a way that it would prove that they really were capable of thinking and feeling. Many lovers, as a result, grew closer than ever before; but others gradually drifted apart. "One really can't be sure about this," said one or another. At tea parties, people yawned with incredible frequency and never sneezed, in order to ward off all suspicion. Spalanzini, as has been noted, had to leave the place in order to escape criminal charges of having fraudulently introduced an automaton into human society. Coppola had also disappeared.

Nathanael awoke as from a deep and frightful dream, opened his eyes, and experienced an indescribable sensation of bliss warmly permeating his body. He lay on his own bed in his own room at home, Klara bending over him, his mother and Lothar standing nearby.

"At last, at last, my darling Nathanael, you have recovered from your terrible illness and are once more mine!" cried Klara with deep emotion, clasping him in her arms. Bright scalding tears streamed from his eyes, so overcome with mingled feelings of sorrow and delight was he, and he gasped, "Klara, my Klara!"

Then Siegmund, who had faithfully stood by his friend in his hour of need, entered the room; and Nathanael shook his hand. "My faithful brother, you have not deserted me."

Every vestige of insanity had disappeared and Nathanael soon recovered his strength again under the tender care of his mother, sweetheart, and friends. Good luck had, in the meantime, visited the house—an old miserly uncle, from whom they had expected nothing, had died and left not only a considerable fortune but a small estate which was pleasantly situated not far from the town. And there they resolved to go and live, Nathanael and Klara, whom he was to marry, and his mother and Lothar. Nathanael had grown more gentle and child-like than ever before, and for the first time could fully appreciate the heavenly purity of Klara's noble spirit. No one ever reminded him, even most remotely, of what had taken place. But when Siegmund said goodbye to him, he remarked, "By heaven, brother, I was on the wrong road. But an angel guided me to the path of light just in time. It was Klara." Siegmund would let him say nothing else for fear that the wounding memories of the past might flare up in him too vividly.

The time came when these four lucky people were to move into their property, and as they were walking through the streets at noon, after having made many purchases, the high tower of the town hall cast its huge shadow over the market place. "Oh!" said Klara, "Let us climb to the top once more and look at the distant mountains!" No sooner said than done. Nathanael and Klara climbed the tower; his mother and the servant went home. Lothar, not wishing to climb so many steps, remained below. There the two lovers stood arm in arm on the topmost gallery of the tower looking down into the fragrant woods beyond which the blue mountains rose up like a giant city.

"Just look at that strange little grey bush," Klara cried. "It really seems to be coming towards us." Nathanael automatically felt his side pocket, where he found Coppola's spyglass, and looked to one side. Klara was standing in front of the glass. Then there was a convulsive throbbing in his pulse. Deathly pale, he stared at Klara; but soon streams of fire flashed and spurted from his rolling eyes. He roared horrendously, like a hunted beast, leaped high into the air, and bursting with horrible laughter, he shrieked in a piercing voice, "Whirl wooden doll! Whirl wooden doll!" And seizing Klara with superhuman strength he tried to hurl her from the tower, but Klara, with a strength born of the agony of desperation, clung tightly to the railing. Lothar heard the madman raving, and he heard Klara's cry of terror. He was seized with a terrible foreboding and raced up the stairs. The door leading to the second flight was shut.

Klara's cries were growing fainter and fainter. Mad with rage and fear, he pushed against the door, which finally burst open. "Help! Save me, save me!" Her voice faded in the air. "She is dead, murdered by that madman," Lothar cried. The door leading to the gallery was also locked, but his desperation endowed him with the strength of a giant and he tore it from its hinges. Good God! Klara was in the grasp of Nathanael the madman, hanging in the air over the gallery railing, to which she barely clung with one hand. Quick as lightening, Lothar seized his sister and pulled her back, at the same instant smashing the madman in the face with his fist so hard that he reeled back and let go of his victim.

Lothar raced down the stairs with his unconscious sister in his arms. She was saved. Nathanael dashed around the gallery, leaping up in the air and shouting, "Circle of fire! Whirl round, circle of fire! Whirl round!" A crowd gathered quickly, attracted by the wild screaming; and in the midst of them there towered the gigantic figure of the lawyer Coppelius, who had just arrived in town and had come directly to the market place. Some wanted to go up and overpower the madman, but Coppelius laughed and said, "Ha, ha! Just wait; he'll come down on his own." And he looked up with the rest. Nathanael suddenly froze, leaned forward, caught sight of Coppelius, and with a shattering scream of "Ah, nice-a eyes, nice-a eyes!" jumped over the railing.

Nathanael lay on the pavement with his head shattered, but Coppelius had vanished in the crowd.

Many years later it was reported that Klara had been seen in a remote district sitting hand in hand with a pleasant-looking man in front of the door of a splendid country house, two merry boys playing around her. Thus it may be concluded that Klara eventually found that quiet, domestic happiness which her cheerful nature required and which Nathanael, with his lacerated soul, could never have provided her.

Councillor Krespel

Councillor Krespel was one of the most eccentric men I ever met in my life. When I went to H——, where I was to live for a time, the whole town was talking about him because one of his craziest schemes was then in full bloom. Krespel was renowned as both an accomplished jurist and a skilled diplomat. A reigning German Fürst—one of no great significance—requested that he draw up a memorandum for submission to the Imperial Court establishing his legal claim to a certain territory. The suit was crowned with unusual success, and because Krespel had once complained that he could never find a house which properly suited him, the Fürst, who had decided to reward him for services rendered, agreed to assume the cost of building a house which Krespel might erect according to his own desires. The Fürst also offered to purchase any site that pleased Krespel, but Krespel rejected this offer, insisting that the house should be built in his own garden, which was located in a very beautiful area outside the town gates. Then he

According to Georg von Ellinger, one of Hoffmann's major editors, Krespel was an historical figure, Johann Berhard Crespel (1747–1813). Goethe mentions him in the second part of the sixth book of his autobiography, *Dichtung und Wahrheit (Poetry and Truth)*. In 1796 Goethe's mother wrote her son a letter containing the following: "Crespel has become a farmer; he has bought estates in Laubach, that is, several forested lots, and is there building a house according to his own invention. But he has in this place neither masons nor carpenters nor cabinet makers nor glaziers—he is all of these himself. A house will come of all of this—like his trousers, which he also makes himself." On the basis of the exact correspondence between this letter and the story, it is probable that Hoffmann heard of the letter, possibly through Brentano.

bought all kinds of building materials and had them delivered there; thereafter he could be seen all day long, dressed in his peculiar clothes—which he always made himself according to his own specific theories—slaking lime, sifting sand, stacking building stones in neat piles, and so on. He had not consulted an architect, nor had he drawn any formal plan. One fine day, however, he called on a master mason in H—— and asked him to appear at his garden at dawn the next day with all of his journeymen and apprentices, many of his laborers, and so on, to build his house for him. Naturally, the mason requested the architect's plan and was more than a little astonished when Krespel replied that there was no need for a plan and that everything would turn out very well without one.

When the mason and his men arrived the next morning, they discovered that an excavation had been dug in a perfect square. "This is where the foundation of my house is to be laid," Krespel said, "and the four walls are to be built up until I tell you that they are high enough."

"Without windows and doors, without partition walls?" the mason interrupted as if shocked by Krespel's crazy notions.

"Do what I tell you, my good man," Krespel replied very calmly. "The rest will take care of itself."

Only the promise of generous payment induced the builder to proceed with this ridiculous building; but never was there one erected under more merry circumstances. The workmen, who laughed continually, never left the site, as there was an abundance of food and drink on hand. The walls went up with unbelievable speed, until Krespel one day shouted, "Stop!" When trowels and hammers were silenced, the workmen descended from the scaffolding and circled around Krespel, every laughing face seemed to ask "So, what's next?"

"Make way!" cried Krespel, who then ran to one end of the garden and paced slowly toward his square building. When he came close to the wall, he shook his head in dissatisfaction, ran to the other end of the garden, and again paced toward the wall, with the same result. He repeated this tactic several times until finally, running his sharp nose hard against the wall, he cried, "Come here, come here, men. Make me a door right here!" He specified the exact dimensions to the inch, and his orders were carried out. Then he walked into the house and smiled with pleasure as the builder remarked that the walls were precisely the height of a well-constructed two story house. Krespel walked thoughtfully back and forth inside. The builders, hammers and picks in hand, followed behind him; and whenever he cried "Put a window here, six by four; and a little window here, three by two!" space was immediately knocked out.

I arrived at H—— at this stage of the operation, and it was very entertaining to see hundreds of people standing around in the garden, all cheering loudly when stones flew out and still another window appeared where it was least expected. Krespel handled the rest of the construction and all other necessary work in the same way. Everything had to be done on the spot, according to his orders of the moment. The comic aspect of the whole project, the growing conviction that everything was turning out better than could possibly have been expected, and above all, Krespel's generosity—which, indeed, cost him nothing—kept everyone in good humor. The difficulties intrinsic in this peculiar method of building were thus overcome, and in a short time a completely finished house was standing, presenting a most unusual appearance from the outside—no two windows being alike, and so on—but whose interior arrangements aroused a very special feeling of ease. Everyone who went there bore testimony to this, and I felt it myself when I grew better acquainted with Krespel and was invited there. Up to that time I had not spoken with this strange man. He had been so preoccupied with his building that he had not even once come to Professor M——'s house for lunch, as had always been his wont on Tuesdays. Indeed, in response to an explicit invitation, he replied that he would not set foot outside his new home before the housewarming took place. All his friends and acquaintances looked forward to a great feast, but Krespel invited no one except the masters, journeymen, apprentices, and laborers who had built his house. He entertained them with the most splendid dishes. Masons' apprentices, without thinking of possible consequences, gorged themselves on partridge pies; carpenters' boys joyfully planed roast pheasants; and hungry laborers for once labored on choicest morsels of *truffes fricassées*. In the evening their wives and daughters arrived, and a great ball began. Krespel waltzed a little with the builders' wives and then sat down with the town musicians, took up his fiddle, and conducted the dance music until daybreak.

On the Tuesday following this festival, which established Krespel as a friend of the people, I finally met him, to my no small pleasure, at Professor M——'s. It would be impossible to imagine

anything stranger than Krespel's behavior. His movements were so
stiff and awkward that he looked as if he would bump into or dam-
age something at any moment. But he didn't, and it was soon obvious that he wouldn't, for the mistress of the house did not bother to
turn a shade paler when he stumbled around the table set with
beautiful cups or maneuvered in front of a great full-length mirror,
or seized a vase of exquisitely painted porcelain and swung it around
in the air as if to let the colors flash. In fact, before lunch Krespel
scrutinized everything in the Professor's room most minutely. He
even climbed up one of the upholstered chairs to remove a picture
from the wall and then rehung it, while chattering incessantly and
with great emphasis. Occasionally—it was most especially noticeable
at lunch—he jumped from one subject to another; then, unable to
abandon some particular idea, he returned to it over and over
again, got himself completely enmeshed in it, and could not disen-
tangle his thoughts until some fresh idea caught him. Sometimes
his voice was harsh and screeching, sometimes it was slow and singsong; but never was it in harmony with what he was talking about.
We were discussing music and praising a new composer when
Krespel smiled and said in his musical voice, "I wish that the
black-winged Satan would hurl that damned music mutilator ten
thousand million fathoms deep into hell's pit!" Then, he burst
out wildly and screechingly: "She is heaven's angel, nothing but
pure God given harmony—the light and star of song!" and tears
formed in his eyes. One had to recall that an hour before he had
been talking about a celebrated soprano.

As we were eating roast hare I noticed that Krespel carefully
removed every particle of flesh from the bones on his plate and
asked especially for the paws, which the Professor's five-year-old
daughter brought to him with a friendly smile. The children had
cast many friendly glances at Krespel during dinner, and now they
got up and moved near to him, but with a respectful shyness, staying
three paces away. "What's going to happen now?" I thought to myself. The dessert was brought in; then Krespel took from his pocket
a little box in which there was a tiny steel lathe. This he immediately screwed to the table, and with incredible skill, made all kinds
of little boxes and dishes and balls out of the bones, which the
children received with cries of delight.

Just as we were rising from the table, the Professor's niece
asked, "What is our Antonia doing now, dear Councillor?"

Krespel made a face like someone biting into a sour orange

who wants to look as if it were a sweet one; but soon his expression changed into a horrifying mask and his laugh was bitter and fierce as he answered with what seemed to me to be diabolical scorn: "Our? *Our* dear Antonia?" he asked in his languid, unpleasant singing tone. The Professor quickly intervened; in the reproving glance he threw at his niece, I read that she had touched a chord which must have jarred discordantly within Krespel.

"How is it going with the violins?" the Professor asked gaily, taking the Councillor by both hands.

Then Krespel's face lightened, and he answered in his firm voice: "Splendidly, Professor, only this morning I cut open that marvelous Amati I told you about recently that fell into my hands through a lucky accident. I hope that Antonia has carefully taken the rest of it apart."

"Antonia is a good child,," the Professor said.

"Yes, indeed, that she is," Krespel screamed, quickly turning around, simultaneously grabbing his hat and stick, and rushing out through the door. I saw in the mirror that there were tears in his eyes.

As soon as the Councillor had left, I insisted that the Professor tell me immediately what Krespel was doing with violins, and especially about Antonia. "Well," the Professor said, "As the Councillor is in general a very remarkable man, he has his own mad way of constructing violins."

"Constructing violins?" I asked in astonishment.

"Yes," continued the Professor. "In the opinion of those who know what it is all about, Krespel makes the best violins that can be found nowadays. Formerly, if one turned out very well, he would allow others to play it; but that has been over for a long time now. When Krespel has made a violin, he plays it himself with great power and with exquisite expression, for an hour or two, then he hangs it up with the rest and never touches it again, nor does he allow anyone else to touch it. If a violin by any of the eminent old masters is on the market, the Councillor buys it, at any price asked. But, as with his own violins, he plays it only once, then takes it apart in order to examine its inner structure, and if he thinks that he has not found what he has been looking for, he flings the pieces into a large chest which is already full of dismantled violins."

"But what's this about Antonia?" I asked suddenly and impetuously.

"Well, now," continued the Professor. "Well, now, that is something that might make me detest the Councillor if I were not convinced of his basic good nature; indeed, he is so good that he errs on the side of weakness, and there must be some hidden explanation behind it all. When he came here to H—— several years ago, he lived like an anchorite, with an old housekeeper in a gloomy house in —— Street. Soon his eccentricities aroused the curiosity of his neighbors, and as soon as he noticed this, he sought and made acquaintances. Just as in my house, people everywhere grew so accustomed to him that he became indispensable. Despite his coarse appearance, even the children loved him, without becoming pests; for in spite of this friendliness, they retained a certain respect for him that protected him from any undue familiarities. You saw for yourself today how he is able to win the hearts of children with various ingenious tricks. We all took him for a confirmed bachelor, and he never contradicted this impression.

"After he had been here for some time, he went away, no one knew where, and returned after several months. On the evening following his return his windows were lighted up more brightly than usual, and this attracted the attention of the neighbors, who soon heard a surpassingly lovely female voice singing to the accompaniment of a piano. Then the sound of a violin struck up and challenged the voice to a dazzling and fiery contest. One immediately knew that it was Krespel playing. I myself mingled with the large crowd which had gathered in front of the Councillor's house to listen to this wonderful concert; and I must confess that the singing of the most famous soprano I had ever heard seemed feeble and expressionless compared with that voice and the peculiar impression it made, stirring me to the depths of my soul. Never before had I had any conception of such long-sustained notes, of such nightingale trills, of such crescendos and diminuendos, of such surging to organ-like strength and such diminution to the faintest whisper. There was no one who was not enthralled by the magic; and when the singer stopped, only gentle sighs interrupted the profound silence.

"It must have been midnight when we heard the Councillor talking violently. Another masculine voice could be heard which, to judge from its tone, seemed to be reproaching him; and at intervals the voice of a girl complained in disjointed phrases. The Councillor shouted more and more loudly until he finally fell into that familiar singsong voice of his. He was interrupted by a loud scream from the girl, and then all grew deathly silent until, suddenly, there was a commotion on the stairs, and a young man rushed out sobbing, threw himself into a carriage waiting nearby, and drove quickly away.

"The Councillor seemed to be very cheerful the next day, and no one had the courage to question him about what had happened the previous night; but the housekeeper, upon being questioned, said that the Councillor had brought home with him a very young lady, as pretty as a picture, whom he called Antonia, and it was she who had sung so beautifully. A young man, who had treated Antonia very affectionately and must have been her fiancé had also come along with them. But, because the Councillor had insisted upon it, he had had to leave quickly. The relationship between Antonia and the Councillor is still a secret, but it is certain that he tyrannizes the poor girl in a most hateful fashion. He watches her as Doctor Bartolo watched his ward in *The Barber of Seville*;[1] she hardly dares to be seen at the window. And if she can occasionally prevail upon him to take her into society, his Argus eyes follow her and he will not permit a musical note to be played, let alone allow her to sing. Indeed, she is no longer permitted to sing in his home either. Antonia's singing on that night has become something of a legend, something romantic that stirs the imagination of the townsfolk; and even the people who did not hear her, often say, when a singer performs here, What sort of miserable caterwauling is that? Only Antonia knows how to sing.' "

You know that such fantastic events are my special weakness, and you can easily guess how imperative it was for me to become acquainted with Antonia. I had often heard the popular comments about her singing, but I had no idea that the glorious Antonia was living in the town, held captive by the mad Krespel as if by a tyrannical sorcerer. Naturally, I heard Antonia's marvelous singing in my dreams the following night, and when she most touchingly implored me to save her in a superb adagio (which, absurdly enough, I seemed to have composed myself), I determined, like a second Astolpho, to break into Krespel's house as into Alzinen's magic castle,[2] and deliver the queen of song from her shameful bonds.

It all came out differently from what I had imagined. As soon

1. Opera by Giovanni Paisiello (1740–1816), upon which the superior *Marriage of Figaro* by Mozart and Rossini's *The Barber of Seville* are based.
2. See n. 5, p. 53, above.

as I had seen the Councillor once or twice and avidly discussed with him the best structure of violins, he himself invited me to call on him at his house. I did so, and he showed me his treasury of violins. At least thirty of them were hanging in a closet, and one of them, conspicuous because it bore the marks of great antiquity (a carved lion's head, and so on), was hanging higher than the rest, crowned with a wreath of flowers that seemed to make it a queen over the others.

"This violin," Krespel said when I asked him about it, "this violin is a very remarkable and wonderful piece by an unknown master, probably of Tartini's time.[3] I am completely convinced that there is something peculiar about its inner construction and that if I take it apart I will discover a secret I have been looking for, but—laugh at me if you like—this dead thing, which depends upon me for its life and its voice, often speaks to me by itself in the strangest manner. When I played it for the first time, it seemed as if I was but the hypnotist who so affects his somnambulist that she verbally reveals what she is able to see within herself. Do not suppose that I am idiotic enough to attribute even the slightest importance to ideas so fantastic in nature, but it is peculiar that I have never succeeded in convincing myself to dismantle that inanimate and dumb object. Now I am pleased that I have never dismantled it; since Antonia's arrival I occasionally use it to play something to her. She is extremely fond of it—extremely."

This was said by Krespel with obvious emotion, and I was encouraged to ask, "My dear Councillor, will you not one day play in my presence?" But his face assumed his sweet-sour expression, and he said in that slow singsong way of his, "No, my dear Herr Studiosus!" And this ended the business; I had to continue looking at all sorts of curiosities, frequently childish ones. Ultimately he thrust his hand in a chest and withdrew from it a folded paper, which he then pressed in my hand, while most seriously saying, "You are a lover of art. Take this present as a true keepsake and value it above all else in the world."

Saying this, he softly clutched both my shoulders and shoved me towards the door, embracing me on the threshold. Actually, I was symbolically thrown out of the house.

When I opened the paper I discovered a piece of an E string

3. Giuseppe Tartini (1692–1770), prominent violinist and composer.

which was about an eighth of an inch in length; and alongside the string was written, "From the E string of the violin used by the deceased Stamitz[4] when he played his last concert."

This unfriendly dismissal at the mention of Antonia suggested that I would never succeed in seeing her; but this was not so, for when I visited the Councillor for the second time I found Antonia in his room, helping him put a violin together. Antonia did not make a strong impression at first sight, but I soon found it impossible to resist her blue eyes, her sweet rosy lips, and her singularly delicate and lovely figure. She was very pale, but if anything was said which was witty and amusing, a fiery blush suffused her cheeks, only to fade to a faint pink glow.

I talked to her without restraint, and I noticed none of those Argus-like glances that the Professor had attributed to Krespel; on the contrary, the Councillor remained absolutely his usual self and even seemed to approve of my conversing with Antonia. And so I often visited the Councillor; and as we grew more familiar, our little circle assumed a warm intimacy which gave the three of us great pleasure. The Councillor continued to entertain me with his eccentricities, but of course it was really Antonia, with her irresistible charm, who drew me there and led me to tolerate a good deal which my impatient nature would otherwise have found unbearable. The Councillor's eccentric behavior was sometimes in bad taste and tedious, and what I found particularly irritating was that as soon as I steered the conversation to music, especially singing, he would interrupt me in his singsong voice, a diabolical smile upon his face, and introduce some irrelevant, often coarse subject. I realized from the great distress in Antonia's eyes at such moments that his sole purpose was to preclude my asking her to sing. I did not give up. The obstacles which the Councillor threw in my way only strengthened my resolution to overcome them. If I was to avoid dissolving in fantasies and dreams about her singing, I had to hear her sing.

One evening Krespel was in an especially good mood. He had been taking an old Cremona violin apart and had discovered that the sound post was so fixed that it was about half a line more oblique than was customary—an important discovery of great practical value! I was successful in getting him to talk very fervently about

4. Karl Stamitz (1746–1801), German composer and violinist.

the true art of violin playing. Krespel mentioned that the style of the old masters had been influenced by that of the truly great singers—Krespel happened just then to be talking about this—and naturally I commented that the practice was now reversed and that singers imitated the leaps and runs of the instrumentalists.

"What is more senseless than this?" I cried, leaping from my chair, running to the piano, and opening it quickly. "What can be sillier than such absurd mannerisms, which instead of being music sound like the noise of peas rattling across the floor!"

I sang several of the modern *fermatas* that run back and forth and hum like a well-spun top, accompanying myself with a few chords. Krespel laughed excessively and cried, "Ha, ha! I seem to hear our German-Italians, or our Italian-Germans, starting some aria by Pucitta or Portogallo,[5] or by some other *maestro di capella*, or rather *schiavo d'un primo uomo*."[6]

"Now," I thought, "is the moment;" and turning to Antonia I asked, "Isn't that right? Antonia knows nothing of such squealing?" And I immediately began one of the beautiful soul-stirring songs by old Leonardo Leo.[7] Antonia's cheeks flushed, her eyes flashed with a newly awakened radiance. She sprang to the piano and parted her lips. But at that very instant Krespel pushed her away, seized me by the shoulders, and shrieked in his shrill tenor voice, "My dear boy, my dear boy!" Then, grasping my hand while bowing most courteously, he led me immediately away, saying in his soft singsong way, "In truth, my esteemed and honorable sir, in truth it would be a breech of courtesy and good manners if I were to express my wish loudly and clearly that you should have your neck softly broken by the scorching claws of the devil who would, one could say, dispose of you quickly; but putting that aside for the moment, you must admit, my dear, dear sir, that it is growing very dark, and since there are no lamps lighted today, you might risk damaging your precious legs, even if I did not kick you out right now. Be good and go home in safety and think kind thoughts of me, your true friend, if it so happens that you never—do you understand me?—if you never happen to find him at home again."

5. Vincenzo Pucitta (1778–1861) and Marcus Antonio Portogallo (1762–1830), both composers, the first Italian, the second Portugese.

6. Literally, "slave of the first singer," i.e., a Kapellmeister bullied by the soloist.

7. Leonardo Ortensio Salvatore di Leo (1694–1744), significant Italian composer.

He thereupon embraced me and, grasping me firmly, slowly turned me towards the door so that I could not get another look at Antonia. You must admit that in my situation I could hardly beat up the Councillor, which he really deserved. The Professor enjoyed a good laugh at my expense and assured me that my break with the Councillor was absolutely permanent. Antonia was too precious to me, too sacred, I might say, for me to play the part of the languishing *amoroso* who stands gazing up at her window or fills the role of the lovesick adventurer. I left H—— completely shattered, but as usually happens in such cases, the brilliant colors of the picture painted by my imagination grew dim, and Antonia—yes, even her singing, which I had never heard—glimmered in my recollection like a gentle, consoling light.

Two years later, when I had settled in B——, I undertook a trip through Southern Germany. The towers of H—— rose up in the hazy red glow of the evening; as I drew nearer, I was oppressed by an indescribable feeling of anxiety which lay upon my heart like a heavy weight. I could not breathe; I had to get out of the carriage and into the open air, but the oppressiveness increased until it became physically agonizing. I soon seemed to hear the strains of a solemn chorale floating on the air. The sound grew more distinct, and I could distinguish men's voices singing a hymn.

"What's that? What's that?" I cried, as it pierced my breast like a burning dagger.

"Can't you see?" said the postillion next to me. "They're burying someone over there in the churchyard."

We were, in fact, close to the churchyard, and I saw a circle of people clad in black standing around a grave which was being filled. Tears welled in my eyes; I felt somehow that all the joy and happiness of my life were being buried in that grave. Moving quickly down the hill, I could no longer see into the churchyard. The hymn was over, and not far from the city gate I could see some of the mourners returning from the funeral. The Professor, his niece on his arm, both in deep mourning, passed close to me without noticing me. The niece had her handkerchief pressed to her eyes and was sobbing convulsively. It was impossible for me to go into town; therefore, I sent my servant with the carriage to the inn where I usually stay, while I hurried off to the neighborhood so familiar to me in an effort to shake off my mood, possibly due to something physical, perhaps the result of becoming overheated on the journey.

When I arrived at the avenue leading to a park, a most extraordinary spectacle took place. Councillor Krespel was being guided by two mourners, from whom he appeared to be trying to escape by making all kinds of strange leaps and turns. As usual, he was dressed in the incredible grey coat he had made himself, but from his small three-cornered hat, which he wore cocked over one ear in a military manner, a mourning ribbon fluttered this way and that in the breeze. A black sword belt was buckled around his waist, but instead of a sword, a long violin bow was tucked beneath it. A cold shiver ran through me. "He is mad," I thought as I slowly followed them. The men conducted him as far as his house, where he embraced them, laughing loudly. They left him, and then his glance fell on me, for I was now standing very close to him. He stared at me fixedly for some time, then called in a hollow voice, "Welcome, Herr Studiosus! You do, of course, understand everything about it." With this he seized me by the arm and dragged me into the house, up the stairs, and into the room where the violins hung. They were all draped in crepe; the violin by the old master was missing; in its place there hung a wreath of cypress. I knew what had happened.

"Antonia! Antonia!" I cried inconsolably. The Councillor, his arms folded, stood beside me as if paralyzed. I pointed to the cypress wreath.

"When she died," he said very solemnly and gloomily, "the sound post of that violin broke with a resounding crack and the soundboard shattered to pieces. That faithful instrument could only live with her and through her; it lies beside her in the coffin; it has been buried with her." Deeply shaken, I sank into a chair, but the Councillor began singing a gay song in a hoarse voice. It was truly horrible to see him hopping about on one foot, the crepe (he was still wearing his hat) flapping about the room and against the violins hanging on the walls; indeed, I could not repress a loud shriek when the crepe hit me during one of his wild turns. It seemed to me that he wanted to envelop me and drag me down into the black pit of madness. Suddenly he stopped gyrating and said in his singsong fashion, "My son, my son, why do you shriek like that? Have you seen the Angel of Death? He's usually seen before the funeral"; and suddenly stepping into the middle of the room, he drew the bow from his belt; and having raised it above his head in both hands, he broke it into a thousand pieces. Then he cried with a loud laugh, "Now you imagine that the staff has been broken over me,[8] don't you, my son? But it's not so. Now I am free, free. I am free! I will no longer make violins—no more violins—hurrah! No more violins!" This he sang to a hideously mirthful tune, again jumping about on one foot. Aghast, I tried to get out of the door quickly, but the Councillor held me tightly and said quietly, "Stay here, Herr Studiosus, and don't think I am mad because of this outpouring of agony which tortures me like the pangs of death. It is all because only a short while ago I made a nightshirt for myself in which I wanted to look like Fate or like God."

The Councillor continued this frightening gibberish until he collapsed in utter exhaustion. The ancient housekeeper came to him when I called, and I was glad when I once more found myself in the open air.

Not for a moment did I doubt that Krespel had become insane, but the Professor held to the contrary. "There are men," he said, "from whom nature or some peculiar destiny has removed the cover beneath which we hide our own madness. They are like thin-skinned insects whose visible play of muscles seems to make them deformed, though in fact, everything soon returns to its normal shape again. Everything which remains thought within us becomes action in Krespel. Krespel expresses bitter scorn in mad gestures and irrational leaps, even as does the spirit which is embedded in all earthly activity. This is his lightening rod. What comes from the earth, he returns to the earth, but he knows how to preserve the divine. And so I believe that his inner consciousness is well, despite the apparent madness which springs to the surface. Antonia's sudden death weighs very heavily upon him, but I wager that tomorrow he'll be jogging along at his donkey trot as usual."

It happened that the Professor's prediction was almost exactly fulfilled. The next day the Councillor seemed to be completely himself again, but he declared that he would never again construct a violin, or play one. As I later learned, he kept his word.

The Professor's theories strengthened my private conviction that the carefully concealed, yet highly intimate nature of the relationship between Antonia and the Councillor, and even her death, had been marked by guilt, which could not be expatiated. I did not want to leave H—— without confronting him with this

8. I.e., condemned to death. In German courts the staff was broken when a sentence of death was delivered.

crime of which I suspected him; I wanted to shake him to the depths of his soul and so compel him to make an open confession of his horrible deed. The more I thought about the matter, the more I convinced myself that Krespel must be a scoundrel, and as the thoughts in my mind grew more fiery and forceful they developed into a genuine rhetorical masterpiece. Thus equipped, and in great agitation, I ran to the Councillor's. I found him calmly smiling, making toys.

"How is it possible," I began the assault, "for you to find a moment's peace in your soul when the memory of your terrible deed must torture you like a serpent's sting?"

Krespel looked at me in astonishment, put his chisel aside, and said, "What do you mean my dear fellow? Do have a seat please, on that chair."

But I grew more and more heated, and I accused him directly of having murdered Antonia and threatened him with the retribution of the Eternal. In fact, as a recently qualified court official imbued with my profession, I went so far as to assure him that I would do everything possible to bring the matter to light and to deliver him into the hands of an earthly judge. I was considerably taken aback, however, when at the conclusion of my violent and pompous harangue, the Councillor fixed his eyes upon me serenely, without uttering a word, as if waiting for me to continue. Indeed, I did try to do so, but it all sounded so clumsy and so utterly silly that I almost immediately grew silent again.

Krespel luxuriated in my perplexity; a malicious and ironical smile darted across his face. Then he became very serious and spoke to me in a solemn voice: "Young man, you may take me for a madman; I can forgive you for that. We are both confined to the same madhouse, and you accuse me of imagining that I am God the Father because you consider yourself to be God the Son. But how dare you presume to force your way into the life of another person to uncover hidden facts that are unknown to you and must remain so? She is dead now and the secret is revealed."

Krespel rose and paced back and forth across the room several times. I ventured to ask for an explanation; he stared at me with fixed eyes, grasped my hand, and led me to the window. After opening both casements, he propped his arms on the sill, leaned out, and looking down into the garden, he told me the story of his life. When he had finished, I left him, deeply moved and ashamed.

The facts of his relationship with Antonia were as follows: About twenty years ago the Councillor's all-consuming passion for hunting out and buying the best violins by the old masters had led him to Italy. He had not at that time begun to make violins himself, nor, consequently, had be begun to take them apart. In Venice he heard the famous singer Angela ——i, who at that time was triumphantly appearing in the leading roles in the Theatro di S. Benedetto. His enthusiasm was kindled, not only because of her art, which Signora Angela had developed to absolute perfection, but by her angelic beauty as well. The Councillor sought her acquaintance, and despite his uncouthness, he succeeded, primarily by his bold and most expressive violin playing, in winning her entirely for himself.

In a few weeks their close intimacy led to marriage, which was kept a secret because Angela did not wish to part from the theater nor surrender the name under which she had become famous nor add the awkward name of Krespel to it. With the most extravagant irony, the Councillor described the very peculiar way Angela plagued and tortured him as soon as she became his wife. Krespel felt that all the selfishness and all the petulance which resided in all the primadonnas in the world were somehow concentrated in her little body. When he once tried to assert his own position, Angela turned loose on him a whole army of *abbates, maestros, academicos* who, ignorant of his true relationship, found in him a completely intolerable and uncivilized admirer who was beyond adapting himself to the Signora's delightful whims. Right after one of these tumultuous scenes, Krespel fled to Angela's country house, trying to forget the suffering the day had brought by improvising on his Cremona violin. He had not been playing long, however, when the Signora, who had followed hard after him, stepped into the room. She was in the mood for playing the affectionate wife, so she embraced the Councillor with sweet languishing glances and laid her head on his shoulder. But the Councillor, who was lost in the world of his music, continued playing until the walls resounded, and it so happened that he touched the Signora a little ungently with his arm and the bow. Blazing into fury, she sprang back, shrieking *"bestia tedesca!"* snatched the violin from his hands, and smashed it into a thousand pieces on the marble table. The Councillor stood like a statue before her; but then, as if waking from a dream, he seized the Signora with the strength of a giant and flung her out of the window of her own country house, after which, without troubling himself about the matter any further, he fled to Venice, then Germany.

It was sometime before he fully realized what he had done. Although he knew that the window was barely five feet from the ground, and though he was fully convinced that it had been absolutely necessary to fling her from the window, he felt troubled and uneasy about it, especially because the Signora had made it clear to him that she was pregnant. He scarcely had the courage to ask about her, and he was not a little surprised when about eight months later he received a tender letter from his beloved wife which contained no mention of what had happened at the country house, but rather informed him that she had given birth to a lovely little girl and concluded with the heartfelt request that the *marito amato e padre felicissimo* come to Venice at once. Krespel did not go; instead he requested a close friend to supply him with details as to what was really going on. And he learned that the Signora had landed that day on the grass as gently as a bird and that the only consequence of her fall had been emotional. As a result of Krespel's heroic deed, she seemed transformed; no longer was there evidence of her former capriciousness or willfulness or of her old teasing habits; and the *maestro* who had composed the music for the next carnival was the happiest man under the sun, for the Signora was willing to sing his arias without a thousand changes to which he would otherwise have had to consent. All in all, there was every reason for keeping secret the method by which Angela had been cured; otherwise primadonnas would come flying through windows every day.

The Councillor grew very excited, ordered horses, and was seated in the carriage when he suddenly cried, "Stop!" He murmured to himself, "Why, isn't it certain that the evil spirit will again take possession of Angela the moment she sees me again? Since I have already thrown her out of the window, what will I do if the same situation were to occur? What would there be left for me to do?"

He got out of the carriage and wrote his wife an affectionate letter, in which he gracefully alluded to her kindness in expressly detailing the fact that his little daughter had a little mole behind her ear, just as he did, and—remained in Germany. A very spirited exchange of letters ensued. Assurances of love—invitations—regrets over the absence of the loved one—disappointment—hopes—and so on—flew back and forth between Venice and H—— and H—— to Venice. Finally Angela came to Germany, and as is well known, sang triumphantly as primadonna at the great theater in F——. Despite the fact that she was no longer young, she swept all before her with the irresistible charm of her marvelous singing. Her voice at that time had not deteriorated in the slightest degree. Meanwhile Antonia had grown up, and her mother never could write enough to her father about the potential she saw in her daughter, who was blossoming into a first-rate singer. Krespel's friends in F—— confirmed this information and urged him to come to F—— to marvel at the rare experience of hearing two such absolutely sublime singers together. They did not suspect the intimate relationship which existed between Krespel and the ladies. He would have loved seeing his daughter, whom he adored from the depths of his heart, and who often appeared to him in his dreams; but as soon as he thought about his wife he felt very uneasy, and he remained at home among his dismembered violins.

You will have heard of the promising young composer B—— of F—— who suddenly disappeared, no one knows how. (Did you perhaps know him?) He fell desperately in love with Antonia and, Antonia returning his love, he begged her mother to consent to a union which would be sanctified by their art. Angela had no objection to this, and the Councillor gave his consent all the more readily because the young composer's music pleased his critical judgment. Krespel expected to receive news that the wedding had taken place, when instead he received an envelope, sealed in black, addressed in an unfamiliar hand. Dr. R—— informed the Councillor that Angela had fallen seriously ill as a result of a chill which she had caught at the theater the evening preceding what was to have been Antonia's wedding day, and had died. Angela had revealed to the doctor that she was Krespel's wife and that Antonia was his daughter. He was therefore to hasten there to assume responsibility for the orphan. Despite the fact that the Councillor was deeply disturbed by this news of Angela's death, he nevertheless soon felt that a disturbing influence had left his life and that now he could breathe freely for the first time.

That very same day he started out for F——. You cannot imagine how dramatically the Councillor described the moment when he first saw Antonia. Even in the very bizarre nature of his language there was a wonderful power of description which I am completely incapable of conveying. Antonia had all of her mother's amiability and charm, but she had none of the meanness which was the reverse side of her mother's character. There was no ambiguous cloven hoof to peep out from time to time. The young bridegroom arrived; and Antonia, who was able through her own affectionate nature intuitively to understand her remarkable father, sang one of the old Padre Martini motets, which she knew Angela had had to sing repeatedly to Krespel when their courtship had been in full bloom. Tears flooded the Councillor's cheek; he had never heard Angela sing so beautifully. The timbre of Antonia's voice was quite individual and rare, sometimes like the sound of an Aeolian harp, sometimes like the warbling of a nightingale. It was as if there were no room for such notes within the human breast. Antonia, glowing with love and joy, sang all of her most lovely songs, and B—— in the intervals played as only enraptured inspiration can play. Krespel was at first transported by delight, but then he grew thoughtful—quiet —introspective. Finally he leaped to his feet, pressed Antonia to his breast, and begged her softly and sadly: "If you love me, sing no more—my heart is bursting—the anguish! The anguish! Sing no more."

"No," the Councillor said the next day to Dr. R——. "When she sang, the color gathered into two dark red spots on her pale cheeks, and I knew that it could not be accounted for by any silly family resemblance; it was what I had dreaded."

The doctor, whose face had shown deep concern from the beginning of the conversation, replied, "Whether it results from her having overexerted herself in singing when she was too young, or whether it results from congenital weakness, Antonia suffers from an organic deficiency in her chest from which her voice derives its wonderful power and its strange, I might say, divine timbre and by which it transcends the capabilities of human song. But it will cause her early death; for if she continues to sing, she will live six months at the most."

The Councillor's heart felt as if it were pierced by a hundred daggers. It was as though a lovely tree and its superb blossoms had, for the first time, cast its shadow over him, and now it was to be cut down to the roots so that it could no longer grow green and blossom. His decision was made. He told Antonia everything and presented her with a choice—she could either follow her fiancé and surrender to his and the world's allurements with the certainty of dying young, or give to her father in his old age a happiness and a peace which he had never known, and thereby live for many years. Antonia collapsed sobbing into her father's arms, and he, aware of the agony the next few minutes might bring, asked for nothing explicit. He spoke with her fiancé, but despite his assurance that no note would ever cross Antonia's lips, the Councillor was fully aware that B—— himself would never be able to resist the temptation to hear her sing—at least the arias he was composing. The musical world, even though it knew of Antonia's suffering, would surely never surrender its claim to her, for people like this can be selfish and cruel when their own enjoyment is at issue.

The Councillor disappeared from F—— with Antonia and arrived at H——. B—— was in despair when he learned of their departure. He followed their tracks, overtook the Councillor, and arrived at H—— simultaneously.

"Let me see him only once and then die," Antonia entreated.

"Die? Die?" the Councillor cried in wild anger, an icy shudder running through him. His daughter, the only being in the wide world who could kindle in him a bliss he had never known, the one who had reconciled him to life, tore herself violently from his embrace; and he wanted this dreadful event to happen!

B—— went to the piano, Antonia sang, Krespel played the violin merrily until the red spots appeared on Antonia's cheeks. Then he ordered a halt; and when B—— said goodbye to Antonia, she suddenly collapsed with a loud cry.

"I thought," Krespel told me, "I thought that she was really dead, as I had forseen; but as I had prepared myself to the fullest degree, I remained very calm and controlled. I seized B——, who was staring stupidly like a sheep, by the shoulders and said" (and the Councillor now returned to his singsong voice) : " 'Now, my dear and estimable piano master, now that you have, as you wished and desired, succeeded in murdering your beloved bride, you will quietly leave, unless you would be good enough to wait around until I run my bright little dagger through your heart, so that my daughter, who you see, has grown rather pale, could use some of your precious blood to restore her color. Get out of here quickly, or I may throw this nimble little knife at you!'

"I must have looked rather terrifying as I said this, for with a cry of the deepest horror, B—— tore himself from my grasp, rushed through the door and down the steps."

As soon as he was gone, Krespel went to lift Antonia, who lay unconscious on the floor, and she opened her eyes with a deep sigh, but soon closed them again as if she were dead. Krespel broke into loud and inconsolable grief. The doctor, who had been fetched meanwhile by the housekeeper, announced that Antonia was suffering from a serious but by no means fatal attack; and she did, in fact, recover more quickly than the Councillor had dared to hope. She now clung to Krespel with a most devoted and daughterly affection and shared with him all of his favorite hobbies, his peculiar schemes and whims. She helped him take old violins apart and put new ones together. "I will not sing anymore, but I will live just for you," she often said to her father, smiling softly, after someone had asked for a song and she had refused. The Councillor tried as hard as possible to spare her from such situations, and therefore, he was unwilling to take her out into society and scrupulously shunned all music. He was well aware of how painful it must be for Antonia to forgo completely the art in which she had attained such perfection.

When the Councillor bought the wonderful violin that he later buried with Antonia and was about to take it apart, Antonia looked at him very sadly and, in a gentle, imploring voice, asked, "This one, too?" The Councillor himself couldn't understand what unknown power had impelled him to spare his violin and to play it.

He had barely drawn the first few notes when Antonia cried aloud with joy, "Why that is me—I am singing again!" In truth, there was something about the silvery bell-like tones of the violin that was very striking; they seemed to come from a human soul. Krespel was so deeply moved that he played more magnificently than ever before, and when he ran up and down the scale with consumate power and expression, Antonia clapped her hands and cried with delight, "I sang that well! I sang that very well!" From this time on a great serenity and happiness came into her life. She often said to Krespel, "I would like to sing something, Father." Then Krespel would take his violin from the wall and play her most beautiful songs, and she was surpassingly happy.

One night, shortly before I arrived in H——, it seemed to Krespel that he heard someone playing the piano in the next room, and soon he distinctly recognized that it was B——, who was improvising in his usual style. He was about to rise, but it was as if there were a heavy weight upon him; he could not so much as stir. Then he heard Antonia's voice singing softly and delicately until it slowly grew into a shattering fortissimo. The wonderful sounds became the moving song which B—— had once composed for her in the devotional style of the old masters. Krespel said that the state in which he found himself was incomprehensible, for an appalling fear was combined with a rapture he had never before experienced.

Suddenly he was overwhelmed by a dazzling lucidity, and he saw B—— and Antonia embracing and gazing at each other rapturously. The notes of the song and the accompaniment of the piano continued, although Antonia was not visibly singing nor B—— playing. The Councillor fell into a profound unconsciousness in which the vision and the music vanished. When he awoke, the terrible anxiety of his dream still possessed him. He rushed into Antonia's room. She lay on the sofa with her eyes shut, her hands devoutly folded, as if she were asleep and dreaming of heavenly bliss and joy. But she was dead.

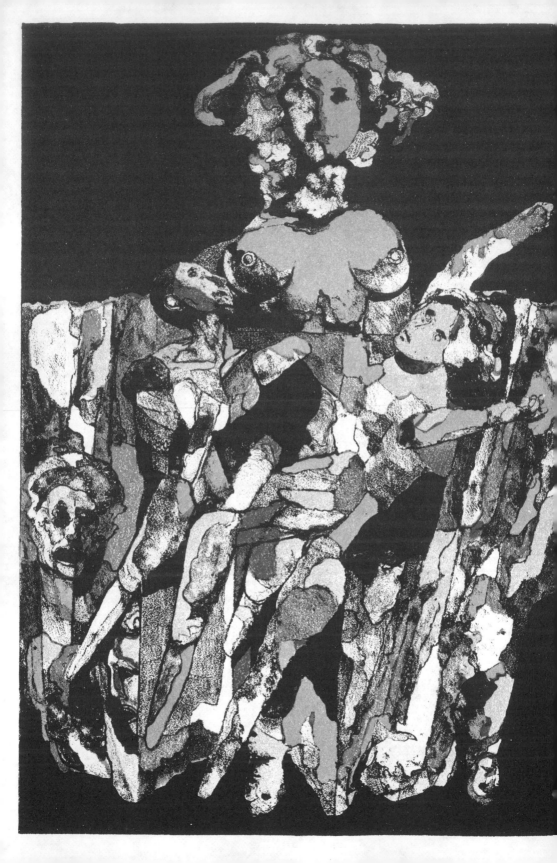

The Mines of Falun

All the people of Göteborg had gathered at the harbor one cheerful sunny day in July. A rich East Indiaman, which had happily returned from distant lands, lay at anchor in Klippa Harbor; the Swedish flags waved gaily in the azure sky while hundreds of boats of all kinds, overflowing with jubilant seamen, drifted back and forth on the crystal waves of the Götaelf, and the cannon on the Masthuggetorg thundered forth resounding greetings toward the sea. The gentlemen of the East India Company were strolling back and forth along the harbor, estimating their handsome profits with happy smiles and rejoicing that their daring enterprises flourished increasingly with the years and that Göteborg's trade was blooming marvelously.

The East Indiaman's crew, about a hundred and fifty men strong, were landing in many boats and were preparing to hold their *Hönsning*—that is the name of the festival which is celebrated on such occasions by the crew and which often lasts several days. Musicians in curious, gay-colored costumes led the way with violins, fifes, oboes, and drums which they played with vigor while singing all kinds of merry songs. The sailors followed them two by two, some with gaily beribboned jackets and caps from which fluttering pen-

Falun is the district capital of Dalarna, Sweden, and is important for its copper, lead and zinc mines.

The sources of this story are in Gotthilf Heinrich Schubert, *Ansichten von der Nachtseite der Naturwissenschaft* [Views of the Night Side of Natural Science] (Dresden, 1808) and Ernst Moritz Arndt, *Reise durch Schweden im Jahre 1804* [Journey through Sweden in the Year 1804] (Berlin, 1806).

nons streamed, while others danced and leaped and all shouted with such exuberance that the sound echoed far and wide.

The joyful throng paraded across the wharf and through the outskirts of the city to Haga, where there was to be feasting and drinking in a large inn.

The finest beer flowed in rivers, and mug after mug was emptied. As is always the case when seamen return from a lengthy voyage, all sorts of pretty girls soon joined them. A dance began; the fun grew wilder and wilder, and the rejoicing louder and madder.

Only one lone seaman, a slim, handsome youth, scarcely twenty years old, had slipped away from the turmoil and was sitting alone on a bench by the door of the tavern.

A couple of sailors stepped up to him, and one of them called out, laughing loudly, "Elis Fröbom! Elis Fröbom! Are you being a wretched fool again and wasting these lovely moments with silly thoughts? Listen, Elis. If you are going to stay away from our *Hönsning*, then keep away from our ship. You will never be a decent, proper sailor. You have courage enough and are brave in times of danger, but you don't know how to drink and would rather keep your money in your pockets than throw it away on landlubbers. Drink, boy, or may the sea devil, Näck,[1] that old troll, take you!"

Elis Fröbom jumped up quickly from the bench, looked at the sailors with glowing eyes, took the goblet that was filled to the brim with brandy, and emptied it at one gulp. Then he said, "You see, Joens, that I can drink like one of you, and the captain will decide whether I am a worthy seaman. But now shut your filthy mouths and get out! I hate your wildness. It is none of your business what I am doing out here."

"Well, well," replied Joens. "I know you are a Neriker man, and they're all sad and dreary and don't really enjoy the good life of a seaman. Just wait, Elis, I'll send someone out to you. You must be cut adrift from that confounded bench that you were tied to by the Näck."

Within a short time a very pretty girl came out of the inn and slid down beside the melancholy Elis, who was again sitting on the bench, silent and withdrawn. It was evident from her finery, from the whole manner of the girl, that she unfortunately sacrificed her-

---

1. A water demon that lures people to their death in the water.

self to evil pleasures; but the wild life had not yet exerted its destructive power on the unusual, gentle features of her charming face. There was not a trace of suppressed insolence; instead, a quiet, yearning sadness glowed in her dark eyes.

"Elis! Don't you want to share your comrades' joy? Don't you feel a little happy that you have come home again and have escaped the terrible dangers of the treacherous ocean?"

The girl spoke thus in a soft, gentle voice while she put her arm around the youth. Elis Fröbom, as though awakening from a deep dream, looked into the girl's eyes and, taking her hand, pressed it to his breast. One could see that the girl's sweet whisperings had found an echo in his heart.

"Alas," he began finally, as if considering what to say. "Alas— as to any gladness there is nothing there. At least I can't share my comrades' revelry. Go back inside, my dear child, and be gay with the others if you can, but leave the dreary, miserable Elis out here alone. He would only spoil all your fun. But wait! I like you very much, and you must think well of me when I am again at sea."

He took two bright ducats from his pocket, pulled a beautiful East Indian scarf from his breast, and gave them both to the girl. Bright tears came to her eyes as she rose, placed the ducats on the bench, and said, "Oh, keep your ducats. They only make me sad; but I will wear the beautiful scarf in remembrance of you. You probably will not find me here at the *Hönsning* next year when you stop in Haga."

The girl slipped away, her hands covering her face, not into the tavern but across the street in the other direction.

Elis Fröbom sank into melancholy reverie again and finally, when the celebration in the tavern became very loud and wild, exclaimed: "If only I lay buried at the very bottom of the sea! There is no one left in this life with whom I can be happy."

Then right behind him a deep, rough voice said, "You must have experienced a very great misfortune, young man, that you should wish for death just when your life should be beginning."

Elis looked around and saw an old miner who was leaning against the wooden wall of the tavern with his arms crossed and observing him with a serious, penetrating glance.

As Elis continued to look at the old man, it seemed to him as if a familiar figure were approaching him offering friendly comfort in the wild loneliness in which he believed himself lost. He pulled him-

self together and recounted how his father had been a fine helmsman but had been drowned in the same storm from which he himself had been rescued in a remarkable way. His two brothers, both
soldiers, had been killed in battle; and he, all by himself, had supported his poor deserted mother from the excellent pay he received
after each voyage to the East Indies. He had had to remain a
sailor, since he had been destined for that calling since childhood,
and it had seemed to him to be a great piece of luck to have been
able to enter the service of the East India Company. The profit had
turned out to be higher than ever this time, and each sailor had
received a good sum of money in addition to his wages; so, with his
pockets full of ducats, he had run to the little house where his
mother lived happily. But unknown faces had looked out the window at him; and a young woman, who finally opened the door and
to whom he explained himself, told him in a rough voice that his
mother had died three months ago and that he could collect at the
town hall the few rags that were left after the burial had been paid
for. His mother's death had lacerated his heart; he felt abandoned
by the whole world, as alone as if shipwrecked on a desolate reef—
helpless, wretched. His whole life on the sea seemed to him like
mad, pointless activity. In fact, when he thought that his mother
had perhaps been badly cared for by strangers and had thus died
without comfort, it seemed to him wicked that he had gone to sea
at all and had not stayed at home to care for his poor mother. His
comrades had dragged him by force to the *Hönsning*, and he had
thought that the gaiety and strong liquor would deaden his sorrow,
but instead, it had soon seemed to him as if the arteries in his
breast were bursting and that he would bleed to death.

"Well," said the old miner. "Well, you will soon put to sea
again, Elis, and your sorrow will be over in a short time. Old people
die. That can't be changed, and your mother has departed a poor,
laborious life, as you yourself said."

"Alas," replied Elis. "Alas, that no one believes in my sorrow!
That I am ridiculed for being foolish and stupid is what alienates
me from the world. I don't want to go to sea any more. The life
there is hateful to me. My heart used to leap when the ship sailed
forth on the sea, the sails spreading like stately wings, the waves
splashing with gay music, the wind whistling through the rattling
rigging. Then I rejoiced with my comrades on deck, and then—if I
had the watch on a still, dark night—then I thought of the return

home and of my good, old mother, of how she would rejoice again when Elis had returned! Then I was able to enjoy myself at the *Hönsning*, when I poured my ducats into my mother's lap; when I handed her the beautiful cloths and many strange objects from foreign lands; when joy flashed in her eyes; when she clapped her hands again and again, quite filled with happiness; when she tripped busily back and forth and fetched the best ale that she had saved for Elis. And when I sat with the old lady evenings, I would tell her about the strange people I had met, of their customs, of all the marvelous things that had happened to me on my long voyage. She enjoyed that greatly and would tell me of my father's remarkable voyages far up north and would serve up many frightening sailors' legends that I had already heard a hundred times and which I could never tire of hearing. Alas! Who can bring me these joys again! No, never again to sea. What should I do among comrades who would only mock me, and how could I take pleasure in the kind of work which would now seem only a tiresome effort without purpose?"

"I listen to you," said the old man when Elis grew silent. "I listen to you with pleasure, young man, just as I have had pleasure watching you for a couple of hours without your having seen me. Everything you did, what you said, proves that you have a pious, childlike nature that is turned inward, and heaven could not bestow a better gift on you. But never in all your life have you been suited to be a sailor. How can the wild, inconstant life at sea agree with you, a quiet Neriker inclined to melancholy?—that you are a Neriker I can see from the features of your face and from your whole bearing. You would do well to give up that life forever. But you won't remain idle? Follow my advice, Elis Fröbom! Go to Falun, become a miner. You are young, energetic. You will make a fine apprentice, then pickman, then miner. You will keep on moving up. You have some good number of ducats in your pocket which you can invest and which you can add to from earnings, and eventually you can acquire a small house and some land and have your own shares in a mine. Follow my advice, Elis Fröbom, become a miner."

Elis Fröbom was almost frightened at the old man's words.

"What are you advising me?" he cried. "Do you want me to leave the beautiful free earth, the cheerful sunny sky which surrounds me and quickens and refreshes me—I am to go down into the fearful depths of hell and like a mole grub around for ores and metal for a miserable pittance?"

"That," cried the old man angrily, "sounds like the common folk who despise what they can't appreciate. Miserable pittance! As if all the fearful torment on the surface of the earth that results from trading was nobler than the miner's work, whose skill and unflagging labor unlock nature's most secret treasures. You speak of a miserable pittance, Elis Fröbom! But perhaps there is something of higher value here. When the blind mole grubs in the earth out of blind instinct, it may well be that in the deepest tunnel, by the feeble light of the mine lamp, man's eyes see more clearly; indeed, in becoming stronger and stronger the eyes may be able to recognize in the marvelous minerals the reflection of that which is hidden above the clouds. You know nothing about mining, Elis Fröbom. Let me tell you about it."

With these words the old man sat down on the bench beside Elis and began to describe in great detail what went on in a mine and tried to give the ignorant boy a clear and vivid picture of everything. He talked about the mines of Falun, in which, he said, he had worked since childhood. He described the huge opening with the blackish brown walls, and he spoke of the immeasurable wealth of the mine with its beautiful stones. His account became more and more vivid, his eyes glowed brighter and brighter. He roamed through the shafts as if through the paths of a magic garden. The minerals came to life, the fossils stirred, the marvelous iron pyrites and almandine flashed in the gleam of the miner's lights; the rock crystals sparkled and shimmered.

Elis listened intently. The old man's strange way of talking about the marvels under the earth as if he were in their midst engaged his whole being. He felt oppressed. It seemed to him as if he had already descended to the depths with the old man and that a powerful magic was holding him fast so that he would never again see the friendly light of day. And then it seemed to him again as if the old man had opened up to him an unknown world in which he belonged and that all the enchantment of this world had long ago been revealed to him in his earliest boyhood as strange, mysterious presentiments.

"I have," the old man finally said, "I have revealed to you, Elis Fröbom, all the splendors of a calling for which nature has actually destined you. Take counsel with yourself, and then do what your mind prompts you to do."

With that the old man jumped quickly up from the bench and

strode away without saying goodbye or looking around again. He soon vanished from sight.

Meanwhile it had become quiet in the inn. The power of the strong ale and brandy had triumphed. Many of the sailors had slipped away with their girls; others lay in corners and snored. Elis could not go to his accustomed home, and at his request, he was given a little room for the night.

Tired and weary as he was, he had scarcely stretched out on his bed when a dream touched him with her wings. It seemed to him that he was drifting in a beautiful ship in full sail on a crystal clear sea, a heaven of dark clouds arching above him. But when he looked down into the waves, he realized that what he had thought was the sea was a solid, transparent, sparkling mass in the shimmer of which the whole ship dissolved in a marvelous manner so that he was standing on a crystal floor; and above him he saw a dome of darkly gleaming minerals, which he had at first thought were clouds in the sky. Driven by an unknown power, he strode on; but at that moment everything around him began to stir and, like curling waves, there shot up all around him marvelous flowers and plants of glittering metal, the blossoms and leaves of which curled upward from the depths and became intertwined in a most pleasing manner. The ground was so transparent that Elis could clearly see the roots of the plants; but when he looked down deeper and ever deeper, he saw in the depths innumerable, charming female forms who held each other locked in embrace with white, gleaming arms, and from their hearts there sprouted forth those roots and flowers and plants; when the maidens smiled, sweet harmony echoed through the dome, and the wondrous metal flowers thrust ever higher and became ever more gay. An indescribable feeling of pain and rapture seized the youth. A world of love, of desire, and of passionate longing expanded within him. "Down—down to you!" he cried, and he threw himself down with outspread arms onto the crystal ground. But it dissolved beneath him and he hovered in the shimmering air.

"Well, Elis Fröbom, how do you like it here among these splendors?" a hearty voice called. Elis saw the old miner beside him; but as he stared at him, the miner changed into a gigantic shape, as if cast of glowing metal. Before Elis had time to be afraid, there was a sudden flash of lightning from the depths, and the solemn visage of a majestic woman became visible. Elis felt the rapture in his breast turn increasingly into crushing fear. The old man seized him and cried, "Take care, Elis Fröbom. That is the Queen. You may look up now."

Unconsciously he turned his head and saw that the stars in the night sky were shining through a crack in the dome. A gentle voice called his name in hopeless sorrow. It was his mother's voice. He thought he saw her figure through the cleft. But it was a charming young woman who stretched out her hand towards the dome and called his name.

"Carry me up there," he cried to the old man. "I belong to the upper world and its friendly sky."

"Take care," said the old man somberly, "take care, Fröbom! Be faithful to the Queen to whom you have given yourself."

But as soon as the youth looked down again into the majestic woman's rigid face, he felt his being dissolve into the shining minerals. He screamed in nameless fear and awoke from the strange dream, the rapture and horror of which resounded deep within his heart.

"That was inevitable," said Elis when he had pulled himself together with an effort. "That was inevitable. I had to dream such strange stuff. After all, the old miner told me so much about the splendor of the subterranean world that my whole head was full of it. But never in my whole life have I felt as I do now. Perhaps I am still dreaming—no, no—I am probably ill. I'll go outdoors. A breath of fresh sea air will cure me."

He pulled himself together and ran to Klippa Harbor where the revels of the *Hönsning* were beginning again. But he noticed that he did not feel happy, that he could not hang on firmly to any thoughts, and that presentiments and wishes which he could not name crisscrossed his mind. He thought sorrowfully of his deceased mother; then it seemed to him as if he were longing to meet that girl again who had spoked to him yesterday in such a friendly way. And then he feared that if the girl should appear in this or that little street, it would really only be the old miner whom he feared, although he could not say why. And yet he would have liked to have had the old man tell him more about the marvels of mining.

Tossed about by all these impelling thoughts, he looked down into the water. Then it seemed to him as if the silver waves were being transformed into a sparkling solid in which lovely, large ships were dissolving, and as if the dark clouds that were rising into the pleasant sky were massing and solidifying into a dome of stone. He was dreaming again; he saw the majestic woman's solemn visage, and that destructive yearning desire seized him anew.

His comrades shook him out of his reverie; he had to go along with them. But now it seemed to him as if an unknown voice were whispering constantly in his ear: "What do you still want here! Away! Away! Your home is in the mines of Falun. There all the splendors that you dreamed of will be revealed to you. Away! Away to Falun!"

For three days Elis Fröbom roamed around the streets of Göteborg, constantly pursued by the strange figments of his dreams, constantly admonished by the unknown voice.

On the fourth day Elis was standing by the gate through which the road to Gefle led. A large man was just passing through ahead of him. Elis thought he recognized the old miner, and irresistibly driven, he hurried after him but was unable to catch up with him.

On and on Elis went without stopping.

He knew very well that he was on the road to Falun, and it was this knowledge that calmed him in a special way, for he was certain that the voice of destiny had spoken to him through the old miner who was now leading him towards his true vocation.

Actually, particularly when he was uncertain of the way, he quite often saw the old man suddenly step out from a ravine or a thick copse or from behind the dark boulders and stride on ahead of him without looking around and then suddenly disappear again.

Finally, after many days of tedious wandering, Elis saw in the distance two large lakes, between which a thick mist was rising. As he climbed higher and higher to the heights on the west, he distinguished a couple of towers and some black roofs in the mist. The old man was standing like a giant in front of him, pointing with outstretched arms towards the mist, and then he vanished again among the rocks.

"That is Falun!" cried Elis. "That is Falun, the goal of my journey!" He was right, for people who were following behind him confirmed that the town of Falun was situated there between Lake Runn and Lake Warpann and that he was just climbing the Guffris mountain where the great *Pinge* or main entrance to the mine was situated.

Elis Fröbom walked on in high spirits, but when he stood before the huge jaw of hell, his blood froze in his veins and he became numb at the sight of the fearful, blighted desolation.

As is well known, the great entrance to the mine of Falun is about twelve hundred feet long, six hundred feet wide, and one hundred and eighty feet deep. The blackish brown sidewalls at first extend down more or less vertically; about half way down, however, they are less steep because of the tremendous piles of rubble. Here and there in the banks and walls can be seen timbers of old shafts which were constructed of strong trunks laid closely together and joined at the ends in the way block houses are usually constructed. Not a tree, not a blade of grass was living in the barren, crumbled, rocky abyss. The jagged rock masses loomed up in curious shapes, sometimes like gigantic petrified animals, sometimes like human colossi. In the abyss there were stones—slag, or burned out ores—lying around in a wild jumble, and sulfurous gases rose steadily from the depths as if a hellish brew were boiling, the vapors of which were poisoning all of nature's green delights. One could believe that Dante had descended from here and had seen the Inferno with all its wretched misery and horror.[2]

When Elis Fröbom looked down into the monstrous abyss, he thought of what the old helmsman on his ship had told him long ago. Once, when he was lying in bed with a fever, it had suddenly seemed to the helmsman that the waves of the sea had receded and that the immeasurable abyss had yawned beneath him so that he could see the frightful monsters of the depths in horrible embraces, writhing in and out among thousands of strange mussels and coral plants and curious minerals until, with their jaws open, they turned rigid as death. Such a vision, the old seaman said, meant imminent death in the ocean, and he actually fell from the deck into the sea accidentally shortly thereafter and vanished. Ellis was reminded of the helmsman's story, for indeed the abyss seemed to him like the ocean depths when drained of the sea; the black minerals and the bluish red metallic slag seemed like revolting monsters that were stretching out their tentacles towards him. It so happened that several miners were just climbing up from the depths, dressed in dark work clothes and with dark burned faces; they looked like ugly creatures who were creeping out of the earth with difficulty and were trying to make their way to the surface.

Elis felt himself trembling with horror, and a giddiness that he had never experienced as a sailor seized him. It seemed to him as if invisible hands were pulling him down into the abyss.

2. See the description of the great *Pinge* at Falun in Hausmann's *Journey Through Scandinavia*, part V, p. 96.—(Hoffmann's note.)

Shutting his eyes, he ran away, and not until he was far from the entrance and was climbing down Mt. Guffris again and could look up at the cheerful sunny sky, was all his fear of that dreadful sight banished from his mind. He breathed freely once more and cried from the bottom of his soul, "O Lord of my life, what are all the horrors of the ocean compared to the frightfulness that dwells in that barren rocky abyss! Let the storm rage, let the black clouds dip down into the foaming flood, the glorious sun will soon reign again and the violent storm grow silent before its friendly face; but the sun's rays will never penetrate that stygian hell, and not a breath of spring air will ever refresh the heart down there. No, I do not wish to join you, you black earthworms; I could never accustom myself to your dreary life."

Elis thought he would spend the night at Falun and then start his journey back to Göteborg at daybreak.

When he came to the market place, which is called Helsintorget, he found a crowd gathered there.

A long parade of miners in full array, their lamps in their hands, musicians in the lead, had just halted in front of a stately house. A tall, slender, middle-aged man stepped out and looked around with a gentle smile. One could see that he was a true Dalkarl[3] from his easy manners, his open expression, and the dark blue, sparkling eyes. The miners formed a circle around him; he shook everyone's hand cordially and spoke a few friendly words with each.

Elis Fröbom found out on inquiry that the man was Pehrson Dahlsjö, the chief official of the district and owner of a fine *Bergfrälse*. Estates in Sweden that are rented for their copper and silver works are called *Bergfrälse*. The owners of such estates have shares in the mines and are responsible for their operation.

Elis was also informed that the court session had just ended on that day and that the miners would then go to the houses of the mine owner, the foundry master, and the senior foreman and would be entertained hospitably.

When Elis observed the handsome, dignified people with their friendly, open faces, he was no longer able to recall those earthworms in the great entrance. The gaiety which inflamed the whole group when Pehrson Dahlsjö came out was quite different from the frenzied revelries of the sailors at the *Hönsning*.

The miners' kind of pleasure appealed directly to the quiet,

3. An inhabitant of Dalarna. They have a reputation for being frugal and industrious.

serious Elis. He felt indescribably at ease, and he could scarcely keep back his tears when several of the younger lads began an old song that sounded the praises of mining in a simple melody that went straight to the heart.

When the song was over, Pehrson Dahlsjö opened the door of his house, and all the miners went inside. Elis followed automatically and stopped at the threshold so that he could see all around the spacious hall where the miners were sitting down on benches. A hearty meal was set out on a table.

Then the rear door opposite Elis opened, and a charming, beautifully attired young girl entered. Tall and slender, her dark hair wound in braids around her head, her neat little bodice fastened with rich brooches, she walked with all the grace of glowing maidenhood. All the miners rose and a happy, subdued murmur ran through the ranks: "Ulla Dahlsjö—Ulla Dahlsjö! God has indeed blessed our valiant chief with this lovely, innocent child of heaven!" Even the eyes of the oldest miners sparkled when Ulla shook their hands in friendly greeting. Then she brought in beautiful silver pitchers, poured out the excellent ale that is brewed at Falun, and served it to the happy company, her charming face aglow with the radiant innocence of heaven.

As soon as Elis Fröbom saw the girl, it seemed to him that a lightning bolt had struck his heart and ignited all the divine joy and all the pain and rapture of love that were enclosed in it. It was Ulla Dahlsjö who had offered him her hand to save him in that fateful dream. He now believed that he had guessed the dream's deeper meaning, and forgetting the old miner, blessed the fate that led him to Falun.

But then, standing on the threshold, he felt like a neglected stranger—wretched, miserable, abandoned. He wished he had died before he had even seen Ulla Dahlsjö, since he must now die of love and yearning. He was not able to turn his eyes away from the charming girl, and when she passed quite close to him, he called out her name in a gentle trembling voice. Ulla looked around and saw poor Elis, who was standing there with a scarlet face and downcast eyes, rigid, incapable of words.

Ulla walked up to him and said with a sweet smile, "Oh, you are a stranger here, dear friend. I can see that by your seaman's clothing. Well, why are you standing there on the threshold? Do come in and be merry with us." She took his hand and pulled him into the hall and handed him a full mug of ale. "Drink!" she said. "Drink, my dear friend, to a warm welcome."

It seemed to Elis as if he were lying in a blissful dream of paradise from which he would shortly awaken and feel indescribably wretched. Mechanically he emptied the mug. At that moment Pehrson Dahlsjö stepped up to him, shook his hand in friendly greeting, and asked him where he came from and what had brought him to Falun.

Elis felt the warming strength of the noble drink course through his veins. Looking the worthy Pehrson in the eye, he became cheerful and bold. He related how he, the son of a sailor, had been at sea since a child; how he had just returned from East India and had found his mother, whom he had cherished and supported, no longer alive; how he now felt completely abandoned in this world; how the wild life on the sea was now quite repugnant to him; how his deepest inclinations were for mining; and how he wanted to try to be taken on as an apprentice miner in Falun. This last remark, which was just the opposite of everything he had decided to do just a few minutes before, came out quite automatically; it seemed to him that he couldn't have told the manager anything different, as if he had expressed his innermost desire, of which he had till now been unconscious.

With a serious expression, Pehrson Dahlsjö looked at the youth as if he wished to see into his heart, and then said, "I do not assume, Elis Fröbom, that mere frivolity has driven you from your previous occupation and that you have not considered carefully all the tedium and difficulties of mining before you made the decision to come here. There is an ancient belief among us that the mighty elements, among which the miner boldly reigns, will annihilate him unless he exerts his whole self in maintaining his mastery over them and gives thought to nothing else, for that would diminish the power that he should expend exclusively on his work in the earth and the fire. But if you have considered your true calling adequately and found it has stood the test, then you have come at a good time. I lack workers in my mine. If you wish, you can stay with me right now and, tomorrow morning, go with the foreman, who will show you your work."

Elis's heart was lifted at Pehrson Dahlsjö's words. He no longer thought about the horrors of that frightful hellish abyss into which he had looked. He was filled with rapture and delight that he would now see the lovely Ulla every day and would live under the same roof with her. He allowed himself the sweetest hopes.

Pehrson Dahlsjö informed the miners that a young apprentice had just reported in, and he introduced Elis Fröbom to them.

All looked approvingly at the sturdy youth and thought that he was a born miner with his slender, powerful build and that he was surely not lacking in industry or application.

One of the miners, already well along in years, approached him and shook his hand heartily, saying that he was the chief foreman in Pehrson Dahlsjö's mine and that he would make it a point to instruct him thoroughly in everything that he needed to know. Elis had to sit down beside him, and the old man began to speak at length —over a mug of ale—about the first duties of the apprentices.

The old miner from Göteborg came to Elis's mind again, and in some special way he was able to repeat almost everything that had been said to him.

"Why Elis Fröbom," cried the chief foreman with astonishment. "Where did you get all that information? You really can't miss. In no time at all you will be the best apprentice in the mine."

The lovely Ulla, who was wandering among the guests and serving them, often nodded at Elis in a friendly way and urged him to enjoy himself. She said to him that he was no longer a stranger but belonged in the house and not to the deceitful sea. Falun with its rich mountains was now his homeland. A heaven full of rapture and bliss opened up to the youth at her words. It was noticed indeed that Ulla liked to linger with him, and even Pehrson Dahlsjö, in his quiet, serious way, observed him with approval.

But Elis's heart beat violently when he stood again by the steaming abyss of hell and, clothed in the miner's uniform, the heavy nailed boots on his feet, went down with the foreman into the deep shaft. At times hot vapors which encircled his breast threatened to choke him; at times the mine lights flared up from the cuttingly cold draughts which streamed through the abysses. They descended deeper and deeper, finally climbing down iron ladders scarcely a foot wide, and Elis Fröbom noticed that all the skill in climbing that he had acquired as a sailor did not help him here.

They finally reached the deepest bore, and the foreman assigned Elis the work that he was to do there.

Elis thought of the fair Ulla. He saw her form hovering like a shining angel above him, and he forgot all the horrors of the abyss, all the difficulties of the toilsome work. It was now clear in his mind that only if he dedicated himself to mining at Pehrson Dahlsjö's with all the strength of his mind and all the exertions that his body could endure would his sweetest hopes perhaps one day be fulfilled, and thus it was that in an incredibly short time he rivaled in work the most skilled miner.

With every day the worthy Pehrson Dahlsjö grew more and more fond of the industrious, pious youth and frequently said quite frankly to him that he had acquired in the young man not so much a worthy apprentice as a beloved son. Ulla's liking for him also became more open. Frequently, when Elis went to work and some danger was involved, she begged him, pleaded with him, bright tears in her eyes, to guard himself against accidents. And when he returned, she rushed out happily to meet him and always had the best ale or some tasty snack ready to refresh him.

Elis's heart beat with joy when Pehrson Dahlsjö once said that with his diligence and thrift, since he had already a good bit of money that he had brought with him, he would surely get a small house and some land or even a *Bergfrälse,* and then there would not be a property owner in Falun who would reject him when he came wooing a daughter. Elis should have said at once how indescribably much he loved Ulla and how all his hopes rested on possessing her, but a shyness he could not overcome kept him silent, although probably it was still the fearful uncertainty about whether Ulla, as he often suspected, truly loved him.

Once Elis Fröbom was working in the deepest bore, wrapped in such sulfurous fumes that his miner's light flickered dimly and he was scarcely able to distinguish the lodes in the rock, when he heard a knocking that seemed to be coming from a still deeper shaft and sounded as if someone were working with a hammer. Since that kind of work was impossible in the bore and since Elis knew that no one besides himself was down there, because the foreman had put his workers in the winding shaft, the knocking and hammering seemed quite uncanny. He put down his hammer and spike and listened to the hollow sounds that seemed to be coming nearer and nearer. All at once he saw a black shadow beside him, and as a cutting blast of air scattered the sulfur fumes, he recognized the old miner of Göteborg, who was standing at his side. "Good luck getting back up!" cried the old man. "Good luck to you, Elis Fröbom, down here among the rocks. How do you like the life, comrade?"

Elis wanted to ask by what marvelous means the old man had come to the shaft, but the latter struck the stone such a powerful blow with his hammer that sparks flew and a noise like thunder echoed through the shaft; and he called out in a terrible voice, "That is a marvelous lode, but you despicable, miserable rogue see nothing but a seam which is scarcely worth a straw. Down here you are a blind mole whom the *Metallfürst*[4] will never favor, and up above you are also unable to accomplish anything and pursue the *Garkönig*[5] in vain. Oh yes, you want to win Pehrson Dahlsjö's daughter Ulla for your wife, and therefore you are working here without love or interest. Beware, you cheat, that the *Metallfürst*, whom you mock, doesn't seize you and hurl you into the abyss so that all your bones are smashed on the rocks. And never will Ulla be your wife; that I say to you."

Anger welled up in Elis at the old man's insolent words. "What are you doing," he cried, "what are you doing in the shaft of my master, Pehrson Dahlsjö, where I am working with all my strength and as is proper to my calling? Get out as you have come, or we will see which one of us can bash in the other's skull."

Elis stood defiantly in front of the old man and raised the iron hammer with which he had been working. The old man laughed mockingly, and Elis saw with horror how he scrambled up the narrow rungs of the ladder as nimbly as a squirrel and vanished in the black cleft.

Elis felt paralyzed in all his limbs; the work would not progress, so he climbed up and out. When the old chief foreman, who was just climbing out of the winding shaft, saw him, he cried, "For God's sake, what happened to you, Elis? You look pale as death. It was the sulfur fumes, which you are not yet used to, that did it, wasn't it? Well, have a drink, boy. That will do you good."

Elis took a good swig of brandy from the bottle the chief foreman offered him, and then, feeling revived, told him everything that had happened in the shaft, as well as the mysterious way he had made the acquaintance of the uncanny miner in Göteborg.

The chief foreman listened quietly but then shook his head thoughtfully and said, "Elis Fröbom, that was old Torbern whom you met, and now I realize that what we relate about him here is

4. "Metal Prince."
5. Literally, "Refined prince." A technical term for refined copper.

more than a legend. More than a hundred years ago there was a miner here in Falun by the name of Torbern. He is said to have been one of the first who really made mining flourish in Falun, and in his time the profits were much greater than now. Nobody else knew as much about mining as Torbern, who with his thorough knowledge, was in charge of all aspects of mining in Falun. The richest lodes were revealed to him as if he possessed a special, higher power. In addition, he was a gloomy, melancholy man, without wife, child, or his own home; and he almost never came into the daylight, but grubbed around unceasingly in the shafts; and so it was inevitable that a story arose that he was in league with secret powers who reign in the bowels of the earth and fuse metals. No one paid any attention to Torbern's warnings—he constantly prophesied that a disaster would occur if it were not true love for marvelous rocks and metals that impelled the miner to work. Out of greed, the mines were constantly enlarged until finally, on St. John's day of the year one thousand six hundred and eighty-seven, a frightful cave-in occurred which created our huge entrance and destroyed the whole structure to such an extent that many of the shafts could only be repaired with tremendous effort and great skill. Nothing more was seen or heard of Torbern, and it seemed certain that he had been killed by the cave-in, for he had been working in the deep bore. Soon after, when the work was going along better and better, the pickmen claimed that they had seen old Torbern, who had given them all kinds of good advice and had shown them the best lodes. Others had seen the old man walking around the main shaft, now complaining sadly, now raging angrily. Other youths came here as you did and maintained that an old miner had urged them into mining and had directed them here. That happened whenever there was a shortage of workers, and it may well be that Torbern looked after the mine in this way. If it really was old Torbern with whom you quarreled in the shaft, and if he spoke to you about a wonderful lode, then it is certain that there is a rich vein of iron in the rock, for as you know, iron-bearing veins are called trap-runs, and a trum is a vein of the lode which divides into a number of parts and probably runs out completely."

When Elis Fröbom, torn in his mind by various thoughts, came into Pehrson Dahlsjö's house, Ulla did not come to meet him in her friendly way as formerly. With her eyes cast down and tear stained as Elis thought he observed, Ulla was sitting in the house beside a fine young man, who held her hand tightly in his and was trying to make all sorts of humorous remarks which Ulla was not particularly listening to. Pehrson Dahlsjö took Elis, who was staring at the couple and was filled with apprehension, into another room and said, "Well, Elis Fröbom, you will soon be able to prove your love and loyalty to me, for even if I have always considered you as a son, now you will be a son in all ways. The man whom you see at my house is the rich merchant Eric Olawsen from Göteborg. I am giving him my daughter, whom he has wooed. He is going to take her back to Göteborg, and then you will stay here alone with me, Elis, the only support of my old age. Well, Elis, you are silent? You have turned pale. I hope that my decision does not displease you and that now that my daughter must leave me, you will not also want to leave. But I hear Herr Olawsen calling my name—I must go back."

With that Pehrson went back into the other room.

Elis felt his soul slashed by a thousand glowing knives. He had no words—no tears. He dashed out of the house in wild despair—away—away—to the huge entrance. If the enormous abyss presented a frightful sight in the daylight, now that night had arrived and the moon's disc was just beginning to gleam, the desolate rocks had a truly terrible appearance, as if an unnumbered crowd of fearful monsters, the frightful offspring of hell, were writhing and twisting together on the smoking ground, their eyes flashing fire, and stretching out their monstrous claws towards a wretched humanity.

"Torbern! Torbern!" Elis cried in such a fearful voice that the desolate abyss resounded. "Torbern, I am here! You were right. I was a vile fellow to yield to the foolish hope of life on the surface of the earth. My treasure,[6] my life, my all lies below. Torbern! Climb up to me; show me the richest trap-runs. I will grub and bore and work there and never more see the light of day. Torbern! Torbern! Climb up to me!"

Elis took his flint and steel from his pocket and lighted his miner's lamp and went down into the shaft which he had yesterday been in without having seen the old man. How strange he felt when he clearly saw the seam in the deepest bore and could recognize the direction of the strata and the edge of the gouge.

---

6. *Schatz* means "treasure," when applied to the mine, and "sweetheart," when applied to Ulla and, possibly, the Queen.

But as he directed his eyes more and more sharply at the vein in the rock, it seemed as if a blinding light were passing through the whole shaft, and its walls became as transparent as the purest crystal. That fateful dream which he had dreamed in Göteborg returned. He looked into the fields of paradise filled with marvelous metal flowers and plants on which gems flashing fire were hanging like fruit, blossoms, and flowers. He saw the maidens; he saw the lofty face of the majestic Queen. She seized him, pulled him down, pressed him to her breast, and there flashed through his soul a glowing ray—he was conscious of only a feeling of drifting in a blue, transparent, sparkling mist.

"Elis Fröbom! Elis Fröbom!" cried a strong voice from above, and the light of torches was reflected in the shaft. It was Pehrson Dahlsjö himself who was coming down with the foreman to look for the youth whom they had seen running towards the main shaft in complete madness.

They found him standing rigid, his face pressed against the cold rock.

"What," cried Pehrson to him, "what are you doing down here at night, you foolish young man! Pull yourself together and climb up with us. Who knows what good news you will hear up above?"

Elis climbed up in complete silence, and in complete silence he followed Pehrson Dahlsjö, who did not cease from scolding him firmly for putting himself in such danger.

It was full daylight when they came to the house. Ulla rushed towards Elis's embrace with a loud cry and called him the most endearing names. But Pehrson Dahlsjö spoke to Elis, "You fool. Didn't I long know that you loved Ulla and that you work in the mine with such industry and zeal only for Ulla's sake? Didn't I long notice that Ulla also loved you from the very bottom of her heart? Could I wish for a better son-in-law than a fine, industrious, decent miner like you, my dear Elis? But it angered me, it offended me that you remained silent."

"Didn't we," Ulla interrupted her father, "didn't we ourselves know that we loved each other inexpressibly?"

"That," continued Pehrson Dahlsjö, "that may well be so. It suffices to say that I was angered that Elis did not speak openly and honorably to me of his love, and therefore, because I also wanted to test your heart, I served up the story with Herr Eric Olawsen, which nearly caused your destruction. You foolish young man! Herr

Eric Olawsen has been married for a long time, and it is to you, dear Elis Fröbom, that I give my daughter in marriage, for I repeat, I could not wish myself a better son-in-law."

Tears of pure joy ran down Elis's cheeks. All of life's happiness had quite unexpectedly descended on him, and it almost seemed to him that he was again in the midst of a sweet dream.

At Pehrson Dahlsjö's command all the miners gathered for a festive meal.

Ulla was wearing her most beautiful dress and looked more charming than ever. Everyone cried, almost simultaneously, "Oh, what a magnificent bride our good Elis Fröbom has won! May heaven bless them both in their goodness and virtue."

The horror of the past night could still be seen on Elis Fröbom's face, and he frequently stared in front of him as if remote from everything around him.

"What is the matter with you, my Elis?" asked Ulla. Elis pressed her to his breast and spoke, "Yes, yes— You are really mine and now everything is well."

In the midst of all his bliss it sometimes seemed to Elis as if an icy hand were gripping his heart and a dark voice were speaking, "Is this your highest ideal, winning Ulla? You poor fool! Have you not seen the Queen's face?"

He felt almost overcome by an indescribable fear. The thought tortured him that one of the miners would suddenly loom up as tall as a giant and that, to his horror, he would recognize Torbern who had come to remind him reprovingly of the subterranean kingdom of precious stones and metals to which he had surrendered himself.

And yet he did not know at all why the ghostly old man was hostile to him or what the connection was between his love and his work as a miner.

Pehrson indeed noticed Elis Fröbom's disturbed behavior and ascribed to it to the unhappiness he had endured and to the trip into the shaft on the previous night. But not Ulla, who was filled with a secret presentiment and pressed her beloved to tell her what horrible thing had happened to him which was tearing him away from her. Elis's heart was about to break. In vain he strove to tell his beloved of the marvelous face that had revealed itself to him in the shaft. It was as if an unknown power held his mouth closed by force, as if the fearful face of the Queen were looking out of his inner being, and that if he should call her by name, everything around him would be turned to dreary, black stone, as occurs when Medusa's dreadful head is viewed. All the splendor which had filled him with the deepest rapture down in the shaft now seemed like a hell full of wretched agony, deceitfully adorned for the purpose of enticing him to his destruction.

Pehrson Dahlsjö commanded that Elis Fröbom stay at home for several days to recover completely from the illness to which he seemed to have succumbed. During this time, Ulla's love, which flowed bright and clear from her childish, innocent heart, dispelled all recollections of that fateful adventure in the shaft. Elis lived in bliss and joy and believed in his good fortune which no evil power could destroy.

When he went down again into the shaft, everything seemed quite different. The most marvelous lodes lay revealed before his eyes; he worked with redoubled zeal; he forgot everything; when he returned to the surface, he had to recall Pehrson Dahlsjö and his Ulla; he felt split in half; it seemed to him that his better, his true being, was climbing down into the center of the earth and was resting in the Queen's arms, while he was seeking his dreary bed in Falun. When Ulla spoke to him of her love and how they would live together happily, then he began to speak of the splendor of the shaft, of the immeasurably rich treasures which lay concealed there, and he became entangled in such strange, incomprehensible speeches that fear and anxiety seized the poor child and she did not know at all how Elis could have changed so suddenly into a quite different person.

With the greatest delight, Elis kept reporting to the foreman, and to Pehrson Dahlsjö himself, how he had discovered the richest veins and the most marvelous trap-runs; and when they found nothing but barren rock, he would laugh disdainfully and say that he alone understood the secret signs, the meaningful writing which the Queen's hand itself had inscribed in the rock and that it was actually enough to understand these signs without bringing their meaning into the light of day.

The old foreman looked sadly at the youth, who with wildly sparkling eyes was speaking of the radiant paradise that flared up in the depths of the earth.

"Alas, sir," the old man whispered in Pehrson Dahlsjö's ear. "Alas, sir, evil Tornbern has bewitched the poor youth."

"Don't believe in such superstitions, old man," replied Pehrson

Dahlsjö. "Love has turned the head of the melancholy Neriker—
that is all. Just let the marriage take place, and trap-runs and treasures and subterranean kingdoms will all be done with."

The wedding day set by Pehrson Dahlsjö finally arrived. Several days before, Elis Fröbom had become quieter, more serious,
and more withdrawn than ever, but never had he been so devoted
in his love to charming Ulla as he was at this time. He did not wish
to be separated for a moment from her, and therefore he did not go
to the mine. He did not seem to be thinking at all of his troubled
activity as a miner, for not a word about the subterranean kingdom
crossed his lips. Ulla was utterly blissful. All her fears that the threatening powers of the subterranean abyss, of which she had often heard
the miners speak, would lure Elis to his destruction had disappeared.
Pehrson Dahlsjö also spoke to the old foreman: "Surely you see that
Elis Fröbom had only become giddy in the head out of love for
my Ulla."

Early in the morning on his wedding day—it was Saint John's
day—Elis knocked at the door of his bride's chamber. She opened
it and reeled back when she saw Elis already dressed in his wedding
suit, pale as death, dark, flashing fire in his eyes.

"I only wish," he said in a soft, hesitant voice, "I only wish to
tell you, my dearly beloved Ulla, that we are standing near the peak
of the greatest happiness that is granted to men on earth. Everything
has been revealed to me in the past night. Down in the shaft the
cherry red sparkling almadine lies enclosed in chlorite and mica, on
which is inscribed the chart of our life. You must receive it from
me as a wedding present. It is more beautiful than the most splendid
blood red carbuncle; and when we, united in true love, look into
its radiant light, we can clearly see how our inner beings are intertwined with the marvelous branch that is growing from the Queen's
heart in the center of the earth. It is only necessary that I fetch this
stone up to the daylight, and that I will do now. Farewell for now,
my dearly beloved Ulla. I will be here again shortly."

Ulla begged her beloved with hot tears to desist from this
visionary undertaking, since she had a foreboding of the greatest
misfortune. But Elis Fröbom assured her that without that gem he
would never more have a peaceful moment and that there was no
reason to fear that any danger threatened. He pressed his bride to
his breast with fervor, and departed.

The guests had already assembled to escort the bridal couple to the Kopparberg Church, where the marriage was to be performed after divine service. A whole crowd of elegantly clad young girls, who were to march in front of the bride as bridesmaids according to the customs of the country, were laughing and joking around Ulla. The musicians were tuning their instruments and were practicing a gay wedding march. It was already nearly midday, and Elis Fröm-bom had not yet appeared. Suddenly some miners, with fear and horror on their pale faces, came rushing in and announced that a frightful cave-in had destroyed the entire excavation at Dahlsjö's mine.

"Elis—my Elis! You are gone! Gone!" Ulla shrieked loudly and fell down as if dead. Pehrson Dahlsjö learned for the first time from the mine inspector that Elis had gone to the great entrance early in the morning and had gone down into it; but no one else had been working in the shaft, since all the apprentices and miners had been invited to the wedding. Pehrson Dahlsjö and all the miners hurried to the main entrance; but their search, which was carried on only at great risk, was in vain. Elis Fröbom was not found. It was certain that the cave-in had buried the unfortunate youth in the rocks. And so misfortune and misery came to the house of Pehrson Dahlsjö at the very moment when he thought he had achieved repose and peace for his old age.

The good owner and overseer Pehrson Dahlsjö had long since died; his daughter Ulla had vanished. No one in Falun remembered anything about them, for a good fifty years had passed since that calamitous wedding day. Then one day miners who were investigating an opening between two shafts found the corpse of a young miner lying in sulfuric acid in a bore nine hundred feet deep. When they brought the body to the surface, it appeared to be petrified.

The body looked as if the youth were lying in a deep sleep, so well preserved were the features on his face and so without trace of decomposition were the elegant miner's clothes, even the flowers on his breast. All the people of the area gathered around the youth who had been carried up from the main shaft, but no one recognized the features of the corpse, and none of the miners could recall that any of their comrades had been buried alive. They were about to carry the corpse to Falun when a hoary woman, ancient as the hills, appeared, hobbling along on her crutches.

"Here comes Saint John's Granny!" cried several of the

miners. They had given this name to the old woman because they had long since noticed that she would appear every year on Saint John's day and would look down into the depths, wringing her hands, groaning sadly and lamenting as she crept around the main shaft; and then she would vanish again.

Scarcely had the old woman seen the petrified youth than she dropped her crutches, stretched her arms towards heaven, and uttered wretched sounds of lamentation. "Oh, Elis Fröbom—oh, my Elis—my darling bridegroom!"

She squatted down beside the body and seized the stiffened hands and pressed them to her withered breast beneath the icy sheath of which, like a holy naptha flame, a heart filled with ardent love was burning.

"Alas," she spoke then, looking around in a circle. "Alas, no one, not one of you, knows poor Ulla Dahlsjö any longer, this young man's happy bride of fifty years ago. When I moved to Ornäs full of grief and sorrow, old Torbern comforted me and said that once again on this earth I would see my Elis, whom the rocks buried on my wedding day, and so I have come here every year and have looked down into the abyss with longing and true love. This blissful reunion has been granted to me this day. Oh, my Elis—my beloved bridegroom!"

Again she put her withered arms around the youth as if she would never leave him, and all those standing around were deeply moved.

The old woman's sighs and sobs became quieter and quieter until they died away into silence.

The miners stepped forward. They wanted to raise poor Ulla up, but she had breathed out her life on the body of her petrified bridegroom. They noticed that the corpse of the unfortunate man, which they had thought was petrified, was beginning to turn to dust.

The youth's ashes, along with the body of his bride, who had been faithful unto death, were placed in the Kopparberg Church, where the couple were to have been wedded fifty years before.

Mademoiselle de Scudéri

A Tale of the Times of Louis XIV

Thanks to the favor of Louis XIV and the Marquise de Maintenon, Madeleine de Scudéri,[1] known for her charming poems, inhabited a small house in the rue Saint Honoré.

One midnight—it might have been in the fall of 1680—someone knocked on the door of this house so hard and with such violence
that the entire hall echoed loudly. Baptiste, who served as cook,
butler, and doorman in Mademoiselle's small household, had, with
the permission of his mistress, gone to the country to attend his
sister's wedding; and thus it happened that La Martinière, Mademoiselle's personal maid, was the only one awake in the house. She
heard the repeated blows, and it occurred to her that Baptiste had
gone away and that she and her mistress were alone in the house,
without any protection. All the crimes of breaking-and-entering, of
robbery, of murder, that had ever taken place in Paris crossed her
mind, and she grew certain that some gang of thugs, aware of the
isolation of the house, was raging outside and, if let in, would com-

1. Madeleine de Scudéri (1607–1701), French author, came to Paris in
1630 and became connected with Mme. de Rambouillet's salon. Later she
formed a literary circle of her own, their "Saturday gatherings" becoming
famous. Her best known work was the ten-volume novel *Artamène ou le Grand
Cyrus* (1649–59); it was followed by *Clélie* (1654–60). Highly artificial, poorly
constructed, flawed by pointless dialogue, her works were popular at the court,
primarily because of their anecdotes about public personages. They served the
parvenu well.

Part of the success of this story results from its combination of realistic
scenes, actual people, and fantastic elements. Almost all of the characters and
places depicted existed in fact.

mit evil against her mistress; and so she remained in her room quaking and quivering, cursing Baptiste and his sister's wedding. Meanwhile, the blows thundered on, and it seemed to her as if a voice were shouting through it all, "Open the door, for God's sake, open the door!" Finally, in growing fear, La Martinière seized a lighted candelabrum and ran into the hall. There she quite clearly heard the voice of a man shouting: "For God's sake, open the door!"

"Well," thought La Martinière, "no robber speaks like that. Who knows, perhaps some persecuted man is seeking refuge with my mistress, who is always charitable. However, let us be cautious." She opened a window and, trying to make her voice sound as masculine as possible, called down and asked who was beating at the door so late at night and waking everybody up.

By the shimmer of the moonbeams, which were just breaking through the dark clouds, she saw a tall figure wrapped in a light gray coat, wearing a large hat pulled down over his eyes. She shouted in a loud voice, so as to be heard by the man below, "Baptiste, Claude, Pierre, get up and see what good-for-nothing wants to break down our house." Then, from below, a soft, almost plaintive voice said, "Oh, La Martinière, I know it is you, dear lady, however much you try to disguise your voice. I know that Baptiste has gone to the country and that you are alone in the house with your mistress. Do not be afraid to open the door. I absolutely must speak with your mistress this very minute."

"What makes you think," La Martinière replied, "that my mistress will speak to you in the middle of the night? Don't you know that she went to bed a long time ago and that nothing on earth could induce me to wake her from her first sweet sleep, which is so necessary at her age?"

"I know," said the person below, "I know that your mistress has just put aside the manuscript of her novel *Clélie*, on which she works so tirelessly, and that she is now writing certain verses which she intends to read tomorrow at Madame de Maintenon's. I beseech you, Madame Martinière, have pity and open the door. I tell you that it is a matter of saving an unfortunate man from ruin, that the honor, freedom, yes, even the very life of a man depend on this moment in which I *must* speak to your mistress. Consider that your mistress's anger would rest on you eternally if she learned that it was you who turned away without mercy the unfortunate man who came to beseech her help."

"But why have you come to appeal to my mistress's compassion at this extraordinary hour? Come again in the morning, at a reasonary time," La Martinière said.

"Does destiny, then," the person below replied, "respect the time of day when it strikes like deadly lightning? When there is but a single moment when it is possible to rescue a man's life, can help be delayed? Open the door for me! You need not fear a defenseless and friendless wretch who is pursued and pressed by a terrible fate, when he wishes to beg your lady to save him from imminent danger!" La Martinière heard him moaning and sobbing with anguish as he uttered those words in a voice at once youthful, soft, gentle, and most touching. Deeply moved, she went to get the keys without further thought.

She had no sooner opened the door when the figure, wrapped in a cloak, burst in violently and, moving past La Martinière into the passage, cried in a wild voice, "Take me to your mistress." In terror, La Martinière lifted the candelabrum she was carrying, and the light fell on the deathly pale, frightfully distorted face of a youth. Terror almost bowled her over when the young man opened his cloak and revealed the shining hilt of a naked stiletto which he was carrying in the open bosom of his doublet. His flashing eyes upon her, he cried, more wildly than before, "Take me to your mistress, I tell you!" La Martinière saw that her mistress was in immediate danger. All her affection for her, whom she honored as if she were her pious, kind mother, inflamed her heart and gave her a courage of which she would not have thought herself capable. Quickly closing the door of her room, which she had left open, she stepped in front of it and said in a voice loud and firm, "Now that you are in the house, your frenzied behavior is very different from your pathetic performance outside. It is clear that my pity misled me. You ought not and shall not speak to my mistress now. If you have no evil intentions, you have nothing to fear from the light of day. Come again tomorrow and state your business. Now, get out of this house!" The young man sighed deeply, glared at La Martinière menacingly, and grasped his stiletto. La Martinière silently commended her soul to God, but she stood firm and boldly returned his glance even as she pressed herself more firmly against the door through which he would have to pass to reach her mistress.

"I tell you to let me go to your mistress!" he cried again.

"Do what you will," La Martinière replied, "I shall not leave this spot. Finish the evil deed already begun. An ignominious death will overtake you on the Place de la Grève, as it did your accursed companions in crime."

"Ha! You are right, La Martinière!" he cried. "I do look like and am armed like an accursed robber and murderer, but my partners are not condemned—they are not condemned!" And glaring at the terrified woman venomously, he drew his stiletto.

"Jesus!" she cried, expecting her deathblow, but at that moment the clatter of arms and the hoofbeats of horses were heard on the street. "The *maréchaussée! The maréchaussée!*[2] Help! Help!" she cried.

"You wish to destroy me, you abominable woman—. All is done for, done for! Take this! Take it, and give it to your mistress today—tomorrow, if you prefer." And with these mumbled words he tore the candelabrum from her, extinguished the candles, and pressed a small casket into her hands. "As you hope for salvation, give this casket to your mistress," he cried and rushed out of the house.

La Martinière had sunk to the floor. With effort she stood up, and groping her way through the darkness to her room, she collapsed into an armchair in a state of complete exhaustion, incapable of uttering a sound. Then she heard the keys which she had left in the front door rattling. The house door was being locked, and soft, hesitant footsteps approached her room. Paralyzed with fear, powerless to move, she awaited the horrible unknown. Imagine her relief when the door opened and, by the light of the night lamp, she immediately recognized honest Baptiste, who looked deathly pale and completely distraught.

"In the name of all the saints," he began. "In the name of all the saints, tell me, Madame Martinière, what has happened? Oh, the fear, oh, the fear I've felt! I don't know what it was, but something drove me violently from the wedding last night. Then I came into our street. Madame Martinière, I thought to myself, sleeps lightly and she will hear me if I tap softly and gently at the door and she will let me in. But when I got to the corner I was confronted by a strong police patrol, on foot and on horseback, armed to the teeth, and they made me stop and refused to let me go on. As luck would have it, Desgrais, the lieutenant of the *maréchaussée,* was among

2. The much-feared mounted police charged with public order.

them, and he knows me very well. When they thrust a lantern under my nose, he said, 'Where are you coming from in the middle of the night, Baptiste? You should stay home and look after your house. It's not safe to be out here. We expect to be making a good catch tonight.' You wouldn't believe, Madame Martinière, how these words disturbed me. And then, as I stepped on the threshold, a man all muffled-up flies out of the house, a naked dagger in his hands, and knocks me down—the house is open, the keys are in the lock—tell me, what does it all mean?"

La Martinière, freed from her terror, told him about everything that had happened. She and Baptiste went into the hall, found the candelabrum on the floor where the stranger had flung it as he fled. "It is only too clear," Baptiste said, "that our mistress was to have been robbed and probably murdered. The man knew, as you told me, that you were alone with her, and he even knew that she was still awake and writing. Undoubtably he was one of those cursed swindlers and rogues who first ferret out information which will help them carry out their plans and then break into a house. And I think, Madame Martinière, that we had better throw the little casket into the deepest part of the Seine. What assurance do we have that some vile monster is not after our good mistress's life and that when she opens the casket she will not fall dead on the spot, as the old Marquis de Tourney did when he opened the letter which he had received from a stranger?"

After a long discussion, the two faithful servants finally decided to tell their mistress everything the next morning and to give her the mysterious casket, which could, of course, be opened after appropriate precautions had been taken. After considering every circumstance surrounding the appearance of the suspicious stranger, they both decided that there might be some mystery involved in this for which they dared not assume responsibility but which they would have to leave for their mistress to uncover.

Baptiste's fears were well founded. At this time Paris was the scene of the most heinous crimes and, concomitantly, the most diabolical invention of hell offered easy means for the execution of these atrocities.

Glaser, a German druggist and the best chemist of his time, occupied himself, like most members of his profession, with conducting experiments in alchemy. He became obsessed with discovering the Philosopher's Stone. He was joined by an Italian named Exili. But this man practiced alchemy only as a subterfuge. His real purpose was to discover the techniques for mixing, boiling, and sublimating the poisonous compounds by which Glaser sought to make his fortune; and he finally succeeded in producing a subtle poison which was tasteless and odorless, that could kill either instantaneously or gradually, that left no trace behind in the human body, and which, therefore, defied all the talent and art of the physicians who, having no reason to suspect poison, invariably attributed death to natural causes. Despite all of Exili's precautions, he was suspected of selling poison and was taken to the Bastille. Soon afterwards, Captain Godin de Sainte-Croix was locked up in the same cell. This man, who for a long time had been living illictly with the Marquise de Brinvilliers, had brought disgrace to her whole family. The Marquis, however, remained indifferent to his wife's misconduct, and finally her father, Dreux d'Aubray, civil lieutenant of Paris, was forced to break up the criminal liaison by ordering the captain's arrest. Passionate, without principle, hypocritically pious, and inclined to all manner and degree of vice from youth on, jealous, vindictive to the point of madness, the captain could not have welcomed anything more than Exili's diabolical secret which would give him the power to destroy all his enemies. He became Exili's eager pupil and soon his master's equal, so that when he was released from the Bastille he was able to continue his work on his own.

La Brinvillier was a dissolute woman; through Sainte-Croix she became a monster. He induced her to poison, one after another, first her own father, with whom she was living under the heartlessly hypocritical pretext of nursing him in his old age, then her two brothers, and finally her sister (her father was murdered for revenge, the others for the rich inheritance). This story of multiple poisoning is a horrible example of the way the commission of such crimes grows into an inexorable passion. Aiming for nothing beyond mere pleasure—like the chemist who conducts experiments purely for his own enjoyment—poisoners have often murdered people about whose life or death they were totally indifferent. The sudden death of several indigents in the Hôtel Dieu later aroused the suspicion that the loaves of bread, which La Brinvillier had distributed there every week in order to be seen as the apotheosis of piety and charity, had been poisoned. In any event, it is certain that she served poisoned pigeon pies to her guests. The Chevalier du

Guet and several other persons fell victim to these hellish meals. Sainte-Croix, his assistant La Chaussée, and La Brinvillier were long able to mask their terrible crimes behind an impenetrable veil; but regardless of the infamous cunning of abandoned men, the eternal power of heaven had decided to judge the criminals here on earth. The poisons compounded by Sainte-Croix were so subtle that if the powder (*poudre de succession* it was called by the Parisians) was even once inhaled as it was being prepared, instantaneous death resulted. Sainte-Croix therefore wore a mask of fine glass when preparing it. One day this mask fell from his face just as he was shaking the finished poison powder into a phial, and inhaling the fine particles of dust, he instantly dropped dead. Since he died without heirs, the court lost no time in placing his possessions under seal. In his home they found the whole infernal arsenal of poisons which he had had at his command locked in a box, but they also found La Brinvillier's letters, which left no doubt about their evil crimes. She sought refuge in a convent at Liège. Desgrais, an officer of the *maréchaussée*, was sent to pursue her. Disguised as a priest, he appeared at the nunnery where she had hidden. He succeeded in engaging in a love affair with this abominable woman and finally, under the pretext of an assignation, enticed her into a deserted garden on the outskirts of town. As soon as the Marquise arrived at the intended rendezvous, she was surrounded by Desgrais' police, while her priestly lover, suddenly converted into an officer of the *maréchaussée*, forced her to enter the carriage which was standing ready outside the garden, and surrounded by police, she was driven straight to Paris. La Chaussée had already been beheaded, and La Brinvillier met the same death. After the execution her body was burned and the ashes scattered to the winds.

The Parisians breathed a sigh of relief now that the world was rid of the monster who had used these secret, deadly weapons with impunity against friend and foe. But it soon became evident that the abominable art of Sainte-Croix had been inherited. Like an invisible, malignant ghost, murder insinuated itself into the most intimate circles of love and friendship and surely and swiftly seized the unfortunate victim. He who on one day was blossoming with health, on the next day was tottering about, sick and debilitated, beyond the skill of the physician to save from death. Wealth—a lucrative position—a beautiful, perhaps too youthful wife—any of these were sufficient for persecution to the death. The most sacred bonds were rent by appalling suspicion. The husband trembled before his wife—the father before his son—the sister before her brother. The food and the wine served a friend were left untouched, and where pleasure and gaiety had once prevailed, truculent glances searched for a secret assassin. Fathers of families could be seen anxiously buying provisions in remote districts and preparing the food themselves in some filthy kitchen, afraid of some devilish treachery in their own homes. And yet the greatest precautions were sometimes in vain.

The King, in order to put a stop to this evil state of affairs, which continued to gain ground, established a special court with the sole duty of investigating and punishing these furtive crimes. This was the so-called *Chambre Ardente* which sat not far from the Bastille, with La Régnie presiding. For a considerable time La Régnie's efforts, as zealous as they were, remained fruitless. It was left to the crafty Desgrais to uncover the most secret haunt of crime.

In the suburb Faubourg Sainte-Germain there lived an old woman, La Voisin by name, who practiced fortune-telling and necromancy and, abetted by her accomplices Le Sage and Le Vigoureux, excited fear and astonishment even in people who were not considered weak or gullible. But this was not all. Like Sainte-Croix a pupil of Exili, she could also brew the subtle poison which left no trace, and in this way she served unscrupulous sons who sought an early inheritance and dissolute wives who sought another and younger husband. Desgrais made his way into her confidence, she confessed everything, and the *Chambre Ardente* condemned her to be burned at the stake; she was executed in the Place de la Grève. In her house was found a list of everyone who had used her services, and so it was that not only did one execution follow another but that grave suspicion fell upon persons of the highest station. Thus it was that Cardinal Bonzy was believed to have obtained from La Voixin the means of bringing to an early death all those to whom, as archbishop of Narbonne, he was obliged to pay a pension. Thus also the Duchesse de Bouillon and the Comtesse de Soissons, whose names were found on the list, were accused of having dealt with the devilish hag; and even François Henri de Montnorenci-Boudebelle, Duc de Luxembourg, Peer and Marshall of the Realm, was not spared. He too was prosecuted by the dreaded *Chambre Ardente.*

He surrendered himself to be imprisoned in the Bastille where the hatred of Louvois and La Régnie resulted in his being incarcerated in a six-foot-long hole. Months passed before it was satisfactorily established that the only crime committed by the Duc was not punishable. He had once had his horoscope cast by Le Sage.

It is clear that the blind zeal of President La Régnie seduced him to acts of terror and brutality. The Tribunal assumed the character of the Inquisition; the slightest suspicion was adequate cause for harsh imprisonment, and it was often left to chance to prove the innocence of a man accused of a capital crime. Moreover, La Régnie, was of repulsive appearance and malicious temperament, so that he quickly aroused the hatred of those he had been appointed to avenge or protect. The Duchesse de Bouillon, asked by him during her trial if she had seen the devil, replied, "I think I see him at this very moment."

While the blood of the guilty and the suspected flowed in streams in the Place de la Grève, and murder by poisoning finally grew rarer and rarer, an outrage of another kind made its appearance and again spread alarm in the city. A band of thieves seemed determined to get possession of all the jewels in Paris. As soon as expensive jewelry was bought, it would unaccountably vanish, regardless of how carefully guarded. What was worse, anyone who ventured to wear jewelry in the evening was robbed or even murdered in the public street or in dark hallways of the houses. Those who had escaped with their lives reported that they had been struck on the head by the blow of a fist which hit them like a bolt of lightning and that, regaining consciousness, they had discovered that they had been robbed and were now in a place very different from that in which they had originally been struck. The murder victims, who were found almost every morning lying in the street or inside houses, all bore the same mortal wound—a dagger-thrust in the heart, so swiftly and surely delivered that, according to the doctors, the victims must have sunk to the ground without uttering a sound. Was there anyone at the salacious court of Louis XIV who was not involved in some clandestine love affair and who did not surreptitiously make his way to his mistress late at night, often carrying a valuable gift? The band of thieves, as if in league with spirits, knew precisely when anything of this kind was going on. Often the unfortunate victim never reached the house where he hoped to indulge his passion; or often he fell on the threshold, or even at the very door, of the room of his mistress, who, to her horror, would find his bloodstained corpse.

Argenson, the minister of police, ordered the arrest of everyone who was the least suspect, but in vain; La Régnie raged and tried to extort confessions, but in vain; watches and patrols were strengthened, but in vain—the tracks of the criminals were not to be found. Only the precaution of arming to the teeth and being preceded by a torch bearer was to some degree effective; but even then there were instances when the servant was beaten off by stones while the master was murdered and robbed at the same moment.

Remarkably enough, investigations conducted in all of the places where jewelry might possibly be disposed of failed to turn up the tiniest specimen of the stolen goods, so that here too clues could not be followed.

Desgrais foamed at the mouth in fury at the way the criminals evaded even his net. The district of the city in which he happened to be was always spared, while in the other sections, where no crime had been anticipated, murder and robbery claimed their wealthiest victims.

Desgrais hit upon the scheme of using several doubles, so similar in gait, posture, speech, figure, and face, that even the police could not identify the real Desgrais. Meanwhile Desgrais, alone and at the risk of his life, spied in the most secret hideouts and followed at a distance this man or that who, at his suggestion, wore valuable jewelry. *This* man remained unscathed; the thieves, then, knew about *this* technique too. Desgrais was at the end of his wits.

One morning Desgrais came to President La Régnie, pale, agitated, beside himself.

"Is there any news? Are you on their tracks?" the President called to him.

"Ha, Your Excellency," Desgrais began, stammering with rage, "last night—not far from the Louvre—the Marquis de la Fare was attacked in my presence."

"Thank heaven," La Régnie rejoiced, "then we have them!"

"You had better hear me out," Desgrais interrupted with a bitter smile. "You had better hear what happened.

"I was standing near the Louvre, all hell exploding in my chest, watching for these devils who are tormenting me. Then a man who did not see me passed close to me with faltering steps,

turning constantly to look back over his shoulder. I recognized
the Marquis de la Fare by the light of the moon. I had expected him;
I knew where he was sneaking. He was barely ten or twelve paces
past me when a figure seemed to spring up from the earth, struck him
down, and fell upon him. Astounded, caught off guard by this moment which would have delivered the criminal into my hands, I
cried out and leapt from my hiding place to attack him, but I became
entangled in my cloak and fell. I saw the man fly away as if on the
wings of the wind; I sprang to my feet; I ran after him—blowing
my horn as I ran—the policemen's whistles responding to me from
the distance—everything burst into life—weapons rattled, horses'
hoofs clattered on all sides. 'Here—here—Desgrais—Desgrais!' I
cried till the streets echoed, and all the while I could see the man
in front of me in the bright moonlight as he dodged here and there
to throw me off the track. We came to the Rue Nicaise; his strength
apparently failing, I exerted myself to the utmost—he was no more
than fifteen paces ahead of me!''

"You caught up to him—you seized him," La Régnie said with
flashing eyes, while he seized Desgrais' arm as if *he* were the escaping
murderer.

"Fifteen paces," Desgrais continued in a hollow voice, breathing heavily, "fifteen paces from me the man leapt aside into the
shadows and vanished through the wall."

"Vanished? Through the wall! Are you mad?" La Régnie cried,
taking two steps back and beating his hands together.

"If you like, Your Excellency may call me a madman from here
on, or you may accuse me of suffering from hallucinations, but all
took place exactly as I told it," Desgrais replied, rubbing his brow
like one tormented by evil thoughts. "I stood dumbfounded before
the wall when several breathless police came running up. The
Marquis de la Fare, who had recovered from the attack, was with
them, a naked dagger in his hand. We lit torches and felt along the
wall; there was not a trace of a door or a window or of any opening.
It is a solid stone wall enclosing a courtyard and attached to a house
which is occupied by people who are above the slightest suspicion.
Just today I carefully inspected the premises again. The devil himself is making fools of us."

Desgrais' story became known throughout Paris. Heads were
imbued with tales of magic, sorcery, exorcisms, and pacts with the
devil made by La Voisin, Le Vigoureur, and the notorious priest

Le Sage; and because human nature is such that belief in the miraculous and the supernatural outweighs reason, the public soon began to accept as fact what Desgrais had said in disgruntlement—that the devil himself was protecting the villains who had sold him their souls. As may be imagined, Desgrais' story became fancifully embellished; and an account of it, complete with a woodcut depicting a ghastly devil sinking into the ground before a terrified Desgrais, was printed and sold on every corner. This was enough to terrorize the public and even to destroy the courage of the police, who now fearfully wandered along the streets at night trembling, hung with amulets and soaked in holy water.

Argenson saw that the efforts of the *Chambre Ardente* were ineffective, and he appealed to the King to appoint a new court which would have even more extensive powers to track down and punish criminals. The King, convinced that he had already vested too much power in the *Chambre Ardente* and horrified at the countless executions which the bloodthirsty La Régnie had imposed, flatly dismissed the suggestion. Another means of stimulating the King's interest in the matter was selected.

In La Maintenon's apartment, where the King was in the habit of spending the afternoons and also of working late into the night with his ministers, a poem was presented to him in the name of imperiled lovers, complaining that the demands of gallantry which required them to bestow gifts upon their mistresses now entailed risking their lives. While it was at once an honor and a pleasure to shed blood for the beloved in knightly combat, it was altogether something else to confront the treacherous assailant against whom arms were no defense. Louis, the lodestar of love and gallantry, was called upon to use his resplendence to dissipate the darkness of night and uncover the black mystery within it. Let the god-like hero, who had shattered all his enemies, draw his victoriously flashing sword, and as Hercules struck down the Lernaean Hydra, or Theseus the Minotaur, let him strike down the dangerous monster that was consuming love's raptures and turning joy into deepest grief and inconsolable mourning.

As serious as the subject was, this poem was not lacking in witty twists, especially in the passages which described how lovers trembled while sneaking to their beloveds and how their fear nipped in the bud the pleasures to be found in love and gallantry. It need only be added that since the poem concluded with a grandiloquent panegyric to Louis XIV, the King read it with visible satisfaction. This done, he quickly turned to La Maintenon, though without lifting his eyes from the paper, and once more read the poem, this time out loud; and then, with a charming smile, he asked her what she felt about the plea of these endangered lovers. La Maintenon, true to her serious cast of mind, with its tinge of piety, replied that those who travel clandestine and forbidden paths do not deserve any special protection but that vile criminals certainly merited being exterminated through special measures. The King, dissatisfied with this inconclusive answer, folded the paper and was about to return to the Secretary of State, who was working in the next room, when his eyes happened to fall on Mademoiselle de Scudéri, who had just taken her place in a small armchair close to La Maintenon. He approached her; the pleasant smile which had first played about his mouth and cheeks and had then disappeared, regained the upper hand. Standing directly in front of Mademoiselle and unfolding the poem once more, he said gently: "The Marquise does not want to know about the gallantries of our lovelorn gentlemen, and her responses to my question evade me in ways that are nothing short of forbidden. But you, Mademoiselle, what is your opinion of this poetic petition?"

Mademoiselle de Scudéri rose respectfully from her armchair; a fleeting blush like the red of the sunset passed across the pale cheeks of the dignified old lady. She curtsied slightly and, her eyes downcast, said:

> "Un amant qui craint les voleurs,
> n'est point digne d'amour."[3]

The king, completely astonished by the spirit of chivalry in these few words, which reduced to rubble the endless tirades contained in the poem, exclaimed with flashing eyes: "By Saint Denis, you are right Mademoiselle! Cowardice shall not be protected through any blind measures which at once affect the innocent and the guilty; let Argenson and La Régnie do their best!"

La Martinière described all of the present horrors in the most

---

3. A lover who is afraid of thieves
    Is not at all worthy of love.

These lines are from one of Hoffmann's sources, a seventeenth-century chronicle by Johann Christoph Wagenseil.

vivid colors when, next morning, she told her mistress about what had happened the previous night and tremblingly and timorously gave her the mysterious casket. Both she and Baptiste, who stood in the corner, pale with anxiety and nervousness, twisting his night-cap in his hand, barely able to speak, implored Mademoiselle in the most melancholy terms, and in the name of all the saints to exercise every possible precaution in opening the little casket. La Scudéri, weighing and testing the locked enigma in her hands, said with a smile: "You're both seeing ghosts! That I am not rich, and that there is no treasure here worth murder the accursed assassins know as well as you or I, for as you yourselves tell me, they spy out the innermost secrets of houses. You think that my life is endangered? Who can have any interest in the death of a woman of seventy-three, who never harmed anyone but the villains and rioters in her novels; who turns out mediocre verse which can arouse the envy of no one; who will leave behind nothing but the finery of an old spinster who occasionally went to court, and a few dozen well-bound books with gilt edges! And as for you, Martinière, regardless of how frighteningly you describe the stranger, I cannot believe that he had an evil purpose in mind. So then—"

Martinière recoiled three paces; Baptiste sank half to his knees with a hollow "Ah!" as Mademoiselle pressed a projecting steel knob which caused the lid to spring open with a bang.

How astonished Mademoiselle was to see a pair of golden bracelets richly set with jewels and a matching necklace sparkling within the casket! She took the jewelry out, and while praising the exquisite craftsmanship of the necklace as La Martinière eyed the valuable bracelets, she repeatedly exclaimed that not even the vain La Montespan had jewelry such as this. "But what is the meaning of all this?" asked La Scudéri. In that instant she noticed a small folded sheet of paper at the bottom of the casket. She rightly hoped to find in it the solution to the mystery. She had barely read the note when it fell from her trembling hands. She cast an eloquent glance to heaven and sank back in her armchair, as if half swooning. Frightened, La Martinière and Baptiste sprang to her side. "Oh," La Scudéri cried with a voice half choked with tears. "Oh, the insult, oh, the terrible shame! Must I suffer this kind of thing in my old age? Have I been guilty of a foolish, wanton act like some giddy young thing? Oh God, are words uttered half in jest capable of being so horribly interpreted? And am I, who have remained virtuous and pious since childhood, to be accused of being involved in crime and of being in league with the devil?" Mademoiselle put her handkerchief to her eyes and wept and sobbed bitterly so that La Martinière and Baptiste, completely bewildered and distressed, did not know how to help their good mistress in her profound distress.

La Martinière picked up the fateful note from the floor. It read:

> Un amant qui craint les voleurs,
> n'est point digne d'amour.[4]

Your ingenious wit, honored lady, has saved us—we who exercise the right of the strong over the weak and the cowardly and acquire valuables which were otherwise to be squandered disgracefully from great persecution. Kindly accept these jewels as a token of our gratitude. They are the most expensive which we have picked up in a long time, though you, worthy lady, should be adorned with jewelry which is much finer. We beseech you not to withdraw your friendship and your gracious remembrance from us.

The Invisibles

"Is it possible," Mademoiselle de Scudéri cried after she had somewhat recovered, "is it possible for shameless insolence and wicked mockery to be carried to such an extreme?"

The sun shone brightly through the curtains of brilliant red silk, and so the gems lying on the table near the open casket blazed with a scarlet gleam. Looking at them, Mademoiselle covered her face in abhorrence and ordered La Martinière immediately to remove the fearsome jewelry to which the blood of murdered men was clinging. La Martinière, after locking the bracelets and necklace in the casket, suggested that the wisest thing to do would be to turn the jewels over to the minister of police and confide in him everything about the terrifying visit of the young man who had delivered the casket.

Mademoiselle de Scudéri rose, slowly and silently paced back and forth in the room, as if only now reflecting upon what should be done. Then she ordered Baptiste to fetch her sedan chair and La Martinière to dress her because she was going to see the Marquise de Maintenon. She had herself carried to the Marquise's apartment at

4. See n. 3 above.

precisely the hour when she knew the Marquise would be alone. She took the casket of jewels with her.

The Marquise was very surprised to see Mademoiselle de Scudéri, usually—despite her age—the personification of dignity and grace and charm, entering pale, disheveled, and with tottering step. "In heaven's name, what has happened to you?" she cried to the poor, frightened lady who, completely beside herself and barely able to stand on her feet, moved as quickly as she could towards the armchair which the Marquise pushed towards her. Finally, able to speak again, Mademoiselle told about the insult, still festering within her, which had resulted from the innocent joke with which she had responded to the petition of the imperiled lovers.

After hearing the rest of the story bit by bit, the Marquise expressed the feeling that Mademoiselle de Scudéri was making far too much of the strange experience and that the derision of the nefarious rabble could never touch a mind as pious and noble as hers; and she finally asked to see the jewelry. Mademoiselle de Scudéri handed the open casket to her, and the Marquise could not restrain a loud exclamation of wonderment when she saw the valuable jewelry. She took out the necklace and the bracelets and carried them to the window where she let the sun reflect on the jewels and then held the intricate gold work very close to her eyes so that she could examine the exquisite workmanship with which every little link in the elaborate chain was crafted.

Suddenly the Marquise turned to Mademoiselle and cried: "Do you realize, Mademoiselle, that these bracelets and this necklace could have been crafted by none other than René Cardillac?"

René Cardillac was at that time the most skillful goldsmith in Paris, one of the most talented and extraordinary men of his day. Of something less than medium height, but broad shouldered and of powerful muscular physique, Cardillac, though well over fifty, still possessed the strength and coordination of a young man; and his thick, curly red hair and heavy-set, glistening face bore witness to his exceptional strength. If Cardillac's reputation throughout Paris had been other than that of a most upright and honorable, altruistic, candid, and guileless man, always prepared to help, the very peculiar expression in his small, deep-set, and flashing green eyes might have resulted in his being suspected of hidden malice and viciousness.

As noted, Cardillac was the most skillful craftsman in his field, not only in Paris, but perhaps anywhere at that time. Intimately acquainted with the nature of precious stones, he knew how to treat and set them so that jewelry which originally was without distinction left his workshop in brilliant glory. Every commission was accepted with burning eagerness, and he would set a price which was so modest that it seemed out of all proportion to the labor involved. Then the work gave him no peace. Day and night he could be heard hammering in his workshop; and often, when the work was almost completed, he would suddenly conceive a dislike for the design and begin to question the daintiness of the setting or of some little link—reason enough for him to throw the entire piece back into the melting pot to begin again. So it was that every piece turned out was a flawless and matchless masterpiece which astounded the patron. But it was therefore almost impossible to regain the completed work from him. Resorting to a thousand pretexts, he would put the customer off week after week, month after month. Offering to pay him double for the work was futile; he would not take a Louis more than the price contracted for. When he was finally forced to give up the jewelry, he could not conceal all the signs of profound regret and inner rage which boiled within him. If he had to deliver a piece of singular importance and value, probably worth several thousands because of the costliness of the gems and the superb intricacy of the craftsmanship, he would, as if distracted, rampage madly, cursing his work and everything around him. But as soon as someone would run after him, calling loudly, "René Cardillac, wouldn't you like to make a lovely necklace for my fiancée —bracelets for my mistress," and so on, he would freeze in his tracks, look at the customer with his little glittering eyes, and rubbing his hands together, ask, "What have you got?" Then the customer would, perhaps, produce a small jewel box and say, "Here are some jewels, nothing much, ordinary things, but in your hands—" Cardillac would not let him finish, but would snatch the jewel box from his hands, take out the jewels, which were really not worth very much, hold them up to the light and cry in delight, "Ha, ha! Ordinary stuff? Not at all! Pretty stones—superb stones—just let me work on them! And if a handful of Louis are of little concern for you, I'll add a few little gems that will sparkle in your eyes like the very sun itself." To which the other would reply: "I'll leave it to you, Meister René, and I'll pay whatever you wish." Regardless of whether he was a rich townsman or a prominent gentleman of the court, Cardillac would fling his arms violently around his neck and hug him and kiss him and tell him that he was absolutely happy again and that the work would be finished in a week. He would dash home exuberantly, rush into the workshop, and begin hammering away; and in a week he would have produced a masterpiece. But no sooner would the customer joyfully come to pay the petty sum asked, than Cardillac would become peevish, rude, and obstinant. "But Meister Cardillac, remember that my wedding is tomorrow." "What do I care about your wedding? Come again in two weeks." "The jewelry is ready, here is the money, I must have it." "And *I* tell you that I still have to make a lot of changes in it and I can't let you have it today." "And *I* tell you that I wish to pay you double your price, but that if you don't give me the jewelry right now, I will immediately return with Argenson's faithful henchmen." "Then may Satan torture you with a hundred glowing pincers and hang a handkerchief on the necklace so that it strangles your bride!" With that, Cardillac would ram the jewelry into the bridegroom's breast pocket, seize him by the arm, and throw him out of the door so roughly that he would tumble down the stairs. Then he would lean out of the window and laugh like the devil at the sight of the poor young man limping out of the house, a handkerchief to his bloody nose.

For some inexplicable reason, Cardillac would often, after enthusiastically accepting a commission, suddenly implore the customer, while evincing signs of deep agitation, violently protesting, sobbing, crying, and appealing to the holy Virgin and all the saints, to release him from the work he had undertaken. Many people, highly esteemed by both the King and the public, had vainly offered large sums for even the smallest piece of work by Cardillac. He had thrown himself at the feet of the King and had begged for the favor of being excused from the necessity of working for him. Likewise, he refused to accept any commission from the Marquise de Maintenon; in fact it was with an expression of revulsion and dread that he rejected her proposal that he make a little ring decorated with emblems of the arts, which she intended to present to Racine.

Accordingly, Marquise de Maintenon now said, "I wager that if I send for Cardillac to find out for whom he made this jewelry he would refuse to come here because he would probably fear that I had some commission in mind, and he is determined not to work for me. Although he seems of late to be somewhat less obdurate, according to what I have heard, he is now working more assiduously than ever before and is delivering his work on the spot, though still regretfully and with averted face."

Mademoiselle de Scudéri, very concerned that the jewelry be returned to its rightful owner quickly, if this was at all possible, suggested that Meister Eccentric might consent to come if it were immediately made clear to him that what was sought from him was not a commission but his opinion regarding certain jewels. The Marquise agreed. Cardillac was sent for, and as if he had already been on the way, he very shortly entered the room.

He seemed to be startled when he saw Mademoiselle de Scudéri, and like someone who forgets the demands of etiquette because he is surprised by the totally unexpected, he first bowed deeply and respectfully to the venerable lady, and only then turned to the Marquise. Pointing to the jewelry which now sparkled on the dark green tablecloth, she abruptly asked him if it were his work. Cardillac hardly glanced at it, but staring the Marquise straight in the face, he quickly packed the necklace and the bracelets into the casket that was beside them and pushed it vehemently away from him; and with an ugly smile suffusing his red face, he said:

"Indeed, Madame Marquise, one must be very poorly acquainted with René Cardillac's work to believe for an instant that any other goldsmith in the world was capable of producing such jewelry. Of course it is my work."

"Well, then tell us, for whom did you make it?" continued the Marquise.

"For no one but myself," Cardillac replied. "Yes," he continued, as both the Marquise and Mademoiselle de Scudéri looked at him in amazement, the former full of mistrust, the latter full of fearful expectation to know what sort of turn the affair would now take. "Yes, you may find it strange, Madame Marquise, but that's how it is. For no reason other than to create something beautiful, I gathered my finest stones and, simply for the sheer joy of it, worked on them more diligently and carefully than ever before. A short time ago the jewels vanished from my workshop in some inexplicable way."

"Heaven be praised," cried Mademoiselle de Scudéri, her eyes sparkling with joy; and she jumped from her armchair as quickly and nimbly as a young girl, walked to Cardillac, and placed both hands on his shoulders saying: "Meister René, take back, take back the property which the infamous thieves stole from you." Then she related in detail how she had come to possess the jewels.

Cardillac heard it all in silence and with downcast eyes, only now and then uttering an indistinct "Um. So! Ah! Aha!"—now clasping his hands behind his back, now gently stroking his chin and cheeks. When Mademoiselle de Scudéri had finished her story, Cardillac appeared to be struggling with some new idea which had just struck him and which confronted him with a difficult decision. He rubbed his forehead, he sighed, he put his hand over his eyes as if to check a welling of tears. Finally he seized the casket which Mademoiselle de Scudéri was offering him, sank slowly on one knee and said, "Destiny decreed that these jewels be yours, noble and worthy lady. Yes, now I realize for the first time that it was of you I thought, for you that I did my work. Do not disdain to accept them nor to wear them. They are among the best things I have made for a long time."

"Oh, oh," Mademoiselle de Scudéri replied in merry playfulness. "What can you be thinking of, Meister René? Would it be right for me at my age to deck myself out with glittering gems? And why should you bestow such an enormously expensive gift upon me? Come, come, Meister René, if I were as beautiful as the Marquise de Fontange and as wealthy, I would not, in fact, let these jewels slip through my hands; but what would these withered arms, this veiled neck offer such glittering gems?"

Cardillac had risen, meanwhile, and speaking as though distracted, with wild eyes, still holding out the casket to Mademoiselle de Scudéri, he said, "Have pity on me, Mademoiselle, and take the jewels. You would not believe how deep a respect for your virtue and your rare qualities I carry in my heart! Accept this meager gift, then, simply as my attempt to express my profound admiration."

But as Mademoiselle de Scudéri still hesitated, the Marquise took the casket from Cardillac's hands, saying, "In the name of heaven, Mademoiselle, you are always talking about your great age, but what have you and I to do with the years and their burdens! Aren't you behaving just like a bashful young thing who longs for the sweet, forbidden fruit which is offered if only she could have it without stretching out hand or finger? Do not reject good Meister René, who freely offers you as a gift what thousands of others cannot obtain despite all of their gold and prayers and entreaties."

The Marquise had, meanwhile, forced the casket on Mademoiselle de Scudéri; and now Cardillac fell to his knees, kissed Mademoiselle's skirt, her hand—groaned, sighed, wept, sobbed, sprang up, ran out like a madman, bowling over chairs and tables in his frenzy, so that china and glasses clattered.

Greatly alarmed, Mademoiselle de Scudéri cried, "May all the saints protect me, what's the matter with the man?" But the Marquise, with an unwonted exuberance born of her gaiety, laughed merrily and said, "There it is, Mademoiselle. Meister René is mortally in love with you and is beginning, according to the proper and ancient custom of true gallantry, to lay siege to your heart with expensive gifts." The Marquise pushed the joke still further, admonishing Mademoiselle not to be too cruel towards her despairing lover; and Mademoiselle, giving full rein to her own inherent spiritedness, was carried away by a flood of witty ideas. She suggested that if this were the true picture of things, she would be unable to avoid being conquered; she would offer the world the unique spectacle of a seventy-three-year-old goldsmith's bride of impeccable nobility. La Maintenon offered to weave the bridal wreath and to instruct her in the duties of a good housewife, since such a young snip of a girl could not, of course, be expected to know much about such things.

When Mademoiselle de Scudéri finally picked up the jewel box and rose to leave the Marquise, she became very serious again, despite all of the spirited raillery. "Madame Marquise," she said, "I will never be able to wear this jewelry. However, come what may, it was once in the hands of those devilish rogues who commit robbery and murder with the audacity of Satan himself, probably even in accursed league with him. I shudder at the sight of the blood that seems to cling to the stones. And also, I must confess, I find even Cardillac's behavior peculiarly disturbing and terrifying. I cannot escape a dark premonition that there is concealed behind all of this some hideous and repulsive secret, but when I consider the matter rationally, in every detail, I still have not the slightest inkling what this secret might be, nor how the honest and upright Meister René, the model of a decent and pious citizen, could be involved in anything which is evil and damnable. But of one thing I am certain— that I will never dare to wear the jewels."

The Marquise felt that this was carrying scruples too far; but when Mademoiselle de Scudéri asked her what her conscience would dictate were their places reversed, the Marquise replied, "I would sooner throw the jewelry into the Seine than ever wear it."

The encounter with Meister René lead Mademoiselle de Scudéri to compose some charming verses, which she read to the King the next evening in La Maintenon's apartment. And it is probable that, conquering her ominous presentiment in regard to Meister René, she painted with vivid colors an amusing picture of the seventy-three-year-old goldsmith's bride of ancient and impeccable nobility. At any rate, the King laughed heartily and declared that Boileau Despréaux had met his master, which led to La Scudéri's poem being regarded as the wittiest ever written.

Several months had passed when Mademoiselle de Scudéri happened to be driving over the Pont-Neuf in the Duchesse de Montansier's glass coach. The appearance of these delicate coaches was so novel that they invariably attracted a crowd of the curious wherever they appeared in the street. Thus it was that a crowd of gaping rabble engulfed La Montansier's glass coach on the Pont-Neuf, almost forcing the horses to halt. Suddenly Mademoiselle de Scudéri, hearing an outburst of cursing and swearing, saw a man fighting his way through the densest part of the crowd with his fists and elbows. As he drew nearer, she met the piercing gaze of his eyes and observed the young man's deathly pale and anguished face. His eyes unwaveringly upon her, he fought his way toward her with elbows and fists until he reached the door of the coach, which he flung open with violent haste; he threw a note into Mademoiselle de Scudéri's lap and disappeared even as he had come, in a flurry of punching and elbowing which he gave and received. As soon as the man appeared at the coach door, La Martinière, who was sitting beside Mademoiselle de Scudéri, screamed out in terror and sank unconscious into the cushions. In vain Mademoiselle de Scudéri tugged the chord and called out to the coachman; he, as if driven by an evil spirit, whipped up the horses, who, spraying foam from their mouths, reared and kicked their hoofs and finally thundered across the bridge at a fast trot. Mademoiselle de Scudéri poured the contents of her bottle of smelling salts over the unconscious woman, who at last opened her eyes and, trembling and shaking and clinging convulsively to her mistress, fear and shock reflected in her pale face, moaned with effort, "In the name of the blessed Virgin, what did that terrible man want? He is the one—yes, the one who brought you the casket on that dreadful night!"

Mademoiselle de Scudéri calmed the poor woman, assuring her that nothing harmful had happened, and that the sensible thing to do would be to find out what the note contained. She unfolded the paper and found these words:

A malicious fate, which you could avert, forces me into an abyss. I beseech you as a son would a mother from whom he cannot part, whom he loves with childish fervor, to return the necklace and bracelets which you received from me to Meister René Cardillac under any pretext—to have them improved—altered—something of the sort. Your well-being, your very life depends upon it. If you have not done this by the day after tomorrow, I will force my way into your house and kill myself before your eyes!

"Now it is certain," Mademoiselle de Scudéri said when she had read this, "that this mysterious stranger, even if he does belong to the band of accursed thieves and murders, intends no evil against me. Perhaps, if he had succeeded in speaking to me that night, who knows but that I might have learned of strange events and dark mysteries about which I now have not the slightest inkling and for which I vainly search in my soul. Be that as it may, I will do as the letter commands, even if it is only to be rid of these accursed jewels, which seem to me like a hellish charm of the devil himself. Cardillac, true to his old habits, will not let them out of his hands so easily again."

Mademoiselle de Scudéri intended to return the jewelry to the goldsmith the very next day. But somehow it seemed as if all the wits in Paris had conspired to assail Mademoiselle that morning with their verses, plays, and anecdotes. La Chapelle had barely finished a scene from a tragedy, with the sly assurance that he would outdo Racine, when Racine himself entered and shattered him with an elevated tirade about some king or other. Then, to escape from an endless disquisition on the colonnade of the Louvre which Dr. Perrault, the architect, was inflicting upon him, Boileau launched his meteor and sent it soaring into the black sky of tragedy.

It was high noon by now, and Mademoiselle had an appointment to visit the Duchesse de Montansier; thus the visit to Meister René Cardillac was postponed until the next morning. Mademoiselle de Scudéri, however, was tormented by a feeling of extraordinary restlessness. The young man appeared continually before her eyes, and from deep within her a dim recollection sought to rouse itself as though she had seen this face, these features before. Her light sleep was disturbed by frightening dreams in which it seemed that her failure to grasp the hand which the unhappy wretch had stretched out to her as he sank into the abyss had been rash, even criminal; indeed, as if it had been within her power to prevent some terrible disaster, some hellish crime! As soon as the sun rose she had herself dressed and set off for the goldsmith's, taking the jewel box with her.

Masses of people were streaming into the rue Nicaise, where Cardillac lived, gathering outside his door, screaming, ranting, raving, trying to storm their way in and prevented from doing so only by the *maréchaussée* who surrounded the house. From the midst of the frantic confusion angry voices shouted, "Tear him to pieces, pulverize the damned murderer!" Finally Desgrais appeared with a sizable force of his men, who made a passage for him through the thick crowd. The door of the house sprang open, and a man weighed down with chains was brought out and dragged off, accompanied by the most hideous curses of the enraged mob. No sooner had Mademoiselle de Scudéri, half dead from shock and terrible forebodings, witnessed this than a shrill cry of distress pierced her ears. "Forward! Keep moving!" she cried, quite beside herself, to her coachman, who scattered the dense crowd with a skillful and quick turn and pulled up directly in front of Cardillac's door. Here Mademoiselle de Scudéri saw Desgrais and, at his feet, a young girl as lovely as day, half naked, her hair hanging freely, an expression of wild anxiety and inconsolable despair on her face, who was clinging to his knees and crying in a voice of heartrendering despair, "He is innocent! He is innocent!" The efforts of Desgrais and his men to tear her away and lift her from the ground were futile. Finally a powerful brute grabbed her with his great hands and tore her forcefully from Desgrais, then clumsily stumbled and dropped the girl, who rolled down the stone steps and lay without a whimper in the street, as if dead.

Mademoiselle de Scudéri could restrain herself no longer. "In the name of Christ, what has happened? What is going on here?" she cried, quickly opening the coach door and stepping out.

The crowd respectfully made way for the worthy lady, who saw that a few compassionate women had picked the girl up and placed her on the step and were rubbing her forehead with spirits. She approached Desgrais and emphatically repeated her question.

"Something terrible has happened," Desgrais said. "René Cardillac was found stabbed to death this morning. His associate, Olivier Brusson, is the murderer. He has just been taken away to prison."

"And the girl?" cried Mademoiselle de Scudéri.

"She is Cardillac's daughter, Madelon," answered Desgrais. "The vile man was her lover. Now she weeps and wails over and over again that he is innocent. She really knows about the deed, and I must also have her taken away to the Conciergerie." As he said this, Desgrais glanced at the girl so slyly and maliciously that Mademoiselle de Scudéri trembled. The girl was beginning to breathe softly now, but unable to make a sound or to move, she lay there with closed eyes, so that no one knew what to do, whether to carry her into the house or to remain with her until she regained consciousness. With tears of sympathy in her eyes, Mademoiselle de Scudéri looked at the innocent angel, and she felt horror for Desgrais and his men. Then the sound of muffled footsteps could be heard on the stairs— Cardillac's corpse was being carried down. Quickly making a decision, Mademoiselle de Scudéri cried in a loud voice, "I am taking the girl with me. You take care of the rest, Desgrais!" A low murmur of approval swept through the crowd. The women lifted the girl up; everyone pressed towards her; a hundred hands came to her aid, and as though floating through the air, she was carried to the coach while blessings from all showered down upon the worthy lady who had snatched an innocent from the bloodthirsty tribunal. The efforts of Seron, the most famous doctor in Paris, were finally successful in bringing Madelon back to consciousness after she had lain in a profound coma for hours. What the physician had begun, Mademoiselle de Scudéri completed by kindling some gentle rays of hope in Madelon's soul until a violent outburst of tears poured from her eyes and brought relief. Then she was able to tell everything that had happened, although she was from time to time overcome by her poignant grief and her words stuck in her throat.

She had been awakened about midnight by a faint knocking at the door of her room and had heard Olivier's voice entreating her to get up at once because her father was dying. Startled, she sprang from her bed and opened the door. Olivier, pale, his face contorted, dripping with sweat, a light in his hand, staggered to the workshop; she following him. There her father lay struggling with death, eyes staring blankly, a death rattle in his throat. Wailing, she rushed towards him, and only then noticed bloodstains on his shirt. Olivier gently drew her away and then busied himself with a wound in the left side of her father's chest, washing it with balsam and bandaging it. While this was taking place, the father regained consciousness; the death rattle ceased; he looked tenderly at Madelon, then at Olivier, took her hand, and placing it in Olivier's, fervently pressed them together. Both Olivier and she had fallen on their knees at her father's bed when he sat up with a piercing cry, but immediately sank back, sighed deeply, and died. Then they both wept and wailed loudly. Olivier told her that he had, at his master's request, accompanied him on his walk in the night; that he had been murdered in his presence, and that he had carried home the heavy man, whose injury he did not think was fatal, with the greatest difficulty. At daybreak the others occupying the house, who had heard the din, the weeping, and the lamenting during the night, had come upstairs and found them still kneeling inconsolably by her father's corpse. Then an uproar broke out, the *maréchaussée* forced their way in, and Olivier was dragged off to prison as his master's murderer. Madelon now added the most touching account of her beloved Olivier's virtue, piety, and faithfulness. She told how he had respected his master as if he had been his own father, and how this affection was fully reciprocated, her father choosing him for his son-in-law despite his poverty, because his skill and fidelity were equal to his nobility. Madelon told all this with the greatest sincerity, and concluded that if Olivier had thrust the dagger into her father's breast in her presence she would more easily have believed it to be an illusion created by Satan than to have believed that Olivier was capable of such a terrible and gruesome crime.

Mademoiselle de Scudéri, most deeply touched by the unspeakable suffering of Madelon and completely disposed to believe in the innocence of poor Olivier, conducted inquiries and confirmed everything which Madelon had said about the personal relationship between the master and his journeyman. The occupants of the house and the neighbors unanimously praised Olivier as the model of virtuous, devout, faithful, and industrious behavior, not one having anything bad to say about him; and yet, when the atrocious deed was alluded to, everyone shrugged his shoulders and thought that there was something incomprehensible about that.

Brought before the *Chambre Ardente*, Olivier, as Mademoiselle de Scudéri learned, denied the deed of which he was accused

with the utmost steadfastness and candor, maintaining that his
master had been attacked and struck down in the street in his presence, that he had carried him back to his home while he was still
alive, where he very soon died. This also agreed with Madelon's
account.

Mademoiselle de Scudéri had the most minute details of the
terrible event repeated over and over again. She carefully sought to
determine whether there had been any dispute between master
and journeyman, whether Olivier was not sometimes afflicted by
sudden violent fits which often affect even the most good-natured
people like a blind madness and cause them to commit acts quite involuntarily. But the more she heard Madelon enthusiastically describing the serene domestic happiness in which these three people
lived, bound by the most sincere affection, the more did every trace
of suspicion against Olivier, who was now on trial for his life, disappear. Meticulously weighing all the circumstances, and proceeding
on the assumption that Olivier, despite all that so loudly spoke for
his innocence, was nevertheless Cardillac's murderer, Mademoiselle
de Scudéri could not discover any possible motive for the horrible
deed, which in any case could do nothing but shatter Olivier's happiness.

"He is poor, but skillful. He succeeded in winning the affection of the most famous of all master goldsmiths. He loves the
daughter. The master approved of this love. Happiness and pros-
perity for all his life awaited him. But supposing that—only God
knows how—he was overcome by anger and actually committed this
murderous attack upon his benefactor, his father, what diabolical
hypocrisy would have been required for Olivier to behave as he
had behaved after the murder!" Firmly convinced of Olivier's innocence, Mademoiselle de Scudéri determined to save the innocent
young man at any cost.

Before appealing for clemency to the King himself, it seemed
to her that it would be best to approach President La Régnie and
call to his attention all the facts that indicated Olivier's innocence,
and thereby arouse in him a conviction of the accused's innocence,
which he might then communicate to the judges.

La Régnie received Mademoiselle de Scudérie with all the
respect which the worthy, who are highly honored by the King himself, might expect. He listened in silence to everything she had to
say concerning the terrible event and Olivier's life and character,

but the only indication that her words were not falling on completely deaf ears was a faint and almost malicious smile with which he heard her protestations and tearful admonitions that, like every judge, he should not be the enemy of the accused but be ready to consider any evidence in his behalf. When Mademoiselle de Scudéri was at last utterly exhausted and had dried her tears and grown silent, La Régnie began:

"It does credit to the kindness of your heart, Mademoiselle, that you, touched by the tears of a young girl in love, believe everything she tells you and that, in fact, you find the terrible crime completely inconceivable; but it is different for the judge, who is accustomed to ripping the mask from insolent hypocrisy. It is not incumbent upon me to reveal the course of a criminal trial to anyone who chooses to inquire. Mademoiselle, I do my duty, and I concern myself little with world opinion. Let those who commit evil tremble before the *Chambre Ardente,* which knows no punishment other than blood and fire. But, Mademoiselle de Scudéri, I do not wish you to look upon me as a monster of severity and cruelty; therefore, permit me to demonstrate in a few words the bloodguilt of this young scoundrel upon whom, heaven be praised, vengeance has fallen. Your acute intelligence will then repudiate the generosity which does you honor but which would be unsuitable in me.

"Well, then: René Cardillac was found stabbed to death in the morning. Nobody is with him except his journeyman, Olivier Brusson, and the daughter. In Olivier's room there is found, among other things, a dagger covered with fresh blood which exactly fits into the wound. Olivier says 'Cardillac was struck down before my eyes during the night.' 'Was the intention to rob him?' 'I do not know.' 'You were walking with him and you were not able to drive off the murderer, to seize him, to call for help?' 'The master was walking fifteen, probably twenty paces in front of me; I was following him.' 'Why in the world were you so far behind him?' 'The master wished it so.' 'What was Meister Cardillac doing in the street so late at night?' 'That I cannot say.' 'But he ordinarily never left the house after nine o'clock, did he?' At this point Olivier hesitates, becomes confused, sighs, cries, protests by everything holy that Cardillac did go out that night and met death in the street. Now, Mademoiselle, note this carefully. It has been established with complete certainty that Cardillac did not leave his house that night; consequently, Olivier's assertion that he went out with him is a barefaced lie. The front door of the house is fitted with a heavy lock which makes a piercing noise when it is opened and shut; further, the door creaks and groans on its hinges, making a noise which, as experiments have proved, even reaches to the top story of the house. Now, on the ground floor, that is to say, next to the front door, there lives old Meister Claude Patru with his housekeeper, a person almost eighty years of age, but still vigorous and active. Both of them heard Cardillac come downstairs, according to his habit, at precisely nine o'clock, lock and bolt the door with a great deal of noise, go upstairs again, read aloud the evening prayer, and then, as could be presumed from the banging of the doors, go into his bedroom. Meister Claude, like many old people, suffers from insomnia. And on that night he could not close an eye; therefore, at about nine-thirty the housekeeper, crossing the entrance hall, struck a light in the kitchen and sat down at the table with Meister Claude and read aloud from an ancient chronicle while the old man mused, sometimes sitting in his armchair, sometimes walking slowly back and forth in the room, trying to invite weariness and sleep. Everything was quiet until after midnight. Then they heard quick steps overhead, a hard fall as though something heavy had dropped to the floor, and immediately afterwards a muffled groaning. They were both filled with a strange anxiety and dread. The horror of the heinous deed which had just been committed swept over them. With daybreak, the light revealed what had been committed in the dark."

"But in the name of all the saints," Mademoiselle de Scudéri broke in, "after considering everything that I told you at such length, can you think of any motive for this diabolical deed?"

"Hm," La Régnie replied. "Cardillac was not poor—he possessed splendid jewels."

"But would it not all have reverted, would it not have reverted to the daughter?" Mademoiselle de Scudéri continued. "You forget that Olivier was to become Cardillac's son-in-law."

"Perhaps he was forced to share, even to murder for others," La Régnie said.

"Share, murder for others?" Mademoiselle de Scudéri asked in complete astonishment.

"You must know, Mademoiselle," La Régnie continued, "that if Olivier's crime were not connected with the thickly veiled mystery which has till now so broodingly lain over Paris, his blood would long ago have flowed in the Place de Grève. Olivier is obviously a member of that accursed band which carries out its crimes with perfect impunity, in contempt of all scrutiny and all the investigative efforts expended. Cardillac's wound is identical with those inflicted on all the people who have been murdered and robbed in the streets and in the houses. Most conclusively, since the arrest of Olivier Brusson, all the murders and robberies have ceased. The streets are as secure at night as they are during the day, proof enough that Olivier was perhaps the leader of the band of murderers. He has not yet confessed, but there are ways to make one talk against one's will."

"And Madelon," cried Mademoiselle de Scudéri, "Madelon, the true innocent dove?"

"Ah," La Régnie said with a venomous smile. "Ah, who can assure me that she was not involved in the plot? What does she feel for her father? Her tears are reserved for the murderer."

"What are you saying?" cried Mademoiselle de Scudéri. "It is impossible. Not for her father! That girl!"

"Oh," La Régnie continued, "just remember the Brinvilliers. You must forgive me if I must soon tear your protégée away from you and have her thrown into the Conciergerie."

Mademoiselle de Scudéri shuddered at this dreadful suspicion. It seemed to her that neither truth nor virtue existed for this terrible man, as if he detected murder and bloodguilt in man's deepest and most hidden thoughts. She rose. "Be humane!" was all that she could say as she left, breathing with difficulty because of her distress. As she was about to descend the stairs, to which the President had accompanied her with ceremonious courtesy, a strange idea came to her—she herself knew not how. "May I be allowed to see this unfortunate Olivier Brusson?" she asked the President, turning around quickly. He scrutinized her thoughtfully, then his face became distorted with the repulsive smile charcteristic of him.

"No doubt," he said, "no doubt you have in mind, my worthy Mademoiselle, to investigate Olivier's guilt or innocence for yourself because you have more faith in your feelings and in your inner voice than you have in what has taken place before our eyes. If you are not averse to the dismal sanctum of crime, if you are not repelled by the sight of depravity in all its stages, the gates of the Conciergerie shall be opened to you in two hours. This Olivier whose fate arouses your sympathy will be brought before you."

In truth, Mademoiselle de Scudéri was incapable of convincing herself of the young man's guilt. Everything spoke against him; indeed, confronted by the evidence at hand, no judge in the world would have acted differently from La Régnie. Yet the picture of domestic bliss which Madelon had so vividly painted for her outshone all evil suspicion, so that she preferred to accept the existence of an inscrutable mystery rather than believe something against which her entire inner being revolted. It was her intention to hear Olivier relate again all that had taken place on that fateful night, and thereby, as far as possible, penetrate into a mystery which judges had been unable to solve because they considered it unworthy of additional investigation.

On her arrival at the Conciergerie, Mademoiselle de Scudéri was taken into a large, well-lighted room. Soon she heard the clanking of chains, and Olivier Brusson was brought in. But as soon as he appeared in the doorway Mademoiselle de Scudéri fainted. When she regained consciousness, Olivier was gone. She vehemently demanded that she be taken to her carriage. She would not for another instant remain in that den of malicious depravity. At the first glance she recognized in Olivier Brusson the young man who had thrown a note into her carriage on the Pont-Neuf, and who had brought her the casket which contained the jewels. Now all doubt was gone; La Régnie's frightful suspicions were completely confirmed. Olivier Brusson was a member of that fearful band of murderers, and he had no doubt also murdered his master! And Madelon? Deluded by her emotions more bitterly than ever before in her life, mortally shattered by the power of hell on earth, in whose very existence she had not believed, Mademoiselle de Scudéri despaired of ever again recognizing truth. The terrible suspicion that Madelon might be implicated and share the heinous bloodguilt was given free rein, for it is the nature of the human mind, once a picture has been admitted, to search diligently and find colors with which to heighten it; and so it was that Mademoiselle de Scudéri, weighing all the circumstances of the crime and the most minute details of Madelon's behavior, found a great deal with which to nourish her suspicion. Many things which had previously been regarded as evidence of innocence and purity now became proof of wanton maliciousness and studied hypocrisy. The heartrending lamentations, the tears of anguish, might well have been pressed from her, not by her mortal dread of seeing her sweetheart bleed—no!—but at her own death at the hands of the executioner.

Resolving that she must immediately cast away the serpent feeding in her bosom, she alighted from her carriage. Madelon threw herself at her feet as she entered the room. Her heavenly eyes—there is not an angel of God whose eyes are more truthful—raised, her hands clasped to her heaving breast, she lamented and implored help and consolation. Mademoiselle de Scudéri, controlling herself with difficulty, trying to give the tone of her voice as much gravity and serenity as possible, said, "Go—go—rejoice that the murderer awaits the just punishment for his shameful crime. May the holy Virgin grant that bloodguilt does not burden you, yourself!"

"Oh, then all is lost!" Madelon cried shrilly and fell unconscious to the ground. Mademoiselle de Scudéri, requesting La Martinière to see to the girl, went to another room.

Completely torn apart inwardly, filled with loathing for everything earthly, Mademoiselle de Scudéri desired to depart from a world so infested with diabolical deception. She cursed the destiny which had granted her so many years in which to strengthen her belief in truth and virtue, only, in her old age, to destroy the beautiful picture which had illuminated her life.

As La Martinière was leading the girl out, Mademoiselle de Scudérie heard Madelon sigh softly and lament, "Oh, *she, she* too has been deceived by the cruel ones. Oh, wretched me—poor, miserable Olivier!"

Mademoiselle de Scudéri was pierced to the heart by Madelon's voice and once again deep within the inmost depths of her soul there dawned the feeling that there was a mystery involved and that Olivier was innocent. Beside herself, torn by the most contradictory emotions, Mademoiselle de Scudéri cried out in desperation, "What hellish spirit has entangled me in this horrible affair which will cost me my life?"

Baptiste entered at this moment, pale and frightened, with the news that Desgrais was outside. Since the despicable trial of La Voison, the appearance of Desgrais in a house had been an absolute precursor of some terrible accusation; hence, Baptiste's terror, about which Mademoiselle simply asked him with a gentle smile, "What is the matter, Baptiste? Has the name Scudéri been discovered on La Voison's list?"

"Oh, in the name of Christ," Baptiste cried, his entire body trembling, "how can you say such a thing; but Desgrais—the horrible Desgrais is behaving so mysteriously and with such urgency that it seems as if he can hardly wait to see you!"

"Well, Baptiste," said Mademoiselle de Scudéri, "bring in at once this man of whom you are so terrified and who does not terrify *me* at all."

"President La Régnie," Desgrais said when he had stepped into the room, "President La Régnie sends me to you with a request which he would not dare expect to see fulfilled if he did not know your goodness and your courage and if the last hope of shedding light upon an atrocious murder did not lie in your hands, and if you had not already taken part in the terrible trial which is now keeping the *Chambre Ardente* and all of us in breathless suspense. Olivier Brusson, since he saw you, is half mad. Once almost ready to confess, he now swears by Christ and everything sacred that he is completely innocent of Cardillac's murder, although he wishes to suffer the death he has deserved. Note, Mademoiselle, that the last remark clearly suggests that he is guilty of other crimes. But all efforts to force one more word from him have been in vain. He entreats and implores us to arrange for him to talk to you. To *you*, to you alone, he will confess everything. Mademoiselle, condescend to hear Brusson's confession."

"What?" cried Mademoiselle de Scudéri indignantly. "Am I to become an organ of the tribunal, am I to abuse the trust of this unfortunate man and bring him to the scaffold? No, Desgrais! Even if Brusson were an accursed murderer, I could never so deceive him. I wish to know nothing of his secrets, which would anyway remain locked in my breast like a holy confession."

"Perhaps," Desgrais answered with a subtle smile, "perhaps, Mademoiselle, you will change your mind after hearing Brusson. Did you not entreat the President himself to be humane? He is being humane by yielding to Brusson's fantastic request and thus making one final attempt to avoid resorting to the torture for which Brusson has long been ripe."

Mademoiselle de Scudéri trembled involuntarily.

"Understand," Desgrais continued, "understand, worthy lady, that no one expects you to return again to those gloomy dungeons which so filled you with horror and loathing. In the still of night Olivier will be brought to your house like a free man. What he says to you will be overheard by no one, though, to be sure, there will be guards in the house; and he may thus freely tell you everything he wishes to confess. I guarantee with my life that you have nothing to fear from that wretched man. He speaks of you with the most profound veneration. He swears that only the grim fate which prevented his seeing you earlier drives him towards his death. Moreover, how much you will tell us of what Brusson confesses to you depends upon you. Can we compel you to do more?"

Mademoiselle de Scudéri stared straight ahead, in deep reflection. It seemed to her that she must obey that higher power which had marked her for the solution of some terrible mystery—as if she could no longer escape the web—in which she had unwittingly become entangled. Making up her mind suddenly, she said with dignity, "God will grant me composure and fortitude. Bring Brusson here. I will speak to him."

As when Brusson had brought the casket, at midnight there was a knock at Mademoiselle de Scudéri's door. Baptiste, who had been alerted to the nocturnal visit, opened the door. An icy shudder leapt through Mademoiselle de Scudéri as she heard from the soft footsteps and the muffled murmer that the guards who had brought Brusson were stationing themselves in the passages of the house. Finally the door of her room quietly opened. Desgrais entered, behind him Olivier Brusson, free of chains and respectfully dressed. "Here," said Desgrais, bowing respectfully, "here is Brusson, worthy lady"; and he left the room.

Brusson sank on both knees before Mademoiselle de Scudéri and raised his folded hands imploringly, a rush of tears streaming from his eyes. Mademoiselle de Scudéri, pale of face and unable to speak, looked down at him. Though his face was distorted by grief and anguish, it radiated true goodness. The longer Mademoiselle allowed her eyes to rest upon his face, the more vivid became her recollection of some person she had loved, but whom she could not see. When her horror left her, she forgot that it was Cardillac's murderer kneeling before her, and speaking in the pleasant tone of serene benevolence which was characteristic of her, she said, "Well, Brusson, what have you to say to me?"

Brusson, still on his knees, sighed deeply with profound melancholy and said, "Oh, noble lady, is there no trace of recollection of me in your mind?"

Mademoiselle de Scudéri, looking at him still more attentively, answered that she certainly recognized in his features a resemblance to someone she had loved and that her ability to overcome her deep repugnance to the murderer and to be able to listen to him quietly was due to this fact. Brusson, heavily wounded by these words, rose quickly to his feet and, looking gloomily at the floor, took a step backwards. Then he asked in a hollow voice, "Have you completely forgotten Ann Guiot? Her son Olivier, the boy whom you often dandled on your knee, it is he who now stands before you."

"Oh, in the name of all saints!" Mademoiselle de Scudéri cried, covering her face with both hands and sinking back into the cushions. There was reason enough for her being so horrified. Ann Guiot, the daughter of an impecunious citizen, had lived with Mademoiselle de Scudéri from her childhood; she had raised her, the dear child, with all affection and loving care. When she grew up, she was courted by a handsome, well-mannered young man named Claude Brusson. Because he was a first-rate watchmaker who was certain to earn a good wage in Paris, and because Ann had fallen completely in love with him, Mademoiselle de Scudéri was not at all hesitant about approving the marriage of her foster daughter. The young couple set up house and lived in serene and happy domesticity, love's bond being tied even more tightly by the birth of a most beautiful boy, the very image of his lovely mother.

Mademoiselle de Scudéri idolized little Olivier, whom she would take from his mother for hours and days at a time so that she could pet and fondle him. Therefore the boy grew attached to her and liked to be with her as much as with his mother. Three years later, the professional envy of Brusson's fellow craftsmen accounting for the diminution in the quantity of work that came his way, Brusson was barely able to provide for his family. In addition, there was Brusson's homesickness for his beautiful birthplace, Geneva. And so, despite Mademoiselle de Scudéri's opposition, and despite her promises of every kind of support, the little family ultimately moved there. Ann wrote a few times to her foster mother and then stopped; Mademoiselle de Scudéri imagined that she had been forgotten in the happiness experienced by the Brussons.

It was now exactly twenty-three years since Brusson had left Paris for Geneva with his wife and child.

"Oh, horror," Mademoiselle de Scudéri cried when she was somewhat recovered. "Are you Olivier? My Ann's son? And now? Like this!"

Quietly and in a composed manner, Olivier replied: "You

probably never thought, worthy lady, that the boy whom you dandled on your knee, whom you gave the sweetest names, having grown to become a young man, would stand before you accused of a horrible murder! I am not completely innocent, and the *Chambre Ardente* can justly charge me with a crime; but, as truly as I wish to die blessed, even though executed, I am innocent of any blood guilt. It was not through me, it was not my fault that the unfortunate Cardillac met his death." As he uttered these words Olivier began to tremble and sway. Silently, Mademoiselle de Scudéri motioned him to a small chair standing beside him. He slowly sat down.

"I have had enough time," he went on, "in which to prepare for this interview with you—which I consider the final favor of a merciful heaven—and to gain the calm and composure necessary to tell you the story of my terrible, unique misfortune. Be so compassionate as to hear me out calmly, regardless of how much the disclosure of a secret of which you assuredly have no inkling may amaze, in fact, horrify you. If only my poor father had never left Paris! As far as my earliest recollections of Geneva are concerned, I remember being sprinkled by the tears of my inconsolable parents and myself crying because of the lamentations which I did not understand. Later there came a clear sense, a full awareness of the oppressiveness in which they lived. All my father's hopes were disappointed. Bowed down, crushed by sorrow, he died just when he succeeded in placing me as an apprentice to a goldsmith. My mother spoke a great deal of you; she wanted to tell you of her misfortunes but was prevented from doing this because of a hopelessness born of poverty. That, and probably also a false shame which often gnaws at mortally wounded spirits, kept her from carrying out her resolution. A few months after the death of my father, she followed him to the grave."

"Poor Ann! Poor Ann!" Mademoiselle de Scudéri cried, overwhelmed by grief.

"Thanks and praise to the eternal power of heaven that she has passed where she cannot see her beloved son fall under the executioner's hand, branded with disgrace!" Olivier cried loudly, looking wildly toward the skies. There was a restlessness outside, the sound of men moving about was heard. "Aha," said Olivier with a bitter smile, "Desgrais is waking his compatriots, as though I could possibly escape from *here!* But to go on: My master treated me harshly, even though I worked hard and was soon one of the best workmen and finally much better than he himself. One day a foreigner happened to come to our workshop to purchase some jewelry. Seeing a necklace I had made, he gave me a friendly slap on the back, eyed the piece of jewelry, and said, 'Well, well, my young friend, this is really a fine piece of work. I know of no one who could outdo you except René Cardillac, who is the finest goldsmith in the world. You should go to him; he would be glad to admit you into his workshop, for no one but you could help him in his superb art, and from no one but him can you learn.' The words of the stranger sank deep into my soul. Geneva offered me no more peace; I felt myself forced from her. Finally I succeeded in freeing myself from my master. I came to Paris, where René Cardillac received me coldly and harshly. I refused to give up. He had to give me work, regardless of how trivial it might be. He told me to make a small ring. When I finished it and brought it back to him, he stared at me with his glistening eyes as though trying to see right through me, then said, 'You are a first-rate journeyman; you may move in with me and help in the workshop. I will pay you well and you will be happy with me.'

"Cardillac kept his word. I had been with him for several weeks without having seen Madelon, who, if I am not mistaken, was staying in the country with one of his cousins. At last she came. Oh, eternal power of heaven, what happened to me when I saw that angelic creature! Has anyone ever loved as I love! And now! Oh, Madelon!"

Olivier was overcome by sorrow and could say no more. He held both hands over his face and sobbed violently. At last, subduing his wild anguish with a mighty effort, he continued.

"Madelon looked on me with friendly eyes. She came more and more often to the workshop. With delight I saw that she loved me. Although her father kept a close watch on us, we stole many hand clasps in token of our bond. Cardillac did not seem to notice anything. I planned to ask his consent to our marriage when I had succeeded in gaining his favor and my mastership. One morning, when I was about to begin work, Cardillac, anger and contempt in his dark gaze, said, 'I need your work no more. You are to be out of this house before the hour is passed, and my eyes are never to rest on you again. There is no need for me to tell you why your presence here is now intolerable. The sweet fruit after which you long hangs too high for you, poor beggar!' I tried to say something, but he seized me with his powerful hand and flung me out of the door. I fell and seriously injured my head and my arm. Furious, torn by deadly pain, I finally found my way to a kind-hearted acquaintance who lived at the far end of the Faubourg Saint-Martin and who found room for me in his garret. I had neither peace nor rest. At night I prowled round Cardillac's house hoping that Madelon might hear my sighs and my lamentations and that she might be able to speak to me from the window without being observed. All kinds of desperate plans which I hoped to convince her to carry out crossed my mind. There is a high wall with niches and old, partly crumbling statues next to Cardillac's house in the rue Nicaise. One night I was standing near one of these statues, looking up at the windows of the house which open to the courtyard that the wall encloses. Suddenly I saw a light in Cardillac's workshop. It was midnight and he was normally never awake at that time, usually going to bed precisely at the stroke of nine. My heart pounded with a terrifying premonition. I imagined that something might take place which would provide me with entry into the house. But the light immediately disappeared again. I pressed myself tightly against the statue and into the niche, but recoiled in horror when I felt the pressure being returned, as if the statue had come to life. In the dim dusk of night I saw the statue rotate slowly and a dark figure slip out from behind it and stealthily make its way down the street. I sprang to the statue. It was again standing close to the wall. Involuntarily, as if driven by a force within me, I crept after the figure. The full light of a bright lamp burning before the statue of the Virgin fell upon its face. It was Cardillac! An incomprehensible terror, an eerie shudder ran through me. As though under a spell, I was compelled to pursue this ghost-like sleepwalker—for that was what I felt my master to be, although it was not the time of the full moon when sleepers are so afflicted. Finally Cardillac vanished into a deep shadow. From a familiar sound he made as he cleared his throat, I knew that he had gone into the entrance of a house. 'What was the meaning of this! What is he up to?' I asked myself in astonishment, pressing myself close against the houses. Not long after this, a man singing and warbling, wearing a white plumed hat, spurs jangling, came out. Like a tiger on his prey, Cardillac pounced upon the man from his dark hiding place. The man immediately sank gasping to the ground. I sprang forward with a cry of horror. Cardillac was bending over the man as he lay on the ground. 'Meister Cardillac, what are you doing?' I screamed. 'Damn you!' Cardillac bellowed, running past me with lightning speed and vanishing. Completely beside myself, barely able to walk a step, I approached

the fallen man. I knelt down beside him, thinking it was still possible to save him; but not a trace of life was left in him. In my desperation I barely noticed that I had been surrounded by the *maréchaussée*. 'Another one struck down by the devils! Hey, young man,
what are you doing here? Are you one of the gang? Away with you!'
This is how they cried out in confusion and seized me. I was barely
able to stammer that I was incapable of committing such a dastardly
crime and that they must release me. Then one of them held a light
to my face and called with a laugh, 'This is Olivier Brusson, the
goldsmith who works with our worthy and honest Meister René Cardillac! Sure—*he's* the kind to murder people in the street! Just the
type—and, of course, one would expect a murderer to lament over
the corpse and allow himself to be nabbed. Come, young man, tell
us about what happened.'

" 'Right before my eyes,' I said to them, 'a man pounced upon
this man, struck him down, and ran away as fast as lightening when
I shouted. I wanted to see whether I could still save the victim.'

" 'No, my son,' one of the men who lifted up the corpse called,
'he's finished, stabbed through the heart as usual.' 'Damn it' said
another, 'again we are too late, just as we were the day before yesterday.' And with this they left with the corpse.

"I really can not tell you what I felt about all of this. I pinched
myself to see whether I was not being deceived by an evil dream; it
was as if I would awake almost at once, amazed at this crazy figment
of my imagination. Cardillac—the father of my Madelon—a vil-
lanous murderer! I sank feebly down on the stone steps of the house.
The morning grew ever brighter. A finely plumed officer's hat lay
before me on the pavement. Cardillac's bloody crime, committed
on the very spot where I sat, appeared to me vividly. And I fled in
terror.

"Completely bewildered, almost unconscious, I was sitting in
my garret when the door opened and René Cardillac entered. 'In the
name of Christ, what do you want?' I cried. Paying no attention to
my question, he approached me, smiling at me with a tranquillity
and serenity which only heightened my inner revulsion. Because I
was unable to get up from my straw bed where I had flung myself,
he pulled up an old rickety stool and sat down beside me. 'Well now
Olivier,' he began, 'how are you, my poor boy? I really was much too
hasty in throwing you out of the house; I miss you at every turn.
Just now I have a job to do which I will not be able to complete

without you. How would it be if you came back to work with me again? No answer? Yes, I know, I have insulted you. I do not want to hide from you the fact that I was angry about your flirtation with my Madelon, but afterwards I thought things over and concluded that, given your talent, your conscientiousness, and your honesty, I could not hope to have a better son-in-law than you. Then come with me and see if you can win Madelon for your wife.'

"Cardillac's words pierced my heart; I shuddered at his wickedness. I could not utter a word. 'You hesitate,' he said sharply, boring through me with his glittering eyes. 'You hesitate? Perhaps you have other things to do today and therefore can not come to me. Perhaps you wish to visit Desgrais or perhaps even D'Argenson or La Régnie. Be careful, fellow, lest the claws you would unsheath to destroy others seize and tear you yourself.' At this my utter indignation suddenly found expression. 'Let those,' I cried, 'who have a horrible crime on their conscience tremble at the names you have uttered. I need not—I have nothing to do with them.' 'In fact,' Cardillac continued, 'you should be honored to work with me! I am the most renowned contemporary master craftsman, and everywhere I am highly esteemed for my honesty and directness, so that any evil slander uttered would fall back heavily upon the head of the accuser. As for Madelon, I must confess that she alone is responsible for my indulgence. She loves you with a passion with which I would not have credited the gentle child. As soon as you were gone she fell at my feet, embraced my knees, and with a thousand tears declared that she could never live without you. I thought that this was merely her imagination—those infatuated young things are always ready to die when the first pale-faced youth looks at them in friendly fashion—but, in fact, my Madelon did really grow ill; and when I tried to talk her out of all this nonsense, she cried out your name a thousand times. Ultimately, what could I do if I did not want to see her surrender to despair? Yesterday evening I told her that I agreed to everything and that today I would go to fetch you. Overnight she bloomed like a rose; and now, beside herself with love-sickness, she awaits you.'

"May the eternal power of heaven forgive me, for I myself do not know how it happened; I was suddenly standing in Cardillac's house, and Madelon was exuberantly shouting 'Olivier—my Olivier —my beloved—my husband!' and pressing me to her breast, her arms around my neck, so that I, in supreme happiness, swore by the Virgin and all the saints that I would never leave her."

Olivier was overwhelmed by the remembrance of this decisive moment, and he had to pause. Mademoiselle de Scudéri, overcome by horror at the crime of a man whom she had looked upon as the personification of virtue and goodness, cried, "Terrible! René Cardillac is a member of the gang of murderers who have for so long turned our good city into a den of thieves?"

"Mademoiselle, did you say 'gang'? There never was any gang; it was Cardillac alone who diabolically sought and found his victims throughout the city. The fact that he was alone accounts for his impunity and is the reason that the police could never track the murderer. But let me go on. What follows will clear up the mystery and reveal the secrets of this man who is at once the most evil and wretched of all men. The situation in which I now found myself in relation to my master anyone can imagine. The step had been taken and there was no going back. At times it seemed to me as if I had become Cardillac's accomplice in murder, and only in Madelon's love was I able to forget for a time the inner pain which tortured me; only when with her could I throw off all the outward signs of the unspeakable horror which burdened me. When I worked with the old man in the shop, I could barely trade a word with him because of the terror which made me shiver just to be in the presence of this abominable man, who displayed all the merits of the tender father and the upright citizen while the night shrouded his crimes. Madelon, pure angelic child that she is, worshiped him. It cut me to the heart to think that she, who had been so deceived by all the diabolical craft of Satan, would find herself the victim of the most abysmal despair if ever vengeance were to fall upon the unmasked villain. This in itself sealed my lips and would have kept them sealed even if my silence were to result in my dying a criminal's death. Although I had heard a good deal from the *maréchaussée,* Cardillac's crimes, their motive and the manner in which he carried them out, were a riddle to me. I did not have to wait long for the solution.

"One day Cardillac, who, to my utter disgust, usually was very light hearted while at work and laughed and joked, was very serious and withdrawn. He suddenly flung away the piece of jewelry on which he was working, pearls and gems scattering in all directions, leapt to his feet, and said, 'Olivier, things cannot go on between us this way. The situation is unbearable. What the most ingenious cunning of Desgrais and his henchmen failed to discover, chance has placed in your hands. You have seen me at the nocturnal work to which I am compelled by my evil star—denial is beyond me. But it was also your evil star which compelled you to follow me and which wrapped you in a mantle of invisibility and gave to your footsteps such lightness that you moved as noiselessly as the smallest animal; so that I, who like the tiger can see in the darkest of nights and can hear the slightest sound, the humming of the flies a street away, did not observe you. Your evil star has made you my accomplice. You can not betray me in your present situation; therefore, you shall know all.'

" 'I shall never ever again be your accomplice, you hypocritical villain!' was what I wanted to cry out, but the horror which over-whelmed me when I heard his words paralyzed my tongue. Instead of words, I could only utter an uintelligible sound.

"Cardillac again sat down on his work bench. He wiped the sweat from his brow and seemed deeply shaken by the recollection of the past and appeared to find it difficult to pull himself together. Finally he began: 'Wise men have much to say about the susceptibil-ity of pregnant women to strange impressions, and about the curious influences which these vivid and involuntary impressions, which stem from the external, may exercise upon the child. A singular story was told to me about my mother. During the first month of preg-nancy she and other women watched a superb court pageant at the Trianon, and she saw a cavalier in Spanish dress wearing a sparkling jeweled necklace from which she could not thereafter remove her eyes. Her entire being longed for the dazzling gems which seemed to her to be supernaturally valuable. This same cavalier, several years earlier, when my mother was not yet married, had made an attempt upon her virtue, but he had been rejected with loathing. My mother recognized him; but now, bathed by the light of the gems, he seemed to her to belong to a higher sphere, to be the very embodiment of beauty. The cavalier noticed my mother's desirous, fiery look and thought that he would be more successful now than he had been before. He contrived to get close to her, to separate her from her friends, and even to lure her to a lonely place. There he passionately clasped her in his arms. My mother grabbed at the beautiful necklace; but at that moment he fell to the earth, dragging my mother along with him. I do not know whether he had suffered a stroke or whether it was for some other reason, but he was dead. In vain did my mother attempt to free herself from the dead man's rigid arms which embraced her. With eyes that were hollow and devoid of light fixed on her, the corpse rolled this way and that with her upon the ground. Her shrieks for help finally reached people who were passing in the distance, and they rushed to her aid and released her from the arms of her gruesome lover. The shock of all this made my mother seriously ill. She and I were given up for lost; but she recovered, and the birth was easier than anyone had expected. But the terrors of that awful moment had marked me. My evil star had risen and flung down sparks which ignited in me a most strange and fatal passion. From my earliest childhood I valued glittering diamonds and the products of the goldsmith above everything else. This was looked upon simply as a childish fancy for lovely things. But it was otherwise, for as a boy I stole gold and jewels wherever I could lay my hands on them. And like the most accomplished connoisseur, I could instinctively distinguished paste jewelry from the genuine. Only the genuine attracted me; I ignored false jewels and rolled gold. This inborn craving was ultimately repressed by my father's severe punishments. But so that I might always be able to handle gold and precious stones, I entered the goldsmith's profession, and working at it with passionate enthusiasm, I soon became the leading craftsman in this field. Then there began a period when my impulse, which had so long been repressed, forced itself to the surface and, growing mightily, consumed everything else. As soon as I had completed and delivered a piece of jewelry, I fell into a state of restlessness and desperation which kept me from my sleep, wrecked my health, and drained my will to live. The person for whom I had made the work haunted me day and night like a ghost—I saw him continually, bedecked in my jewelry, and a voice whispered in my ear, "It's yours! Take it, it's yours, it's yours, take it! What use are diamonds to the dead?" Ultimately I began to steal. I had access to the houses of the great, and I quickly took advantage of every opportunity. No lock resisted my skill, and soon my jewelry was back in my hands again. But even this was not sufficient to calm my uneasiness. The eerie voice made itself heard again, jeering at me and saying, "Aha, a dead man wears your jewels!" I did not know how it happened, but I began to harbor an indescribable hatred towards those for whom I had made jewelry. Even more, in the depths of my soul there began to seeth an impulse to murder before which I myself shuddered. It was then that I bought this house. I had concluded the terms with the owner, and we were sitting together in this room, drinking a bottle of wine in honor of the completed transaction. Night had fallen; he was about to leave when he said to me, "Listen, Meister René; before I go, I must inform you of a secret about this house." He opened the cupboard built into the wall, pushed the back of it aside, stepped through into a small closet, where he bent down and raised a trap door. We descended a steep and narrow staircase, arrived at a narrow gate, which he opened and which let us out into the open courtyard. Then the old gentleman went up to the encircling wall, pushed at a piece of iron which slightly projected from the wall; immediately a part of the wall revolved so that a man could step out through the opening into the street. You must see this device, Olivier. It must have been made by the cunning monks of the monastery which once existed here so that they were able to slip in and out secretly. It is wood, but mortared and whitewashed on the outside; and a statue, also of wood, but which looks as if it were made of stone, is fitted into the side; the wall and the statue rotate together on hidden hinges. When I saw this device, dark thoughts surged up in me. It seemed a presentiment of deeds which were as yet hidden even from myself. I had just delivered an opulent ornament to a gentleman of the court, which I knew was to be presented to a dancer at the opera. I was terribly tortured—the ghost haunted my steps—the whispering devil was in my ear! I went back into the house. Drenched in the sweat of anguish, I tossed and turned on my bed, sleepless. In my mind's eye I saw the man slipping off to the dancer with my beautiful jewelry. Infuriated, I sprang up—threw on my coat—climbed the secret staircase—went out through the wall into the rue Nicaise. He came, I fell upon him, he screamed, but I seized him from behind and plunged my dagger into his heart—the jewelry was mine! This done, I felt a peace and contentment in my soul such as I had never known before. The ghost had disappeared, Satan's voice was no more. Now I knew what it was that my evil star demanded. I had to obey or perish!'

" 'Now you understand my actions and that which drives me, Olivier. Do not think that because I do that which I am compelled to do I am devoid of all feelings of pity or of compassion, which are said to be intrinsic in man's nature. You know how difficult it is for me to deliver a piece of jewelry; that there are some for whom I will not work at all because I do not wish them to die; that sometimes, knowing that my ghost will be exorcized with blood the next day, I forestall this with a powerful blow of my fist which flattens the

owner of my jewels on the ground so that I can get them back into my hands!'

"Having said all this, Cardillac led me into his secret vault and allowed me to look at his jewel cabinet. The King does not own a finer one. Each article had attached to it a small label stating exactly for whom it had been made and when it had been taken back by theft, robbery, or violence. 'On your wedding day, Olivier,' Cardillac said in a hollow, solemn voice, 'you will swear a sacred oath with your hand on the crucifix that as soon as I am dead you will immediately reduce this opulence to dust with a technique which I will teach you. I want no human being, least of all Madelon and you, to come into possession of this blood-bought hoard.'

"Trapped and snared in this labyrinth of crime, torn by love and revulsion, I was like the accursed soul whom a beautiful, softly smiling angel, beckons aloft, while Satan holds him back with red hot claws, and the holy angel's loving smile, in which is reflected all of the bliss of paradise, becomes the most agonizing of his tortures. I thought of flight, even of suicide—but Madelon! Blame me, blame me, worthy lady, for having been too weak to smash forcefully a passion which chained me to crime, but am I not to atone for it by a shameful death?

"One day Cardillac came home in unusually good spirits. He caressed Madelon, cast a most friendly look at me, drank a bottle of vintage wine at dinner—something which he only did on special occasions and holidays—sang, and was merry. Madelon had left us, and I was about to go into the workshop. 'Sit still, boy,' Cardillac cried, 'no more work today. Let us drink to the welfare of the most worthy and excellent lady in all of Paris.' After we had clinked glasses and he had emptied his at a gulp, he said, 'Tell me, Olivier, how do you like these lines?

> Un amant qui craint les voleurs
> N'est point digne d'amour.'

"He then told me what had happened between you and the King in the Marquise de Maintenon's apartment, adding that he had always revered you above any other human being and that before your lofty virtue his evil spirit would never arouse in him any vile thoughts of murder, even were you to wear the finest piece of jewelry he had ever made. 'Listen, Olivier,' he said, 'to what I have decided to do. A long time ago I was commissioned to make

a necklace and bracelet for Henrietta of England, supplying the
gems myself. This work turned out to surpass anything I had ever
done before, and it broke my heart to think that I must part with
these ornaments, which had become treasures of my soul. You know
of the Princess's unfortunate death by assassination. I kept the jewelry, and now I will send it to Mademoiselle de Scudéri, in the name
of the persecuted gang, as a token of my respect and gratitude. Besides, if I deliver these jewels to Mademoiselle de Scudéri as a symbol
of her triumph, it will be heaping upon Desgrais and his men the
contempt they deserve. You shall take the jewelry to her.' Mademoiselle, as soon as Cardillac mentioned your name, it was as if
black veils had been pulled aside, and the beautiful bright picture
of my happy early childhood rose again before me in gay and glowing
colors; a wonderful sense of consolation came into my soul, a ray
of hope before which the gloomy shadows vanished. Cardillac must
have seen the effect that his words had upon me, and he interpreted
this in his own way.

" 'My plan,' he said, 'seems to please you. I may confess that
in doing this I was responding to a voice deep within me which was
so very unlike the voice which demanded of me blood sacrifice as if
from a voracious beast of prey. At times a strange feeling comes over
me—an inner anxiety, the dread of something malicious, the terror
of which seems to float across the earth from the world beyond, seizes
me. At such times I feel that those things that are committed through
me by my evil star may be charged to my immortal soul, which plays
no part in it. In one of these moods I determined that I would make
a stunning diamond crown for the Holy Virgin in the church of
Saint-Eustache. But whenever I attempted to start making it, I was
filled with an·ever increasing, incomprehensible anxiety, until I
finally gave up. But now it seems to me that in sending to Mademoiselle de Scudéri the most splendid jewelry I have ever crafted I
will be humbly bringing a sacrifice to the very model of virtue and
piety and imploring effective intercession.' "

"Cardillac, who was familiar with every detail of your mode
of life, Mademoiselle, told me precisely how and when I was to
deliver to you the jewelry which he had encased in a rich jewel box.
My entire soul was imbued with happiness, for heaven itself seemed
to be showing me, through the sacrilegious Cardillac, a way to
escape from the hell in which I, a banished sinner, was languishing.
This is what I thought. Completely against Cardillac's wishes, it was

my intention to meet with you personally. As Ann Brusson's son and your foster child, I intended to throw myself at your feet and to tell you all, everything. Moved by the unspeakable misery which the disclosure of the secret would have brought upon poor, innocent Madelon, you would have maintained the secret, but your brilliant mind would surely have been able to find the way to control the accursed wickedness of Cardillac without revealing it. Do not ask me through what means this could have been done, I do not know. But the conviction that you would rescue Madelon and me was as deeply ingrained in my soul as my belief in the consoling help of the Holy Virgin.

"You know, Mademoiselle, that my plan fell through that night. I did not abandon hope that I would be more fortunate another time. But then Cardillac suddenly lost all his gaiety. He crept around gloomily, stared into space, muttering unintelligible words, and hit the air with his hands as if he were fighting off something hostile; his mind seemed full of evil thoughts. This continued for a whole morning. At last he sat down at the workbench, peevishly sprang up to his feet again, looked out of the window, said in a grave and gloomy voice, 'I wish Henrietta of England had worn my jewelry.'

"These words filled me with terror. I knew now that his insane mind was once more possessed by the specter of malignant murder and that the voice of the devil was again loud in his ears. I saw that your life was threatened by the accursed demon. If Cardillac could only regain possession of his jewels, you would be safe. Every instant increased the danger. Then I met you on the Pont-Neuf, broke my way into your carriage, and threw you the note in which I implored you to return the jewelry you had received from Cardillac. You did not come. My anxiety mounted to despair when, the next day, Cardillac spoke of nothing but the priceless jewelry that had appeared before his eyes during the night. I could only surmise that this was a reference to your jewelry, and I was certain that he was brooding upon a murderous attack which he undoubtedly had determined to pursue that night. I had to save you even were it to cost me Cardillac's life. When Cardillac, as usual, shut himself up in his room after evening prayers, I entered the courtyard by climbing out of the window, slipped out through the opening in the wall, stationed myself close by in deep shadow. It was not long before Cardillac came out and softly crept down the street. I followed him. He went towards the rue Saint Honoré. My heart quivered. All at once he vanished. I determined to station myself at your door. Then, just as chance had once made me witness to Cardillac's murderous attack, it intervened again, and an officer who was singing and warbling passed by without seeing me. But at that very instant a black form sprang out and attacked him. It was Cardillac. I wanted to prevent this murder. Shouting loudly, I was on the spot in two or three bounds—it was not the officer—it was Cardillac who sank to the earth mortally wounded, the death rattle in his throat. The officer dropped his dagger, and under the impression that I was the murderer's accomplice, unsheathed his sword and assumed a fighting stance; but he quickly left when he noticed that I paid him no attention but merely examined the corpse. Cardillac was still alive. After retrieving the dagger which the officer had dropped, I lifted Cardillac to my shoulders and, with difficulty, carried him home and up the secret passage to the workshop.

"You know the rest. You see, Mademoiselle, that my only crime consists of my not having betrayed Madelon's father to the courts, thereby ending his crimes. I am innocent of any bloodguilt. No martyrdom will tear from me the secret of Cardillac's outrages. I do not wish that now, contrary to the everlasting power which concealed from the virtuous daughter her father's atrocious crimes, I should be responsible for unleashing upon her all of the misery of the past which would mean her death, nor that the world's vengeance shall exhume the corpse from the soil which covers it and that the executioner shall brand the moldering bones with shame. No, my soul's beloved will mourn for me as an innocent victim. Time will assuage her grief and her sorrow, but her anguish for her father's atrocious crimes could never be assuaged!"

Olivier grew silent, but then suddenly a torrent of tears burst from his eyes; he threw himself at Mademoiselle de Scudéri's feet and implored, "You are convinced that I am innocent—I'm sure you are! Have pity on me, tell me how Madelon is."

Mademoiselle de Scudéri summoned La Martinière, and a few minutes later Madelon flung her arms about Olivier's neck.

"Everything is well now that you are here—I knew that this noble-hearted lady would save you!" cried Madelon over and over again; and Olivier forgot the fate which awaited him and all that threatened him. He was free and blissful. In the most moving way they both lamented what each had suffered for the other and then embraced each other again and wept for joy at having once more found each other.

Had Mademoiselle de Scudéri not already been convinced of Olivier's innocence, she must have been convinced of this now as she saw them both forgetting, in the rapture of profound and sincere love, the world, their misery, and their indescribable torment. "No," she called, "only a pure heart is capable of such blissful forgetfulness."

The bright rays of morning broke through the window. Desgrais knocked softly on the door and reminded them that it was time for Olivier Brusson to be taken away because it could not be done later without attracting attention. The lovers had to part. The dim presentiments which had possessed Mademoiselle de Scudéri when Brusson first appeared in her house now assumed a fearful actuality. She saw the son of her beloved Ann as being innocent, but as being so enmeshed by events that there was no apparent way of saving him from a shameful death. She honored the young man's heroism which led him to prefer dying with the burden of apparent guilt rather than to betray a secret which would result in Madelon's death. In the entire realm of possibility she could think of no way to tear the unfortunate youth from the cruel court. And yet, firmly imbedded in her soul was the conviction that no sacrifice should be spared to prevent the crying injustice which was being committed. She tortured herself with all sorts of projects and plans, some of which were completely impractical and all of which were rejected as soon as they were formed. Every glimmer of hope grew more and more faint until she was but a step from despair. But Madelon's unhesitating, pious, child-like trust, and the change which came over her when she spoke of her beloved—who, a freed man, she would soon embrace as a wife—touched Mademoiselle de Scudéri's heart and inspired her to new efforts.

In order to do something, Mademoiselle de Scudéri wrote a long letter to La Régnie, in which she informed him that Olivier Brusson had proved to her absolute satisfaction his complete innocence in the death of Cardillac and that only his heroic resolution to carry to his grave a secret whose disclosure would result in the ruin of true innocence and virtue, prevented him from offering to the court a statement which would not only absolve him from the terrible suspicion of having murdered Cardillac, but also of having been a member of the accursed gang of murderers. In her effort to soften La Régnie's hard heart, she put into her letter all the burning zeal and brilliant eloquence at her command. A few hours later La Régnie replied, saying that he was sincerely pleased that Olivier had succeeded in convincing his noble and worthy patroness of his innocence. As for Olivier's heroic resolution to carry into the grave a secret relating to the murder with which he was charged, he regretted that the *Chambre Ardente* could not honor such heroism but must, rather, attempt to break it by the most powerful means necessary. Within three days he hoped to possess the amazing secret which would result in light being cast on miraculous events.

Only too well did Mademoiselle de Scudéri know what the terrible La Régnie meant by the means which would be used to break Olivier's heroic silence. It was now clear that the unfortunate young man was to be tortured. In her mortal anguish, it at last occurred to Mademoiselle de Scudéri that the advice of a lawyer would be helpful, even if it were only to obtain a postponement. Pierre Arnaud d'Andilly was at that time the most celebrated lawyer in Paris. His profound knowledge and his comprehensive intelligence were equal to his integrity and virtue. She went to him and told him everything she could without divulging Olivier's secret. She thought that d'Andilly would enthusiastically accept the innocent man's defense, but her hopes were bitterly smashed. D'Andilly listened calmly to all that she had to say and then, smiling, responded with Boileau's words: "Le vrai peut quelquefois n'être pas vraisemblable."[5] He showed that the evidence against Brusson was of a most powerful kind, that the procedure followed by La Régnie was neither brutal nor precipitous, but, on the contrary, entirely within the bounds of law, and that, in fact, he could respond in no other way if he were not to neglect his responsibility as a judge. D'Andilly did not believe that even the most skillful defense could spare Brusson from torture. Only Brusson could accomplish that, either by fully confessing or, at the least, by accurately relating the circumstances surrounding Cardillac's murder, which might then result in fresh facts being brought to the surface.

"Then I shall throw myself at the King's feet and plead for mercy," Mademoiselle de Scudéri said, beside herself, in a voice half choked with tears.

"Do not do that, for heaven's sake do not do that, Made-

5. "Truth may sometimes look improbable."

moiselle," d'Andilly cried. "That should be reserved as a last resort. If you attempt it prematurely and do not succeed, it will be lost to you forever. The King would never pardon such a criminal at this point, for if he did he would expose himself to the most bitter reproaches of the people who feel themselves to be endangered. It is possible that Brusson, by revealing his secret, or by some other means, may succeed in exonerating himself in the eyes of the populace. Then would be the time to beg the King for mercy, who would not ask what had or had not been established legally but would be guided by his own inner conviction.

Mademoiselle de Scudéri could not but agree with what d'Andilly's broad experience suggested. Deeply worried, brooding without end about what she could do—in the name of the Virgin and all the saints—to save Brusson, she was sitting in her room late that evening when La Martinière entered and announced that the Comte de Miossens, a colonel of the King's Guard, urgently wished to speak to Mademoiselle.

"Pardon me, Mademoiselle," said Miossens, after bowing with soldierly courtesy, "for disturbing you so late; we soldiers do things that way; moreover, just a few words will excuse my behavior. I am here on behalf of Olivier Brusson."

Extremely interested in what she was going to hear, Mademoiselle de Scudéri cried out, "Olivier Brusson? The most unfortunate of all men? What have you to do with Brusson?"

"I thought," said Miossens, laughing again, "that your protégé's name would assure me a sympathetic hearing. The whole world is convinced of Brusson's guilt. I know that you think otherwise, although I have been told that your opinion is supported only by what the accused has told you. In my case it is different. No one can be more certain than I am that Brusson had nothing to do with Cardillac's death."

"Speak, oh, speak!" cried Mademoiselle de Scudéri, her eyes glistening with delight.

"I," Miossens said emphatically, "it was I who struck down the old goldsmith in the rue Saint Honoré, close to your house."

"In the name of all of the saints, you? You!" cried Mademoiselle de Scudéri.

"And I swear to you, Mademoiselle," he continued, "that I am proud of my deed. Know that Cardillac was the most detestable and hypocritical villain, and that it was he who cunningly murdered and robbed at night and for so long escaped every snare. I myself do not know what aroused my suspicion of the old villain when, obviously distressed, he brought me the jewelry I had ordered, asked in great detail for whom I intended it, and most shrewdly asked my valet about when I was in the habit of visiting a certain lady. It had long ago occurred to me that the unfortunate victims of this repulsive robber all had the same mortal wound, and I understood that the murderer had practiced a particular thrust which killed instantaneously and on which he depended. If he failed in this, it would mean a fight. I therefore took a precaution which is so simple that I am astounded that others had not thought of it before and saved themselves from the cowardly murderer. I wore a light breastplate beneath my vest. Cardillac attacked me from behind. He grasped me with the strength of a giant, but his deadly accurate thrust glanced off the iron. I broke free from his grasp at the same instant and stabbed him in the breast with a dagger I held ready."

"And you have said nothing?" asked Mademoiselle de Scudéri. "You have not made a statement to the authorities regarding what happened?"

"Allow me," said Miossens, "allow me to remark that such a statement, even if it did not cause my ruin, would at least involve me in a most loathsome trial. Would La Régnie, who scents crime everywhere, immediately believe me if I accused the honest Cardillac, the very embodiment of complete piety and virtue, of attempted murder? What if the sword of justice were pointed at me?"

"That would not be possible," cried Mademoiselle de Scudéri, "your birth, your rank—"

"Ah," Miossens interrupted, "remember the Maréchal of Luxembourg, who was locked in the Bastille because he was suspected of poisoning, as a result of having his horoscope read by Le Sage? Know, by Saint Denis, neither one hour of my freedom nor the lobe of my ear would I sacrifice to the raving La Régnie, who would be delighted to put his knife to all our throats."

"But in this way you will bring the innocent Brusson to the scaffold," interrupted Mademoiselle de Scudéri.

"Innocent?" Miossens responded. "Are you calling the accursed Cardillac's accomplice innocent, Mademoiselle? He who assisted him in his crimes and who has deserved death a hundred times over? No, in truth, he will justifiably bleed; and if I have related to you the actual facts of the case, Mademoiselle, it was on the presumption that you would somehow know how to make use of my secret in the interests of your protégé without delivering me into the clutches of the *Chambre Ardente.*"

Mademoiselle de Scudéri, completely delighted at the convincing confirmation of her conviction of Olivier's innocence, was not at all reticent about telling the Comte everything, since he already knew of Cardillac's crimes, and she requested that he accompany her to d'Andilly who would, when the entire story had been told to him under the seal of secrecy, advise them on what was next to be done.

D'Andilly, after Mademoiselle de Scudéri had told him as precisely as possible what had happened, asked again about the most minute particulars. He especially asked Comte Miossens if he was absolutely positive that it was Cardillac who had attacked him and whether he would be able to identify Olivier Brusson as the one who had carried the corpse away.

"Aside from the fact that I distinctly recognized the goldsmith in the moonlit night," Miossens replied, "I have also seen at La Régnie's the dagger with which Cardillac was stabbed. It is mine; it is distinguished by delicate work on the handle. I was standing only a pace from the young man, whose hat had fallen from his head, and I saw every feature distinctly. I would have no difficulty recognizing him."

D'Andilly sat in silence for a few moments, staring into space, then said: "There is absolutely no way to snatch Brusson from the hands of justice by ordinary methods. Because of Madelon, he refuses to name Cardillac as a robber and murderer. He may keep to this because even if he were to succeed in proving this accusation by revealing the secret entrance and the hoard of stolen jewels, he would nevertheless be condemned to die as an accomplice. The same would occur if Miossens were to inform the judges about what truly happened to the goldsmith. All that we can look forward to accomplishing for the time being is delay. Let Comte Miossens go to the Conciergerie and be confronted by Brusson so that he may identify him as the man who carried Cardillac's corpse away. Let him then hasten to La Régnie and say, 'I saw a man struck down in the rue Saint Honoré, and while I was standing next to the corpse, I saw another man dart forward and bend down over the body and, finding that there was still life in it, lift it over his shoulders and carry it away. In Olivier Brusson I recognize that man.' This statement will result in Brusson's once more being questioned by La Régnie in the presence of Miossens. Brusson will not be tortured and additional investigations will be conducted. Then will be the time to approach the King himself. Mademoiselle, doing this in the most diplomatic manner possible will be left to your discretion. It is my opinion that it would be best to reveal everything to the King. Comte Miossen's statement will support Brusson's confession, which may additionally be confirmed by a secret investigation of Cardillac's house. The matter cannot be handled through the Court's verdict, but must rather be resolved through a decision of the King, who, drawing upon intrinsic feeling, will grant pardon where a judge would mete out punishment."

Comte Miossens precisely followed the advice of d'Andilly, and everything took place precisely as he had predicted it would.

The next step was to approach the King. This was the major difficulty because he had such an intense aversion to Brusson, whom he believed to be singly responsible for the atrocious robberies and murders which had for so long held all of Paris in a reign of terror that the slightest allusion to the infamous trial enraged him. Madame de Maintenon, consistent with her principle of never speaking to the King of unpleasant subjects, refused to act as an intermediary. Brusson's fate was, therefore, utterly in the hands of Mademoiselle. After extended reflection she came to a decision upon which she immediately acted. She put on a black dress made of heavy silk, bedecked herself in Cardillac's magnificent jewelry, added a long black veil, and attired in this fashion, appeared at La Maintenon's at the hour when the King would be there. Dressed in this solemn manner, the venerable lady had about her an air which was designed to kindle reverential respect even from those jaded people who are wont to expend their trivial existences in the royal antechambers. Everyone made way for her; and even the King, in great surprise, rose when she entered and came forward to meet her. The stunning diamonds in her necklace and bracelets dazzled him, and he exclaimed, "By heaven, that is Cardillac's jewelry!" Turning to La Maintenon, he then smiled charmingly and said, "See, Madame La Marquise, how our lovely bride mourns her bridegroom."

"Oh, Gracious Sire," Mademoiselle de Scudéri said, as though following up the jest, "how would it become an agonized bride to bedeck herself in such magnificence? No, I have totally abandoned the goldsmith, and were it not that the terrifying image of his corpse being borne close before me keeps appearing before my eyes, he would be absent from my thought."

"What," the King asked, "you saw the poor devil?"

Mademoiselle de Scudéri then told him in a few words (not mentioning Brusson's role in the business) how chance had brought her to Cardillac's house immediately following the discovery of the murder. She described Madelon's frantic grief, the deep impression made upon her by the heavenly child, and how she had rescued the poor girl from the grasp of Desgrais amid the cheers of the populace. With continually heightening effect, she described the scenes with La Régnie, Desgrais, and Olivier himself. The King, transported by the very great vividness with which Mademoiselle de Scudéri told the tale, did not notice that they were talking about the notorious trial of that very Brusson whom he found so repulsive, and he listened wordlessly, only occasionally expressing his involvement through an exclamation. Before he was aware of what was going on, while still in a turmoil from the fantastic story just told to him, Mademoiselle lay at his feet begging mercy for Olivier Brusson.

"What are you doing?" the King exclaimed, taking both her hands and seating her in an armchair. "What are you doing, Mademoiselle? You have astonished me. It is a terrifying story. Who can vouch for the accuracy of Brusson's story?"

"Miossens' statement—the search of Cardillac's house—an inner conviction—oh, Madelon's virtuous heart that recognized the identical virtue in the unfortunate Brusson!" Mademoiselle de Scudéri responded.

The King was about to reply when he was distracted by a noise coming from near the door. Louvois, who had been at work in the next room, entered with a troubled expression. The King rose and left, Louvois following. Both Mademoiselle de Scudéri and La Maintenon considered this interruption to be dangerous because the King, having been caught by surprise once, might avoid falling into the trap again. But he returned in a few minutes, walked quickly back and forth two or three times, then, his hands behind his back, he stood before Mademoiselle de Scudéri and, without looking at her, said in a soft voice, "I would like to see your Madelon!"

To this, Mademoiselle de Scudéri replied, "Oh, gracious Sire, what great, great joy you are bestowing upon this poor, unfortunate child. You have only to give a sign, and the little one will be at your feet." Saying this, she tripped to the door as quickly as her heavy clothing permitted, called out that the King wished to have Madelon Cardillac admitted to his presence, and returned, weeping and sobbing with joy and gratitude. Having anticipated this favor, Mademoiselle de Scudéri had had Madelon accompany her, leaving her to wait with the chambermaid of the Marquise, with a short petition drawn up by d'Andilly in her hands. A few moments later she was lying prostrate at the King's feet. Fear, confusion, shyness, love and anguish forced the boiling blood of the poor girl to surge through her veins ever more quickly. Her cheeks glowed red, her eyes sparkled with pear-like teardrops, which now and then fell from her silky lashes onto her lovely lily-white bosom.

The King seemed to be moved by the wonderful beauty of the angelic child. He gently raised the girl and moved as if to kiss the hand which he was holding. He let it fall and looked at the precious child through eyes wet with tears which testified to deep emotion. La Maintenon whispered softly to Mademoiselle, "Isn't the little thing the very image of La Vallière. The King revels in the sweetest memories. Your game is won!"

Despite La Maintenon's having spoken softly, the King appeared to have heard. A blush came to his face; he cast a glance at La Maintenon; he read the petition which Madelon had given to him and then said, gently and kindly, "I find it easy to believe, dear child, that you should be certain of the innocence of your beloved, but let us hear what the *Chambre Ardente* has to say about it."

A light movement of the hand dismissed the little one, who was swimming in tears.

To her terror, Mademoiselle de Scudéri noted that the recollection of La Vallière, as propitious as it had appeared at first, had changed the King's intention as soon as the name had been mentioned by La Maintenon. It was perhaps felt by the King that he had been rudely reminded that he was about to sacrifice stern justice to beauty, or that he was like a dreamer who discovers that the beautiful image created by sleep quickly disappears even as he prepares to embrace it when he is awakened by a loud call. Perhaps he no longer could see his La Vallière before him, but thought only of Soeur Louise de la Miséricorde (La Vallière's cloister name among the Carmelite nuns), whose piety and penitence tortured him. There was nothing which could now be done other than to await the decision of the King.

Meanwhile, the statement made by Comte de Miossens to the *Chambre Ardente* had become known, and as often happens, public opinion being easily swayed from one extreme to the other, the man who had so recently been cursed by the mob as the vilest of murderers and threatened with being torn to pieces before reaching the scaffold, was now lamented as the innocent victim of a barbarous justice. His neighbors only now recalled his decorous behavior, his great love for Madelon, his faithfulness and complete devotion to the old goldsmith. Masses of people began assembling in front of La Régnie's palace and shouted threateningly, "Release Olivier Brusson, he is innocent"; and they even flung stones at the windows so that La Régnie was forced to seek protection from the incensed rabble with the *maréchaussée*.

Several days passed without Mademoiselle de Scudéri hearing anything new about Olivier Brusson's trial. Very disconsolate, she went to see La Maintenon, who assured her that the King was keeping absolutely silent on the subject and that it did not seem advisable to remind him of it. When she then, with a peculiar smile, asked how the little La Vallière was doing, Mademoiselle de Scudéri became convinced that inwardly the proud lady was grieved by the affair which threatened to entice the susceptible King into a realm whose magic spell was beyond her control. Consequently, nothing was to be hoped from La Maintenon.

With d'Andilly's help, Mademoiselle de Scudéri was ultimately able to discover that the King had had a long discussion with Comte de Miossens; also, that Bontems, the King's most trusted valet and deputy, had been to the Conciergerie and had spoken to Brusson; and finally, that the same Bontems had, in the company of several men, been to Cardillac's house and had spent a long time there. Claude Patru, the ground floor tenant, assured them that there had been rumbling noises overhead throughout the night and that he was certain that Olivier Brusson had been there because he had clearly recognized his voice. That the King was himself attempting to discover what the facts were was thus far clear, but what remained puzzling was the long delay in reaching a decision. La Régnie must have been exhausting every means to preclude his victim's being torn from his grasp. This nipped all hope in the bud.

Nearly a month had elapsed when La Maintenon sent word to Mademoiselle de Scudéri that the King desired to see her that evening in her, La Maintenon's, rooms.

Mademoiselle de Scudéri's heart beat furiously. She knew that Brusson's case was about to be decided. She informed poor Madelon, who fervently prayed to the Virgin and all the saints that they succeed in convincing the King of Brusson's innocence.

And yet it seemed as if the King had forgotten the entire matter; as usual, he passed the time engaged in pleasant conversation with La Maintenon and Mademoiselle de Scudéri, not directing a single syllable to poor Brusson. Finally Bontems appeared, approached the King, said a few words to him so softly that neither of the ladies understood any of it. Mademoiselle trembled inwardly. Then the King rose, walked to Mademoiselle de Scudéri and, his eyes radiant, said, "I congratulate you, Mademoiselle! Your protégé Olivier Brusson is free!" Mademoiselle de Scudéri, tears streaming from her eyes, unable to utter a word, was about to throw herself at the feet of the King. He prevented her from doing this, saying, "Now, now, Mademoiselle, you should be Lawyer of the Court and argue lawsuits on my behalf, since by Saint Denis, no one on earth is able to resist your eloquence. But," he added with greater seriousness, "but is not he who is protected by virtue not secure from every evil accusation, from the *Chambre Ardente* and from every court in the world?"

Mademoiselle de Scudéri now found words again, and glowing gratitude poured forth. The King interrupted her, told her that far more enthusiastic thanks awaited her at home than he could claim from her, because the happy Olivier was, at that very instant, undoubtedly embracing his Madelon. "Bontems," the King concluded, "is to pay you one thousand louis; present them to the little one in my name, as a dowry. Let her marry her Brusson, who does not deserve such a treasure, but then they are both to leave Paris. This is my wish."

La Martinière rushed to meet Mademoiselle de Scudéri, followed by Baptiste, both with faces beaming with joy, both triumphantly crying, "He is here—he is free! Oh, the dear young people!"

The ecstatic couple fell at the feet of Mademoiselle de Scudéri.

"Oh, I knew that you, only you, would rescue my husband," Madelon cried.

"Oh, my faith in you, my mother, stood firm in my soul," Olivier cried, and both kissed the hands of the worthy lady and shed a thousand burning tears. And then they embraced again and declared that the divine bliss of this moment outweighed all the unspeakable sufferings of the past, and they swore never to part till death.

A few days later a priest's blessing bound them to each other. Even if it had not been the King's wish, Brusson could not have remained in Paris, where everything reminded him of the heinous period of Cardillac's outrages, and where his tranquil existence might at any moment be shattered forever by some accidental disclosure of the evil secret now known to but a few. Immediately following the wedding, he and his young wife moved to Geneva, accompanied by the blessings of Mademoiselle de Scudéri. Handsomely equipped with Madelon's dowry, highly gifted in his profession, endowed with every civic virtue, he soon established a happy and carefree life there. In him were fulfilled the hopes whose frustration had led his father to the grave.

A year had passed since the departure of Brusson when a public proclamation signed by Harloy de Chauvalon, Archbishop of Paris, and Pierre Arnaud d'Andilly, Lawyer of the Court, appeared, stating that a repentant sinner had, under the seal of confession, turned over to the church a hoard of stolen jewelry. All who had, up until about the year 1680, been robbed of jewelry, particularly through a murderous attack in the open street, were invited to make a claim to d'Andilly, and if the description provided by the claimant precisely tallied with any of the jewelry and there was no reason to doubt the legitimacy of the claim, it would be returned to him.

Many who were described in Cardillac's list as having been merely struck down with a fist rather than having been murdered, gradually came to d'Andilly and, to their amazement, received the jewelry that had been stolen from them. What remained went to the treasury of the Church of Saint-Eustache.

The Doubles

The innkeeper of the Silver Lamb snatched his cap from his head, threw it on the ground, and stamping on it with both feet, shouted, "*Thus—thus*—you trample on integrity, on virtue, on love of your fellow man, you dishonorable neighbor, you godless innkeeper of the Golden Ram! Didn't that fellow just have his damned ram over the door newly gilded at great expense so that it gleams just to spite me, my dainty little silver lamb in contrast looking quite miserable and pale, all the customers passing me by to go to the glittering beast? That wretch lures away all sorts of rabble, like tightrope dancers,. strolling players, and conjurers, so that his inn is always swarming with people who are enjoying themselves and swilling down his vinegary, sulfurous wine, and I myself must drink up my excellent Hochheimer and Nierensteiner just to give it to a man who appreciates true wine. The actors have hardly left that damned Ram when the wise woman comes in with her raven, and the whole world streams in again and has its fortune told and ruins itself eating and drinking. I can just imagine how my evil neighbor treats the people that frequent his place, for that handsome young gentleman who was there a few days ago and has just come back, is not staying there but with me. But he will be waited on here like a prince. Oh hell! The young gentleman is going to the Golden Ram—That damned wise woman—he probably wants to see her. It is noon—his young lordship is heading towards the Golden Ram —he scorns the food at the Silver Lamb! Sir! Your Grace!"

Thus the innkeeper shouted out through the open window, but Deodatus Schwendy (that was the young man) let the torrent of people sweep him along to the neighboring inn.

Everyone was jammed together in the entrance and courtyard, and a gentle expectant murmur coursed back and forth. Several people were allowed into the main room; others came out, some with troubled faces, some with thoughtful ones, some with happy ones.

"I do not know," said a serious old man who had retreated to a corner with Deodatus, "I do not know why this disorder is not regulated by the authorities."

"Why?" asked Deodatus.

"Oh," the man continued, "Oh, you are a stranger here. Therefore you do not know that from time to time an old woman comes here who makes a fool of the populace with prophecies and oracles. She has a large raven with her who tells the people truly, or rather falsely, about everything they want to know. For although it is true that, in some strange way, many of the clever raven's pronouncements come true, I am still convinced that he utters hundreds of lies. Just look at the people when they come out, and you will easily notice that the woman with the raven cheats them. Does such ruinous superstition have to exist in our age, which, thank God, is completely enlightened—"

Deodatus heard nothing more of the excited man's chatter, for just at that moment a handsome young man, pale as death, tears sparkling in his eyes, emerged from the room which he had cheerfully and smilingly entered a few minutes ago.

Then it seemed to Deodatus that, hidden behind the draperies through which the people slipped, there really was a dark mysterious power who revealed future disasters to happy people, thus spitefully destroying the pleasure of the moment.

The thought occurred to him of going in himself and questioning the raven about what the next days or even moments were going to bring him. Deodatus had come from far away, sent to Hohenflüh by his father, old Amadeus Schwendy, in a mysterious fashion.

Here, at the peak of his life, his future was to be decided by a marvelous occurrence that his father had prophesied in dark, mysterious words. With his own eyes he was to see a being who had so far been entangled in his life only as in a dream. He was to test whether this dream, which, from the spark tossed into his soul, was growing stronger and brighter, could become a part of his external, ordinary life. If this was so, he was to take action.

He was already at the door to the room; the curtain was already lifted. He heard a repulsive, croaking voice, and an icy shudder passed through him. It seemed as if an unknown power was pushing him back, but other people thrust ahead of him; and so, without consciously being aware of it, he climbed the stairs and came to a room where the noon meal was being prepared for the numerous customers of the inn.

The innkeeper approached him in a friendly way. "Well, well, Herr Haberland! How nice! Even though you are staying across the way in that wretched Silver Lamb, you mustn't miss the world-famous meals at the Golden Ram. I have the honor of preparing this place for you."

Deodatus knew very well that the innkeeper had mistaken him for someone else; however, he was so completely constrained by a disinclination to speak, which every violent inner turmoil occasioned, that he did not bother to clarify the error, but rather sat down in silence. The wise woman was the object of the table conversation, and various opinions were expressed. Some declared that it was all a childish conjuring trick, whereas others actually credited her with an absolute knowledge of life's mysterious intricacies and with the gift of prophecy.

A little, old, plumpish gentleman, who frequently helped himself to tobacco from a golden box, after rubbing it on his sleeve, smiled very cleverly and said that the highly intelligent Council, of which he had the honor of being its least member, would soon put a stop to the accursed witch, primarily because she was a bungler and not a true and proper witch. And it was not such a trick to have everybody's life in her pocket and to have the raven predict it in peculiarly bad and stylized sentences. After all, at the previous fair there had been a painter and picture seller in whose booth everyone could find his own likeness.

Everybody laughed.

"That," cried a young man to Deodatus, "that is something for you, Herr Haberland. You yourself are a fine portrait painter, but you haven't yet developed your art to such a high point!"

Now that he was addressed for the second time as Herr Haberland, who, he assumed, was a painter, Deodatus could not suppress an inner shudder, for it suddenly seemed to him as if he were, in his shape and being, the sinister specter of this Haberland, who was unknown to him. This inner dread intensified to horror when, before he could reply to the one who had addressed him as Haberland, a young man in traveling clothes rushed up to him and, embracing him violently, cried loudly, "Haberland—my dearest George—I have finally found you! Now we can happily continue our journey to beautiful Italy! But you look so pale and distracted?"

Deodatus returned the embrace of the unknown stranger as if he really were the long-sought painter George Haberland. He noticed clearly that he was entering the circle of marvelous occurrences of which his father had warned him by all sorts of hints. He must submit to everything the dark powers had ordained. But a deeply ironical anger toward an unknown, remote, arbitrary control under which one must strive to maintain one's own ego overwhelmed him. Burning with anger, he held the stranger firmly in his grasp and cried, "Indeed, unknown brother, why shouldn't I seem muddled, since I and my ego have just put on another person as if he were another overcoat, one which is too tight here and two wide there, and which still squeezes me. Indeed, young man, am I really the painter George Haberland?"

"I don't know," said the stranger, "what you seem like to me today, George. Are you trapped again in that strange state that attacks you like a periodic illness? What I really wanted to ask is what you meant by all the incomprehensible nonsense that filled your last letter."

With that the stranger pulled out a letter and opened it. As soon as Deodatus looked in it, he cried out as if he had been painfully touched by an invisible hostile power. The handwriting in the letter was exactly like his.

The stranger cast a quick glance at Deodatus and then slowly and softly read the letter:

" 'Dear brother-in-art Berthold. Alas, you do not know what a somber, painful, and yet soothing melancholy possesses me the farther I wander. Would you believe that my art, indeed, my whole life and everything I do, often seems flat and paltry? But then the sweet dreams of my happy, carefree youth awake. I lie stretched out on the grass in the old priest's little garden and gaze upwards, while the lovely spring rides in on the morning's golden clouds. The little flowers, awakened by the glow, open their dear little eyes and scatter their fragrance like a marvelous hymn of praise. Oh, Berthold, my heart is nearly bursting with love, with longing, with fervent desire! Where will I find her again, she who is my whole life, my whole being? I am planning to meet you in Hohenflüh, where I am spending several days. It seems to me that something special will happen to me in Hohenflüh, but where this belief comes from I do not know!'

"Now tell me," continued the engraver Berthold—that is who the stranger was—after he had read the above. "Now tell me, brother George, why you have succumbed to such effeminate ravings when you are in your carefree youth and on a wonderful journey to the land of art."

"Dear brother-in-art," replied Deodatus, "it is a crazy, peculiar thing that is wrong with me. Just as it is quite comic that I did write from the depths of my soul what is written there and that I nevertheless am not George Haberland at all, whom you—"

At that moment the young man who had earlier greeted Deodatus as George Haberland came in and said that George was right to have come back to see the wise woman. He should not pay any attention to the chattering at the table, for even if the raven's prophecies did not mean very much, it was still most amazing when the wise woman herself performed, spouting forth mysterious sayings in a wild rapture like a second Sibyl or Pythia, while hollow, mysterious voices sounded around her. She was about to give such a performance, which George should be sure not to miss, in a spacious woodsy part of the garden.

Berthold went off to attend to a number of essential matters in Hohenflüh. Deodatus stayed to drain a couple of bottles with the young man and thus passed the time until sunset.

The company that had assembled in the room finally broke up to go to the garden. A tall, haggard, well-dressed man, who seemed to have just arrived, passed them on the threshold. He was on the point of entering the room, but turning around again, his glance fell on Deodatus. His hand still on the latch, he stopped as if rooted to the ground! A wild fire glowed in his melancholy eyes, while a

deathly pallor crossed his twitching face. He took a few steps toward
the company, but then, as if suddenly thinking better of it, turned
around again, ran into the room and slammed the door behind him.
Nobody could understand what he was muttering.

The others were more aware of the stranger's behavior than was
Deodatus, who had not paid him any particular attention. They
went to the woodsy area.

The last rays of the afternoon sun were shining on a tall figure
wrapped from top to toe in a massive muddy-yellow garment, her
back turned toward the spectators. Beside her on the ground lay a
large raven, with drooping wings, as if dead. Everyone was captivated by the strange, horrible sight; the whisperings ceased, and in
oppressive silence, all waited to see what the figure would do.

A rustling sound like splashing waves resounded through the
dark shrubbery and then turned into audible words.

"Phosphorous has been subdued. The kettle gleams in the west!
Eagle of the night, fly up to the awakened dreams!"

Then the raven lifted his head, beat his wings, and flew upwards, croaking. The figure stretched out her arms, her garment
slipped down, and a tall, splendid woman stood there in a white
pleated robe with a belt of sparkling stones, her black hair piled
high. Her bare neck, and arms were youthfully rounded.

"That's not the old woman!" whispered the spectators.

Then a distant, somber voice began, "Do you hear the howling
and crying of the evening wind?"

A still more distant voice murmured, "Sorrowing will begin
when the glowworm shines!"

Then a horrible lacerating shriek resounded through the air.
The woman spoke: "Distant sorrowing sounds, have you freed yourselves from the breast of man so that you can raise yourselves in a
mighty choir? But you must die away in delight, for the power enthroned in the blessed heavens that command you is desire."

The somber voices howled more loudly, "Hope has died! Desire's delight was hope. Desire without hope is nameless agony!"

The woman sighed deeply and cried out in despair, "Hope is
death! Life the cruel sport of the dark powers!"

Then Deodatus cried out involuntarily from the depths of his
soul, "Natalie!"

The woman spun around, and an old, fearfully distorted

woman's face stared at him with glowing eyes. Rushing at him angrily with outspread arms, the woman shrieked, "What do you want
here? Away! Away! Murder pursues you! Save Natalie!"

The raven dove through the trees toward Deodatus, croaking
horribly, "Murder! Murder!"

Seized by a wild horror, nearly out of his senses, Deodatus fled
towards his dwelling.

The innkeeper told him that in the meantime a strange, richly
dressed gentleman had inquired for him several times, describing
Deodatus exactly without mentioning him by name, and that he
finally had left a note.

Deodatus opened the note that the innkeeper handed him and
which was correctly addressed to him. He found the following
words:

> I do not know whether to call it an unheard-of-impertinence
> or insanity that you let yourself be seen here. If you are not a
> dishonorable villain, as I must now assume, depart at once
> from Hohenflüh or you can expect that I will find means to
> cure you forever of your folly.
>
> Graf Hektor von Zelies[1]

"Hope is death. Life the cruel sport of the dark powers!"
Deodatus murmured to himself gloomily when he had read the
above. He was determined not to be driven out of Hohenflüh by
an unknown person's threats that were based on some curious mistake, but rather to oppose with firm courage and manly strength
that fate which some dark power had ordained for him. His whole
soul was filled with an anxious presentiment, his heart was about to
burst, and he yearned to get outside into the open. Night had descended when he hurried out through Neudorfer Gate, his
loaded pistol in his pocket, mindful of his unknown menacing pursuer. He had already reached the open space in front of the gate
when he felt himself seized from behind and dragged backwards.

"Hurry—hurry! Save Natalie! The time has come!" someone
murmured in his ear. It was the horrible woman who had seized
him and was dragging him along.

A carriage stopped nearby, the door was opened, the old woman

---

1. "Graf" is comparable to an earl in England and to a count on the
Continent. The German word is used throughout, as is the title Fürst, for which
there is no precise English equivalent, "sovereign prince" being the closest.

helped him in and climbed in after him. He felt himself encircled by soft arms, and a sweet voice whispered, "My dear friend! At last! At last you have come!"

"Natalie, my Natalie!" he cried, clasping his beloved in his arms, almost fainting with rapture.

They drove on quickly. The bright glow of torches suddenly flared up through the leaves of the thick forest.

"It is they!" cried the old woman, "one step forward and we are lost!"

Deodatus, who had come to his senses, had the carriage stopped, climbed out, and cocked pistol in hand, crept quietly towards the gleam of the torches, which suddenly vanished. He hurried back to the carriage, but stopped, rooted in horror, when he saw a male figure, who had his voice, say, "The danger is past!" and then climb in.

Deodatus was about to dash after the rapidly vanishing carriage when a shot from the bushes knocked him to the ground.

2

It is necessary to tell the gentle reader that the distant place from which old Amadeus Schwendy sent his son to Hohenflüh was a country estate in the neighborhood of Lucerne. The little town of Hohenflüh, in the principality of Reitlingen, was, however, situated about six or seven hours from Sonsitz, the Residence of Furst Remigius. If there was gaiety and noise in Hohenflüh, there was, contrariwise, as complete a quiet in Sonsitz as perhaps in Herrnhut or Neusalz.[2] Everyone tiptoed around as if wearing socks and even a necessary quarrel was carried on in muffled voices. The usual pleasures of a Fürst's Residence, such as balls, concerts and plays, did not exist, and if the wretched people of Sonsitz, who were doomed to sadness, for once wanted to have a good time, they had to go over to Hohenflüh. The following explains why that was so.

Fürst Remigius, formerly a friendly, high spirited gentleman, had been for years, probably for more than twenty, plunged into a deep melancholy that bordered on insanity. Never wishing to leave Sonsitz, he wanted his abode to resemble a wilderness, ruled by the gloomy silence of desolate grief. He cared to see only his most intimate councillors and the most necessary servants, and even these did

2. The Herrnhuter monastic order was located in those two towns in Saxony and Silesia. Silence and patience were two of their rules.

not dare to speak unless the Fürst addressed them. He drove around in an enclosed carriage, and nobody was allowed to indicate by even a gesture that he knew the Fürst was in the carriage.

There were only vague rumors as to the cause of this melancholy. So much was certain, that at the time when the wife of the Fürst gave birth to the Crown Prince, and the whole country resounded with joy, the mother and child vanished a few months later in some incomprehensible fashion. Many thought that the wife and son had been kidnapped as victims of a shocking intrigue, but others claimed that the Fürst had repudiated her. To support this opinion they pointed out that Graf von Törny, the first minister and the Fürst's decided favorite, had been removed from the court at the same time and that it seemed certain that the Fürst had uncovered an illicit relationship between the Fürstin and the Graf and that he doubted the legitimacy of his son.

But all those who were closely acquainted with the Fürstin were completely convinced that such a moral lapse on the part of the Fürstin, a woman of purest, spotless virtue, was quite unthinkable, quite impossible.

Nobody in Sonsitz, on pain of severe punishment, was allowed to utter a single word about the disappearance of the Fürstin. Spies were lurking everywhere; the sudden arrest of all those who discussed it anywhere except in their own rooms indicated the incredible extent of the eavesdropping. Similarly, no one was allowed to speak a word about the Fürst, his sorrow, or about all his activities; and this tyrannical control was the greatest grievance of the inhabitants of any little town with a Resident Fürst, who liked nothing better than to discuss their Fürst and his court.

The Fürst's favorite abode was a little country house with an extensive hedged-in park situated close to the city gates of Sonsitz.

One day, when the Fürst was strolling along the gloomy, overgrown paths of the park, surrendering himself to the devastating sorrow which raged in his breast, he suddenly heard a peculiar noise close by. Inarticulate sounds—a moaning—a groaning—at times a repulsive squeaking—a grunting—and then curse words muttered as if in a choking rage. Furious at whoever had dared to enter the park in direct violation of the strictest prohibition, the Fürst quickly stepped forth from the shrubbery and saw a sight that would have made the most morose Smelfungus[3] burst out laughing.

3. One of the outrageous characters in Lawrence Sterne's *A Sentimental Journey through France and Italy* (1768).

Two men, one tall and emaciated, the other a lively little Falstaff dressed in the very smart Sunday clothes of the typical townsman, were engaged in a violent fistfight. The tall man was jabbing with his long arms, his clenched fists not unlike maces, so mercilessly at the little man that further resistance seemed useless and nothing but quick flight advisable. Like the Parthians, the little man was about to flee while fighting courageously, when the tall one firmly seized his opponent's hair. A poor idea! The wig remained in his hand while the little one, strategically using the cloud of powder which encircled him, ducked quickly, and with outstretched fists darted in so nimbly and cleverly at the tall one that the latter somersaulted backwards with a piercing cry. Then the little one hurled himself on the tall one and, using the curled fingers of his left hand as a hook, clawed at his opponent's collar and, with his knees and his right fist, belabored him so mercilessly that the latter, purple as a cherry, uttered horrible sounds. But then the tall one dug his sharp fingers so powerfully into the little one's sides and with the strength of despair gave such a violent jerk that the little one was hurled into the air like a ball and landed on the ground right in front of the Fürst.

"You dogs!" shouted the Fürst in the voice of an enraged lion. "You dogs! What devil let you in? What are you up to?"

One can imagine the horror with which the two furious gymnasts picked themselves up from the ground and how they stood before the enraged Fürst, like poor lost sinners, quaking and trembling, incapable of uttering a word or even a sound.

"Be gone!" cried the Fürst. "Be gone at once. I will have you driven out with whips if you stay a moment longer!"

Then the tall one fell on his knees and roared in utter despair, "Your most Serene Highness—most Gracious Sovereign—justice— blood for blood!"

The word "justice" was still one of the few that affected the Fürst's ear intensely. He looked at the tall one sharply and spoke more moderately. "What is it? Speak, but avoid all stupid words and make it brief."

The gentle reader may have already suspected that the two valiant warriors were none other than the two famous innkeepers of the Golden Ram and the Silver Lamb from Hohenflüh. Because of their ever-increasing animosity, they had come to the insane conclusion that since the wise Town Council had not been helpful, they should bring to the attention of the Fürst all the wrongs that they imagined they had suffered from each other; and it so happened that both had arrived at the same moment before the outermost gate of the park, which a simple-minded gardener's boy had opened for them. From now on, both can be very conveniently designated by the names of their inns.

So—the Golden Ram, encouraged by the Fürst's calmer question, was about to begin when such a fearful croaking and coughing fit attacked him, as a result of his having been half-choked, that he was unable to produce a single word.

The Silver Lamb promptly availed himself of this unfortunate occurrence and with great eloquence described all the harmful things the Golden Ram had done to him—enticing away all his customers by taking in all kinds of clowns, charlatans, prophets, and other rabble. He described the wise woman with the raven; he spoke of her despicable tricks, of the prophecies with which she was duping people. That seemed to capture the Fürst's attention. He had the woman described from top to toe; he asked when she had come and where she was staying. The Lamb said that, for his part, he considered the woman nothing but a deceitful, half-mad gypsy, whom the wise Council in Hohenflüh ought to arrest.

The Fürst directed a sparkling, penetrating glance at the poor Lamb, who immediately sneezed violently as if he had looked into the sun.

The Golden Ram profited from this, having meanwhile recovered from his coughing fit and having been waiting for the moment when he could interrupt the Lamb. The Ram reported in sweet and gentle sounding words that everything that the Lamb had said about his taking in dangerous, unauthorized rabble was the most disgraceful slander. The Ram especially praised the wise woman, whom the cleverest, most brilliant gentlemen, the greatest geniuses of Hohenflüh, gentlemen to whom he daily had the honor of serving dinner, claimed was a supernatural being to be respected more highly than the most trained somnambulists. Oh, but things were dreadful at the Silver Lamb. The Silver Lamb had enticed away from him a charming, handsome young gentleman when he had returned to Hohenflüh, and in the very next night a murderous attack had been made on him in his room, and he had been wounded by a pistol shot and was hopelessly ill.

In his rage, forgetting all caution and all respect for the Fürst, the Silver Lamb cried out that the person who claimed that the young gentleman George Haberland had been attacked and wounded in his room was a most contemptible rascal and the most out-and-out scamp that ever wore leg-irons or swept the streets. Rather, the superb police in Hohenflüh had ascertained that on that night he had been taking a walk by the Neudorfer gate, that a carriage had stopped from which a feminine voice had called, "Save Natalie!" and that the young gentleman had then immediately sprung into the carriage.

"Who was the woman in the carriage?" asked the Fürst in a severe voice.

"They say," stuttered the Golden Ram, just to be able to talk again, "they say that the wise woman—"

The words stuck in the Golden Ram's throat at the Fürst's frightful expression; and when the latter asked in a deadly voice, "Well? What else?" the Silver Lamb, who was standing in the shade outside the path of those rays, interrupted, stammering, "Yes, the wise woman and the painter George Haberland—he was shot in the woods—the whole town knows that—they fetched him out of the woods and brought him to me early in the morning—he is still at my place—but he will probably recover because of the care he will receive at my place—and the strange Graf—the Graf Hektor von Zelies—"

"What? Who?" cried the Fürst so loudly that the little Silver Lamb recoiled a few steps. "Enough!" the Fürst then continued in a rough, commanding voice. "Enough! Be off with you at once! Whoever serves his customers best will have the most trade. If I hear of the slightest quarreling between you two, the Council will tear down the signs from your houses and have you put out of the gates of Hohenflüh!"

After this brief, vigorous decree, the Fürst left the two innkeepers and vanished quickly among the trees.

The Fürst's anger had calmed their agitated tempers. Completely crushed, the little Silver Lamb and the Golden Ram looked at one another sorrowfully, tears rolled from their gloomy eyes, and with the simultaneous cry "Oh godfather!" they fell in each other's arms. While the Golden Ram embraced the Silver Lamb tightly and, bending over, sprinkled the grass with floods of tears, the latter sobbed with bitter sorrow on the breast of his reconciled opponent. It was a sublime moment!

But the two royal gamekeepers who were hurrying thither did

not seem to appreciate such emotional scenes, for without further
ado they seized the Golden Ram as well as the Silver Lamb by their
pinions, as one usually says, and threw them both out of the gate
with anything but gentleness.

3

Though I've wandered hither thither
Over meadow, lea, and field,
I have only seen hopes wither
Only seen joys vanish thither
In the giddy, noisy world.

What can end his timid hoping?
What the pain that's in my heart?
Aching sorrow, bitter moping,
Useless striving, helpless groping—
Will all joy fore'er depart?

Will I ever hope be sharing?
Does a gleam still light my star?
Must I longer pain be bearing?
Won't my sorrow be declaring
If she's near or if she's far?

She who is my inner being,
She who is my joy always.
Lost in blissful, distant dreaming,
Drunk with love my eyes are gleaming,
Trembling in her eyes I gaze.

My beloved, sweet, appealing,
Now has vanished in the night.
Will I never find true healing,
Never friendship's ease be feeling,
Has that vanished from my sight?[4]

Berthold, the copper engraver, while humming this song composed by his friend the painter George Haberland, was stretched
out under a large tree on a slight rise and was trying to sketch

---

4. The translators are embarrassed by this rendering. They would have
it known that the original is hardly better.

accurately in his notebook a section of the village that lay below him in the valley.

At the final words, tears streamed from his eyes. He thought vividly of his friend, he whom he had often roused, by a cheerful word or by a lively discussion of art, from the depressed, desperate mood to which he had been succumbing for some time, and from whom an inexplicable misfortune had now separated him. "No," he cried finally, quickly packing up his equipment and leaping to his feet. "No, being consoled by your friend is not lost to you, George! I am off to seek you out and not to leave you until I see you in the lap of happiness and peace."

He hurried back to the village that he had left a few hours before and was about to continue on to Hohenflüh.

It was a Sunday. Evening was coming on; the country folk were hurrying to the taverns. An oddly dressed man marched into the village, blowing a merry march on a *Papagenoflöte* which was braced on his chest, and vigorously beating a drum which was hung around his neck. An old gypsy woman, valiantly striking a triangle, followed him. Ahead of them, slowly and carefully, strode a stately donkey, laden with two fully packed baskets on which two cunning little monkeys were skipping about and frolicking. From time to time the man stopped blowing and began a peculiar, screeching song, in which the gypsy woman, straightening up a bit, joined with a piercing voice. When the donkey also joined in with his mournful brays, and the monkeys squeaked, everything combined to a cheerful, amusing chorus, as one can readily imagine

The young man captured Berthold's entire attention, for it was evident that he was young, although his face was smeared with all kinds of ugly colors and was distorted by a huge doctorial wig on top of which rested a tiny little braided cap. He also wore a shabby red velvet coat with large, gold cloth facings, an open Hamlet collar, black silk britches in the latest fashion, shoes with large, gaily colored rosettes, and an elegant sword hung at his side.

He was making funny faces and leaping around gaily, causing the peasants to laugh uproariously; but this person seemed to Berthold to be the mysterious ghost of insanity; and besides that, when he looked the crazy man in the eye, feelings which he could not explain seemed to arise within him.

The man finally stopped in the middle of the grassy square in

front of the tavern and beat out a loud roll on his drum. At this sig-
nal the country folk formed a large circle, and the man announced
that he was now going to produce before the honorable audience a
spectacle as fine as any that potentates and gentlemen would get to
see.

The gypsy woman then went around the circle offering coral
beads, ribbons, and holy pictures for sale while making all sorts of
nonsensical remarks and gestures, sometimes telling a fortune to
this or that young girl by looking at her hand and sending the blood
to her cheeks by talking about a fiancé, a wedding, and a baptism,
while the other girls giggled and laughed.

Meanwhile the young man had unpacked the basket, set up a
small framework, and hung it with curtains. Berthold recognized
preparations for a puppet play, which was then performed in the
customary Italian manner. Punch was particularly lively and behaved very bravely, saving himself from dangerous situations with
skill, and always getting the upper hand over his enemies.

The play seemed over when suddenly the puppeteer, with a
fearfully distorted expression, stuck his head up into the puppet
stage and stared out at the audience with lifeless, glazed eyes. Punch
on one side and the doctor on the other seemed appalled at the sight
of the gigantic head; then they recovered, carefully inspected the
face through their spectacles, touched his nose, mouth, and forehead, which they could scarcely reach, and began a very deep,
scholarly argument about the nature of the head and about the
body to which it might be attached, and whether or not a body
could be presumed to belong to it. The doctor advanced the most
absurd hypotheses; Punch, on the other hand, showed a good deal
of common sense and had the most amusing notions. Finally they
both agreed that they could not assume that a body belonged to the
head or that there was a body; but the doctor said that when
Nature had created this monstrosity she was making use of a figure
of speech, a synecdoche, in which a part is used for the whole.
Punch, however, insisted that the head was an unfortunate fellow
whose body got mislaid because of all his thinking and his crazy
thoughts and who, completely lacking any fists, could defend himself from boxes on the ear and pokes in the nose only by cursing.

Berthold soon noticed that this was not the kind of joking that
amuses curious folk, but that it was the dark spirit of the irony
which arises in the person whose soul is at war with itself. His happy,

friendly spirits could not endure it, so he went to the tavern and had a modest supper served at an isolated table.

Soon he heard drums, pipes, and triangles in the distance. The country folk were streaming toward the tavern; the play was over.

At the very moment when Berthold was about to continue his journey, the droll puppeteer rushed toward him with a loud cry.

"Berthold—my dearest brother!" He snatched the wig from his head and quickly wiped the makeup from his face.

"What! George! Is it possible?" Berthold stammered with effort, nearly paralyzed.

"What is the matter with you? Don't you know me?" George Haberland asked in astonishment. Berthold explained that unless he wished to believe in ghosts he could not doubt that it was his friend he was seeing, but he could not figure out how this could possibly be so.

"Didn't you come," continued Berthold, "didn't you come to Hohenflüh as we had arranged? Didn't I meet you there—didn't something strange happen to you with a mysterious woman at the Golden Ram? Didn't unknown people want to use you to help carry off a girl whom you yourself called Natalie? Weren't you severely wounded by a pistol shot in the forest? Didn't I take my leave of you with a heavy heart when you were lying on your bed, weakened and mortally wounded? Didn't you speak about an inexplicable event—of a Graf Hektor von Zelies?"

"Stop! You are stabbing my soul with glowing daggers!" George cried with frenzied pain. "Yes," he then continued more calmly, "yes, brother Berthold, it is very certain that I have a second ego, a doppelgänger, who pursues me, who wishes to do me out of my life and rob me of my Natalie!"

Completely silenced by his misery, George sank onto the grassy bank.

Berthold sat down beside him and sang softly while he gently pressed his friend's hand:

> Friendship's ease you'll soon be feeling,
> It's not vanished from your sight.

"I understand you completely," said George, while drying the tears that streamed from his eyes. "I understand you completely, my dear brother Berthold! It is not right that I did not long ago open my heart to you, that I didn't tell you everything. You have

long been able to guess that I am in love. The story of this love—
it is so simple, so ordinary, that you can read about it in any insipid
novel. I am a painter, and so it is in the ordinary course of events
that I should fall deeply in love with a lovely young girl I was drawing. That really did happen to me during my stay in Strasbourg
when I was doing a lot of bread-and-butter work—you know that by
that I mean portrait painting. I acquired the reputation of being
an excellent portraitist who could steal likenesses for miniatures
right out of mirrors; and so it happened that an old lady who ran a
pension turned to me and begged me to paint a young lady who was
staying with her for a distant father. I saw, I painted Natalie. O ye
eternal powers! My fate was sealed! Now truly, brother Berthold,
there is nothing special in all that, is there? But do listen—much
may still be of interest. Let me tell you that since my earliest childhood the picture of a divine woman, towards whom all desire and
love were directed, has hovered in my dreams and presentiments.
The crude attempts of the artistic boy reveal this picture, as do the
more finished paintings of the maturing artist. It was Natalie! That
is extraordinary, Berthold! I can also tell you that the same spark
which inflamed me had also fallen in Natalie's breast so that we saw
each other secretly. O love's vanished happiness! Natalie's father,
Graf Hektor von Zelies, arrived; the little picture of his daughter
pleased him; I was invited to paint him also. When the Graf saw me,
he became strangely moved, I might say dismayed. He asked me
with noticeable anxiety about the circumstances of my life, and
then screamed rather than spoke, while his eyes gleamed, that he
didn't want to be painted, but that I was a fine painter, that I should
go to Italy immediately, and that he would give me money if I
needed it!

"I go? I, separate myself from Natalie? Well, there are ladders,
bribable maids—we saw each other secretly. She was in my arms
when the Graf entered. 'Ah, as I suspected!', screamed the Graf in a
rage and rushed at me with a drawn dagger. Without his being able
to stab me, I ran past him and escaped. The next day he had vanished with Natalie, without leaving a trace!

"It so happened that I came upon the gypsy woman, whom you
saw with me today. She jabbered out such strange prophecies that I
did not want to pay any attention to them, but to go my way. Then
she spoke in a tone that penetrated my very soul, 'George, child of
my heart, have you forgotten Natalie?' Whether witchcraft exists or

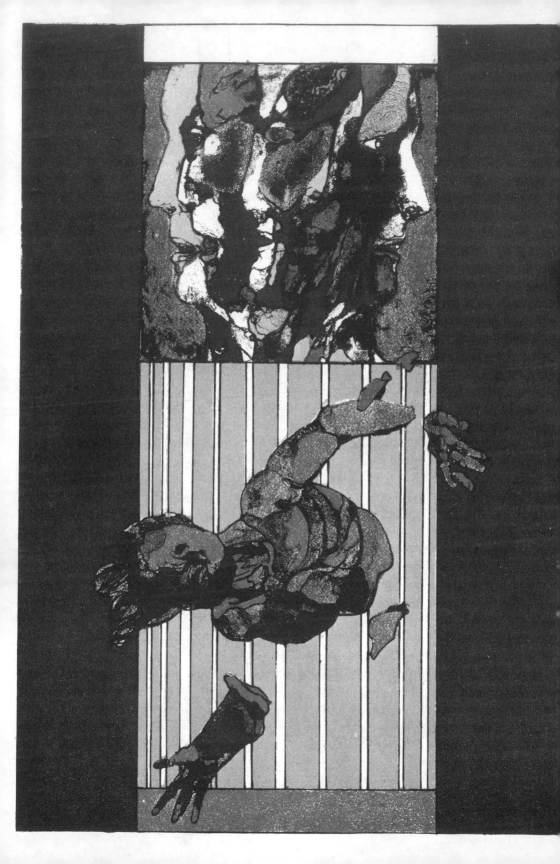

not, at any rate the old woman knew about my love affair, knew exactly how everything had occurred, indicated that through her I would possess Natalie, and ordered me to arrive in Hohenflüh at a particular time, where I would find her, although in a quite different form. Well, Berthold, don't let me make too long a story of it —my breast was burning—a carriage rolled up to me—stopped— the riders were coming nearer— 'Jesus,' cried a voice in the carriage —it was Natalie's voice—the riders turned aside. 'The danger is over,' I said and climbed into the carriage— At that moment a shot rang out—away we went! My suspicions had not deceived me—it was Natalie; it was the old gypsy woman—she kept her word."

"Happy George!" said Berthold.

"Happy?" repeated George, a wild laugh bursting forth. "While we were still in the forests, the military police caught up with us. I leapt out of the carriage, the gypsy woman after me. She seized me with her great strength and dragged me into the dark bushes—Natalie was lost. I was in a rage. The gypsy woman knew how to calm me, to convince me that resistance was impossible but that all hope was not yet lost. I trusted her blindly, and the way you see us here is her plan for escaping pursuit by a bloodthirsty enemy."

At that moment the old gypsy came up and said in a croaking voice, "George, the glowworm is already shining; we must away across the mountains."

It seemed to Berthold that the old woman was fraudulently deceiving George so as to trick him out of more money. Angrily he turned to the old woman and declared that he, as George's best friend, would no longer allow him to sacrifice his art for a filthy vagrant life and base tricks, and that George was to go with him to Italy; and he asked what claim she had on his sworn friend.

Then the old woman rose; her expression seemed to become ennobled; dark fire blazed from her eyes; and suddenly her whole being was dignity and majesty itself. She spoke in a firm, rich voice. "You ask me what claim I have on this youth? I know you very well. You are the engraver Berthold. You are his friend, but I—O ye eternal powers—I am—his mother!"

Then she clasped George in her arms and pressed him stormily to her breast. But suddenly a convulsive trembling overcame her; averting her head she pushed George away. Exhausted, half fainting, she slipped down on the grassy bank, whimpering while she veiled her face with the large cloak she had put around herself. "Do not stare at me so, George. Why do you constantly reproach me for my crime? You must go—go!"

"Mother!" cried George, hurling himself at the gypsy's feet.

She clasped him violently in her arms, sighing deeply, for she was incapable of words. She seemed to sink into a sleep. But soon she rose with an effort, spoke again, quite the gypsy, in a croaking voice: "George, the glowworm is already shining. We must away across the mountains!" and strode slowly away.

George hurled himself speechless on his friend's breast, whose tongue was tied by an astonishment that bordered on terror.

Soon Berthold heard the drumming, the piping, the ringing, the horrible singing, the donkey's braying, the monkeys' squeaking, and the shouts of the accompanying country folk, until everything died away in the far distance.

4

Foresters, who were roaming through the forest early in the morning, found young Deodatus Schwendy lying unconscious in his blood. Brandy, which they were carrying in hunting flasks, performed the service of recalling him to life. They bound up the wound in his breast as best they could, placed him in a carriage, brought him to Hohenflüh to the inn, the Silver Lamb.

The shot had only grazed his breast; the bullet had not penetrated him, and therefore the surgeon declared that there was no fear for his life, although the shock and night cold had produced a state of exhaustion. Powerful remedies, however, would soon ease that.

If Deodatus had not been able to feel pain in his wound, the whole inexplicable occurrence would have seemed to him like a dream. It seemed clear to him that the secret to which his father had referred in dark words had been about to reveal itself, but then some hostile being had interfered and destroyed his hopes. This hostile being—who else could it be but the painter George Haberland, who was so like him that he was everywhere confused with him.

"And what," he said to himself, "if Natalie, love's beautiful dream, who has always been a premonition in my life, should only belong to *him*, my unknown doppelgänger, my second ego; what if he should rob me of her, if all my desires, all my hopes, should remain forever unfulfilled?"

Deodatus lost himself in mournful thoughts. Ever-thicker veils seemed to conceal his future; all his reveries faded; he realized that he could only hope for some chance event that might perhaps reveal secrets to him which were probably ominous, even dangerous, since his father, old Amadeus Schwendy, had not dared to reveal them to him.

The surgeon had just left Deodatus. He was alone when the door was quietly opened and a large man, wrapped in a cloak, came in. When he threw back the cloak, Deodatus immediately recognized the stranger whom he had met at the threshhold of the inn, the Golden Ram, and he guessed that he must be the same person who wrote him the inexplicable letter, namely, Graf Hektor von Zelies. It was he.

The Graf seemed to be making an effort to soften the somber, piercing glance which seemed peculiar to him, and he even forced himself to a certain friendliness.

"Probably," he began, "probably you are astonished to see me here, Herr Haberland, but you will be even more astonished when I explain to you that I am here to offer you peace and reconciliation in the event that certain conditions—"

Deodatus interrupted the Graf, assuring him vehemently that he was absolutely not the painter George Haberland, that there must be some unfortunate mistake which seemed to be about to hurl him into a labyrinth of enigmatical events. The Graf stared him in the face and then said, with a look in which the devil was smiling a little, "Did you not wish, my dear Herr Schwendy, or my dear Herr Haberland, or however you like to call yourself, to abduct Natalie?"

"Natalie, O Natalie!" sighed Deodatus from the depths of his soul.

"Aha," said the Graf with the most bitter anger. "You love Natalie very much, no doubt?"

"More," replied Deodatus, sinking back on his cot in weakness, "more than my life. She will be mine; she must be mine. Hope and desire glow in my innermost soul."

"What unheard of impertinence!" the Graf flared up in rage. "Why didn't the bullet hit—" Stopping suddenly, suppressing his anger with effort, the Graf, after a few moments of silence, continued with feigned calm, "You may thank your condition that I spare you; under other circumstances I would avail myself of laws that would destroy you. But I only demand now that you tell me immediately how it was possible for you to see Natalie in Hohenflüh."

The tone with which the Graf spoke filled Deodatus with very great resentment. Pulling himself together, in spite of his weakness, he sat up and spoke in a firm, manly tone. "It can only be the law of insolence, of which you believe you can avail yourself, when you force your way into my chamber and trouble me with questions that I cannot answer. You are completely unknown to me; I have never had anything to do with you and this Natalie, of whom you speak. Do you really know that she is the divine image who dwells in my heart? Neither in Hohenflüh nor anywhere else did my own eyes see the—but it is sacrilege to speak to you of secrets which I hide deep in my heart."

The Graf seemed to be overcome by amazement and doubt; he stammered scarcely audibly, "You have never seen Natalie? And when you painted her? What if this Haberland—this Schwendy—"

"Enough!" cried Deodatus. "Enough! Depart! I have nothing to do with the dark spirit which an insane error drives along behind me and which is aiming at my death. There are laws which protect against artful assassination. You understand me, Graf."

Deodatus rang the bell loudly.

The Graf clenched his teeth and measured Deodatus with a fearful glance.

"Take care," he spoke. "Take care, boy. You have an unlucky face—take care that your face does not displease another besides myself."

The door opened, and in came the little old plumpish gentleman with the golden snuffbox, whom the gentle reader has seen as a member of the wise Council at the innkeeper's table in the Golden Ram, and has heard arguing very cleverly.

The Graf retired through the door with a threatening gesture towards Deodatus, leaving so wildly and violently that the little Councillor and his entourage were astonished and amazed.

Behind the Councillor came a very tiny, deformed little person, who was carrying a large bundle of paper under his arm, and two summoners, who promptly placed themselves by the door as guards.

The Councillor greeted Deodatus with a serious official expression; with difficulty, the little man pushed a table near to the bed, placed his papers on it, took his writing materials out of his pocket, climbed up on a chair that had also been dragged over with difficulty, and placed himself in a posture for writing, while the Councillor sat down on a chair beside the bed and stared at Deodatus with wide open eyes.

Deodatus was impatient to know what this was all about. Finally the Councillor solemnly began: "Herr Haberland or Herr Schwendy, for you, sir, who are lying in bed before me, like to have two different names, notwithstanding that that is a luxury which no proper authority should permit. Well—I hope that you will not delay your arrest by useless lies, plots, and tricks, since the all-knowing Town Council is already very exactly informed about everything. For at this minute you are arrested as you can see by, among other thing, the stance of these loyal, honorable guards."

Deodatus asked in surprise what crime he was accused of and by what right he could be arrested, since he was a transient traveler.

But the Councillor charged that he had violated most horribly the gracious Fürst's recently passed ban against duelling, by actually duelling in the forest, which the pistols found in his coat pocket adequately proved. So would he please, without further ado, name the impertinent opponent, as well as any possible seconds, and relate very nicely just what had happened from the beginning to the end.

In answer to this, Deodatus assured him calmly and firmly that it was not a question of a duel but of a murderous attack on his person. An incident that was incomprehensible to himself and would be even more so to a wise Council had led him to the forest, not at all by his own intent. The dangerous threats of a completely unknown persecutor were the cause of his having armed himself, and the wise Council would be better attending to its duty of maintaining peace and order if it investigated the murderous attack, rather than ordaining an arrest and investigation on a baseless suspicion.

Deodatus stuck to that story although the Councillor asked this and that; and when the latter wished to learn more about the facts of his life, Deodatus referred him to his pass, which, as long as there was no real basis for suspicion, would have to content the wise Council.

The Councillor wiped the sweat from his brow. Eager to write, the little man had repeatedly dipped his goose quill into the little inkpot and kept watching the Councillor. He seemed to be looking in vain for words. So the little man wrote boldly and read in a croaking voice, "Document, Hohenflüh, the— At the command of the local wise Council, the undersigned deputy had—"

"My dear Birdbrain," cried the Councillor, "divine actuary, the undersigned deputy had—the undersigned deputy—that's me— I had—"

It had been decided in the councils of Heaven that the undersigned deputy was not to complete his work, nor to sign, but rather to absolve Deodatus from the unfortunate accusation.

An officer of the Fürst's bodyguard, accompanied by the innkeeper, entered and asked the latter whether Deodatus was really the young man who had been wounded in the forest. When the innkeeper affirmed it, the officer approached Deodatus' bed and explained to him with modest good manners that he had been commanded to bring George Haberland to the Fürst at Sonsitz immediately. He hoped that his condition would not prevent this. At any rate, all the arrangements had been made so that the journey would not be detrimental to him, and in addition, the Fürst's own physician would be constantly at his side.

Suddenly released from the errand that had made him perspire with fear, the Councillor, beaming, approached the officer and while making a submissive bow, asked whether he should perhaps have the prisoner handcuffed for safety's sake. The officer stared at him in surprise and asked whether the Councillor was out of his mind and what prisoner was he talking about? The Fürst wished to talk to Herr Haberland to ascertain all the circumstances of an event that had aroused his anger. The Fürst could not understand how a notorious assassin was allowed to pursue his trade in his country, especially so near Hohenflüh, and therefore was going to call to account the authorities who were responsible for the safety of the citizens.

One can imagine how this made the plump Councillor tremble; the little secretary quickly somersaulted down from his chair, whimpering that he was nothing but a poor, wretched actuary who would be in serious trouble if he ever uttered aloud the doubts which he had long harbored about the wisdom of the wise Council.

Deodatus protested, to obviate any mistake, that he was not the painter Haberland, whom he must greatly resemble, but was called Deodatus Schwendy and had come here from Switzerland, as he could prove to their satisfaction. The officer assured him that the name was not important since the Fürst wanted to speak with the young man who had been wounded in the forest. Then Deodatus declared that, in that case, he was the one the Fürst meant and that he felt strong enough to go to Sonsitz, since his wound was minor. The Fürst's physician confirmed this. Deodatus was packed into the Fürst's very comfortable carriage and was on his way to Sonsitz.

All of Hohenflüh became very excited when Deodatus was driven through the streets, and there was no end to their amazement, since it was quite unheard of that the Fürst should have a stranger brought to Sonsitz. The people of Hohenflüh were even more astounded when they saw the two neighbors who had been mortal enemies for so many years, the innkeepers of the Golden Ram and the Silver Lamb, chatting together in a friendly way in the middle of the street on the so-called broad stone, even whispering intimately in each other's ears.

The gentle reader already knows how the Golden Ram and the Silver Lamb became reconciled, and the two found an even more effective reason for their sudden reconciliation in their common burning curiosity as to who the stranger could be to whom such an extraordinary thing was happening.

5

The raging thunder had quickly vanished over the mountains on the wings of the storm and only muttered angrily in the far distance. The setting sun blazed through the dark bushes; and the thousand sparkling drops of crystal, as they were shaken from the branches, bathed themselves with delight in the warm surging air. The Fürst was standing as if rooted to the ground in a place enclosed by Babylonian willows in the park at Sonsitz—with which the gentle reader is already acquainted. His arms were crossed, and he was looking up into the azure of the cloudless sky as if he wished to call back vanished hopes, and as if his life were lost to sorrow and pain. Then the officer of the guard, whom the Fürst had sent to Hohenflüh, appeared. The Fürst signalled impatiently to him and commanded that the young man, whom the officer announced, be brought to him immediately and that a sedan chair be used for the purpose. All was done as the Fürst commanded.

As soon as the Fürst saw Deodatus, he seemed to be deeply moved, and involuntarily the words escaped him, "Oh God! My premonition! Yes—it is he!"

Deodatus got slowly up and was about to approach the Fürst respectfully.

"Stay where you are!" cried the Fürst. "Stay where you are. You are weak, exhausted. Your wound is perhaps more dangerous than you imagine. My curiosity will not be detrimental to you. Bring two armchairs."

The Fürst said all this barely audibly and disjointedly; one could see that he was trying to master the storm that was raging within him.

When the armchairs had been brought, when Deodatus had sat down in one of them at the Fürst's command, and when the others had withdrawn, the Fürst paced up and down with growing agitation. Then he stopped in front of Deodatus. In the look with which he stared at him lay lacerating pain and deepest sorrow; and then all seemed to be submerged in the glow of a sudden flaming anger. An invisible, hostile power seemed to rise between him and Deodatus; and full of horror, the Fürst recoiled and paced even more violently up and down again while secretly glancing at the youth, whose astonishment mounted with every second and who did not know how the scene, which constricted his heart, would end.

The Fürst seemed to have to accustom himself to the sight of Deodatus; he finally pulled his chair a bit to one side, away from Deodatus, and sat down completely exhausted. Then he spoke in a subdued, almost gentle voice. "You are a stranger here, sir. You entered my country as a traveler. 'What concern are my affairs to a strange Fürst, whose country I am passing through?' Thus you might ask—but perhaps, unknown to you, there are certain affairs, certain mysterious connections—but—enough. You have my royal word that it is not empty, childish curiosity, or any other improper intent, which forces me—but, I will, I must know everything!"

The Fürst spoke the last words as he rose from the armchair in a flaming rage. But then, thinking better of it, he pulled himself together, sat down again, and spoke as gently as before. "Give me your complete confidence, young man, do not conceal any of your circumstances; tell me in particular where you came from and how you came to Hohenflüh and how your experiences in Hohenflüh are related to prior events. Most especially, I would like to know exactly what the wise woman—" The Fürst hesitated, then he continued, as if composing himself, "It is silly, crazy nonsense—this illusion is an offspring of hell, or—well—speak, young man, speak openly, no secret, no lie—"

The Fürst, about to leap violently up again, quickly composed himself and did not utter the word that was on his tongue.

From the deep emotion which the Fürst was trying in vain to suppress, Deodatus could easily see that there were secrets here in which the Fürst himself was involved and which might be a threat to him.

Deodatus, for his part, could see no reason for not being as forthright as the Fürst demanded, and he began to tell about his father, about the years of his boyhood and of his youth, and about his lonely life in Switzerland. He related how his father had sent him to Hohenflüh and had indicated in mysterious phrases that the turning point in his life would occur there, that he himself would feel inspired to a deed which would decide his fate. He accurately told everything that had taken place with the wise woman and the strange Graf.

Several times the Fürst expressed the liveliest astonishment, and he leaped up as in a sudden fright when Deodatus mentioned the names of Natalie and the Graf von Zelies.

Deodatus had finished his story; the Fürst remained silent, his head bowed in thought; then he arose, rushed to Deodatus, and cried, "Oh, the villain! The bullet was to pierce this breast; he wanted to kill the last hope, to destroy you—you, my—"

A flood of tears choked the Fürst; full of sorrow and pain, he embraced Deodatus and pressed him violently to his breast.

Then suddenly, as before, the Fürst recoiled in horror and cried, his clenched fist stretched out, "Away, away, you serpent, you who wish to nest in my heart—away! You satanic phantom, *you* shall not kill my hopes, you shall not destroy my life!"

Then a distant, strangely somber voice called, "Hope is death! Life the cruel sport of the dark powers!" Croaking, a black raven fluttered off into the shrubbery.

The Fürst fell to the ground unconscious. Too weak to assist him, Deodatus called loudly for help. The physician declared the Fürst had had a stroke and was in critical condition. Deodatus did not know what ineffably painful feeling of deepest pity surged in his breast; he knelt beside the stretcher on which the Fürst had been placed, kissed his shriveled, limp hand, and wet it with his ears. The Fürst became conscious; his eyes, which had been fixed as in death, acquired their power of vision again. He saw Deodatus, waved him away, and cried with trembling lips that could scarcely be understood, "Away—away!"

Deeply shaken by the scene that seemed to touch the roots of his life, Deodatus was close to fainting; and the doctor found his condition so serious that it was not thought advisable to take him back to Hohenflüh.

The physician said that even if the Fürst had expressed the wish that the young man should go away, for the moment he could be cared for in a distant wing of the manor house; and there could be no concern that the Fürst would find out about this, for he would not be allowed to leave his room for a long time. Deodatus was actually so exhausted that he was incapable of any desire or even of resistance, and he was glad to remain at the Fürst's estate.

It had been quiet and dreary at the manor house before, but now that the Fürst was ill the silence of the grave reigned, and Deodatus knew that others were there only when a servant took care of his needs or the surgeon visited him. This monastic solitude was beneficial to Deodatus, who had been assaulted on all sides, and he thought of the Fürst's manor as an asylum in which he was saved from the menacing secret that threatened to trap him.

In addition, the bare but friendly and comfortable arrangements of the two little rooms which he occupied and the marvelous view from the windows which he enjoyed contributed to the beneficial feeling of ease that cheers up the gloomiest spirits. He could see the loveliest part of the park, at the end of which, on a hill, were the picturesque ruins of an old castle. Behind them loomed the blue peaks of the distant mountains.

Deodatus used the time, when he had become calmer and the surgeon permitted him such activity, to write his old father in detail about everything that had happened to him. He entreated him not to remain silent any longer about what lay ahead of him in Hohenflüh, but to put him in the position of being informed about his own situation so that he could arm himself against the wiles of unknown enemies.

A small section of the main building of the tumble-down castle, the ruins of which Deodatus could see from his window, still stood almost intact. This section adjoined a built-out alcove which hung out airily like a swallow's nest because the other side of the main wall had fallen in. Deodatus ascertained with his spyglass that this alcove was covered with shrubs that pushed through the cracks in the walls and formed a leafy roof that was lovely to see. Deodatus thought that it must be quite livable there, although it seemed impossible to climb up to it because the steps had collapsed. Deodatus was all the more astounded, when he looked out of the window one night, to see quite clearly in the alcove a light that vanished again after an hour. Not only that night, but also during the following nights, Deodatus observed the light; and one can imagine that the young man, who was already entangled in inexplicable secrets, assumed that this was another portentous adventure.

He shared his observation with the surgeon, who said, however, that the appearance of a light in the alcove could have a natural explanation. In that undamaged part of the main building, on the ground floor, there were several rooms that had been fixed up for the gamekeeper who had charge of the royal park. Although he was convinced from frequent inspection of the ruins that one could not climb up to the alcove, at least not without danger, still it was possible that the huntsmen had climbed up to that swallow's nest to carry on their affairs undisturbed.

Deodatus was not at all satisfied with this explanation; he vividly imagined some intrigue that was hidden in the castle ruins.

The doctor finally allowed Deodatus to wander through the park at dusk, but he was to take great care to avoid that part which could be seen from the windows of the room where the ailing Fürst was living. The Fürst had recovered to the extent that he was able to sit at the window and look out; and Deodatus would not escape his sharp eyes and would, if discovered, unquestionably have to leave. At least, the doctor had to assume this from the way the Fürst had previously waved the young man away with an expression of abhorrence.

As soon as the doctor had given him his freedom, Deodatus at once walked over to the ruined castle. He met the gamekeeper, who acted very surprised at seeing him; and when Deodatus told him everything—how he had got there and what had happened— the former said quite bluntly that the gentlemen who had installed him in the manor without the Fürst's prior knowledge were playing a daring game. If the Fürst should find out anything about it, it might be that he would throw the young gentleman out of his sanctuary and all his protectors after him.

Deodatus wanted to see the interior, undamaged part of the castle; but the gamekeeper dryly assured him that this was not possible, since a rotten ceiling or a piece of the wall could cave in at any moment, and in addition, the steps were so rotten that there was no safe way to climb up, and one ran the danger of breaking one's neck any moment. But when Deodatus told the gamekeeper that he had often seen a light in the alcove, the latter replied in a coarse, rude tone that that must simply be a mistake and that the young gentleman would do well not to bother about anything but himself and not to go out snooping. He could thank heaven that he, the gamekeeper, had pity on him and didn't go immediately to the Fürst and tell him at once how his express command had been dis-obeyed.

Deodatus could see that the gamekeeper was trying to con-ceal a certain embarrassment by his rudeness. Deodatus found his suspicion that a secret lay hidden here confirmed when, crossing the castle courtyard, he saw, in a rather concealed corner of the wall, a narrow, wooden outside stair that had been built recently and that seemed to lead to the upper floor of the main building.

6

The Fürst's illness, which became more and more critical, aroused not a little dismay and concern. The gentle reader has already learned that the Fürst's consort and the child she had born had vanished in a mysterious way. The Fürst was therefore without an heir, and his successor to the throne was a younger brother who had made himself hated by the court and the people by his arrogant behavior and his many vicious inclinations which he insolently indulged. A dim rumor accused him of the vilest treason against the Fürst and suggested this as the reason why he had had to leave the country without anyone knowing his present secret where-abouts.

The people of Hohenflüh racked their brains wondering what would happen when the Fürst died. They trembled at the thought of the tyrannical brother and wished him at the bottom of the sea.

There was a lot of talk about this at the dinner table in the

Golden Ram; everyone gave his opinion, and the well-known Councillor stated that a wise Council could take over a bit of the government of the country along with the government of the town until something else turned up. An old man, withdrawn and silent for a long time, spoke next, in a tone of deepest emotion: "What bitter troubles are coming to our poor country; some unheard of doom has seized the best of Fürsts and robbed him of all life's happiness, all peace of soul, until he has finally succumbed to the terrible pain. We have everything to fear from his successor, and the only man who can stand as firm as a rock in the ocean, who would be our refuge and our salvation, has gone!"

Everyone knew that the old man meant none other than Graf von Törny, who had left the court soon after the Fürstin vanished.

Graf Törny was an excellent man in all respects. He combined the noblest spirit, the liveliest sense of everything that was good and beautiful, with the sharpest intelligence and the most flexible brilliance which wishes only what is right and has the power to achieve it. He was the protector of the oppressed, the indefatigable pursuer of the oppresser. It was inevitable that the Graf not only won the Fürst's love but also the love of the people; and only a very small section of them dared to credit the rumor that pictured him as guilty and which the Fürst's brother, who hated the Graf from the bottom of his heart, had made every effort to spread.

With one voice, everyone at the dinner table cried, "Graf Törny, our noble Graf Törny! Oh, were he only with us in our hour of need!"

The Graf's health was drunk. As they went on to talk about the Fürst's critical illness, it was natural that they should recall the young man in whose presence the Fürst suffered a stroke.

The clever Councillor suspected the most dreadful things. It was certain, he said, that the young man who had been foolish enough to try to deceive the wise Council about his person with two diverse names, had been a rascal of the highest order, one who had evil purposes in mind.

It was not for nothing that the Fürst had had him brought to Sonsitz, to his manor house, to question him about all sorts of hellish plots; and the officer's politeness, the comfortable carriage, the doctor, had all been a mask to keep the criminal happy and cheerful so that he would confess everything immediately. The Fürst would certainly have succeeded if the cold damp night air had not brought on a stroke and if the young man had not used the confusion to escape quickly. He only wished that the good-for-nothing would show up again in Hohenflüh, because he would not escape the justice of the wise Council a second time. The Councillor had just finished saying this when the young man about whom they were talking entered, greeted the company silently and solemnly and sat down at the table.

"A right good welcome, my dear Herr Haberland," said the innkeeper, who could not share the Councillor's bad opinion. "A right good welcome! Well— You don't feel any hesitancy about appearing in Hohenflüh again?"

The young man seemed to be very surprised by the innkeeper's address. Then the plump little Councillor struck an attitude and began very solemnly, "Sir, I hereby declare to you—," but then the young man looked him right in the eye with such a sharp and penetrating glance that he hesitated and, bowing automatically, stuttered, "Your most obedient servant."

The gentle reader may have already observed that there are people who will immediately bow with guilty humility if one looks them straight in the eye.

The young man ate and drank without saying a word. An oppressive, expectant silence lay over the whole company.

The old man, who had spoken earlier, finally addressed the young man, asking him if the wound in his breast, which he had received in the forest near Hohenflüh, was already completely healed. The young man replied that he must mistake him for someone else, since he had never been wounded in the breast.

"I understand," continued the old man, grinning slyly. "I understand, Herr Haberland. You have recovered completely and do not wish to talk any more about that unpleasant occurrence. But since you were present when our good Fürst suffered a stroke, you will best be able to tell us how it happened and what there is to hope or fear for his condition."

The young man replied that this was the same mistake, since he had never been at Sonsitz, nor had he ever seen Fürst Remigius. But he had heard about the Fürst's illness and wished to learn the details.

Perhaps, said the old man, Herr Haberland did not wish or was not allowed to speak much about his stay at the Fürst's, perhaps

rumor had distorted much that had occurred at Sonsitz, but so
much was certain: the Fürst had had the young man, who had been
wounded here, and whom he, the old man, had to assume was Herr
Haberland, brought to Sonsitz, and the Fürst had suffered a stroke
during his private conversation with this same young man. The
servants who had withdrawn nearby had heard a strange, hollow
voice cry, "Hope is death! Life the cruel sport of the dark powers!"

The young man sighed deeply, his color changed, everything
betrayed deep inner turmoil. He dashed down several glasses of
wine, ordered a second bottle, left the room. Dinner was over. The
young man did not return. The doorkeeper had seen him hurrying
to Neudorfer Gate. Payment for the dinner lay on his plate.

Then the Councillor became very officious, spoke of pursuit,
warrants, etc., but the old man reminded him of a great occasion
when he got his knuckles rapped by the state authorities for un-
timely activity over a similar instance and said it would be better
not to bother any more about the young man and to leave the
matter alone.

The entire company seconded this opinion, and the Councillor
really did let the matter rest.

While this was going on in Hohenflüh, Haberland's doppelgänger, young Deodatus Schwendy, had stepped into a new magical
cycle of dangerous intrigue.

Early one evening, when he was standing in front of the
mysterious alcove and was looking up at the concealed window with
a longing that he himself could not explain, it seemed to him as
if he saw a white figure; at the same moment a stone dropped at his
feet. He picked it up and unwrapped the paper which was around
it. He found the following words, scribbled in pencil, in a scarcely
legible script.

George—my George! Is it possible? Am I deceived by my
aroused senses? You, here! O ye eternal heavenly powers!
My father lies in these ruined walls as if in ambush—alas,
brooding only evil! Fly, fly, George, before father's anger
reaches you! But no—stay—I must see you—a single moment
of blissful rapture, then fly! Father is away until midnight.
Come! Cross the castle yard—the wooden stairs! But no; that
is impossible. The gamekeeper's men—and if they are asleep,

the dogs will attack you. On the south side, there is another stair which leads to the rooms, but it is rotten and broken. You must not venture it, but I will come down. O George, what can all of Hell's craftiness accomplish compared with a loving heart. Natalie is yours—yours forever!

"It is she," cried Deodatus, quite beside himself. "There is no longer any doubt. Yes, it is she, the dream of the boy, the passionate longing of the young man! Away to her! Never to leave her again! My father's dark secret shall be made clear! But—is it I? Am I George?"

Like a mortal cramp, the thought seized Deodatus that it was not he, that it was that unknown doppelgänger whom Natalie loved and whom she believed to have found again. And yet—thus the burning passion reasoned in his heart—and yet could it not be the doppelgänger who is deceiving her, can it not be I to whom she belongs, to whom secret bonds hold her? Away to her!

As soon as night had come, Deodatus slipped out of his room. He heard voices whispering in the park not far from the manor house, and he ducked behind a bush. Two men wrapped in cloaks passed close by him.

"Therefore," said one of them, "therefore, the doctor thought today that the Fürst could last a long time?"

"So it is, Your Grace," replied the other.

"Well," continued the first, "one must try other means—"

The words were no longer audible. Deodatus raised himself. The full light of the moon fell on the speaker's face. With horror, Deodatus recognized Graf Hektor von Zelies.

Trembling from the thought that a black fiend, that death, was lurking in the darkness, and at the same time driven by an irresistible force, by a burning passion, by a fierce desire, Deodatus crept away. By the light of the moon he found the dilapidated steps on the south side, but he was almost in despair after he had climbed a few steps and realized the impossibility of continuing in the blackness that now surrounded him. Suddenly a light from the building shone towards him. He climbed all the way up the stairs, though not without danger, and came into a high, wide hall. The charming image of his dreams stood before him, blinding in her beauty and grace. "Natalie!" cried Deodatus and hurled himself at the feet of the glorious woman.

Natalie murmured melodiously, "My George!" and embraced the youth. Not a word—only a glance, only a kiss, the language of hot, stormy passion.

Then Deodatus cried in the madness of a mortal anguish and a fervent rapture, "Mine—you are mine, Natalie! Believe in my ego. I know that my doppelgänger wanted to smash your heart, but he hit me—it was only a bullet; the wound is healed, and my ego lives. Natalie, just tell me if you believe in my ego, otherwise death will seize me right before your eyes. I am not called George, but I am still my own ego and none other."

"Alas," cried Natalie, releasing the youth from her embrace. "George, what are you talking about? But, no, no! A hostile fate has confused your senses! Be calm, be completely my George."

Natalie opened her arms and Deodatus embraced her, pressed her to his breast as he cried, "Yes, Natalie, I am the one, I am the one you love. Who will dare, who can tear me from this heavenly rapture! Natalie—let us fly, let us fly—away—so my doppelgänger cannot catch you—fear nothing—It is my ego that will kill him!"

At that moment muffled steps were heard, and "Natalie! Natalie!" echoed through the high room.

"Away!" cried Natalie, pushing the youth towards the stairs and handing him a lamp that she had brought along. "Away, or we are lost. My father has come. Come again tomorrow at the same time. I will follow you."

Half unconscious, Deodatus clambered down the stairs. It was a miracle that he did not fall down the dilapidated steps. At the bottom he extinguished the lamp and threw it into the shrubbery. He had scarcely gone a few steps when he was seized from behind by two men who hurried him away, lifted him into a wagon that was standing before the gate, and drove off with him at a furious gallop.

Deodatus might have been riding for an hour when the wagon stopped in the thick of the forest in front of a charcoal-burner's hut. Men with torches stepped from the hut and begged the youth to get out of the carriage, which he did. A stately old man came quickly towards him, and Deodatus fell on his breast, crying "My father!"

"I have saved you," said old Amadeus Schwendy, "I have saved you from the snares of trickery and malice, I have snatched you from death, by dear son! That which is secret will soon be revealed; what you could not even surmise will soon be made clear."

7

The Fürst awoke very early in the morning from a deep and peaceful sleep. He seemed refreshed, his illness broken, and he impatiently demanded his doctor. The latter was not a little surprised when the Fürst gently ordered him to bring the young man to him who he knew very well was concealed in the manor house.

The doctor tried to excuse his action, explaining that the condition of the young man required quiet and the most careful medical treatment, but the Fürst interrupted him with the assurance that there was no need for any excuses since he, the doctor, had unintentionally done him a very great service. Besides, the young man's presence had only been revealed to him yesterday by the gamekeeper.

But Deodatus had vanished without a trace; and when the Fürst learned that, he became visibly upset. He repeated several times, in the most pained voice, "Why did he run away? Why did he run away? Didn't he know that foolishness yields in the face of death?"

At the Fürst's command, the President of the State Council came, as well as the President of the High Court and two Councillors. The doors were locked immediately; one could assume that the Fürst was making his will.

On the following day the somber sound of the bells announced to the inhabitants of Sonsitz the death of the Fürst, who had peacefully passed away following a second stroke.

The State Council, the highest officials, gathered at the castle; the Fürst's last will was to be opened, since it could be rightfully presumed that, there being no heir, directions would be contained in it as to how the state government was to be carried on, at least for the present.

The solemn act was about to begin when the Fürst's long-lost younger brother suddenly arrived, as if evoked by magic, and declared that he, as reigning Fürst, had sole command and that all the Fürst's arrangements that in any way diminished the brother's right to the throne were and must remain null and void; therefore, there was no need to hurry and open the will.

Fürst Isidor's unexpected appearance was a baffling riddle to
everybody, for no one knew that Fürst Isidor, changed by age and
disguised by false hair and make-up, had been living in the principality and that during the most recent days had been lurking in
the ruined castle waiting for his brother's death.

Immediately after he had left the principality of Reitlingen so
long ago, he had assumed the name Graf Hektor von Zelies and had
skillfully erased all traces of where he had been.

The President of the State Council, a worthy old man, looking Fürst Isidor straight in the eye, assured him that he could not
consider the brother entitled to the throne until after the opening
of the last testament of Fürst Remigius. Certain secrets might be
revealed which would change matters.

The President spoke the last sentence in a loud voice, and
Fürst Isidor suddenly turned pale.

The will was then opened with the usual ceremonies, and
everyone except Fürst Isidor was happily astonished at the contents. The Fürst explained that the mere suspicion of unfaithful-
ness, which an evil villain had known how to arouse in him, had
caused him to do a wicked injustice to his virtuous wife by repudiat-
ing her and the child and locking them up in a distant castle on
the border. She had escaped from there, and he had never been
able to find even the slightest trace of her. Thanks to the heavenly
powers, he had found his son, for he had the deepest conviction
that the young man with the name Deodatus Schwendy, who had
been brought to him, was none other than his son whom he had cast
out in a satanic delusion. Graf von Törny could remove any doubt
about the identity of the young man, for he had saved the boy and
raised him as Amadeus Schwendy in complete concealment in a
manor house near Lucerne. It was self-evident that the wicked suspicion that he had harbored in regard to the legitimacy of his son
did not obtain. The rest of the will was filled with expressions of the
deepest repentance, of assurances that all suspicions were erased
from his mind; and he directed warm paternal words to his son and
future ruler.

Fürst Isidor looked around with amused scorn and said then
that all that was based on the dying Fürst's dream and that he did
not at all intend to sacrifice his well-earned rights to insane fantasies.
At any rate, the so-called heir to the throne was not there, and it
would depend a great deal on what Graf von Törny would say and

how he would succeed in explaining all the circumstances mentioned by the Fürst in such a credible way that no doubt could
arise about the young man who had suddenly dropped from Heaven
as an heir to the throne and who was, perhaps, an adventurer. For
the moment, therefore, he would ascend the throne immediately.

Fürst Isidor had scarcely spoken these words when old
Amadeus Schwendy, or rather Graf von Törny, came in, very dignified, richly clothed, a sparkling star on his breast, and leading by
the hand a young man who had been thought to be his son Deodatus
Schwendy. All eyes were directed at the young man; all cried in
one voice, "It is the Fürst, it is the Fürst!"

The day's miracles were still not exhausted, for as soon as
Graf von Törny began to speak, the jubilant shouts of the people
in the streets were heard. "Long live the Fürstin! Long live the
Fürstin!" resounded; and soon a tall, majestic woman strode into
the hall followed by a young man.

"Is it possible?" cried Graf von Törny, quite beside himself.
"Is it not a dream? The Fürstin—yes, it is the Fürstin whom we
believed lost!"

"Oh happy day, oh blessed moment—mother and son are
found!" cried the entire gathering.

"Yes," said the Fürstin. "Yes, the death of an unhappy husband restores to you, loyal people, a Fürstin, and even more! Behold the son whom she bore, behold your Fürst, your sovereign!"

Then she led the youth who had come with her to the middle
of the hall. The young man who had come with Graf von Törny
strode quickly toward him; and the two, not only resembling each
other, but the one the doppelgänger of the other in features, build,
gestures, etc., stopped in horror and remained rooted to the floor.

This might well be the place to tell the gentle reader everything that had occurred at the court of Fürst Remigius.

Fürst Remigius had grown up with Graf von Törny; both
felt firmly bound to each other, being similar in intelligence and
nobility of spirit, and so it came to pass that when the Fürst
ascended the throne the friend who was closest to his heart, whom
he could not desert, became first in the government after him. The
gentle reader has already learned that the Graf had won love and
confidence everywhere.

Both the Fürst and Graf von Törny had fallen in love at the
same time while on a visit to a neighboring court, and it just so hap-

pened that Princess Angela, whom the Fürst had chosen, and Gräfin Pauline, whom the Graf loved, had been from childhood equally closely bound together in love and friendship. They celebrated their nuptials on the same day, and nothing in the world seemed able to destroy a happiness that had its base deep in their hearts.

A dark fate decreed otherwise!

The more the Fürstin saw Graf Törny, the more clearly was his inner being revealed to her and the more strongly and wonderfully she felt attracted to the splendid man. Possessing the purest, most divine virtue, the most irreproachable faithfulness, the Fürstin discovered finally, to her horror, that she was being consumed by a flaming passion. She thought and felt only for him; a mortal emptiness was in her heart when she did not see him; all of heaven's raptures filled her when he came, when he spoke! Separation or flight were not possible, and yet the fearful state of wrestling with her burning passion was unendurable. If often seemed as if she must breathe out her love and with it her life on the bosom of her girlhood friend. Bathed in tears, she convulsively clasped the Gräfin in her arms and spoke in a lacerating voice, "You blessed woman! Paradise glows for you, but my hopes are death!"

The Gräfin, who was far removed from suspecting what was occurring in the Fürstin's heart, felt so deeply stricken by the Fürstin's nameless pain, that she mourned with her and wept and also wished for death, so that the Graf was not a little concerned about the sudden melancholy of his formerly cheerful wife.

Since their earliest childhood, hysteria, bordering on the neurotic, had been observed at times in both the Fürstin and the Gräfin; the doctors, therefore, with perfect justice, felt that they could ascribe all these strange attacks, which were particularly noticeable in the Fürstin, to the condition in which the two women found themselves. They were both with child.

By a strange quirk of fate—or it might be called by a miraculous doom—both the Fürstin and the Gräfin bore sons in the same hour, actually at the same moment. That was not all! Week by week and day by day the two babies developed such a complete similarity, such a complete likeness, that it was quite impossible to distinguish them. Both clearly had Graf von Törny's features. Even if this could be chance or an illusion, the quite superior formation of the skull and a small moon-shaped mole on the left temple affirmed the complete similarity.

Hostile mistrust and evil suspicion, which always live in a degenerate heart, had betrayed the Fürstin's secret to Fürst Isidor. He made every effort to inject the same poison into the Fürst's mind, but the Fürst dismissed him with scorn. But then the moment arrived which seemed appropriate to Fürst Isidor to renew his attacks on Graf von Törny and also on the Fürstin, both of whom he mortally hated, since they constantly resisted his evil influence.

The Fürst vaccillated, for the mere resemblance of the child to Graf von Törny would never have forced him to any kind of horrible decision, if the Fürstin's behavior had not been decisive.

The Fürstin found no peace. She mourned day and night as if lacerated by the deepest pain, by a nameless torment. Sometimes she covered the child with the tenderest kisses, sometimes she put it down, her face averted with an expression of the deepest aversion. "Just God, you punish my sin so severely!" Several people had heard the Fürstin cry and could not but interpret it as referring to an illicit deed which was being bitterly repented.

Several months passed; finally the Fürst came to a decision. During the night he had the mother and child removed to a barren, remote castle on the border, and he dismissed Graf von Törny from court. His brother, also, the sight of whom the Fürst found unendurable, had to leave.

Only the spirit had sinned; earthly desires had had no part; faithfulness stood firm; but the Fürstin considered even the sin of the spirit a punishable crime for which only deepest repentance could atone.

Living in the desolate castle, the strictness of the guard, everything contributed to bringing the Fürstin's convulsive condition to near madness.

Then one day a gypsy troop arrived with their gay songs and camped right next to the castle walls.

It seemed to the Fürstin as if thick veils had suddenly slipped away and she could see out into a bright and varied life. Ineffable longing filled her breast. "Away! Away into the outer world! Take me! Take me!" she cried as she stretched out her arms through the open window. A gypsy woman seemed to understand her, for she waved to her cheerily, and quick as a flash a gypsy boy scrambled up the walls. The Fürstin took her child, ran downstairs; the door was open. The gypsy boy quickly lifted the child over the wall. The

Fürstin stood sadly by the wall, unable to scale it. But immediately a rope ladder was let down, and in a few seconds she was free.

The gypsy band greeted her jubilantly, for in their superstition they saw in the noble lady who had escaped from her prison a lucky star that had risen for them. "Aha," said an old gypsy woman. "Don't you see how the royal crown sparkles on her brow? Such a glow can never be extinguished."

The gypsies' wild, nomadic life, their practice of black lore and mysterious arts, were beneficial to the Fürstin; and she became reconciled with life, for her eccentricities that bordered on insanity were permitted free expression. The gypsies cleverly arranged for the baby to be cared for by an old pious country priest. It need scarcely be said that it was the Fürstin who had appeared as the wise woman with the raven after she had become calmer and had left the gypsies. This also explains why Fürst Isidor believed the painter George Haberland and the young Deodatus Schwendy to be one and the same person—namely, the young Fürst—and tried every possible way to get rid of him, since only he could supersede him in claiming the throne.

It is remarkable that both Haberland and Schwendy had been dreaming for a long time of the beloved creature who then came into their lives. It is remarkable that this person was Natalie, the daughter of Fürst Isidor, and that both Graf von Törny and the Fürstin viewed her as chosen to end the reign of the unknown doom by her union with the Fürst, and that both had, therefore, used all means at their disposal to unite a pair whom, they believed, a mysterious force had predestined for each other.

You now know how all the plans came to nought because the doppelgängers' paths crisscrossed each other. You also know how all those who had been banished by the Fürst's commands, gathered together again near him when he became mortally ill.

8

So—stiff with horror, rooted to the floor, the doppelgängers faced each other. An oppressive uneasiness lay on the company; each searched his heart, wondering, "Which one is the Fürst?"

Graf von Törny broke the silence, calling with painful happiness to the young man who had come in behind the Fürstin, "My son!"

The Fürstin's eyes gleamed with fire, and she said with shattering dignity, "Your son, Graf von Törny? And who is he who stands beside you? The thief of the throne that belongs to the one I nourished at my breast?"

Fürst Isidor turned to the gathering and said that, since complete uncertainty obtained about the person of the young Fürst and heir, it was only natural that neither of the pretenders could ascend the throne, and that it depended on which of the two could best establish proof as to the legitimacy of his birth.

Graf von Törny assured everyone that such a procedure was not at all necessary since he was in the position to convince the gathering in a few minutes that his progeny was the son of the deceased Fürst Remigius and therefore the legitimate heir.

Graf von Törny related the following to the gathering.

The intimate servants of Fürst Remigius were too devoted to the Graf not to have informed him of the Fürst's decision, even to the moment that was set for removing the Fürstin and her child. The Graf was aware of the danger to which the heir was exposed, the confusion which the resemblance of the child to his could in some future time occasion, and the misfortune which could occur after the Fürst's death. He decided to take preventive measures.

He succeeded in entering the Fürstin's antechamber late in the night, accompanied by two trusty councillors, by the guardian of the secret archives, by the doctor, by the surgeon, and by an old valet. The old nurse, who had also been made privy to the plan, brought the child in while the Fürstin slept. The surgeon burned a little mark on the left breast of the child, which lay in a slumber induced by narcotics; then Graf Törny took the child and handed his own to the nurse. A precise document was drawn up describing all the circumstances and containing a drawing of the brand mark. The document was signed by all present, sealed, and handed over to the archivist to keep in the royal secret archives.

Thus it was that Graf Törny's son was taken away with the Fürstin and the young Fürst was raised by the Graf von Törny as his own son.

His wife, the Gräfin, bowed with sorrow and inconsolable at the evil fate of her bosom friend, died shortly after their arrival in Switzerland.

Of the people present at the time of the deposition, the surgeon, the archivist, the nurse, the valet still lived and were at the castle as arranged by Graf von Törny.

The archivist produced the document, which was opened in the presence of the above mentioned persons and read aloud by the President of the State Council.

The young Fürst bared his breast; the mark was found; all doubts vanished; and lusty cheers echoed from the hearts of the loyal vassals.

Fürst Isidor had left with an expression of very deep anger while the document was being read. When the Fürstin found herself alone with Graf von Törny and the two young men, she felt no longer able to conceal the multitude of emotions in her heart. She threw herself stormily on the Graf's breast and cried, as if dissolved in painful rapture, "Oh, Törny! You cast off your son, your child, to save the one that I bore! But I am returning your lost son to you! Oh, Törny, we no longer belong to the earth, no earthly sorrow has power over us from this time forth! Let us enjoy Heaven's peace and blessedness! A conciliated spirit hovers over us! But what have I forgotten! The blessed bride is waiting!"

The Fürstin went into a side room and returned with Natalie, who was dressed as a bride. Incapable of speech, the young men had been staring at each other with glances reflecting a sinister fear. At the very moment the young men saw Natalie, a burning flame seemed to animate them. With a loud "Natalie!" both rushed to the angelic child. But a deep horror seized Natalie when she saw the two youths, a double image of the beloved whom she carried in her heart.

"Ha!" cried the raging young Törny. "Ha, Fürst! Are you a doppelgänger come from Hell who has stolen my ego, who is plotting to steal my Natalie and to snatch my life from my lacerated breast? Vain, mad thought! She is mine, mine!"

The young Fürst replied, "Why are you thrusting into my ego? What do I have to do with you that you ape my features, ape my figure! Away with you! Natalie is mine!"

"Choose, Natalie!" cried Törny. "Speak! Did you not pledge me your troth a thousand times in those blissful hours when I painted you, when—"

"Ha!" the Fürst interrupted. "Think of that hour in the ruined castle when you wanted to follow me—"

And then they both cried together, "Choose, Natalie, choose!" Then one said to the other. "Let's see which one succeeds in getting rid of the doppelgänger—you shall bleed—bleed, if you are not a satanic illusion of Hell!"

Then Natalie cried in sorrowful tones of utter despair, "Just God, who is it, which of the two do I love? Has my heart broken and yet can live? Just God—let me die, die in this moment—" Tears choked her voice. Then she bowed her head, held both hands before her face as if she wished to look into her own heart. She sank on her knees, raised her tear-stained face and her folded hands as if praying fervently, and spoke softly in a tone of deepest anguish, "Renounce!"

"It is the angel," said the Fürstin with transfigured rapture. "It is the angel of eternal light who is speaking to you."

The young men were still staring at each other, fire in their eyes. Then suddenly a flood of tears poured from their eyes, they fell in each other's arms, they pressed one another to their hearts and stammered, "Yes! Renounce—renounce—forgive—forgive me, brother—"

Then the Fürst said to young Törny, "For my sake your father cast you off—for my sake you have suffered. Yes, I renounce her!"

Then young Törny said to the Fürst, "What is my renouncing to yours! It was you, the Fürst of the country, for whom the princess had been chosen."

"Have thanks," cried Natalie, "have thanks, O eternal Might of Heaven. It is over!" Then she pressed a farewell kiss on the young men's foreheads and tottered away, supported by the Fürstin's arm.

"I am losing you again," said Graf von Törny with the deepest pain when his son was about to leave.

"Father," he cried, "give me time, give me freedom lest I succumb, that my lacerated heart may mend!" Silently he again embraced the Fürst, his father, and hurried away.

Natalie retired to a remote nunnery, becoming Abbess there. The Fürstin, deceived of her last hope, had the border castle where she had been imprisoned comfortably furnished and chose it as her solitary dwelling. Graf Törny remained with the Fürst. Both were happy that Fürst Isidor had left the country again.

All Hohenflüh was intoxicated with joy and gaiety. The carpenters' guild, supported by worthy construction workers, climbed up on the stately triumphal arches, ignoring the danger, and hammered away merrily, while the painters, ready to begin at a moment's notice, stirred their pots of paint, and the gardeners' boys created innumerable wreaths of yew and gaily colored flowers. The

orphan boys were already jammed into the market place, attired in
their Sunday clothes; the schoolboys were already rehearsing, blub-
bering out, *"Heil dir im Siegeskranz"*;[5] from time to time a trumpet
squawked as if clearing its throat, and a whole bevy of girls from the
solid citizen class were resplendent in newly washed clothes, while
the mayor's wife, Tinchen, attired in rustling white brocaded satin,
sweated profusely because the young degree candidate, who was by
profession the poet of Hohenflüh, would not stop reciting to her
the address to the Fürst that he had composed in verse, neglecting
not a single declamatory effect.

The two reconciled innkeepers of the Golden Ram and the
Silver Lamb strolled up and down the street, both glowing in the
thought that they supplied hospitality to their gracious sovereign,
both happily admiring the *Vivat Princeps!* that was being written
in oil above their doors and which would flame high that evening
when the town was illuminated. The Fürst was expected in a few
hours.

The painter George Haberland (young Graf Törny did not
want to be anyone else at the present) quietly slipped through Neudorfer Gate, dressed for a journey, with his pack and portfolio on
his back. "Hey!" Berthold called to him, "Well met! The best of
luck to you, brother George! I know everything! Thank God you
are not a reigning Fürst   all would be over. Your being a Graf does
not bother me, for I know you are and will remain an artist. And
the girl you love? She is not a creature of the earth, she does not
live in the world, but in you yourself as the high and pure ideal of
your art, which inspires you, which breathes from your works,
which is enthroned above the stars.

"Brother Berthold!" cried George, his eyes shining with a divine fire. "Brother Berthold, you are right. She, she is art, in which
my whole being breathes. I have lost nothing, and if earthly sorrow
seizes me and bows me down when I have turned away from the
divine—then you—your ever cheerful nature—

> Friendship's ease you'll soon be feeling,
> It's not vanished from your sight."

The young men wandered on over the mountains!

5. "Hail to thee in the wreath of victory."

XIII
XIV

107   your belief gives him power
108   transformation of artist — self?
110

183

    the stranger — the encounter, the revelation of strangers
       full nature
    role of mother and father

    poetic possession of your inner mind
    Atlantis, spirit of elements
    role of physician — friend to further transformation, or foe?
    vigil — chapter?
    mystery of the golden pot — unknowable in advance
    crisis of belief
    role of different loves, different kind of loves
    exile of voice of nature
    farther of the role of salamanders — power, nature of
                       but recognize Jungian method
    male, female archetypes — female to female, male to male, her
    calligraphy, poems
                                  unconscious
    trials, shattering, rediscovery, manipulation of true vision
    bliss and terror, alternating — ambivalence of love? + dream
    role of hag — temptation
    courage — moral, intellectual, physical
    equinox — natural cycles.
                             effort?
    self — discovery?
         entirely different men — how is transformation.
    power of vision, awaking from dream   unconscious
    water — surface + depths - psychological states — mirror,
    role of vigil — waiting for … what? Trials of the hero
    pain of leaving through departure, (
    copying manuscripts — imbibing, assimilating their meaning
    signs, make
  Summary. repetition of themes, story,
       banish evil from your mind
       childish terrors live to infect adult mind
       how to effect transformation, rather than
       succumb to horror?